Cathy Woodman lives in Winchester with her young family. A qualified vet, Cathy is now a full-time writer. Her debut novel, UNDER THE BONNET, was joint winner of the Harry Bowling First Novel Award and is also available from Headline.

Also by Cathy Woodman

Under the Bonnet

Our House

Cathy Woodman

headline

First published in 2005
by HEADLINE BOOK PUBLISHING

First published in paperback in 2005
by HEADLINE BOOK PUBLISHING

1

ISBN 0 7553 0958 8

Typeset in Book Antiqua by Palimpsest Book Production Limited,
Polmont, Stirlingshire

Printed and bound in Great Britain by
Mackays of Chatham plc, Chatham, Kent

Headline's policy is to use papers that are natural, renewable and
recyclable products and made from wood grown in sustainable
forests. The logging and manufacturing processes are expected to
conform to the environmental regulations of the country of origin.

HEADLINE BOOK PUBLISHING
A division of Hodder Headline
338 Euston Road
London NW1 3BH

www.headline.co.uk
www.hodderheadline.com

To Mum and Dad

Acknowledgements

I should like to thank my family,
my agent Laura Longrigg at MBA,
my editor Sherise Hobbs,
and the team at Headline
for their encouragement and support.

Chapter One

I, Sadie Keith, have many desirable properties, as well as a few less attractive ones that I'd rather keep quiet about. (Did I say quiet? I don't do quiet.)

If, as my best friend Helen has suggested, I should find myself putting a Lonely Hearts ad in the *Surrey Comet* or *South London Press*, I would describe myself as being generously, rather than elegantly proportioned, and having an open outlook. From the front aspect, I have a great figure for a thirty-nine-years-young mother of twins i.e. curvy in all the right places. It's not so impressive side on – my belly and bum stick out like counterbalances. My hair is a bit of a thatch in the mornings before I've washed it. It's auburn, and shoulder-length, with a softly feathered fringe and sides.

Unique Selling Point? My eyes, which are blue-grey and ringed with long, dark lashes. The Wow Factor? My boobs, which I make the most of by wearing scoop-neck tops.

There's no scoop-neck top today though. I'm wearing my Saturday-afternoon clothes – a red and white striped shirt with a Paisley print bow tie, and a pair of outsized dungarees in sunshine yellow. I made them myself from a pair of old curtains that I bought for 50p in a car-boot sale in Cheam.

I glance down towards my covered assets, very briefly because I'm driving along Coombe Hill, taking advantage of the downhill slope and hoping that the light on the fuel gauge of my aged Peugeot 406 might prove to be an electrical fault. It isn't, and the car – which is on its second trip around the clock – stutters to a stop in the middle of the road.

'Oh damn and bother it!' (Actually, I don't put it quite like that.) I pump the accelerator, but nothing happens. In front of me, the road clears. Behind, the traffic builds, then slowly overtakes. An ensemble of horns blasts my eardrums. My face grows a little warm. Beads of perspiration start to ooze through layers of theatrical make-up. I grimace into the rearview mirror. My alter ego, Topsy the Clown, grimaces back, the spots of rouge on her cheeks contrasting with the rest of her china-white complexion.

The driver of a black Mercedes that has slewed to a stop close to my rear bumper grimaces too. He gestures for me to drive on. I shrug my shoulders. I can't go anywhere, and even if I could, I wouldn't now that he is giving me a furious, two-fingered salute with one hand and leaning on his hooter with the other.

'I'm stuck,' I mouth, saluting him back, at which there's an unnerving crunch of crumpling metal and plastic, and I am jerked forwards. I think I knock my forehead on the windscreen. I'm not sure. I am just relieved that Lorna and Sam, my eight-year-old twins, are with Dan, my ex-husband, today and not in the car with me.

The enraged driver appears at my window. He beats his fist against the glass which I wind down quickly to avoid any further damage that I can ill afford.

He's young, charmless and vaguely familiar.

'This isn't a bloody car park,' he begins in a condescending tone which has a similar effect on my temper as water on a chip-pan fire.

'I never claimed it was, smart arse,' I interrupt.

'What did you call me?' His face colours up and the veins on his forehead start to bulge.

'Look what you've done to my car!' Slightly dazed, I climb out, angling the hoop that supports my dungarees at the waist so I can get through the door.

'That isn't a car. It's more like spare parts for *Scrapheap Challenge*. It shouldn't be on the effing road, and neither should you, dressed like that and distracting other drivers!'

'I pay my Road Tax. I have as much right to be on the road as you.' I've lost it. I'm squawking like a manic jackdaw. '*More* right! Your driving's rubbish!'

'Don't blame me. You're the hazard. I didn't drive into *you*. You rolled back into *me*!'

'How could I? I'm facing downhill.'

The driver hesitates very briefly, but long enough for me to know that I'm in the right. He doesn't like it. He steps up very close until the front of his jacket is touching the edge of my hoop, and stares. My heart pounds. He's going to hit me, or worse. What if he has a knife tucked in his pocket? Or a gun? Warily, I keep my eyes fixed on his, but suddenly, he's not looking at me any more.

I follow his gaze to where a white pick-up van has pulled up on the opposite side of the road, mounting the verge and leaving a trail of crushed daffodils behind it. I say it's white, but it's better described as biscuit beige, the grime on its panels patterned with slashes of last week's rain and crude lettering made by a fingertip: CLEAN ME and DRIVEN BY A DIRTY BASTARD. Underneath these, in green print, are the words BRYANT BUILDERS FOR ALL YOUR – word smudged out – REQUIREMENTS.

Sunlight reflects from the windscreen, so I can't see the driver's face as he opens his door. I see his feet before anything else – big feet encased in muddy boots. My first thought is to recall what Helen says about men with big feet. My second is to ask myself why on earth he has got a chain padlocked to his left ankle? My third, as long legs emerge, sheathed in smart, dark-grey trousers, is to wonder why he is wearing boots and a chain with what looks like half a morning suit? This guy is also wearing a bow tie, shirt and waistcoat, but no jacket.

He slams the door then strolls across the road, stopping the traffic by his mere presence. He walks very straight, with his thumbs in his trouser pockets and forefingers pointing towards his groin. My heart skips a beat, then two. This is exactly the kind of man I would advertise for, if Helen should ever persuade me.

'Can I help?' he says, addressing me. He's about six foot tall, and more than a head taller than I am. His eyes are blue-green, the colour of the sea. He has a healthy tan, and short brown hair, run through with wax. He reminds me of good times, of skimming pebbles on the beach, of sunbathing at the base of rugged cliffs on a long, hot summer day. 'Well?'

'No, thanks. This young gentleman –' (I'm being ironic here) '– is just about to give me his insurance details.' The young gentleman in question starts to open his mouth, but before he can get a word in edgeways, I continue, 'And get down on his knees with a grovelling apology for ramming my car.'

'I bloody well am not.'

My have-a-go hero muscles in and starts fingering the back of the road-rage driver's collar. I was angry before, but this irritates me beyond all measure. *I* am dealing with this. I don't need any help, thank you. I especially don't need assistance from a man. I never have needed a man – although, yes, I am prepared to admit that after a year on my own, I'm beginning to miss having a man around. I miss that feeling you get when you drift out of sleep the morning after the night before and find your lover's hand sliding between your thighs. I miss making love naked in the rain – well, the possibility of it, at least. (Dan, my ex-husband, was never quite brave enough to go through with my fantasy.) What I don't miss is the macho posturing, even if it does work like magic in situations such as this.

'It was an accident,' the road-rage driver blusters. 'My foot slipped on the accelerator.'

'Shall I call the police?' the pick-up driver asks me.

'Look – I'll give you my name, address and the name

of my firm's insurance company,' the road-rage driver concedes. 'I've paper and a pen in my car.' He fetches them, scribbles the details down on a scrap of paper and hands it over to me with a business card. *Presley & Partners Estate Agency.* He doesn't recognise me, but I recall now where I've seen him before.

Last summer, when he came to value our house, he made disparaging comments about it, suggesting calling in the *House Doctor* to deal with our clutter – Dan and I were living separate lives by this time. He also criticised the colour of the bathroom suite, which is Air Force blue in case you're wondering. I could gloat and tell him how we sold it through another agent at the full asking price within a couple of weeks of putting it on the market, but I'm already running late so I let him go.

The Mercedes squeezes between my car and the pick-up, then shoots off at high speed with its tyres screaming. A removal lorry tries the same manoeuvre, but can't quite make it. There's a lot more waving and hooting.

'I think we'd better get you off the road, don't you?' the pick-up driver suggests.

'I thought you'd gone,' I say sharply.

'I can't leave you like this, can I?' he says, waving towards my car.

'I can manage,' I protest. 'I don't need any more help, thank you.'

'Forgive me,' he says, 'but I thought you'd broken down.' He speaks with an accent like mine, more South London than Surrey, but the resemblance ends there.

His voice has the gravelled edge of mortar being poured out of a mixer like the one on the back of his pick-up.

'I haven't broken down exactly. I've just run out of diesel.'

'Same difference, isn't it? Your car's blocking the road. There'll be gridlock soon, thanks to you.'

'I can handle it,' I insist.

He raises one eyebrow. That's all it takes for me to realise that I have to admit defeat.

'Okay,' I say grudgingly, 'you could give me a push.'

'Go on then, hop in and release the handbrake,' he says with a grin. 'I'll see if I can bump you up onto the pavement.'

It isn't that easy, and my car ends up in front of a pair of gates at the entrance to one of the grand houses on Coombe Hill. It's called *Haze on the Hill* – either the owners made their fortune in air fresheners, or it's a reference to the traffic fumes from the A3.

I put the handbrake back on, get out again and move round to the boot as the traffic files past. My hero is hanging around beside me. I can smell the sharp citrus scent of soap or shower-gel. I can't help staring at him. He's cleanshaven, his neck lacerated with fresh nicks from a razor. The ridge of his nose is misshapen – I guess he's broken it at some time – but this makes him no less perfect.

'Thanks,' I say belatedly.

'Is there anything else I can do for you?'

'Nothing. Nothing at all.' I'm in denial. What I'd really like him to do for me has much more to do with my body than with my car. It's been well over a year since Dan and I separated, and I haven't had anything more intimate than verbal intercourse with a member of the opposite sex for at least two. I had assumed that my internal workings had rusted through, but I realise now that all it would take is a quick servicing to get them going again.

'I can drive you down to the garage to pick up some diesel.'

'No time, I'm afraid. I'm on my way to a party,' I explain, opening the boot where I keep my boxes of props, too proud to admit that I haven't got any money to buy diesel with. In fact, I'm completely brassic, thanks to Dan. 'If I run like Kelly Holmes with the wind behind me, I might just make it.'

The corners of the pick-up driver's eyes crease as he breaks into a grin.

'I thought you might be running away from the circus.'

'Me?' I say, puzzled.

'The clown outfit?'

In all the excitement I'd completely forgotten my state of dress. I whip off my red foam nose and stuff it into my pocket. I hang on to the curly, multi-coloured wig because I'm unsure what condition my own hair is in underneath it.

'I prefer to call myself a self-employed magic operative,' I say, more stiffly than I intend since I'm smarting at being such an idiot as to imagine that this gorgeous man is chatting to me because he finds me physically attractive!

'A self-employed what?'

'Magic operative.' I've learned that giving your occupation as 'clown' when trying to obtain quotes for car insurance is financial suicide.

'What's your name?'

'Topsy.'

The man frowns.

I give him my best smile. 'I'm also known as Sadie.'

The man reaches out and takes my hand. 'I'm Gareth,' he says. 'Gareth Bryant.'

Tremors of lust and longing judder up my spine. I take in the broad shoulders, and the chain that's wound four times around his ankle, secured with a padlock.

'Are *you* on the run?' I ask, wondering if I'm speaking to an escaped convict. He does have a hint of wickedness around the eyes.

'I'm on my way to start a life sentence, in a manner of speaking,' he says, still clinging to my hand as if I am all that stands between him and Alcatraz. A gust of wind whisks a swirl of cherry blossom from the tree beside us. It settles like pink confetti in his hair. 'I'm getting married.' He drops my hand.

'That's wonderful,' I say flatly, thinking, Congratulations, Sadie. You've found the perfect man without having to place an ad in the paper, and he's marrying someone else.

'I hope all the fuss is worth it, the diets and the dress fittings,' he goes on.

'I can't quite see you in a dress,' I joke, to try and lighten the situation. It works, temporarily. He flashes me a heartstopping smile then returns to unburdening himself.

I don't know what it is about me that makes people want to reveal their innermost thoughts. I am reminded of the plumber who broke down over a weeping tap in my kitchen and confided that his wife had told him she was bored with being married to him. She kicked him out, refused him access to his two children, changed the locks and screwed him for as much money as she could get. She did let him take the dog, a blind and incontinent poodle, as a kind of souvenir. He really couldn't see what he'd done wrong, but maybe that was the problem – what he had failed to do. Not only did he fail to repair his marriage, he failed to mend my tap as well.

'She wants me to wear this bloody awful tie.' Gareth tugs at the insipid, salmon-pink bow which scrunches into a knot as tight as the knot of disappointment that has formed in my belly. I watch him fiddle with it for a moment.

'Let me try.' I angle my hoop so I can step up close to him and reach my hands up to the base of his neck.

'I spent half of last night chained naked to a lamp-post. I could have died from exposure,' he continues as I pick at the knot, 'and my best man's stolen my shoes.'

'What strange friends you have.'

'They belong to the Rugby Club,' he says, as if this explains everything – his physique at least.

'I suppose you can be grateful that they didn't stick you on the overnight train to Edinburgh.' I pause. 'Keep still, will you?'

'I can't. You're tickling me.' He grins again, then adds softly, 'I think you're enjoying this.'

'You can think what you like.' I let my fingers linger a little longer than necessary once I've unfastened the knot in the tie, absorbing the heat and texture of the skin beneath his chin. I take a step back. 'There you go – you're undone.'

'Hey, I couldn't borrow your boots, could I?' he says. I hesitate, looking down at the outsize Doc Martens that I bought from one of the charity shops on New Malden High Street, and sprayed silver.

'You could, but—'

'They're big, but not big enough,' Gareth finishes for me. 'She'll kill me, you realise, when I turn up looking like this.'

I take it that he's referring to his bride.

'I don't think she'll have anything to complain about. You look pretty good to me.' I pause. 'Apart from the chain maybe, and the mud.' I watch him kick his boots one at a time against the high redbrick wall that blocks the view of *Haze on the Hill* from envious eyes like mine.

'Better?' he says.

'No. If you want to know what I think—'

'You're going to tell me anyway,' he interrupts.

'You're having last-minute premarital jitters. Everyone I've ever met has been overwhelmed by nerves on their big day.'

'Are you married?' Gareth asks.

'Divorced.'

'I'm sorry.'

'Don't be. Marrying Dan was the greatest mistake of my life. I realise that now.'

11

Gareth's lips form an O. Very sensual. Incredibly sexy. 'So you think I'm doing the wrong thing?'

'Definitely.' Me and my big mouth. 'Er, possibly,' I backtrack. 'It's my turn to apologise. I have a bit of a downer on marriage at the moment, but that's just me. I'm sure you and your wife will be very happy. Me and Dan were for a while, quite a long while. Listen, I shouldn't have said what I did. I don't know anything about you, or your fiancée. Most marriages work out really well.' And I think of my mother putting on a brave face each time she learned of one of Dad's many affairs until his public fling with her best friend drove her to divorce. Of Annette my sister and her husband Sean, fixated on trying to make a baby. Of my friend Helen, always on the lookout to make sure her husband Michael doesn't run off with a younger model – which is what he did when he left his first wife for her.

'You don't look convinced,' Gareth says quietly.

'It isn't all bad. There are some advantages to being married.'

'Give me one, then.'

I gaze into the boot of my car and pick up the collapsible wand that has fallen out of one of the boxes. I give it a little shake to straighten it out, and drop it back in alongside the magic colouring book.

'Go on. You can't, can you?'

'I'm thinking. How about . . .' I pause for a moment, glancing down at Gareth's great, muddy boots. I can't quite bring myself to mention sex. It's a funny thing, but when you have sex available on tap, you find you're not really bothered about whether you have any or not, but when you don't, it becomes quite an attractive proposition. Forget the panting and the sticky bits. It's being so close and in love with another human being that does it for me.

'When two people are head over heels in love, marriage can strengthen the bond between them,' I begin. 'You do love your fiancée?'

Gareth frowns as if he hasn't considered this question before. 'Yeah, I suppose I must do,' he sighs. 'When I proposed, it seemed like a good idea at the time. I'm almost forty, and all my friends have settled down.'

'You shouldn't get married just because you feel left out,' I comment.

'It's too late to analyse my motives now. I have to go through with it. I gave my word.'

'What time is the wedding?'

Gareth glances at his watch and swears. 'In five minutes.'

'You'd better go. You might just make it, although it is usually the bride who's late, not the groom.'

'I'll have to break with convention.'

I wonder if perhaps, rather than breaking with convention, Gareth would be better off breaking his word, but for once I keep my mouth firmly shut. Somewhere, not far away, some poor bride, surrounded by a clutch of bridesmaids in flouncy, salmon-pink dresses, is waiting for the man she wants to spend the rest of her life with to turn up.

'Thanks again.' I watch Gareth stride across the road to his pick-up. 'Good luck!' I yell over the sound of the traffic, but I don't really mean it. Secretly I hope that

13

Gareth's new wife's bouquet wilts and her veil slips. I hope that the wedding charms, the naff silver-coated plastic horseshoes and ribbons, fall apart in her hands, and that she receives twenty identical toasters and no kettle. I hope that Gareth drops her at the threshold of their marital home.

You see, I do have bad points. An inability to finish what I started. A tendency not to look before I leap. I'm not good with money and, as Dan used to keep telling me, I can't stop myself acting like a jealous cow.

Chapter Two

As I stand watching Gareth drive away and out of my life, the pick-up disappearing in several puffs of black smoke from its exhaust, a song comes to mind. 'Tears of a Clown' by The Beat from way back when I was about thirteen, when I spent hours pogo-dancing in front of a mirror in my bedroom, and tried to pierce the skin on the back of my right hand with a safety pin, sterilised in vodka. I still bear the scar.

I'm gasping for a cup of tea, I have no diesel, and no money until Topsy has magicked her way through her next performance.

Afraid that the owners of *Haze on the Hill* might have my car clamped or towed away while I'm at the party, I find a pen in the glove compartment and scribble on the back of a school newsletter about nit control, DOCTOR ON CALL, and place it on the dashboard. I unload my two boxes overflowing with props from the back of the car. My boots are not conducive to running, so I walk, reassuring myself that it is all downhill from here to the venue, a house in a new development tucked away on the site of an old warehouse on the other side of the A3.

Although the house is only mock-Georgian, its honey-gold stucco reflects the afternoon sunshine, making it look like something out of Jane Austen. I almost expect Colin Firth to wander around the corner past the wisteria to greet me. I stagger up the drive between low hedges of box that appear to have been trimmed with nail scissors, and stop to catch my breath by the front door. For the first time before a party, I have butterflies dancing in my belly. I put it down to Gareth with the sea-green eyes . . .

I knock. The door flies open and I am faced with a wall of small children, all girls, jumping up and down and squealing with excitement.

'It's Topsy. Topsy, Topsy, Topsy!'

A tall slim woman in her early thirties pushes her way through. No Colin then . . .

'Mrs Oaten, I presume?' I say, taking in the bob of shiny ash-blonde hair and the slightly crumpled white linen suit. With her snub nose, flat chest and stomach, she looks as if someone's taken an iron to her, and run out of steam for smoothing out her trousers.

'That's right. Are you the children's entertainer?' she asks primly.

'No, I've come to read your meter,' I joke.

Mrs Oaten exhales a quiet hiss of disapproval.

'I'm Topsy.' I hug the boxes tight, at which the flower on my lapel shoots a slug of water straight at her face. Mrs Oaten tries to take this generously, with a *moue*

16

tighter than a cat's bottom, while the girls shriek with laughter.

'Oh, I'm sorry, so sorry. I have a hankie somewhere.' I rummage through my pockets with one hand and pull something out – a blue hankie with white spots which is knotted to a green one which is knotted to a red one ... The girls keep laughing, but Mrs Oaten is not amused.

'Do come in,' she says, unsmiling.

It might sound a risky thing to do to your customers, but I always like to do this – it gives the kids a laugh, puts them on my side, and provides a useful test of the level of humour that will be appreciated by the audience. There's no point using double entendres in this house. Mrs Oaten won't get them.

'Which one of you is the birthday girl?' I ask as I step inside the hall.

'My daughter Katya, who is in the playroom,' Mrs Oaten says. 'Come this way.'

'Katya's in a strop,' pipes up one of the girls.

I find that I am to perform in the playroom, a room three times the size of my living room at home, that can easily accommodate me, my props and an audience of twenty-five, or twenty-four since Katya, the birthday girl, makes it perfectly clear that she's not in the mood for a party.

'I don't want to be four,' she wails, 'and I don't want *you* here,' she adds, pointing at me.

At first I wonder if it's because she'd prefer the act that someone has set up locally in competition with mine. Theirs is in the style of Harry Potter. Mine is more

Grimaldi, but without the acrobatics. I don't do acrobatics. (I do wonder sometimes if my act is getting a little tired. Helen would make a great straight man to my Topsy, but she won't contemplate it. 'Don't make me laugh,' she says whenever I suggest it.)

While Katya stamps her feet on the lilac and pink floor, and wipes her nose on the batwing sleeve of a blue velvet dress, her mother tells me that Katya is upset because she no longer wants a clown for her party, but a disco like the one her friend Amber had for hers. At first I wish Katya had had a disco too, but gradually, with the help of the magic colouring book and wand, I win her round.

I sit myself on the folding Director's chair that I always bring with me, and weave tales of magic and mystery, taking the girls to other worlds where anything can happen, where I don't have to entertain boisterous children hyped up with food colourings and fizzy drinks, and where I fall in love with a handsome and eligible prince.

It goes better than I expected. I fail to conjure myself up a prince, but Katya falls in love with Ricky, a streak of stripy fur with glass eyes that passes for a racoon, and at the end of the performance, she cries because she doesn't want Topsy to leave. I beg a cup of tea from a grudging Mrs Oaten and make Katya an animal from a modelling balloon in an attempt to console her. They are all variations on the dog. She chooses a rabbit, which is a dog with big ears and a bobble for a tail.

While the caterers – no expense has been spared on this occasion – deliver trestle tables and elaborate sandwiches such as baguettes made into snakes with grapes for eyes, and red pepper tongues, to the play-room, I take Mrs Oaten aside and press an invoice into her hand. She recoils as she reads it, as if I have performed a trick at her expense.

'That's rather excessive, isn't it?' she queries. Her eyes, which glitter like the diamonds on her finger, are small and mean, and I swear that if I had the power to turn this woman into a frog, I'd do it.

'That's what we agreed.'

Mrs Oaten shakes her head slowly. 'I think it's absolutely extortionate for a couple of hours of puerile acting and unsophisticated illusions.'

'I'm a clown. That's what clowns do,' I protest, 'and the children loved it.'

'I took your number from the advert on the infor-mation board at my eldest daughter's school. I was expecting an educational experience.'

I know the school, the private one where my sister Annette teaches geography. She put the card up for me.

I am gobsmacked, but not for long. 'If you'd wanted something educational, you should have taken them on a trip to the Natural History Museum.' I watch Mrs Oaten re-read the invoice.

'How about giving me a discount?' she says next. 'That way, everyone will be happy.'

'Hang on a mo. *I'm* not happy!' I stamp one Doc Marten down on the floor. 'I don't do discounts, Mrs Oaten. You might assume that because I'm a clown, you don't have to take me seriously, but this is my job,

19

my career. It isn't something I do for fun. I'm a single parent with twins. It's up to me to pull the rabbit out of the hat, metaphorically speaking, to support them.' I look down the playroom. Twenty-five faces are looking up at me from their sandwiches with great interest. 'If you don't pay me in full, in cash, poor Topsy will have to sell her magic colouring book and give Ricky away to the zoo.'

'Who, or what, is Ricky?' interrupts Mrs Oaten.

'Oh, your silly mummy wasn't paying attention, was she?' I aim this at Katya, who is at the head of the nearest table. Katya stands up and places her hands on her hips.

'Don't you know, Mummy, that Ricky is Topsy's racoon,' she says superiorly.

'Tell me,' says Mrs Oaten, trying but failing to join in with the spirit of the party, 'did you name him after Rikki-Tikki-Tavi?'

I frown.

'The mongoose from *The Jungle Book*,' she continues.

'It's Rick-ay,' I explain, 'from *EastEnders*.' I am unable to suppress a smug smile as Mrs Oaten doesn't appear to have heard of either Rick-ay or *EastEnders*. In fact, I am beginning to understand why she wanted an educational experience. Her education is sadly lacking. 'Anyway, if the zoo won't take him, I shall have to have him put down.'

'What's put down?' asks Katya, tugging on my hoop.

'Shh!' hisses Mrs Oaten, trying to steer me towards the playroom door.

I stand my ground. 'Topsy will starve to death.'

'Please pay Topsy, Mummy,' begs Katya, clinging to her mother's linen trousers. 'You have to . . .'

Mrs Oaten gives into a chorus of emotional blackmail. I win, but I have to have my full fee as a cheque, not in cash, which is inconvenient to say the least. I still have no money, and my car's still stuck halfway up Coombe Hill parked across someone's drive.

When I return, I pack my props boxes back into the boot and decide to call Helen on my mobile. However, the battery's flat so I can't ask her for a loan until the cheque's been cleared at the bank, and even then the bank will probably want to hang on to it to reduce my overdraft.

There's only one thing for it. I head on foot to New Malden High Street. *New* Malden? The newest concepts here, among the rows of commuter-belt houses, are the ubiquitous one-way signs, speed humps and other traffic-calming measures that only serve to agitate the most tranquil driver. Oriental food shops like SeoulPlaza, and MKate Supermarket stand on the High Street alongside Safeway and Tudor Williams, an old-fashioned department store. There's Pizza Hut, B'Wise, and Shoefayre, and it's always busy, a fact that I am depending on . . .

Embarrassed? I don't do embarrassed although I will confess to a prickling heat that is breaking out between my breasts, the same sensation that came over me when I was in Tesco this morning.

I was standing at the check-out, my stomach growling in response to the mingling aromas of croissants, crispy bacon and stewed coffee, while the woman at the till rang up the last items – a half-price Smarties egg left over from Easter and spare toothbrush heads. I'd picked them up for Dan, forgetting that I'm no longer responsible for his oral health.

The woman at the check-out swiped my Clubcard and credit card, and her blank expression changed to one of mild interest.

'Your credit card's been rejected,' she said.

I handed over my debit card.

'That's come up *refer to bank*.'

'I don't understand.' I dug around in my purse for cash, and found the sum of 28p. 'Hold on a mo, I'll get some cash.' I dashed off across the shop, ignoring the groans and tut-tutting from the people in the queue behind me. I tried both cards in the cash machine. No luck. I called Dan on the mobile on my way back to the check-out. 'It's me, Sadie. What the hell's going on?'

'What do you mean?' Dan blustered.

'You know very well,' I snapped down the phone. 'I'm in the middle of Tesco with no money!' The line fizzed. 'Don't you dare hang up on me!'

Dan cleared his throat. He always clears his throat when he's nervous. 'I'm out of work,' he blurted out.

'When? For how long?' When I am excited or stressed, my voice rises by an octave and more than a few decibels, a reflex over which I have no control. I became aware that everyone was staring in my direction.

'It's been three months since my last contract ran out.'

'Why didn't you tell me?'

'I hoped something would come up, but the job market's like a burned-out motherboard.'

I hesitate, wondering if this is Dan's latest idea of an insult to my mothering skills.

'It's dead,' he adds in explanation. Dan is a computer programmer. Some might classify him as a nerd. If I hadn't been the main attraction in Tesco, I might have found myself feeling sorry for him because his self-esteem, as well as our financial security, depends on his work.

'What am I supposed to do?'

'You and the twins will be all right. You'll have the money from the sale of the house soon.'

It's true. The home that Dan and I shared when we were married, and where I live with the twins, has been under offer for months, and I'm supposed to be looking for somewhere else for us to live.

'I need money now. I can't wait until we complete the sale. Listen, Dan, you get yourself down here right now, and pay for my shopping.'

'I've told you, I've given you all the money I possess. You've stripped me of all my worldly goods, apart from my clothes and my U2 CDs.'

'Thank goodness I don't have to listen to *those* any more.'

'You have an appalling taste in music, Sadie.'

'Haven't!'

'Abba, Stevie Wonder and Mike Oldfield's *Tubular Bells* are all so middle of the road,' he taunts.

'You can talk. That knitted pullover you were wearing last time I saw you reached the end of the road several millennia ago.'

'Oh Sadie, don't exaggerate.'

23

'I'm not exaggerating.'

'You are!'

'Excuse me,' the woman at the check-out cut in, 'but are you going to pay for this shopping, or not?'

'I am not!' I was neither exaggerating, nor about to pay for my shopping. Dan and I were still bickering like a married couple, and I couldn't think of anything else for an outrageous bohemian like me to do, except cut Dan off, then walk as quickly and as nonchalantly out of the supermarket as I could.

The prickling heat between my breasts intensifies now as I position myself outside the Old Town Hall, a redbrick building which is now Waitrose, and alongside an unshaven middle-aged man with a dog and a tartan shopping trolley.

'G'day,' he says in an Australian accent. '*Big Issue*?'

'Er, not yet, thanks. I'm brassic.'

He frowns.

'Boracic lint. Skint,' I explain.

'Ah. No brass? No lolly?'

'That's right. Would you like a balloon?'

'Love one.'

I model him a hat with a flower on the top to start things off. It isn't very good, but he's pleased.

'That's beaut,' he says, pulling it down to his ears. 'A real ripsnorter.'

I have modelled balloons on the street before for practice and for fun, but not out of desperation. It's a pound a go. I do dogs and cats, but no more hats. One of the dads who stops to order a sword for his son which turns out quite well, asks me if I am collecting for charity. I am, if you believe that charity should start at home, but I do start to worry that I might need a licence, and that one of the Big Guns from the PTA might recognise me and ask me to do a session at the school fête in June and, even worse, that Dan and the children might turn up.

Yes, I'd like Dan to see what he has reduced me to, to make him sick with shame, but I don't want Lorna and Sam to find out that I'm working on the streets for money. Lorna would live in a state of perpetual worry about our financial security, and Sam would lose all credibility with his friends, the few that he has left. In his head he is Jackie Chan fighting the baddies of the world, but the violence of his Kung Fu moves tends to put any would-be friends off.

An hour later, and I am doing quite well. I add up the money during a lull. I've done it. My ordeal is over. I have enough cash for a container of diesel, a ready meal for one, and a copy of the *Big Issue*. Relieved, I tuck my balloon pump inside my dungarees.

'Mum! Hey, Mum!' Lorna is waving and calling from the other side of the High Street. 'Mum! It *is* you, isn't it?'

I can hardly deny it. Running isn't an option. Nor, for obvious reasons, is blending into the crowd. I stand and wait, watching Lorna skipping along in an outfit as colourful and uncoordinated as Topsy's: a pink long-sleeved top with sparkling *Princess* logo on the front, a lime-green and mauve striped 'skort', teamed with long blue and cream socks.

Dan and Sam are behind her, Dan straightbacked and scowling, and Sam with his hands in his jeans pockets, head bowed and pretending he hasn't seen me. Dan, Sam and Lorna: three freckled redheads. Am I pleased to see them? Of course I am. I haven't seen the twins since seven o'clock last night when Dan came to collect them for the weekend and take them back to the house that he's renting just off the Kingston Road. It's a two-storey hutch of a house, hardly big enough for a rabbit, and a dwarf one at that.

Dan steers the twins across the High Street.

'You should have used the pedestrian crossing,' I say protectively.

'You fuss too much,' he replies, blinking hard as if he has an attack of hayfever. 'What the hell are you doing, Sadie?' The sound of Dan's voice, which used to fire me up with joy and desire, niggles me. My make-up starts to melt as my face burns hotter than a red chili pepper.

'What does it look like?' I snap back.

'As if you're out begging.'

'I've been selling balloons.'

'Mum, you're so embarrassing,' Sam groans.

'This isn't embarrassing,' says Dan. 'It's tantamount to child abuse. How could you? How can you let your children down like this?'

'My children?'

'Our children,' Dan corrects himself quickly, and I smile to myself. He must have been having a bad time with the twins this weekend as the children are always mine, not his, when they misbehave. I expect Lorna's been going on at him about having her ears pierced, and I dread to think what Sam's been up to. Sam was the one I had to keep strapped in the trolley at all times whenever we went to the supermarket. That was until he learned how to undo the straps and fell out onto his head. After that, I had to keep him out of the super-market altogether.

Three pairs of hazel eyes gaze at me. I concentrate on Dan's. He isn't wearing his glasses. I peer closer, not difficult as we are the same height when I'm wearing Doc Martens. He blinks hard again. His eyes look red and slightly tearful.

'You're wearing contact lenses?'

A deep flush drowns Dan's freckles.

'Dad's trying them out,' Lorna interrupts. 'We have to guide him back to the optician's after an hour.'

Dan's had his hair cut short too. Like the twins, his hair has a tendency to curl, but the curls have gone, and the remaining hair has been waxed up into a Hoxton fin.

'Are you seeing someone?' I ask.

'I don't think that's any of your business,' Dan says.

'I'm just taking an interest.' I was going to add, 'in your affairs,' but affairs are a no-go subject for me and Dan. That was it, you see. I'm not sure to this day that Dan ever had any affairs while he was married to me. He says that his infidelities were all in my head, and it was my jealous streak that drove us apart.

Dan walked into me, literally, spilling a bottle of Diamond White down my front at the Fountain pub. He was celebrating his eighteenth birthday. I was twenty-two. I dragged him outside and we meandered, arm-in-arm, along the banks of the Beverley Brook in the dark, until he'd sobered up enough to remember where he lived so that I could escort him home. It took me seven years to decide to accept his proposal of marriage, and we were happily married for another nine.

Happily might be stretching the point a little, but the time passed agreeably enough until I noticed that Dan was becoming increasingly blasé about our wedding anniversaries. The number of Belgian chocolates in my annual gift-wrapped box seemed to diminish exponentially with the number of years we had been married, and I began to believe that I loved him far more than he loved me.

Our troubles didn't so much start as come to a head during the season of office parties, the Christmas before last. One night, Dan didn't come home. He said he'd drunk too much to drive. I accused him of sleeping with one of the women he was working with at the time. Dan denied it, and I never had any proof either way, but it was too late. Dan sat me down with a glass of wine, and said that we needed to talk. The conversation is etched on my memory.

'What is it you want?' I asked. 'An open marriage? Time out?'

'I'm getting to the point where I'm beginning to hate you,' he said. 'I don't want to hate you, Sadie.'

'I shall hate you if you ask me for a divorce.'

'You'll have to hate me then,' he said quietly.

Was it a shock? I suppose it was. Among the usual little niggles, Dan had begun complaining about my body hair. He was appalled when he noticed that I hadn't done anything about my bikini line when we took the twins swimming together, but I put that down to him looking at too many copies of *FHM*. It wasn't a shock to my mother, who claimed that she always knew that Dan and I weren't right for each other, that we would inevitably split up because we didn't possess a garden shed into which Dan could retreat in times of stress. I didn't force her to confront her powers of logic by pointing out that she and my father once owned two garden sheds *and* a greenhouse – which didn't stop them divorcing.

My father's dead now. He died from a heart attack at sixty, a consequence perhaps of the stress he created for himself, trying to hide his rampant promiscuity behind the façade of 'The Perfect Marriage'. I came to forgive him and my mother for the lie that they lived while Annette and I were growing up, but I can't quite forget.

'Mum, can I have a balloon?' Lorna asks, bringing me back to the present.

'If you give me a pound.'

'I haven't got a pound.' Lorna's face falls. My heart twists.

'Do you really think I'd try to make money out of my own children?' I tease.

'Well, yes,' says Lorna.

'You haven't given us our pocket-money for weeks,' Sam cuts in.

'Your dad's supposed to give you pocket-money.'

'I'm skint,' Dan says, turning his trouser-pockets inside out to prove the point.

'Nice trousers,' I comment.

'They're new,' says Lorna. 'We helped him choose them when we went into Kingston this morning.'

'I can tell. Look.' I point to the label that's hanging out of the waistband beneath his leather jacket. 'You will be skint if you go around buying new clothes as well as contact lenses.' A helpless anger rises like bile in my throat. 'For goodness sake, Dan, you're not working. Where's the money coming from?'

'That's none of your business either,' Dan growls, tearing at the label and ripping it off.

'Of course it bloody well is! How am I supposed to manage? I expect you've already contacted the CSA to reduce your payments.'

'I haven't,' says Dan, looking hurt.

'No, I suppose there's no point if you're refusing to contribute anything at all!'

'Listen, Sadie, I'm trying to beat the competition by projecting a more youthful image so I can get a new contract. It's dog eat dog out there at the moment.'

'You expect me to believe that?' I am close to combusting spontaneously.

'Please, Mum. Stop shouting.' Lorna looks up at me, wide-eyed through long lashes. 'You promised that you wouldn't shout at Dad any more.'

'I'm not shouting.'

'You are,' Dan says.

I turn away from his smug, self-righteous expression and take a deep breath. Sam is standing a little way away, staring into the travel agent's window, wishing no doubt that he was on the other side of the world.

The *Big Issue* seller has stuffed his belongings into his tartan trolley, and is slipping a rope lead around his dog's neck, ready to move on.

'All right, I'm sorry.' I reach out and dab at Lorna's freckled nose with one forefinger. 'What kind of animal would you like?'

'Can I have a parrot, please?'

I frown. A parrot can hardly be classed as a variation on the dog.

'Parrots aren't in fashion,' I say, taking a balloon from my pocket and pump from my dungarees. 'Apparently, dogs are incredibly trendy at the moment.'

'Don't you mean cool?' says Lorna.

'Maybe. Hey, Sam,' I call as I blow up a balloon and tie a knot in the end. 'Come over here and choose a balloon.'

He turns his back.

'Don't you turn your back on me!'

He spins round on the flashing heel of his trainer, and sticks his tongue out.

'Sam!'

'Leave me alone!'

'Let it drop, Sadie,' says Dan, restraining me with a hand on my arm. 'He's upset.'

'So am I, but that's no reason for Sam to be rude to me. I didn't choose to do this,' I say, pulling my arm away and twisting up Lorna's balloon. 'It's your fault that I'm almost destitute.'

There's a flicker of warmth in Dan's eyes. 'Can I make it up to you and invite you to have tea with us? We're going to McDonald's.'

'I thought you said you hadn't got any money.'

'I have one last ten-pound note,' Dan says, tapping his breast-pocket.

I decline the offer of tea because I can see that he's right about me embarrassing Sam, and I don't want to be mistaken for a passing Ronald McDonald.

'See you tomorrow night then, Mum,' Lorna says. Her lip quivers slightly as she gives me a kiss goodbye, putting her arms up across my hoop and wrapping them around my neck. Of the four of us, I believe she is the only one who still harbours secret dreams of Dan and me getting back together.

'Bye, darling,' I murmur. I approach Sam, but he shrinks away from my embrace, and wipes off the smudge of white make-up that I leave on his cheek. He thinks he's too old to kiss – in public anyway.

'I'll drop them back at six tomorrow, if that's all right,' says Dan. 'I know it's a bit earlier than usual—'

'No, that's fine,' I cut in. By six I am normally pacing the house, waiting for the twins to return. For all his faults, Dan is a great dad, but I can't help begrudging him the time they spend with him.

I watch them go, Lorna skipping along on one side of Dan, and Sam swaggering along on the other, before I slip into Waitrose to buy my dinner. I choose a pasta meal, then fail to decide between Raspberry Tiramisú, and Two Islands of Passion with Apricot Coulis. I put the pasta back, and buy both desserts, then head off to purchase diesel before I collect the car. It's still outside *Haze on the Hill*, but some (other) clown has left a hand-written note tucked under one of the windscreen wipers.

Dear Dr who? Please leave your name and address so I can contact your surgery to complain about your inconsiderate parking. Illegible signature.

I scribble a note back, and leave it spiked onto one of the double gates.

Address – Tardis, Edge of the Universe. I shall be back. The Doctor.

Back inside the car, I switch on Magic FM and drive home the long way round because the High Street is clogged with traffic. I'm on my way along a cut-through, cursing the speed humps, when I catch a glimpse of a *For Sale* board peeping out from an overgrown hedge. What makes me pull in and stop? The dazzling glare of the sun reflected by the windows of the house behind it? The figures that I conjure up from the shadows in the front garden, ladies from another age, dressed in bonnets and shawls? I tell myself not to be silly, that I've borrowed too many sagas from the library since Dan and I split up.

It is just a house, a dilapidated Edwardian mid-terrace, caught between its more respectable neighbours and their tarmacked front gardens. A few steps lead up to an aluminium replacement door which is completely out of keeping with the style of the house, but it wouldn't take much for someone to change it.

I sink into my seat as far as I can with Topsy's hoop digging into my back and study the end-on gable and bay windows in more detail. There's blue paint peeling from the window-frames, and a few tiles missing from the roof, but the redbrick walls look sound. My heart starts to beat faster than it did when the man from

Presley & Partners Estate Agents ran into the back of my car. I'll soon have the whole of my divorce settlement. The twins and I need somewhere to live. Why not live here?

Yes, the house appears to need some work to turn it into a home, but that shouldn't be beyond me. I know from telly programmes like *Property Ladder* that the most unlikely people are buying houses nowadays, doing them up and selling them on for profit. In fact, I've considered it myself when trying to dream up more lucrative alternatives to my career as a clown, but not that seriously.

However, with Dan out of work, I need to earn more money than Topsy can ever provide for food and clothes, and paying the bills. I could do with an occupation that offers me and the twins a more secure financial future than we have now: holidays, a pension, deposits for Lorna and Sam to buy homes of their own one day. Not only that, there are only so many fresh routines that Topsy can conjure up – I'd love a new challenge.

Why not go into property development? It would be a laugh, much more fun than clowning about as Topsy. It might be hard work, but when has there ever been anything I cannot do? (I'm ignoring parking a car, and keeping a marriage going.) I have experience of running my own business, and I know my PVC from my MDF. All I need now is a partner.

Chapter Three

I am sitting in Helen's conservatory, waiting for her to bring coffee through from the kitchen. The conservatory has a dwarf wall. This is important, according to Helen's husband Michael. It puts you one up on people who have a conservatory without one, and of course miles above people like me who haven't got a conservatory at all.

Helen enters, carrying a tray. She is tall, slender and moves with the lanky elegance of a giraffe, and I mean that sincerely. This morning she's wearing straight-cut blue jeans and a pink hooded top, and nothing on her feet. She has a pair of tiny earrings and a simple gold chain around her neck.

'I don't know why you can't tell me where we're going,' she grumbles as she sits down with a creak that I hope has more to do with the rattan colonial-style suite than her thirty-five-year-old joints. 'Let me guess, you're taking me to meet someone. You've met a new man at last. Oh Sadie, that's fantastic, but why the black jacket?'

I'm wearing the one smart jacket I possess, the one I used to wear for meetings with the solicitor who dealt with my divorce.

'I'll die if you tell me he's a funeral director,' Helen continues.

'A wealthy and drop-dead gorgeous funeral director,' I say, stroking my chin.

Helen plunges the cafetière down so hard that coffee splurges out of the spout and drips through the rattan coffee-table onto the ceramic tiled floor.

'Don't be ridiculous. I wouldn't be seen dead with a funeral director,' I say, laughing. 'I'm not seeing anyone.'

Apparently reassured, Helen pours two glasses of coffee. Yes, glasses, not mugs. A bit over the top, if you ask me.

If I were a man, I would fancy Helen. She manages to look infuriatingly stunning whatever she's wearing, yet she has one or two flaws that mean you can forgive her for it. The blonde highlights that run through the untamed curls that tumble down to her shoulders, contrast perhaps a little too strongly with her own shade of brunette, and her teeth are a tiny bit yellowed, in spite of the hours she spends trialling different brands of whitening toothpastes. Helen claims that the yellow is an indication of how strong her teeth are, but I think it's an unfortunate consequence of her having attended too many coffee mornings when her daughter Charlotte was a baby. She's talking about having her front teeth veneered. Is it vanity or insecurity on Helen's part? I might feel insecure if I was married to Michael.

Michael is a self-made man, a jack-the-lad from the East End, with ambition, a streak of ruthlessness and the gift of the gab. He has made his fortune importing, dealing and double-dealing in all those things you find in discount shops, things you didn't realise you couldn't live without until you see them. There's the pink pig, twist-and-ping kitchen timer that I have to set for ten minutes to get three and a half for a boiled egg. Perhaps time moves more quickly in Taiwan, or their hens lay smaller eggs. There are the boxes of fifty hair clips that I buy for Lorna that all snap or are lost within a couple of days of purchase, and the light-up Father Christmas with the dirty laugh that I bought on 23 December last year, and threw out on Boxing Day.

'So where are we going?' Helen tries again.

'You'll see when we get there.' I change the subject. 'Now, I was telling you about my weekend. Where did I get to?'

'The check-out, Tesco.'

'That's right. Dan said he hadn't worked for three months, so he hadn't paid any money into my account.'

'The bastard.' Helen breathes steam from her coffee glass.

'I didn't have any money to buy food or diesel, so my car broke down, and someone ran into the back of me on the way to Topsy's party, and then this macho builder muscled in and took over when I was managing the situation perfectly well myself.' I gaze at the view from the conservatory. It faces an area of new decking enclosed by a palisade fence. When I told Helen that it reminded me of a hitching post in a Mid-west town where Clint Eastwood might tie up his horse, she thought I was joking. Still does. There is a lawn with daffodils beyond it, and a not-so-very-distant vista of the neighbours' conifer hedge. My house, which is across the road from Helen's, faces in the opposite direction so the view from my back garden is a playing-field and an electricity pylon.

'Go on,' says Helen, leaning towards me. 'Tell me more.'

'Oh, I let him play the hero.'

'A man likes to think he can be somebody's hero,' says Helen thoughtfully as she starts tidying up. She closes the catalogue that's open on the table, hiding the description of a Neoprene tankini she's ringed with blue biro. I've already looked. It's a size 12.

'He didn't do much,' I explain. 'He saved me from a road-rage attack, then pushed my car off the road.'

'Did you turn a few tricks for him in return?' Helen grins.

'I wish,' I sigh. 'I wish I'd waited to get changed and made-up at the party. I mean, my bum looks big enough already without Topsy's dungarees.'

Helen rearranges the photo frames beside the catalogue. One contains a Red Indian nuptial prayer about roaming buffalo, love and fire. Its sentiments of everlasting faith and commitment make me feel slightly nauseous, as if I've eaten a plateful of onion bhajis for breakfast, but maybe if Dan and I had had one and we'd read and acted on it every day, our marriage might have survived, like Helen and Michael's. Maybe not. Helen picks up a photo of a man who resembles

Pierce Brosnan, gazing up fondly into the eyes of his younger bride. Helen was twenty-six then, and Michael was forty-one. Helen gives it a quick blow and a brush with her hand to remove some imagined dust, and puts it back down, while the burr of the fan with integral spotlights competes with the hum of traffic out on the main road.

'Would you like me to leave?' I ask.

She looks up, her brow furrowed in spite of all the rejuvenating AHAs that she uses.

'I seem to be getting in the way of you doing your housework.'

'No, you're not. I'm just . . .'

'Is something bothering you?'

Helen bites her lip for a moment, then shakes her head and forces a smile. I don't press her – she'll tell me when she's ready.

'So this man, he was all right?' she prompts me. 'Fanciable?'

'Eminently. If I were looking for a man, which I'm not, not really, he would have been perfect.'

'Oh Sadie, do you know what this means?' says Helen excitedly. 'You're finally over Dan.'

'I've known that for ages.'

'No, you haven't. You've been going round oblivious to the charms of other men. Last week, if Brad Pitt had walked into this room, you wouldn't have noticed.'

'I would because you would have screamed, and jumped all over him.'

Helen ignores me. 'Don't you see, this man you're talking about is the first one you've taken any interest

39

in since your divorce. Did you get his phone number?' She pauses as I shake my head. 'His name?'

'Gareth. Gareth Bryant.' A shadow crosses Helen's face. 'You don't know him, do you?' I suppose it shouldn't surprise me if she does, since she's lived in New Malden for most of her life. I'm a relative newcomer, having moved here from Croydon a mere twenty-one years ago when my parents broke up.

'The name's very familiar . . .'

'Please, don't tell me he was one of your conquests,' I interrupt.

'You said that he's a builder, so it can't be the same one. My Gareth got a commission to go into the Army.' Helen grins, and adds, 'At least, one of my Gareths did.'

I am relieved. I couldn't bear the thought of Gareth being one of her cast-offs. Officially, Helen had three lovers before Michael. Unofficially, when she's under the influence of a couple of glasses of wine, and Michael's out of earshot, she's had many more. I wonder sometimes if I missed out, holding on to my virtue until Dan proposed to me under the flyover at the end of Burlington Road, and remaining monogamous thereafter.

'Can't you trace him, find his number in the *Yellow Pages*, or send a letter to the paper saying that you want to thank your knight in armour in person?' Helen suggests.

'There's no point. He was dressed in a morning suit, not armour, and he had a chain, not chainmail, padlocked to his ankle.'

'He sounds like some kind of pervert to me.'

'He was on his way to his wedding,' I say glumly.

'Sadie, I'm sorry . . .'

'I spent the rest of the weekend on my own.'

'We're going to have to do something about this,' says Helen.

'There's no time.' I finish my coffee. I drink it too quickly, scalding my throat. 'We've got to go.'

'For goodness sake, I can't get wound up about this adventure of yours if you won't tell me where we're going.'

I stand up.

Helen follows suit reluctantly. 'Why are you keeping me in suspense?'

'I'll show you. We'll take your car.'

'Do I need to get changed?'

'No, you're fine as you are. Let's go.'

Helen whistles up her keys (the bleeping keyring is one of Michael's imports) and we are off. Helen drives. I give directions over Coldplay on Radio 1 while we tailgate a pick-up truck along the High Street. It isn't Gareth's, which is a pity because if it was, I'd have made Helen follow it so I could run into him just one more time. Instead, we park in front of a Mercedes with its front bumper caved in outside the house I saw on Saturday.

'Well?' says Helen.

'Look. Over there.'

She frowns.

'The house.' I wave my arms as expansively as I can in the passenger seat of a Mini Cooper. Michael bought it in metallic silver for Helen's birthday. I'd have preferred a yellow VW Beetle myself. For someone so tall, Helen folds up very neatly inside it, like one of Michael's ultra-cheap, fast-selling clothes horses.

'You remember that you were saying only the other day when we were talking about careers and fulfilment and the rest of our lives, how keen you were for us to get into property development?' I begin. I ignore her protestations of *was I?* and continue, 'Here is our perfect opportunity.'

'It looks a bit tatty.' Helen cricks her neck to look out of the side window.

'That's the whole point. You buy a property that needs some work, but not too much, then you do it up and sell it for a handsome profit. Don't jump to a decision yet. You have to see inside it first to appreciate its potential.'

'You've been inside already?'

'On Saturday afternoon. As I said before, it was an eventful weekend.' I push the car door open and slide out. My new friend from *Presley & Partners* is on the pavement holding out the keys. His name is Marcus, and he can be quite polite when he's not behind the wheel of a Mercedes – positively fawning, in fact.

'I'll wait in the car,' he says.

'We might be some time.'

'Take as long as you like, Mrs Keith,' he simpers.

Helen and I walk the few paces across the overgrown front garden and the five steps up to the front door.

'That's the nutter who rammed my car on Saturday.' Water drips onto my shoulder from the branches of a rampant lilac. I brush it off. 'That's why he's being particularly smarmy, even for an estate agent.'

'So that's what this is all about. You're giving him the runaround as some kind of revenge.' Helen sighs. 'Sadie, you are the limit, dragging me over here when I could have been hanging out my first load of sheets.' She turns and heads back down the steps.

'Where are you going?'

'Home.'

'No, stop!' I run after her, grab her arm. 'I want you to look at this house with me. This has nothing to do with revenge.'

Helen raises one eyebrow.

'Well, maybe a little,' I concede. 'Now that we're here though,' I dangle the keys, 'we might as well have a look inside, mightn't we?' I march up the steps without waiting for an answer. Helen follows.

'It was you who put the idea of property development into my mind, Helen.' I insert the key in the lock and jiggle it before it will turn. 'You said that Michael had some money he wanted to invest outside the business.'

'I'm surprised you remember – you were completely sozzled.'

We'd just finished Michael's last bottle of rum. Rum and Coke is Michael's favourite tipple at home. When he's impressing his business associates at the Golf Club, it's a single malt with a splash of highland spring water. Helen insisted on drinking the rum in a fit of pique because Michael had been having a dig about her not going out to work.

43

Helen has always given me the impression that Michael likes her being a stay-at-home mum. It gives him a certain status, being able to show everyone that he makes enough money for Helen not to have to work, but times are changing, and one by one as the children of his business associates start school, their wives return to work, and there is more status in being able to say, 'My wife is setting up a shop to sell secondhand baby equipment and children's clothes,' than 'My wife is at home, bleaching the kitchen worktops.'

'I'm not sozzled now. I'm sober and perfectly serious. I've sold my house, subject to contract. I could buy this one, and release some capital to live on while I do it up.' I correct myself. 'While *we* do it up.' I push the front door open to let Helen in. 'What do you think?' I ask, stepping into the hall behind her.

'I think you're mad.' Helen wrinkles her nose. 'It's a bit small.'

'I bet you don't say that to Michael.' I am not smiling. I am a little hurt that Helen doesn't like the house as much as I do.

'I faked it last night,' she says. 'Michael's taken to watching the clock when we're making love. When he thinks I have my eyes closed and I'm in the grip of passion, he sneaks a look at his alarm. I thought I might be able to hurry things up by pretending I was having an orgasm. You should have seen me, like Meg Ryan in *When Harry Met Sally*.'

'I'd rather not, thanks,' I cut in quickly as Helen reminds me indirectly of what I am missing in my life.

'I've never had to fake it before.'

'It's probably nothing to worry about. Why don't you talk to Michael about it, explain that quality is more important than quantity when it comes to making love?'

'You're right, Sadie. Enough of my sordid sex-life.'

I show Helen into the front reception room to get her mind back on the house. On a second inspection, the house seems rather sordid too. The front room is unfurnished apart from a carpet and curtains. The woodchip wallpaper, which is painted mustard, has been scratched to pieces below knee height. Strange odours of musk, cold chips, and cat's pee emanate from the brown and gold swirls underfoot. I lift the edge of the carpet to find floorboards. Perfect.

'It's darker than a Tarantino film,' Helen observes.

'If we redecorate in a light colour, and get rid of those old curtains it will look fantastic,' I assure her. 'In fact, it'll be so bright, you'll need to wear shades.'

Helen is not convinced.

'The location is perfect,' I insist, but my words are drowned out by a fearsome rumbling and the house starts to shake as if we're at the epicentre of an earthquake.

'What did that measure on the Richter scale?' says Helen as the rumbling dies down.

'All right, the house backs onto the railway line, but it's very convenient for the station.'

Helen moves on. 'There's a catflap in the back door.'

'It has all the mod cons.'

'Don't tell me this is supposed to be the utility?' she continues.

'There isn't a utility. This is the kitchen.'

'Oh, it can't be . . .' I watch Helen run her eyes over the beige mock marble worktop, the cupboards painted in shiny pea-green, and the dank hell-holes left for a cooker and fridge-freezer. 'How can you contemplate doing up this house? It's absolutely filthy.'

'A splash of bleach should do it.'

'You'll be telling me next that a bottle of Febreze can fix the carpets.'

'We'll take the carpets up. There are boards underneath that we can strip and polish. It'll be as cheap as chips. What do you think?'

Helen seems to be warming to the idea. 'I can see a neutral, hessian-style carpet throughout, and ceramic tiles with underfloor heating in the bathroom,' she says. 'We'll have to rip the kitchen out and start again.'

'That's a bit drastic, isn't it? I thought we'd change the doors and paint the tiles.' I know I've fallen in love with the house, but it's supposed to be an investment opportunity. 'I haven't budgeted for a complete refit.'

Helen's biting at her lip. She is tempted, isn't she? I must be careful not to put her off.

'I suppose I can juggle with the figures,' I suggest helpfully.

'I'll ask Michael to have a look at them.' Helen turns away to the kitchen wall and thumps it. 'We can have this wall taken out,' she says, 'and make the dining room open-plan into the kitchen. We'll have brushed steel appliances and maplewood units. It'll look fab.' She pauses. 'Do you think we could scrape up enough money for an extension?'

'I don't think so. I've done the sums,' I continue, which is pretty amazing when you consider that I got a D the first time I took O-level Maths, and an E the second, 'and this is the type of property we can afford if we go in fifty-fifty. It'll never be Beckingham Palace, but it's a good place to start. Who knows? In a few years' time, we could be renovating a mansion, or doing up a farmhouse in Tuscany.'

'Michael's always wanted to move to Tuscany,' says Helen. 'Sometimes I wish that he would when he goes on about me not having a job.'

'Just think how pleased he'll be when he can tell his associates down at the Golf Club that his wife's a property developer.'

'What if it doesn't work out?' Helen grumbles. 'None of your other scams have.'

'They were schemes, not scams.' I've known Helen for eight years, since Dan and I moved into the house opposite. During that time, we've tried various money-making ideas. Helen still has heaps of junk in her garage from our car-booting enterprise. We never did find the elusive Fabergé egg for 50p. I have stacks of jigsaw puzzles up in my loft from our foray into handmade wooden toys that we peddled around the craft fairs until we decided that it would be more fun to make novelty birthday cakes. In between times, I have worked in Market Research, and delivered the *Yellow Pages*, while Helen had a brief spell as a trainee veterinary receptionist before returning to the pursuit of extreme housework.

'I don't think I want the commitment,' she tells me now. 'I have more than enough to do already.'

'Like what?'

Helen shrugs. 'Michael likes the house to look reasonable, and for me to have his dinner on the table when he gets home.'

'That's a pretty pathetic excuse.'

'I have Charlotte to look after too.'

Helen has a point regarding Charlotte, their eight-year-old daughter. All around their house are pictures of Charlotte in various guises: as school swot, Brownie Sixer, prima-donna ballerina, disco diva, aspiring international gymnast and future Olympic swimmer. Apart from the clothing, Charlotte always looks the same with her big blue eyes, straight brown hair and a deadpan expression that makes me wonder if she enjoys any of these activities at all.

'A new career would be quite a topic of conversation for the mums at ballet.'

'But I have loads to talk about already,' Helen protests.

'Like what? The price of limescale removers, and the number of cyclones in your vacuum cleaner?'

'We're different, Sadie. I don't need a career. I'm not like you – I'm not allergic to housework.'

'I know you have less reason to work than the rest of us with Michael being loaded, but what are you going to do with the rest of your life? You aren't going to have another baby to keep you at home, are you?'

'I'd have liked a boy like Sam.' Helen corrects herself quickly. 'Almost like Sam.'

Much as I love him, I know what she means.

'So Michael hasn't changed his mind?'

Helen shakes her head. Her eyes glitter with tears, and I wish I hadn't raised the subject of a brother or sister for Charlotte. Helen's emotions are still very raw even though Michael told her before they married that he didn't want any more children as he already has one son, Tom, with his first wife. Charlotte was the compromise.

I can understand why Helen didn't argue at the time. It's easy when you're in love with a bloke to go along with what he wants. Sadly, it's just as easy to change your mind afterwards.

'I don't regret it,' Helen says. 'Our marriage is based on love and respecting each other's opinions.'

'What about you, though? Michael's never respected your opinion.' Words continue to spill from my mouth, like sugar strands from a tub switched from 'sprinkle' to 'pour'. 'You've always wanted another baby.'

'I don't want to talk about it any more,' Helen says sharply.

'I'm sorry, I shouldn't have—'

'Apology accepted,' Helen cuts in. 'Now let's go home.'

'You haven't seen upstairs yet.' We move back through the house and up the stairs to the main bedroom. 'Just look at that view,' I sigh at the window.

'What view?'

'Those houses,' I hesitate. 'Birds, sky . . .'

'It's nothing special.' Helen runs one finger along the dust on the sill and recoils in disgust, while I turn the emotional screw.

'Listen, Helen, Dan and I have sold our house. Our

49

buyers are threatening to pull out of the sale if I'm not gone by the end of next month.'

'That's good, isn't it? You'll be able to stay there.'

'Dan has no work. I can't afford to keep the mortgage going on my own. The twins and I will be homeless. Unless . . . Oh Helen, if we bought this together, we could stay in New Malden.'

'I'm not sure.' She twists the gold chain up tight around her neck so it digs into her skin.

'I'll be lucky to be able to afford a caravan in North Wales on my own.'

'There's nothing wrong with North Wales,' Helen says sniffily, and I recall that one of her grandmothers is Welsh.

'I didn't mean that there's anything wrong with Wales,' I say quickly. 'It's just that it's so far away that we'd never see you, or Charlotte again.' Or Michael, but that wouldn't worry me too much. 'We won't be able to go for picnics in Richmond Park. We won't be able to go shopping together in Kingston.' I realise that I'm having to be devious here to persuade Helen to come in with me on the development, but the thought of not seeing her every day really does choke me. 'I don't think I could bear it.' I pull a tissue out of my jacket-pocket and examine it for wear and tear. It looks quite safe to use – the upside-down smile of smudged lipstick is mine. I blow my nose. Loudly. 'You've been such a support to me, especially during the divorce.'

'Oh Sadie.' Helen slides her arm around my shoulders and gives me a squeeze. 'We'll work out a way you can stay, but not by buying this house.'

I blow my nose again. Very loudly.

'I shan't let you go,' Helen promises. 'You're like a sister to me.'

Not ever having had a sister, my friend has a romantic view of sisterly love – enforced, I suspect, by images of the Nolans on stage in the 1980s, dancing to the same rhythm and singing in harmony. She's wrong, of course. Annette and I have always fought like mad.

'I thought this would make such a fantastic master bedroom,' I sniffle.

'How? Look at the mould on the ceiling!'

'Where?'

'There,' she says, pointing at an area of damp that's eaten half the ceiling away.

'It's purely cosmetic,' I argue, using the exact words Marcus used on Saturday when he showed me round. 'All it needs is a couple of coats of paint.' I change the subject quickly. 'I'm sure you can think of ways of making the room feel more spacious than it is. You have to admit that you have a flair for interior design.' I was going to say design in general, to include exterior, but remember that palisade fence just in time.

'Have I?' Helen hesitates, then smiles. 'I suppose I have.'

'There'll be a fair amount of shopping to do.'

Her face lights up. I am winning.

'Please, Helen, the course of my life depends on your decision.'

'I suppose it wouldn't hurt if you had a word with the agent to find out what kind of offer the owner would be prepared to accept.'

'I already have. I put an offer in on Saturday, and it's been accepted.'

'Sadie!' I watch Helen's face, holding my breath. Will it be yes or no? Suddenly, her shoulders relax and she breaks into laughter. 'You are impossible!'

The deal is done, with Helen anyway. I grab her hands and we dance around the room, squealing with excitement.

'Mrs Keith? Mrs Keith! It's Marcus here.'

I skip to the top of the stairs and lean over the banisters.

'Excuse me,' he grovels, 'I was beginning to think you'd moved in already. Will you be much longer, only I'm supposed to be back at the office?'

'Give us another five minutes,' I say.

We make him wait another fifteen.

'It shouldn't take too long to exchange contracts on an empty house,' I say as we leave. 'We could start work within weeks.'

'If we go ahead,' Helen adds.

My heart plummets like a lift from a severed cable. 'What do you mean? I thought you'd decided.'

'I'll have to persuade Michael.'

'How?'

'I'll seduce him over a lamb chop and a bottle of wine. I'll let him lick Häagen-Dazs off my nipples even though it gets all over the sheets. I'll wear a string, although it makes me feel like I'm straddling a circular saw.'

'And if he doesn't agree?'

'He will. Don't worry, Sadie.'

*   *   *

I do worry. I spend the evening at home, sitting in near-darkness, watching the flame from the tealight inside the burner casting patterns on the walls, and inhaling the soothing fragrance of blended lavender and rosewood oils. Wearing a string would be nothing compared to the agony of uncertainty that I am suffering.

Restless, I get up and pad across to the window. I pull the curtain aside and gaze out. The light from the streetlamps catches slanting streaks of rain, turning them silver. All Helen's curtains are closed. I wonder how she's getting on, whether I should phone to find out, or if phoning would interrupt her at a critical moment?

'Mum?'

I turn. Lorna's shadowy shape stands in the doorway.

'You should be asleep, my fairy,' I say.

'I can't get to sleep.'

'Go and count sheep or something.'

'I can't sleep because you keep disturbing me. Who are you talking to?'

'Oh, come here,' I say, reaching out my arms. 'I must have been talking to myself.' Lorna stares at me as if I'm slightly mad. 'Let's have a hug.' We sit down on the sofa. I bury my face in her hair, which smells of cherries and almonds. 'I could eat you, you know,' I murmur.

'No, don't. It's the shampoo,' she chuckles, pretending to fight me to escape.

When I release her, she relaxes and snuggles against my breast. 'How was school today?' I ask.

'I got nine out of ten for my spellings.'

'Well done.'

'And Sam got into a lot of trouble with the dinner-ladies. He stole the cheese out of Harry's Dairylea Lunchable. Harry's in Sam's class.'

I am torn between telling Lorna to shut up and stop being a snitch, and letting her go on so I can hear her version of what Sam's been up to. Sam came home with a red card today, a note that reads, *Your child suffered an injury to his/her* Bump on Head. *Whilst adequate treatment was given, it may require your attention at home.*

'Was that after Harry hit Sam on the head?'

'Before,' Lorna confirms, 'then Sam gave Harry a Chinese burn.'

'Miss Watson didn't mention it when I picked you both up from school.' Miss Watson is Sam's class-teacher.

'That's because Sam said he'd give Harry another one if he told anyone.' Lorna changes the subject. 'Mum, why do you sit down here on your own in the dark? Are you lonely?'

'Sometimes.'

'I think Dad must be lonely too.'

I want to say, *Serves him right*, but I don't. 'Lorna, would you be terribly upset if I found a boyfriend one day?'

She grins, her eyes reflecting the flame of the tealight. 'You're much too old to have a boyfriend, Mum.'

'Thanks a lot. How old do you think I am?'

'Twenty-one.'

'Who told you that?'

'You did. Last birthday, you told everyone you were

twenty-one.' I can't help smiling as Lorna continues, 'You did, you said you were twenty-one again. Sam says you can't have the same birthday twice, but you did.'

'It's something that happens to you when you get older,' I say.

'Like ear-piercing?'

'I'm sorry, you've lost me.'

'I'd like to have my ears pierced, but Charlotte says you have to wait until you're older.'

'You can have your ears pierced any time you like as long as your dad agrees. Now, come on, it's time you went back up to bed.' I hold Lorna's hand up to her room, and tuck her into bed.

'Goodnight, my fairy,' I whisper as I kiss her cheek.

''Night,' she mumbles.

On the way back downstairs I look in on Sam who is sleeping the deep sleep of the innocent. This afternoon he let me dab his bruises with a packet of frozen peas wrapped in a flannel. He let me believe he was the injured party when he was the one who started it.

'Goodnight, Sam,' I say, letting my fingertips rest briefly on the bruise on his forehead. 'Tomorrow, we shall have to have words.'

I retire to bed myself, worrying about Sam's behaviour, and whether or not Michael will take on the development, but later, I dream that I am with Gareth, the man with the gorgeous green eyes. I dream of making love naked in the rain.

Chapter Four

The trouble with being an optimist is that you're liable to be permanently disappointed in life. If I can't have Gareth, then I don't want any man, so I try to recreate that bitter, man-hating state of mind that I sank into when Dan and I separated, when I slouched around in faded fleeces and jaded joggers, and ruined my tendons skulking about in trainers instead of my usual precipitously high heels, and the doctor offered me Prozac, which I declined when I heard the dreaded words, 'Avoid alcohol'.

Men! It isn't difficult to hate them.

I phoned Dan first thing this morning – he wasn't answering his phone last night. I don't have to tell him anything any more, but I prefer to do so before the twins give him their version of my plans. Of course, I should have known that I could rely on Dan to point out the disadvantages of my course of action.

'The trouble with you, Sadie,' he said, 'is that you change your career as often as you change your . . .' he hesitated, '. . . your socks.'

'I don't wear socks,' I pointed out. I was being awkward. Dan was going to say knickers, but didn't because he'd just remembered that we're divorced and no longer have the right to mention anything that might remind us of past intimacies.

'You know what I'm trying to say. I don't think property development is that brilliant an idea.'

That's right, I thought. Squash me flat. Dan has the power to make me feel like a spider crushed underfoot, which is what he does to spiders when he finds them in the bath. If I find one, I drag a towel along the bottom of the bath, encouraging the spider to grip on to it so I can bundle it up and throw the whole thing, spider and towel, out of the window.

'Helen and I are going into partnership,' I said.

'Is that wise?' said Dan. 'You might fall out.'

'Of course we won't. We never fall out.'

'Where are you and the kids going to live?'

'At the property.'

'You can't.'

'We'll have to. Don't worry, we'll be fine. The children can always stay with you if the water has to go off.'

'Don't expect to move in with me,' he spluttered. 'There isn't room at my place.'

'There's room for the twins.'

'Yes, at weekends. I couldn't have them all week as well. I'll be out at work again soon. Sadie? Are you there?'

'Yes.'

'I thought you'd gone, you went so quiet.'

'I was just thinking how strangely you're behaving for a father who at one time wanted to apply to the courts for full custody. Really, Dan, if we have to stay anywhere, we'll stay at Helen's. There isn't any structural work to do on the house. All it needs is a quick bleaching and a lick of paint.'

'It might look like that at first glance, but you can guarantee you'll find more problems when you start working on a project like that,' said Dan.

'Gloom-monger!'

'I'm being practical.'

'What do you know about property development? You never so much as laid a finger on a paintbrush when we lived together.'

'As you've never failed to remind me,' Dan said flatly. I'd hurt him. We can still hurt each other. I suppose we always will. That's one of the problems with men, isn't it? Like Achilles, the insensitive bastards do have the odd vulnerable spot – not their heels, but their egos.

It turns out that in spite of Helen's protestations to the contrary, Michael is no different from any other man. He keeps us in suspense all day with his decision on the development.

'When did you say Michael would be in touch?' I ask her once we are settled with two coffees at a table in the café at the Malden Centre, our local sports venue.

'I didn't,' Helen says.

'Couldn't you phone him and find out?'

'He'll let us know when he's seen the accountant this afternoon.'

'I hope he realises how important this is.'

'I've made it quite clear,' Helen smiles. 'Michael had the best night of his life last night. He was shuffling about the house like a bowlegged jockey with arthritis this morning.'

'But did he say yes? Did he at least agree in principle?'

'I think so.'

'You have got your mobile switched on? Will you check?'

'Sadie! Will you shut up and watch the children. Lorna's been waving and you haven't waved back once.'

Struck down with guilt that I haven't been paying attention, I turn towards the window that looks out from the café to the swimming pools. Charlotte is doing Bend, Star, Pencil at the deep end, while Sam sits shivering on the edge, waiting for his turn. I believe that his teacher takes malicious delight in making him sit on the edge of the pool for as long as possible. In fact, I don't know why I pay six quid each for the twins to do a few widths of the main pool every Tuesday after school when I could take them myself on a family ticket for half that. Dan and I started it though, and we've let the children down in so many other ways that I can't bear to face them and say, 'Sorry, no more swimming lessons,' so here we are.

Charlotte and Sam are in the Intermediate lesson, while Lorna is still a struggling Beginner. I'm not a swimmer myself, and all I can remember of swimming lessons at school was getting caught trying to peer into the boys' changing-rooms.

Meanwhile, Lorna paddles in small circles like a fly stuck in the top of a glass of lemonade in the Teaching Pool. Once I'm certain that she isn't drowning, I offer Helen a KitKat.

'I shouldn't really,' she says half-heartedly. 'Oh, go on then.'

On the way to the pool I bought a copy of the local paper and two chunky KitKats, the type I imagine the gorgeous Gareth would eat, though why I'm still fantasising about a married man, I don't know. I suppose he's gone somewhere hot for his honeymoon, somewhere his new wife can strut about without her clothes on. I bet she's young, blonde and slim – anorexic, probably. I bite straight through my KitKat, then try to flick crumbs of chocolate out of my cleavage, but it's so hot in here that some of them have already melted onto my skin like moles.

'Hey, did you see what Sam did then?' Helen interrupts.

I peer through the window.

'That boy's strangling him.' I stand up and start waving, trying to attract the swimming teacher's attention.

'Sam started it.' Helen sits back smugly. 'He dragged him underwater.'

The swimming teacher ignores me, and makes Sam sit shivering with his back to the wall beneath the clock.

'That's not fair!'

'Sadie, sit down again,' Helen soothes.

'Sam didn't do anything to that boy!' I sit down,

but remain with the edge of the seat digging into my buttocks.

'He did,' Helen argues. 'You're going to have to accept that swimming with Sam is like swimming with Roboshark.'

'Are you trying to tell me that you think he's a bully?'

'Well, yes, actually. He ruined Charlotte's new poster the other day.'

'I'm sure he didn't mean to.'

'He drew whiskers and an exploding boil across Gareth Gates's chin.'

'Is that so bad?' I ask lightly although I am seething inside, at Helen for stating the obvious, and at Sam for the trouble he causes.

'Sam doesn't respect other people's property,' says Helen. 'He doesn't know how to behave.'

'I'll show him how to behave when I get my hands on him,' I scowl.

'That's exactly what I mean. He doesn't take a blind bit of notice of you.'

I recall how Sam looked at me when I tackled him about the Chinese burns this morning. I told him that if he looked at me like that again, I'd give him a slap, and he laughed, and I didn't give him a slap because I couldn't bring myself to, and then I told him that he wouldn't be able to go swimming tonight instead, and he said he didn't care because he didn't like swimming much anyway, at which I gave up and told him not to get into any more trouble otherwise I'd go straight to his dad.

'What's this about Sam attacking Harry?' Helen goes on.

'How did you find out?'

'I was speaking to Caroline at school this morning. Harry's her son.'

My blood runs cold in spite of the heat. Caroline is one of the Big Guns of the PTA. She's a big woman too, bigger than me in all dimensions, and Harry has a reputation. He nutted his mother in the eyeball while she was trying to persuade him to read to her – she had to be treated for a detached retina.

'You and Dan aren't firm enough,' Helen continues. 'Sam knows he can do what he likes. It's time you stopped feeling guilty for letting him down over the divorce, and took him in hand. He'll thank you for it when he's older.'

'Since when have you been the perfect parent?' I bluster just as Helen's mobile rings.

'That'll be Michael,' she says, digging about in her tan leather backpack. 'He's changed the ringtone on my mobile again.'

It takes me a few moments to realise that Helen's phone is playing 'I'm Too Sexy', by Right Said Fred. Michael must have had a good night last night.

'What does he say? Is it yes?'

'Sadie, I haven't answered it yet,' Helen sighs as she pulls out the phone and puts it to her ear. There seems to be a problem. She nods, chews her lip, nods again.

'Well?'

She glares at me, meaning 'shut up', and my future flashes before me. Me and the twins in a one-bedroomed mobile home on a windswept mountain in North Wales, with sheep bleating plaintively outside the door, begging to come in from the cold. Me and the twins surviving on Welsh rarebit and leek stew. I reach forward and press my palms against the glass in front of me. I feel the nudge of an elbow in my ribs, and hear Helen's voice.

'Michael says "yes". Did you hear me? We're property developers!'

'Yes, yes, yes!' I hammer on the window, then turn shrieking to Helen to embrace her until an announcement comes across the Tannoy from somewhere in the direction of the ticket-booth.

'This is a polite warning,' says an anything but polite voice. 'Spectators will be removed from the café if they continue to disrupt the swimming lessons!'

Helen and I sit down again, still grinning. I try to attract Lorna's attention to give her the news, but she won't look at me. I suppose I shouldn't be surprised.

'You have a new career, Sadie,' Helen says once we've calmed down a little. 'All you need now is a new man.' She picks up my newspaper and flicks through it, folding it open at the Lonely Hearts ads. She runs one bitten fingernail down the columns until she reaches *Men For Women*. 'What do you fancy?'

'Someone with a GSOH,' I say, thinking about the laughter-lines at the corners of Gareth Bryant's eyes. Someone tall and sexy with bizarre dress sense.

'How about this one? "Athletic lover seeks slim, unassertive girlfriend" – that's you out, then.' Helen laughs. 'Or: "Stallion seeks long-legged filly for light exercise and munching hay. Maybe leading to stable relationship." Do you think he's a fetishist?'

'A pervert, more like.' I glance across at the adverts. 'There's no one there I'd want to date.'

'You'll have to put an ad in yourself. You could use the property angle to make it interesting now that we're property developers.'

'How about: "Feisty, generously proportioned woman seeks bungalow, nothing up top, everything down below"?' I suggest.

'You're not taking this seriously.' Helen frowns. 'How about: "Hot property required by woman with open outlook"? I'll phone up for you, if you like.'

'How about: "A man with period charm"?' I giggle. I don't for a million years believe that Helen will go ahead with it. '"Who needs some updating"?' I add, thinking of the phrase that appears in the estate agent's details of *St Ives*, which is what our property is called, according to the sign outside the front door.

'You don't want anyone so old that he depends on Viagra for his performance.'

'How about: "Man with drive"? Oh Helen, put that paper down.' She can advertise all she likes, but the man I want will never reply.

'You can't be on your own for ever,' Helen says, closing the paper. 'You're in your prime.'

'I'm almost forty.'

'Exactly. It's time you found someone else, and there are men all over the place if you look. There's a lifeguard over there.'

'He's too young.'

'Very fit though. I went out with a lifeguard once.'

'You didn't! You haven't told me about a lifeguard before.'

'Haven't I? I guess he wasn't one of the more interesting ones, all bod and no brain. You won't tell Michael, will you? It would break his heart if he knew what I used to get up to.'

'Course I won't.' I pause. 'Isn't Michael a little hypocritical, expecting you to have an unsullied history? I'm sure he's seen plenty of action in his lifetime. He is almost fifty, isn't he?'

'Fifty this year, and no, he knows I'm not unsullied. My history of three ex-lovers is just right, enough to show a degree of honesty about my past life, and not so many that I look like a complete slag.'

Much as I admire Helen's eclectic tastes in men, my requirements have always been much more refined. I look around the pool. The lifeguard has changed shift. The children have gone too. In our excitement, we hadn't noticed that the lessons had finished, and we find Charlotte and Sam shivering outside the showers, waiting for their swimming towels.

'Where's Lorna?'

Charlotte shrugs. Sam ignores me.

'Lorna!' There is no sign of her. My heart begins to flutter with panic. I start to head for the pool in case she should be lying unconscious at the bottom after failing to make it across the width.

'Mum, I want my towel!' Sam yells from behind me.

I turn and throw it at him at the same time as Helen returns from the showers, shouting that she's found Lorna and she's all right. It turns out that Lorna has attached herself to another girl, presumably in the hope that her mother will accidentally adopt her and take her home.

I try to talk to Lorna and Sam at tea-time.

'I've been making plans for our future,' I begin. 'Helen and I are buying a house together.'

Lorna's jaw drops. 'You mean, we're going to be like Karisma at school who has two mums?'

I put her straight very quickly. I don't want it reported back to school that Helen and I are a pair of lesbians.

'I don't want to move,' says Sam, getting up from the table and leaving his plate of bacon and chips half-eaten.

'Where do you think you're going?'

'To play football.'

'I'm talking to you.'

'Going on at me, you mean.'

I am just about to tackle Sam over his cheek when the phone rings. It's Lisa from *Mums and Tots*, and one of Helen's old schoolfriends, confirming Topsy's next booking. I wonder if I have taken on too much, whether I shall drown in my Olympic-sized swimming pool of commitments: the twins, the new development, love-seeking lonely heart, and self-employed magic operative?

Although I'm not booking any more parties for her, Topsy has a handful more obligations to meet before she can hang her wig up for good. Today she is entertaining *Mums and Tots*. It's fun. It's informal. We all go – me and Helen, the twins and Charlotte, because school is closed for a teacher training day. We meet Lisa at the church hall early so I can dress and make myself up before the mums and tots start to arrive, while the children racket around on plastic trikes and tractors which are far too small for them.

While I'm painting the circles of rouge on my cheeks in the mirror that I bring with me as part of Topsy's equipment, Helen shows me a copy of the local paper.

'Look,' she says, opening it up. *'Women For Men.'*

My brush slips, leaving a gash of red across my face. 'You haven't?'

'I have,' she grins. 'Here it is.'

Once I've read the advertisement Helen has placed on my behalf, I relax slightly. She's made me sound like Jennifer Aniston, Sarah Jessica Parker, and J-Lo rolled into one. She's also made me completely unrecognisable.

'I'm not trying to find you another husband, Sadie, just someone you can meet for a drink or a meal once in a while. Let's see if you have any replies.'

I find I am warming to the idea of a little lighthearted dating.

Helen switches on her mobile, and rings the special number.

'Well?'

'Nothing yet.'

My self-esteem pops like one of Topsy's balloon creations.

'Sadie, it's no reflection on you – the ad only went in today. Wait till tomorrow and you'll have so many replies you won't know which one to choose.'

'Do you think so?'

'I know so.' Helen takes a piece of tissue and wipes the red gash from my face. 'Now, get a move on. They'll be here soon.' She starts packing up my make-up. 'How's Annette? Is she pregnant yet?'

'She'd have told me if she was.'

'Hasn't she ever considered a sperm donor? That's what I'd do if I was in her position. I'd have a quick fling with someone other than Sean, preferably someone who's got kids so I knew he was fertile. No one would need to know.'

'Not even Sean?'

'No.'

'Isn't that a little unethical, Helen?'

'Maybe, but it would save Annette a lot of heartache and Sean a lot of money, and we all know how important saving money is to Sean,' Helen adds impishly.

'It won't happen because it's Annette's problem,' I say firmly. 'It's Annette who's infertile, not Sean.'

'What is wrong with her?'

'She's never said exactly. Something to do with her ovaries, I think.'

'Are she and Sean coming to the picnic?' Helen asks. The May picnic in Richmond Park is becoming an annual tradition for us.

'I'll ask them,' I say, before wondering whether it would be better if I didn't invite them, considering what's happening – or not happening – in their lives at the moment.

Although Helen denies it, I suspect that she tolerates Annette and Sean for my sake, rather than because she enjoys their company. Sean isn't the most tactful person in the world, and I have no idea what state Annette will be in, whether she'll be quiet and bitter, or overly jolly. IT, as I call the foetus, is always there, present in its absence.

'Your audience is arriving,' Helen says.

I arrange my props with the help of several toddlers who have to be dragged away kicking and screaming by their mothers. Another, Lisa's three-year-old daughter, Brooke, has to be dragged kicking and screaming towards me. She cannot be persuaded by any amount of cajoling and bribery to remain in the same room as Topsy, and she is taken round to the kitchen which opens into the hall via a hatch, so she can listen from what she considers to be a safe distance.

Helen makes Charlotte, Lorna and Sam sit at the back. Charlotte and Lorna sit together, drawing studs on each other's earlobes with blue biro.

'Hi, everyone,' I begin, waving my hands. 'I'm Topsy.' I do the ball inside the handkerchief routine, asking for a volunteer to hold the wand. A boy called Jake does the honours. As he is about to take the wand, it collapses. Most kids laugh at this point, but Jake is concerned.

'It broken,' he says, frowning.

I give the wand a shake, straighten it up and offer it again. You've guessed. It collapses. So does Jake, in tears, and he runs back to his mother sobbing that it's no good. Another mother press-gangs me into choosing her child, Gemma, to take centre-stage.

I demonstrate the ball, and the handkerchief. I make a great fuss of showing that I am wrapping the ball inside the handkerchief. I palm the ball in my right hand, while I squash the handkerchief into my left fist.

'You have to do the magic, Gemma,' I say. 'Wave the wand – that's right. Give it a good waggle. Now, what's the magic word?'

'Please,' says Gemma.

That raises a laugh at least.

'Let's try *abracadabra*.' Of course it takes several goes with full audience participation before the magic works, and I open my hand to reveal that the ball has disappeared from the handkerchief. Gemma's eyes widen with surprise.

'Shall we see if we can magic the ball back?'

'Yes,' she nods.

'Everyone knows there's no such thing as magic,' interrupts a voice from the back. 'That isn't Topsy the Clown. It's my mum, and she's hiding the ball up her sleeve.'

'Sam!'

'I saw you do it,' he continues in muffled tones as Helen drags him out of the hall in an armlock.

I'm not sure that the toddlers in Topsy's audience understand what Sam is saying, but I run through the magic colouring book routine to prove he is wrong. One boy starts picking his nose. Another wets himself. Yet another wanders off to sit on a trike. As I lose my audience one by one, I realise there is only one thing I can do to regain their attention. I pump up and release a series of farting balloons.

It works and, once we have had a rendition of several verses of 'The Wheels on the Bus', the performance is over, and we can gossip over cracked china cups of tea and stale Bourbon biscuits.

'Helen told me about your new venture, Sadie,' Lisa says. 'My old man's got some paving slabs if you're interested. He's a chippie. He picks up bits and pieces from work.'

'A chippie?'

'A carpenter,' Lisa explains. 'You have a lot to learn about the property business.'

'How many slabs?' Helen interrupts.

'Seventy or eighty or thereabouts.'

'They'll be perfect for that patio we're planning to lay at the back of the house,' I consider.

'Are you sure we need that many? The garden's tiny,' says Helen.

'You have to remember to allow for a few breakages,' Lisa reminds us 'and you can always sell on any surplus.'

We do a deal. In return for Topsy's fee, Helen and I are the proud owners of eighty paving slabs, and Lisa pockets the cash that the mums have paid to *Mums and Tots*.

'I think you rushed into that deal with Lisa,' Helen says in the car on the way back home. 'I know we're due to complete and exchange contracts on the house next week, but it might all fall through yet.'

It's scary, isn't it, when your best friend starts to sound like your ex-husband.

'We can't leave the external space as it is,' I insist, trying to ignore Helen's pessimism.

'I take it that by external space, you're referring to

the garden.' Helen snorts with laughter. 'You're sound-ing like a property developer already.'

I don't look like one, I think as I glance into the wing mirror on my side of Helen's Mini as we travel home. I look like an ageing clown. My make-up has settled in the creases on my face like Polyfilla spread across a crazed plaster surface. Selling houses? I'm more worried about how I'm going to sell myself to a new man – if one ever replies to my advert.

Chapter Five

Needs some updating. A phrase that could apply equally well to me as the new house, it turns out when Helen arrives on the doorstep of my old house on the morning of the move some weeks later.

'You look like you've been to Faliraki and back,' she says, smiling.

'How can you say that? I haven't got a tan, or shagged for Britain. I haven't even been drinking.'

'You look absolutely shattered.'

'Okay, there's no need to rub it in. I couldn't sleep for all the excitement.' I touch the skin beneath my eyes. It feels sticky, reminding me that I've massaged half a tube of pile-shrinking cream into the bags I found there this morning. They still remind me of black bin-liners. So much for *that* so-called beauty tip!

'Have you finished packing?' Helen asks. She's an angel – has taken Charlotte and the twins to school so that I could have a nervous breakdown in peace.

'Almost.'

'You get on with that then, and I'll put the kettle on for coffee.'

'I've packed the kettle.'

'I'll fetch mine.'

Most of our furniture is in storage. I'm taking the rest of our belongings to *St Ives* in a hired van. Helen makes us both a mug of coffee and stands about chatting while I throw the last few bits and pieces into plastic carrier bags.

'Tom arrived on our doorstep at midnight last night, with his guitar slung over his shoulder,' she tells me.

'Tom?'

'My stepson.'

How could I forget? Tom came to stay with Helen and Michael once when he was about twelve. Within twenty-four hours he was round at mine, asking if he could move in with us until his mother, Suzanna, could pick him up. He's a nice boy, very quiet, and not like Michael at all.

'He's staying for a couple of days. Suzanna says she won't have him back. She said she'd be responsible for him until he was eighteen, and now he's on his own.'

'I thought he was at university?'

'He says he needs a break.' Helen puts her mug down on the kitchen worktop. 'So do I.'

'A break from what?' I rinse her mug under the tap, dry it and stuff the mug and tea-towel into my last plastic bag.

'All this hassle.' She waves her hand in the direction of the bags and boxes that are stacked up in the hall.

'Helen, we've hardly started!' For the very first time,

I wonder if I'm doing the right thing, trying to shoe-horn a housework fanatic like Helen into the role of property developer. She doesn't seem at all excited that we are on the verge of starting the project. She seems more intent on wittering on about Tom, and how pleased she is that he's turned up.

'I know that Tom and I have never seen eye to eye, but I have a feeling that this is the beginning of a truce. He sees me more as fairy godmother than the wicked stepmother who broke up his family.'

'I'll bet he does if you're paying for his keep. What about Michael – what does he think?'

'He's over the moon. He hasn't seen Tom since October.'

'Why don't you ask him to give us a hand today? We could do with some muscle.'

'He's still in bed,' says Helen. 'It wouldn't be fair to wake him up. He's exhausted, poor boy.'

Later, I try not to compare the luxurious surroundings that Tom is sleeping in, Helen's spare room with its built-in wardrobes and illuminated display shelves, Arctic Fox faux-fur throw and chrome bedside lamp, with my new boudoir that is dirtier, gloomier and smellier than I remember from when I first looked around the house. I wonder if we shouldn't have handed St Ives over to the National Trust for preservation as a historic monument.

Helen has flung herself full-length on her back on my double mattress that we have just lugged up the stairs. I sit down on the edge.

'You should at least have run the vacuum cleaner

over the floor.' Helen lifts one hand to her hair to scrape it back from her forehead. She is perspiring lightly. I am sweating like a slice of salted aubergine.

'I'll do that later.'

'You won't.'

'Okay, I won't.'

'I don't know why you didn't bring the bed to put the mattress on,' says Helen. 'It doesn't make a very good impression.'

'I've never liked my old bed. It reminds me of Dan. He chose it.'

'He always did have old-fashioned taste in furniture.'

'When we dress the house to sell, we'll hire a bed, or knock one up from MDF,' I say confidently.

'I wasn't thinking about when we sell the house. I meant that this old mattress on a dirty floor isn't going to make a good impression on the men you'll be bringing back here, is it?'

'I'm not looking for an orgy. I'd like one man, someone who'll provide some grown-up conversation and cook a meal for me now and then.'

Helen raises one eyebrow. 'If you want conversation and someone to cook for you, you'd have more luck advertising in the *Women For Women* section of the ads, wouldn't you? When have you ever met a man who can hold a grown-up conversation without resorting to dirty jokes and innuendo to impress?'

'Did I have any replies?' I ask, trying desperately to sound as if I don't care.

'I haven't checked today,' says Helen, sitting up. She takes her mobile out of her pocket and dials. 'Three more,' she giggles, passing the phone over. 'It's really time you dated one of these guys, you know, Sadie.' We try to listen at the same time, our heads pressed together.

The first one, who says his name is Roger, is downright rude with a message along the lines of, 'Heard you're vacant and ready for occupation, let me be the one to stick my key in your lock.' The second, John, sounds pleasant, yet hesitant. The third is from the Stallion.

'I'll say nay to that one. I don't want to get frisky with him. In fact, I don't like the sound of any of them.'

'Come on, Sadie. John sounds pretty normal.'

'Ordinary, you mean?' I realise that I can't be content with ordinary any more, not since I met Gareth Bryant. If I hadn't met him, I might have been grateful to receive a reply from any member of the male species, even Mr Bean.

'Go on. Give him a ring.'

'There's no point now, is there? He'll be at work.'

'You can always leave a message.'

'I've changed my mind. I've just got rid of one man, and made a life for me and the twins.' I drop the mobile onto the mattress. 'I don't want, or need another one.'

'It would be useful to have one around here to help now and then,' Helen says.

'This is our house. This is our project. I don't want to have anyone else interfering in it. I want to be able to say that we did it all ourselves when we come to sell up.'

'A man would be useful for getting spiders out of

the bathroom. I don't know whether you've noticed, but there's a massive one in the sink.'

'I'll deal with it. I'll do my trick with the towel.'

'Let's go and set the television up first,' says Helen.

We go downstairs and pull the carpet up from the front-room floor before we rig up the telly, and I begin to worry that we're not going to get very far with the development at the rate Helen works. However, after a coffee, she is up banging on the walls again.

'I've prepared a mood-board for each space,' she says. 'I'll bring them with me tomorrow to show you the artwork for the living-room walls. I thought we'd take some photos of you and the twins, cut them up and make collages in driftwood frames, to symbolise the kind of people that give the house its life, and its atmosphere.'

'I think we should let our ideas evolve a little more organically,' I say tactfully just before three or four trains rattle past in close succession, and what sounds like a steamroller rumbles slowly along the road at the front. 'I'd like to live here for a few days and get a feel for the house.'

'You said yourself that time is money. We can't afford to hang about when we have a six-month deadline.'

'You're right, Helen. We should get started straight away.' I am on a high. I am Superwoman, single with two kids and a career. I will write To Do lists and stick to them. I will cook a full roast dinner once a week. I will pay to have my bikini-line waxed if I want to.

Helen and I are flicking through some copies of *House Beautiful* that she's brought along with her when

Michael turns up. Helen lets him in, and I hear them exchange cheeping kisses in the hall.

'Thanks, Mikey,' she says. 'Lunch and champagne?'

'Chicken tikka masala sandwiches and a bottle of Bolly to celebrate your new enterprise.' Michael strolls into the front room followed by Helen carrying his generous offerings. 'Hi, Sadie. I thought I'd got the wrong house. It looks like a building site with all those paving slabs dumped outside.'

'What are you talking about?'

'The slabs in the front garden. I hope you've ordered a skip to get rid of them.'

Helen and I reach the window at the same time. There's a heap of slabs, some broken, in all shapes and sizes, and colours, humped across the overgrown patch of lawn that passes as the front garden. My heart sinks.

'Lisa's old man must have dropped them off.'

'I said it was too good to be true,' Helen says stiffly, 'eighty paving slabs in return for Topsy's fee.'

'You never said that!' I protest.

'It seems as if everyone except Topsy knows that Lisa's old man Dave's nickname is Dodgy,' says Michael, smiling.

'What are we going to do?' says Helen. 'Those were for the Cotswold stone patio.'

'It looks as if it'll have to be crazy paving instead.' Michael is laughing. It isn't terribly funny. I could grab that shiny, metallic grey tie he's wearing, and pull it tight around his neck.

'What are you waiting for?' he continues. 'Aren't you going to give me the grand tour?'

'We're glad you turned up,' says Helen as we head for the kitchen. 'We could do with a hand.'

'No, we couldn't,' I say.

Helen turns on me. 'There's still half a vanload of bits and pieces out there, and I've got to pick Charlotte up at three.' She turns back to Michael. 'Please, Mikey.'

'I would if I could, but I've booked a round of golf for two o'clock and I have to go home and change first.' He rubs his hands together. 'You did iron my golf shirt this morning, didn't you, Hels?'

Helen's hand flies to her mouth. 'I didn't have time,' she gasps.

'You'll have to do it yourself,' I cut in, 'or employ a Molly Maid now that Helen has a full-time job.'

Michael flashes me a look, warning me not to interfere in his domestic arrangements, while Helen apologises for neglecting her duties. They make up with a kiss, Michael winking at me around Helen's shoulder. I'm not sure why he does that. He doesn't fancy me, so maybe he's expressing sympathy for my single status in the face of all this marital understanding.

Helen starts describing the minutiae of her plans for the kitchen – Zimbabwean black granite worktops at £300 a metre, stainless steel T-bar handles, and feature utensil drawers, but Michael is more interested in the skirting beside the back door. He pulls a pen from his pocket and digs it into the wall above. A chunk of plaster falls out, followed by crumbs of redbrick.

'What did the surveyor say about this damp?' Michael asks.

Helen frowns.

'You did have a survey?'

'Did we, Sadie?'

'The estate agent didn't think there was much point . . .'

Michael runs his hands through his dark wavy hair, and swears. 'Didn't it occur to either of you that a property of this age would need a professional eye cast over it?'

'Not really,' says Helen. 'It looked all right, and as Sadie said, if a surveyor picked up a few things that needed doing, we'd buy it anyway.'

'You could have dropped your offer accordingly.' Michael taps the wall higher up. 'The whole of this wall is sodden. It's in a terrible state.' His temper doesn't improve when we show him the main bedroom upstairs. 'This is going to cost six or seven grand to put right. What with repairs to the damp-proof course, and a new roof, you'll be lucky to break even on your investment.' He corrects himself. 'On *my* effing investment. I'd have been better off putting the money on the dogs.'

'What new roof?' Helen says.

Better keep quiet, I think. There was me hoping a lick of paint would do the trick.

'There's no point in doing up the inside when you've got water pouring in through the roof every time it rains,' Michael scowls. 'You need a builder, and bloody fast, before that ceiling caves in.' He glances at his watch. 'I've got to go.'

'So soon?' says Helen, looking downcast. 'We haven't opened the champagne yet.'

83

'What the hell is there to celebrate?' Michael says. 'You and Sadie can drown your sorrows together as long as she doesn't drown in her bed first.'

'Michael!'

'I'll be late tonight. I'm having dinner at the Club.'

'What about Charlotte?' Helen says. 'She missed you this morning because you were out before she woke up. She'll be very disappointed if she doesn't see you tonight.'

'Tell her I'm sorry, but I'll make it up to her,' Michael says. He brushes Helen's cheek with his lips then turns to me. 'I'll see you at the picnic on Sunday, Sadie, if you're not too busy.'

Helen sees Michael out then rejoins me in the bedroom, where we stand a little apart at the window, watching him drive away in his car.

'I think I made a boo-boo,' I say eventually, breaking the silence that hangs between us.

'What's a boo-boo between friends?' Helen asks. 'We all make mistakes.' She smiles suddenly, which doesn't make me feel any better, and adds, 'Some bigger than others. Seven thousand pounds' worth! Oh Sadie. What are we going to do?'

'Look for a builder, of course. It'll be all right, Helen. We can still make a profit.' I pause. 'I'm sorry Michael's so angry about it.'

'He's angry because I haven't ironed his shirt,' Helen says with a shrug.

'I don't know why you put up with that. I wouldn't.'

'Sometimes I envy your sister. Sean does all the housework, doesn't he, including the ironing.'

I don't point out that if Michael did it, it wouldn't reach Helen's exacting standards.

'Our marriage is like one of Michael's deals,' Helen continues. 'He brings the money in, and I make his life comfortable. Now that I'm working, the rules have changed, and we don't know what they are yet. Oh, don't worry about Mikey. He needs something to take his mind off Tom.'

'I thought you said he was pleased to see him.'

'He was last night, but he didn't seem quite so happy this morning.' Helen sighs. 'Perhaps he envies Tom's youth, and opportunities.'

I nod in agreement. Tom's presence must bring into focus the fact that Michael is about to hit his half-century.

We open the champagne. Helen has one mugful as we haven't unpacked the glasses yet and she has to collect Charlotte from school to take her to ballet. Dan offered to collect the twins today, so I drink the rest. I don't do anything by halves. I don't do half-cut. I do completely sozzled – which is what I am by the time Helen has gone and Dan arrives with the twins. I'm glad, because I didn't have to run the gamut of the Big Guns of the PTA and explain that I can't afford to give them the money Sam and Lorna raised during the sponsored spell just yet. I've never seen Sam so keen on a school event until he realised it was a glorified spelling test, and nothing to do with Harry Potter.

Lorna gives me a hug. Sam edges past me. I grab him by the upper arm.

'Is there anything you need to tell me about today?' I ask.

'He's got a letter from Miss Watson,' says Lorna.

'I wasn't asking you. I'm asking Sam.'

Sam squats down and yanks his rucksack open, tosses out three empty crisp packets and a squashed blackcurrant Winder before he finds a dog-eared envelope, addressed to me.

'There you are,' he says, throwing it in my direction. 'And before you go on at me, I didn't do it.'

'Do what?' I open the envelope and read the note, Miss Watson requesting that I make an appointment to see her.

'Whatever she says I did.' His face creases up in tears. 'I didn't do it. I didn't throw stones at Harry in the playground. I didn't.'

'Oh, Sam.' My heart softens, and I wrap my arm around his skinny shoulders. You assume that they're so grown-up at eight, but he's still my little boy. He sniffs a couple of times, and wipes his nose on the sleeve of his sweatshirt. 'Do you mind? You've got to wear that one again tomorrow.'

'Mum, you're always going on at me. Miss Watson's always going on at me.' Sam stamps his foot. 'I *didn't* throw stones at Harry in the playground.'

'You threw them at him outside in the car park,' says Lorna, 'and you hit Miss Watson's car.'

Sam shouts at Lorna. I shout at Sam. Dan shouts at us all to shut up shouting, then tells the twins to hop it. They both hop away, giggling – one of their standard jokes – to explore, leaving me and Dan looking at each other.

'There are alternative ways of dealing with Sam other than yelling at him,' Dan says gently.

'I can't help it when the little toe-rag lies and answers me back.'

'I suppose he's confused about the divorce and the move. It's very unsettling for him.' Dan scratches his head. 'I think it'd be a good idea for you to go and have a word with Miss Watson anyway.'

'If anyone should go and see Miss Watson, it's you since you haven't got a job.'

'We'll both go,' says Dan, 'to see how we can work with the school before they start talking about excluding him.'

'They wouldn't do that. Sam's not that bad. I expect it's six of one and half a dozen of the other.'

'It's time you realised how difficult Sam really is, and accepted some responsibility for his behaviour, Sadie. You are his mother.'

'And you're his father.'

Dan ignores me. 'I wish Sam would take the lead from Lorna. She's such a good girl.'

'Sam has a spark about him,' I protest. 'It means he can stand up for himself. Lorna can't. She acquiesces, tries to please everyone . . .' I wish she was a little more like Sam, and Sam was a little more like her.

'Like I do,' says Dan with a glimpse of a smile. 'Let's not argue any more. I came to see the new house.' He holds out a rather mean-looking bunch of yellow carnations, with half of the price label ripped off.

'Are those for me?' I take them, and bury my nose briefly in the blooms. They make me sneeze. 'You didn't used to give me flowers,' I splutter.

'That's why, I expect,' says Dan.

He looks so serious that I can't help giggling, and that in combination with the sneezing, leads on to an attack of hiccups.

'Have you been drinking?' Dan raises one eyebrow.

'Helen and I opened a bottle of champagne to celebrate the move. Michael brought it as a moving-in present.' I'm not sure why Dan's still here. 'How are the contact lenses?'

Dan blinks. 'They're great. Oh, stop changing the subject, Sadie.'

'You're looking good. You've lost weight,' I continue, playing on his vanity.

'I've been going to the gym.' He pinches the spare tyre of flesh that hangs over his belt.

'Spending money we haven't got?'

'I have a free three-month trial subscription.' He looks around the hall. 'You know, I really think you've made a mistake. I give you six weeks and you'll be resurrecting Topsy, or planning another madcap scheme, like making edible greetings cards, or running a gymnastic club for toddlers. It'll be anything but developing property, and you and the children will be homeless. Have you seen the state of the roof?'

'Of course I have, Dan. I didn't go into this with my eyes closed. I'm not stupid.' I don't tell Dan about the builder. I don't want him rubbing his hands and saying, 'I told you so.'

'Come into the kitchen,' I offer. 'I'd better throw these into some water.' I slench back a mug of cold water to quell my hiccups, refill it and stick the flowers into it, leaning them against the cracked tiles beside the microwave so that they don't fall over. Sam and Lorna must have heard us go into the kitchen because they turn up, asking for drinks and biscuits. I oblige, and offer Dan an orange squash, but he declines.

'Those flowers are beautiful, aren't they, Mum?' says Lorna as she leaves her glass on the draining board.

'Where's the other bunch?' says Sam. Dan looks at the floor as Sam continues, 'Shall I get them out of the car for Mum?'

'Er, no,' says Dan, looking up at me. 'I'm taking them home. They were on offer, buy one get one for free.'

'BOGOFF,' says Sam, delighted to be able to use rude words legitimately in front of his parents.

I want Dan to BOGOFF home now for it can only mean one thing. 'The flowers? You've met someone else,' I say quietly.

Lorna interrupts again before Dan can respond.

'Daddy, Daddy, have you decided about me having my ears pierced yet? You said you'd think about it.'

That's so typical of Dan to stall a decision so as not to upset Lorna, but I know, even if Lorna doesn't yet, that that is his way of saying no.

'I'm still thinking, princess. Now, go away. This a grown-up conversation.'

'Boring,' says Lorna, and she skips off with Sam.

'Well?' I whisper. 'Don't tell me you've taken up flower arranging. Who is she?'

'I am not seeing anyone, Sadie.'

'If you are,' I say, unconvinced, 'I'd be embarrassed to show her that handful of wilting carnations in case she sees them as a symbol of your ardour and esteem. They're an insult.'

'Daddy, Daddy, you said you'd come and see my bedroom,' Lorna yells from upstairs.

Dan invites himself upstairs and stops at the bathroom door.

'This is in a worse state than our old house,' he says, prodding at some mould that's sprouting between the peach tiles that someone once imagined looked fantastic with an avocado suite with gold taps. 'There's a spider in the sink.' He makes to grab it between his pinched finger and thumb.

'Leave it,' I snap. 'I'll deal with it.'

'You've always hated spiders.'

'I've learned to love them since you moved out.'

Dan backs off. 'I was only trying to help.'

'Helen and I don't need any help. When we've finished doing this place up we're sure to be invited on one of those "before and after" TV DIY shows.'

'There's no need to be quite so touchy.'

'Daddy!' Lorna and Sam are on the landing.

'I'd better not keep Lorna waiting any longer,' Dan observes. 'Which is your bedroom, Lorna, and which is Sam's?'

'They're sharing the second bedroom,' I say.

'I'm not sleeping with *her*!' Sam exclaims.

'No way am I going to sleep in the same room,' Lorna joins in.

'Helen and I are going to make a start on the smallest bedroom, then one of you can move in there.'

'Can I put my Arsenal posters up?' Sam wants to know.

'Can I put my magnetic fairy board up?' Lorna says at the same time.

'Yes, yes, yes. Perhaps you can get on with that now, so that your room's ready to show Auntie Annette when she arrives.'

'Will she talk about babies?' sighs Lorna. 'She always talks about babies.'

'Her insides are broken,' I explain. 'It makes her feel sad sometimes.'

'She's always sad,' says Sam. 'She's a saddo.'

'Sam!'

'Saddo, saddo,' Sam chants.

I turn my back on him, and show Dan into the main bedroom. I watch his expression as he casts his eyes over our old mattress on which we used to sleep together. That mattress is full of history – spilt wine, particles of cornflakes, chocolate digestives and dust mites. As if he's recalled some of that history, Dan averts his eyes to the ceiling.

'What a hideous mess,' he says. 'You'll never do it, Sadie.'

'Sod you,' I murmur under my breath, in case the twins are eavesdropping. Sod everyone who doesn't believe in me. *Sod 'em all.*

When Dan leaves, I redirect my creative energies into rechristening the house, making a sign with Lorna's Crayola Crazy Colouring Pens on a piece of cardboard I've ripped off one of the packing boxes. I hang it in the front window. *Llamedos.* I take down the sign that reads *St Ives* from beside the front door and turn it face down on top of one of the paving slabs in the front garden.

I feed the kids on microwaved pizza and chips, and tomato ketchup, and tuck them up in bed.

'Goodnight, Sam,' I say, but he's already asleep. 'Goodnight, Lorna.'

'What did Dad say about me having my ears pierced?' she asks, stalling bedtime.

'I think you'll have to work on your dad for a bit longer. Goodnight,' I say more firmly.

Later, when I am alone downstairs, sitting on Topsy's Director's chair in front of the television which stands on a tea-chest, I have time to wonder what I have done. What exactly have Helen and I taken on? A phone call from Annette interrupts me briefly.

'I'm so sorry I didn't turn up today,' she says.

'I thought that with you having no sense of direction, you'd lost your way and were orbiting London on the M25.' Annette doesn't laugh and tell me not to exaggerate like other people would at that suggestion because she has done it before, travelling from Mitcham to Orpington via Chertsey, Heathrow and Dartford.

'I had a detention,' she sighs, 'and when I finally arrived home, Sean was in the middle of cooking dinner, and then . . .' Annette pauses. 'Oh, why lie about it? I can't face coming to see you, Sadie. I'm not in the mood.'

When I was ten or eleven, I'd have rushed in and pulled Annette's hair, or scribbled over her homework, but I no longer take her slights personally. Annette's reluctance to visit is about how she feels about not being able to have a baby, not how she feels about me, and my encounter with Gareth Bryant has reminded me that if you can't have something, you want it even more . . .

'Another time then,' I say.

'I'll be over at the weekend. Bye, Sis.'

I put the phone down, and sit listening to the rain pattering against the window. The atmosphere inside the house is damp, making it seem much colder than it is, and I can't get the boiler in the kitchen to fire up to give the heating a blast. Helen and I didn't think to check that, either. In the end, I retire to bed, and lie on my mattress in the dark, staring up at that ceiling. Michael was wrong about the roof at least. There's no sign of the rain coming in.

'Mum?'

'Yes?' I roll over to face the doorway. Two shadowy figures draped in fleece throws creep towards me. 'Don't tell me you can't sleep because of the trains.'

'There's a big cat in our room,' Sam says.

'I think it's a tiger,' whispers Lorna.

'Don't be silly,' says Sam.

'There is. Come and see.'

We switch on all the lights, and investigate, but there is no tiger as Sam and I suspected.

'Go back to bed,' I yawn. 'You've got school tomorrow.'

'I can't get to sleep. I'll sleep with you.' Lorna ends up in my bed, and so does Sam in spite of his protestations that tigers don't exist in the middle of New Malden. We snuggle down, and there is a blessed silence. Then:

'Did you hear that?' says Lorna, grabbing my arm.

'What?' I mutter.

'That thud.'

I did, but I deny it.

'Perhaps it's a ghost,' says Sam helpfully.

I can feel Lorna's heartbeat hammering against my chest as she cuddles up against me. Something – a weight – lands on my legs. I can't help it. I scream. Lorna screams too. Whatever it is flees lightfooted down the stairs.

'I told you there was a tiger in this house.' Lorna sits up, sobbing. 'I hate this place. I want to go home.'

'Shh!' We sit and listen. I hear a faint meow from the hall. 'It's a cat!'

It is waiting in the kitchen for us as if it's expecting us to feed it. It's a skinny tabby with a white bib – a boy, I think.

'Perhaps he comes with the house,' Lorna says, reassured and letting the animal butt its head against her hand. 'Can we keep him?'

'I don't know.'

'He isn't wearing a collar.'

'I suppose he can move in if he wants to,' I say, recalling that it's a cat's prerogative to choose its owner, not the other way round. I can't say I'm unhappy about it. Dan hated the idea of keeping a pet.

'What shall we call him?' says Lorna. 'Atomic Kitten? Pilchard?'

'How about something unusual like Bram or Alvin?' I suggest.

'Alvin,' says Lorna.

Alvin it is. We feed him some ham from the fridge,

then return to snuggle down together on my mattress. None of us can sleep so we sing 'I'm a Spring Chicken' followed by 'Johnny's Lost His Marble' but without the actions that this song involves: ramming a broomstick, clothes-prop, policeman and some gunpowder up a drainpipe. I drift off thinking quietly of another kind of ramming, and it doesn't involve John or the Stallion, but guess who?

I dream of a new life as Sadie, the successful property developer, who can afford a house like *Haze on the Hill*. I can do it. I can do anything. I can walk on water. I am walking on water. I am lying in water, and it's icy cold, and I'm beginning to shiver. I fumble around under my pillow and pull out my torch. I switch it on. The duvet is saturated. I aim the beam towards the ceiling and catch the glint of a drop of water as it falls through the darkness.

I wake the twins, and take them downstairs where we console ourselves with a midnight feast of apples and mint Aeros. So what if the roof is leaking? So what if I have to go and face Miss Watson's wrath? So what if Dan's found a new lover and I haven't?

'Mum, I feel sick,' moans Sam.

'How many of those Aeros did you have?'

'Three, and some of Lorna's.'

I pass him the washing-up bowl.

It's true what they say. It never rains, but it pours.

Chapter Six

Why is it so difficult to find a builder? I've rung seventeen out of the *Yellow Pages*. They are busy. They're on holiday. They are booked up until the January after next. I wanted to get hold of Gareth Bryant, but I can't find his number. It appears that he doesn't need to advertise.

It is Thursday, and I am driving about in my old car with three strips of 3-metre length skirting in the boot, along with a bucket of white gloss trade undercoat and topcoat from B&Q. I turn right into the High Street at the Fountain roundabout – and there is Gareth's pick-up right in front of me! It is clean this time. The words *Bryant Builders* stand out from its gleaming panels but, more importantly, Gareth himself is at the wheel.

The sun breaks through the clouds above and my pulse begins to thrill. I can't resist the urge to follow him. I try to tell myself that I want to see Gareth because I'd like to find out if he made the same mistake as I did in getting married. It's idle curiosity, nothing more.

I jump a set of lights. Now that I've found a builder at last, I can't afford to lose him.

He turns right into Waitrose car park, and parks the pick-up so that it's overlapping two spaces. I drive along the same row of car-parking, until I find a space I can drive into forwards. I haven't reversed into a parking space since I took my driving test. I don't do reversing. I plan my angle of entry, then have to reverse anyway as I've overshot, and by the time I've parked, Gareth has disappeared. (I blame the skirting for obscuring my view.)

Having sprinted from the far end of the car park to the shop, I'm gasping and wishing I was wearing a heavy-duty sports bra. Have I lost him? I track the fading trail of prints that his big muddy boots have left across the floor to where he stands in front of the fruit display. He's even more gorgeous than I remember. Devastatingly handsome. I grab a basket and pause, wondering how best to approach him.

Gareth hooks the basket he is carrying over his left forearm, and pulls a piece of paper out of one of the many pockets he seems to have attached to his distressed khaki cargo pants. His brow creases then smooths again as he scans what has to be a shopping list. I find myself silently cursing my bad luck. In my experience, men don't make shopping lists. They take the lists forced on them by their wives and girlfriends with all good intentions, then turn up at home with lager instead of loo rolls. Any hope I had that Gareth might have broken his word and cancelled his wedding collapses like the kitchen unit did this morning when

I clambered on top of it to force the window open. Gareth is married.

However, I do need a builder and there is no reason why I shouldn't admire the way Gareth's biceps swell and ripple beneath his T-shirt as he stretches out his fingers towards the peaches on the top shelf. I watch, transfixed, as he picks up a peach, caresses it and gives it a gentle squeeze. He lays it carefully in the bottom of the basket then moves on, picking up milk, orange juice, digestive biscuits and a fruit cake. Someone has a healthy appetite.

He stops to re-read his list, and heads for the alcoholic drinks, where he squats down to select a bottle of gin. His trousers slip slightly, revealing a hint of his bare loins, ridges of hard, well-defined muscle on either side of his spine that are covered with lightly tanned skin. The view is quite breathtaking. My heart skips a beat then another and another until I fear that I'm having a cardiac arrest. I press my hand to my chest, and follow Gareth as he heads back on himself to the frozen items.

He selects a tub of ice cream – vanilla with toffee chunks and swirls of caramel sauce, my favourite – and one of Waitrose's 'perfectly balanced' meals for two. I can't do this. I can't have this man working in my house and keep my hands off him. It would be a torment worse than working in a chocolate factory, watching it melt and set, breathing its heady aroma while being forbidden to eat it. I am gutted. I am about to turn away, but it is too late. Gareth looks up and fixes me with those gorgeous eyes of his.

'I'm beginning to feel like Michael Douglas in *Fatal Attraction*. Are you stalking me?'

Suddenly, I find that I *do* do embarrassed after all. I feel the heat rush up my neck and smother my face. 'Er, no, not really. It's just that you're a builder, aren't you?'

He tugs at the back of his trousers. 'I didn't realise it was that obvious.'

'I didn't mean you had a builder's bum. I recognised your pick-up back at the roundabout, and I followed you here.'

Gareth looks from me to the fruit cake in his basket, and back. I can guess what he's thinking.

'I need a builder as soon as possible. It's urgent.' I am not making myself clear. 'I woke up this morning, dripping wet. My sheet, my duvet, my nightie were all saturated.'

'It sounds as if you need to see a doctor.'

'No, you don't understand. It's my roof. It's leaking.'

'I'm very sorry to hear that, but I'm incredibly busy.' Gareth makes to move away, but I grasp his arm firmly.

'I wondered if you'd come back to my place so you can give me an idea of what you can do, and how long it will take.'

'Do I know you?' Gareth's forehead creases. 'Have we met before? Have I quoted you for an extension or a conservatory?'

'We met on Coombe Hill when my car broke down. I'm Sadie.'

'The magic operative?' Gareth whistles through his

teeth as he looks me up and down. 'You look different.'

I let go of his arm, and take a step back. I suppose I do. I'm in a pair of old jeans that don't quite do up around my middle, and a man's shirt that I found in a charity shop, over a fuchsia pink scoop-neck top. I've dragged my hair back into one of Lorna's denim scrunchies with my fingers as Lorna borrowed my hairbrush because she couldn't find hers, and hasn't put mine back where I can find it.

Gareth keeps on staring. A shiver runs down my spine and it has nothing to do with the fact that I have my back to the freezers.

'I've got another job on at the moment,' Gareth says as I am starting to wonder if I have lipstick on my teeth, or Shredded Wheat stuck to my chin.

'I can't wait. My ceiling's close to collapse.'

'I suppose I can't let Topsy's wig get wet,' he says, breaking into a smile. 'Would nine o'clock on Monday morning suit you? I believe the forecast is for good weather over the weekend, so you should stay dry until then.'

I am just about to open my big mouth to complain that Monday is ages away, but realise in time that that would sound ungrateful. I thank Gareth instead, and give him my address and telephone number, and follow him through the check-out, so that when he leaves with his shopping, I can grab the shopping list that he has screwed up into a little ball and left in the bottom of his basket.

'Would you like to go through first?' he asks politely.

'No, you first. I realise how busy you are.'

101

'You're not likely to hold me up, are you?' he grins, glancing towards my basket. 'You haven't got any shopping.'

I can't help grinning back.

'I only came in for a builder.'

'Where else, other than Waitrose, could you find a fresh, quality item like me?' Gareth banters back. I squeeze past him even though I could quite easily have gone back the other way, and I wait while he packs and pays for his shopping. If he finds this odd, he doesn't let on.

'I'll see you on Monday morning,' I say, palming Gareth's shopping list from the basket where he's left it.

Once I'm back in my car, I tug the ball of paper out from up my sleeve, and spread it out to check the handwriting.

I'm no graphologist, but I've gleaned enough information from various magazine articles to be able to recognise that the list is written in the hand of a control freak, the loops on the Ts capturing the letters on either side of them. The letters slant backwards too, indicating a pessimistic nature, which only confirms what I already know: that Gareth has made a big mistake marrying the woman who wrote it, even if she does have good taste in ice cream.

I have found a builder. One problem solved. I still have Miss Watson to deal with. I meet Dan at the school gates at lunchtime, and we find Miss Watson's grey head bowed over some papers in her classroom.

'Sam's in the dinnerhall,' she says, slipping her reading glasses off so that they hang around her neck. 'I thought it would be best if we had this conversation in his absence. Sit down, Mr and Mrs Keith.'

Dan perches on the edge of one of the low tables that serve as desks, and I squat like a garden gnome on a toadstool of a tiny chair, while Miss Watson remains sitting on the only full-sized piece of furniture in the room.

'This is my fed-up chair,' she says. 'The children know that when I'm sitting on it, I am unhappy with their behaviour.'

I think she's trying to tell us something. I glance towards Dan who is biting his lip as if it's him who is about to be criticised, not Sam.

'We understand that Sam's been playing up,' he says.

'It's a little more than that, Mr Keith. Another parent is accusing your son of a physical assault.'

'He's a boy,' I protest. 'Boys can be rough. They don't know their own strength.'

'Sam is a bully,' says Miss Watson. 'If we are going to be able to help him, we must all recognise that, and take appropriate steps to correct him.' There are murmurings of exclusion and home tutors.

'I don't want him home all day,' I argue. 'Exclusion isn't a punishment. What do you think will happen if you tell a boy who hates school that he'll be sent home if he misbehaves?'

'I suggest that we work together to make sure that Sam understands the consequences of his actions.' Miss Watson relaxes slightly. 'I shall do what I can at school but you, as his parents, have the greater role in keeping him on the straight and narrow.'

I want to say that I'm doing my best, but I realise that Miss Watson will only mark me down as 'could do better'.

'Children have the best chance of reaching their potential if they have a stable and loving home-life,' Miss Watson goes on. 'I understand from Sam's home-work in which he had to draw his own house and compare it with one on the island of St Lucia, that he's just moved into a derelict house without proper cooking facilities, Mrs Keith.'

Miss Watson stares at me through narrowed eyes. Dan looks at me accusingly.

'Sam's lying,' I say quickly.

'Then it isn't true that the roof's letting water in, that he's having microwaved chips for every meal?' the teacher enquires.

What can I say? Dan takes over, explaining how I've turned to property developing in order to give my children a brighter future, while Miss Watson argues that what's important isn't money, but enabling chil-dren to control their aggressive impulses so that they can grow up to be well-adjusted adults. Sam doesn't need Jackie Chan. He needs grown-ups who can inspire his respect. At no time does Miss Watson suggest that Dan and I make suitable role models for a delinquent eight year old.

'Sam's schoolwork is poor too,' Miss Watson remarks, to add insult to injury. 'His handwriting is illegible. He doesn't try with his spellings.' She pauses as a bell rings out on the playground. 'I have to stop there for now. We'll reassess Sam's behaviour later in the term.'

Outside in the corridor among the plimsoll bags and backpacks, Dan tries to make repairs to my battered ego. I know now how my mother used to feel when she was called into school to talk about me.

'Cheer up, Sadie,' says Dan. 'Sam will turn out all right in the end. You did.'

I catch a glimpse of my reflection in the glass doors to the gym. My hair is sticking out above my left ear, and my face is deeply flushed. I should be working on the house. I should be the perfect parent. Bowing under the weight of all this responsibility, I find that I don't feel all right at all.

What makes me feel better? Lying on my back in a clearing in Richmond Park, trying to conjure up pictures of Gareth on the backs of my eyelids. It's Sunday morning, and although the children have abandoned their games under the trees at least three times to complain that they're starving, and my stomach is threatening to digest itself, Helen insists that we wait for Sean and Annette to arrive before we can start on the picnic.

'So you're definitely doing the school run tomorrow?' says Helen, interrupting my daydreams.

I sit up abruptly from my pillow of grass, and brush an unfurling frond of bracken from my face. My scarlet V-neck T-shirt clashes with Helen's pink sleeveless top. I wear navy Capri pants with ethnic embroidery around the hems, and mules. She wears a white skirt that reaches just below the curve of her buttocks, and pink jewelled flip-flops.

'No, you are!'

Helen grins. 'Don't panic. I know you want to be alone with this Gareth bloke. You have the hots for him something chronic.'

'I don't.' I gaze towards the sky, watching flashes of sunlight glance off the bellies of the jets flying in and out of Heathrow. What with them and the traffic crawling along the roads that run through the park, it isn't as peaceful as you might expect.

'Doesn't it bother you that he's married?'

'Of course it does. That's what broke up my marriage, some silly tart leading Dan astray.'

'Allegedly,' says Helen rather coolly, and I remember that that is exactly what *she* did. She led Michael astray and broke up his first marriage. As if reading my mind, she goes on, 'When I met Michael, his marriage to Suzanna was already under strain. Michael says that falling in love with me made him realise how unsuited they really were.'

And how old Suzanna was, I think, looking out over the glittering ponds – about the same age as I am now. As far as I know she remains single, an attractive and available man being as rare as a Patagonian Toothfish.

'When are you going to meet John?' Helen asks. 'You did call him?'

'John?'

'The Lonely Heart. You haven't, have you? Sadie, you are the limit. The one thing that will help take your mind off a man you can't have, is a man you can. Promise me you'll ring him?'

'I promise.' I cross my fingers behind my back, and hope that Helen will forget the whole idea. I am not optimistic. Although, as I've said before, Helen moves with the elegance of a giraffe, she also possesses the memory of an elephant.

'Where are Annette and Sean?' Helen says, slipping on a pair of shades.

I gave Annette explicit instructions to help her find us, but I'm not optimistic about that either.

'I'm sure they'll turn up eventually,' I say without conviction. I scan the path but there's no sign of them. Tom is playing football with Sam. The ball flies into the pond, scattering ducks and feathers. Tom wades out thigh-deep in his trainers and knee-length shorts to fetch it, ignoring the signs warning of the dangers of blue-green algae. Michael is making up for the time he hasn't been spending with Charlotte recently, playing hide and seek around the trees with her and Lorna.

Suddenly, a large grey whiskery creature with a long whip-like tail comes bounding over to join us, landing in the middle of the picnic blanket.

'I'm so sorry,' Annette's voice rings out. 'Homer, darling, come here!'

Sean rushes in and hauls the dog off, holding Homer's collar so tight that his tongue goes almost the same blue-grey colour as his coat.

'You think that life's one great game, don't you, you big softie?' Sean bends down and Homer licks his face. I smile to myself. With Sean, it's definitely a case of love me, love my dog. Annette's potty about it too, but if she'd wanted a dog as a surrogate baby, I wish she'd chosen something smaller than an Irish Wolfhound.

'I'm so sorry we've kept you all waiting,' Annette says, holding out a bottle of wine and a packet of crisps. I take them, and hand the bottle to Michael who turns up to take charge of the drinks. 'We were delayed.'

'Traffic?' says Helen politely.

'Annette's spent the last half-hour on her back,' Sean elaborates.

'It's all right. You don't have to explain,' I cut in quickly, but Sean does anyway.

Annette uses an ovulation thermometer to work out her 'fertile' days when she and Sean have to shag like rabbits. She still refers to this desperate coupling as making love, and afterwards she spends hours on her back, with her feet pressed up against the wall in the bedroom to optimise her chances of conception. I can tell from the expressions on Helen and Michael's faces that they'd prefer not to hear any more details, while Sean remains oblivious to the embarrassment that he's causing.

Sean is a firefighter, and so fit that Michael once accused him of abusing steroids. I can hardly forgive him for some of the tactless comments he's made about me and my friends, but I do admire his enthusiasm for personal fitness. He releases Homer who stands drooling over the picnic basket while Annette spreads out a second blanket.

Annette is two years older than me, the pretty sister with the academic achievements that I failed to emulate.

She sits down, stretching her slim, denim-clad legs out in front of her, and ties her long auburn hair back into a plait.

'I saw Dan in the gym the other night,' Sean says, slipping out of his tracksuit bottoms and limbering up in a pair of muscle-hugging, shiny shorts and vest. He runs his hands through his short blond hair, then performs a couple of squat thrusts on the grass.

'What was he doing?' I ask. 'Pumping iron?'

'Sadie doesn't want to hear about Dan,' Helen interrupts.

I find that I do. If he wasn't pumping iron, perhaps he was pumping somebody else. 'Well?'

'When I ran into him he was half-dead. He'd just had an induction session with Washboard Wendy on weights. She's a killer, but she gets results.' Sean pulls himself to his full height and sucks in his stomach. 'Not that Dan has a hope in hell of ending up with a physique like mine.'

'I hope he doesn't hurt himself.'

'I didn't think you'd care, Sadie,' says Annette, pulling her fraying bra-strap back onto her shoulder so that it's hidden beneath her olive green T-shirt.

'Whatever Dan did to me, he's still Lorna and Sam's dad. I'd hate to have to tell them that their father killed himself in the pursuit of the perfect body.'

'Champagne, everyone?' Michael offers, pulling out from the coolbox one of the bottles he and Helen brought with them.

'Please,' says Sean far too quickly. I wish he'd temper his enthusiasm for Michael's champagne with the memory of how he insulted him at the picnic last year by telling him that golf was a girls' game, and how he disapproved of capitalist bastards making money off the backs of poverty-stricken children working under appalling conditions in undeveloped countries. I'm not saying that I disagree with Sean's sentiments, it was the way he communicated them . . .

'One glass can't hurt, can it?' says Annette, glancing towards me.

I am surprised. She usually refuses alcohol, adding some light-hearted comment to the effect that she doesn't wish to pickle the eggs she may, or may not have left in her dysfunctional ovaries. However, she can't fool me. She can't disguise the pain that comes across in her voice whenever she mentions her inability to conceive.

'Tom!' Michael yells. 'Get your arse up here, will you? I want to drink a toast.'

Tom comes ambling up from the edge of the pond, with Sam following behind with the football. I sit up straight. I haven't had a chance to have a good look at Tom yet.

Michael swaggers and pats Tom on the back as he introduces everyone. Tom reminds me of Darius Danesh with his dark hair and brown eyes, but there the resemblance ends as he obviously doesn't make any effort over his appearance. He's wearing a T-shirt with a print of a woman's nude silhouette on the front, dark green combat shorts, and filthy old trainers without socks.

'He's making a flying visit, aren't you, Tom?' This is a statement of fact rather than a question, I gather, from the tone of Michael's voice. Helen nods forcibly in agreement.

'Aren't you at university?' says Annette.

'Yeah, I'm studying Conservation and the Environment,' Tom mutters, rubbing his palms up and down the sides of his shorts.

'Sounds interesting.'

'Yeah, it is . . .'

Helen hands out tall flutes made from blue-tinged glass that coordinate with the plastic picnic set, one of Michael's cheap imports. I watch Michael untwist the wire that restrains the cork in the champagne bottle. He drops it on the ground, then holds the bottle in front of him and works around the bulbous end of the cork with his thumbs, until it flies out, chased by a spurt then a slow drip of creamy froth.

Michael pours and we drink toasts to Tom and his continuing education.

'I'm thirsty too,' moans Sam. 'Can I have champagne?'

Michael glances towards me, eyebrows raised.

'Sam can try mine.' I hold out my glass. Sam takes a sip and screws up his face. 'Do you like it?' He wipes his mouth with the back of his hand and nods. 'You don't . . .'

'Do,' he says, snatching at my glass. I keep hold of it, and slench the rest down.

'It's too good for little boys,' says Michael, grinning.

'I'm not little,' says Sam. 'I'm eight.'

'Wait until you're eighteen then and I'll buy you a whole bottle. I promise.'

'Will you?' Sam ducks behind Michael's back. 'Just checking you're not crossing your fingers like Mum does,' he grins. 'If you keep your fingers crossed when you tell a lie, it doesn't count. That's what Mum says.'

'I don't.'

'I saw you earlier crossing your fingers behind your back while pretending to promise me that you'd ring John,' Helen says.

'Who's John?' asks Annette.

'Someone who wants to go on a blind date with Sadie,' says Helen, and I am grateful to her for not revealing that John is a desperate Lonely Heart. 'Get away, dog!' Helen tries to push Homer away from the picnic basket, but the more she pushes, the more Homer leans. Helen hits him on the nose with a Tupperware container.

'Oh, poor Homer. Come to Mummy,' says Annette as Homer backs off. 'Isn't it time you fed him, Sean?'

'Please do, if it'll stop him salivating into the bloody sandwiches,' says Michael.

Sean feeds the dog tripe from a tin while Helen and I unpack baby tomatoes, pasta salad, two types of grapes, fairy cakes and chocolate muffins. The girls come running up.

'Lorna pushed me off the tree-trunk,' Charlotte announces.

'I didn't. Charlotte slipped.' Lorna pulls her scrunchie out of her hair and twists it back into a ponytail, elbowing me in the face. She sniffs and holds her shoulders very taut, as if she's about to cry. I wish Lorna would stand up for herself. It always seems to be Charlotte who makes the rules.

Annette is frowning at me, thinking no doubt with the smug assurance of a childless person, that if Lorna was her daughter, she wouldn't behave like this. I hope, and I mean that sincerely, that she finds out how difficult childrearing is one day.

'Look at my knee.' Charlotte takes several sharp intakes of breath between her teeth and points to a speck of red on her knee. 'I'm bleeding.'

'That's mud, isn't it?' Helen pulls a tissue out of her pocket, spits on it and presses it against Charlotte's knee, but Charlotte has already forgotten that she's supposed to be in agony and at risk of imminent death from a massive haemorrhage.

'Lorna called me minging because I haven't got my ears pierced.'

'Neither has Lorna,' I point out.

'I'm going to,' says Lorna. 'I'm going to have gold hoops.'

'Is that true?' Helen says, looking at me.

'Dan won't let her.'

'I should think not, at her age.'

'I think Dan's being mean,' I say.

'I think Dan's right not to overcompensate for the divorce by letting Lorna have her own way all the time,' Helen says. 'Come on, let's eat. Everyone will feel better.'

We eat with the stench of tripe hanging thick in the air. Lorna and Charlotte forget their differences and run off to play with Sam who has persuaded Annette to let him borrow her picnic blanket. Helen is rather protective over hers – she hates putting washing through her machine if it's muddy.

Sean is making eyes at Annette. Michael lies with his head in Helen's lap, a lazy smile on his face. Helen's legs are stretched out in front of her, freshly tanned from a respray at the salon yesterday, and her skirt rides high up her thighs. As well as feeling light-headed, I feel choked. Am I missing out? I didn't think I would ever feel like this again. Didn't want to.

'Shall we go for a walk, Tom?' I suggest. 'We can take Homer.'

We pull Homer away by the collar because we can't find his lead, and walk through dappled sun and shade. The tripe smell accompanies us. It's Tom though, not the dog, I think, as we walk straight into an ambush. We are pelted with grass and twigs from behind the trunk of a fallen tree. Sam leaps out of nowhere with a thud and much hollering, keeping his face partially hidden by the picnic blanket that he's wearing as a cloak. Charlotte and Lorna follow behind.

'Stand and deliver!' Sam yells.

'Your money or your life!' says Charlotte.

Lorna remains silent. Charlotte is holding one end of Homer's lead. The other end is tied around Lorna's wrist.

Tom acts scared, falling to his knees.

'I surrender,' I say, trying but failing to keep a straight face.

'Where's your money then?' says Charlotte.

Tom and I dig around in our pockets. Between us, we find and hand over the sum of 15p.

'Who are you anyway?' I ask. 'Robin Hood?'

'Charlotte's a Roman, and Lorna is our slave,' Sam

says. 'I'm an Angry Saxon,' he adds, scything his hands through the air. Mission accomplished, the raiders run off giggling.

'I didn't realise that the Anglo-Saxons were great exponents of the Oriental martial arts,' Tom says, laughing as we stroll on.

'Neither did I.' I hesitate. 'Helen says you've boomeranged for a while. That's the technical term, isn't it?'

'Dad thinks I'm going back to uni, but I'm not. I've had it up to here with studying.' Tom tips his head back and wipes his hand horizontally across his neck as if he's cutting his throat.

'Oh?' I don't really want Tom to unburden himself to me because I shall feel obliged to tell Helen what he said. I don't do confidential very well.

'Molluscs have rights, you know. They have the right to live their lives without interference, without fear . . .'

'You've lost me.'

'I walked out on a matter of principle. One of the lecturers designed an experiment to calculate the dry matter supported by one area of chalk downland. It involves incinerating hundreds of live snails.' Tom shudders with disgust. 'I went to uni to learn how to conserve nature, not destroy it.'

'What about your friends there?' I enquire.

'I don't suppose they'll notice I've gone,' Tom cuts in bitterly, and I find myself wondering if his return has more to do with girlfriend trouble than snails.

There is a disturbance ahead of us, a second ambush,

perhaps, and Homer comes gambolling out of the undergrowth, followed by a whirling dervish of a tan and white terrier that's snapping and snarling at his heels. The terrier is followed by a woman, yelling, 'Vinnie! Vinnie! Stop!' She grabs it by the collar and detaches it from where it's hanging on to Homer's back leg, then hauls it out of snapping distance.

'Come here, you little shit!' The terrier turns on her. She slaps it on the nose, picks it up and hugs it to her chest, and that's when I realise that she's naked from the waist up and pretty well naked from the waist down unless you count the skimpiest thong bikini bottom in shiny red Lycra as clothing. 'Is your dog all right? Vinnie's a little sod,' she says, dropping the terrier to the ground again and revealing a pair of what some might call enviably pert breasts, a stomach like a mudflat, and a navel glittering with a jewelled piercing.

I'd imagined that Tom wouldn't know where to put himself but he seems completely unfazed that we're talking to an almost naked woman in the middle of Richmond Park. He doesn't goggle or gawp, just goes and inspects Homer who's sitting, holding up one paw.

'You great wimp,' I say.

'Wuss,' Tom agrees.

'A right little Saddam, aren't you, Vinnie?' I recognise that voice. I lived with its owner for almost sixteen years, didn't I? Dan emerges from the bracken, fiddling with the fly on his shorts.

'There you are, my rutting stag,' says the woman with the terrier, but Dan appears not to notice her compliment on what I assume is his sexual prowess. His eyes remain fixed on me.

'Hello, Sadie,' he mumbles. 'We were – um – we were looking for one of my contact lenses.'

The Hoxton fin is not in evidence today. A breeze ruffles Dan's hair, disturbing the parting that he has forced along a line where it doesn't naturally fall. I feel sick. I feel hurt and angry, but I don't think that's un-reasonable when I am face to face with my ex, and his girlfriend, the girlfriend whose existence he denied to my face only last week.

'Would you like me to help you find it?' I suggest.

'Find what?' Dan's complexion suddenly clashes with his hair.

'Your contact lens.'

'Don't worry. I have some spares at home.' He tugs nervously at one earlobe. 'I wasn't expecting to see you here. Wendy,' he says, turning to the woman. 'This is my ex-wife.'

Wendy runs one hand through her unnaturally blonde hair, pushing it back from her face while we stare at each other. I suppose this Wendy is none other than the fitness instructor Sean mentioned earlier.

What does Dan expect me to do? Congratulate him on his success in snagging a new girlfriend, and a young one at that, because in spite of the fine lines at the corners of her eyes that suggest an unhealthy addic-tion to tanning, she can't be more than twenty-five.

Wendy slaps at her forearm, and gives it a good scratch. 'Bloody horseflies,' she mutters.

'I'd advise you to bring some insect repellent to keep

the little bastards away next time,' I say sharply. I turn to Homer, and drag him away by his collar with as much dignity as I can muster. Tom follows.

'Are you all right?' he asks.

'I didn't realise Dan had a girlfriend.'

'Do you mind?'

'I mind because he didn't have the guts to tell me.'

'My mum pretends she doesn't care what Dad's up to, or who he's with, but she's still in love with him.'

'I'm not in love with Dan any more. What I mind most is that he doesn't like pets. Not only was I not allowed to have a cat when we were together, but I wasn't allowed to have a dog, and now he's going out with one.'

'That's being uncharitable,' says Tom.

'You're right. That Wendy isn't a dog. She's more of a scrawny cow.' I pause. 'Look – if you're intending to stick around for a while, I could do with a man about the place.'

Tom gives a nervous cough.

'I don't mean in that way.' I find myself laughing. I invite Tom to come and do some of the heavy work in the garden at *St Ives*, but he says he prefers to chill out for a while. When I offer to pay him, he informs me that a few quid here and there isn't going to be much help to him when his dad is threatening to disown him if he leaves university before his finals. Apparently, Tom is already five grand down.

I watch Tom jog ahead down the hill to find Sam and the girls who are making a shelter out of some sticks and Annette's picnic blanket. I can hear Sam chuckling as I stroll back to the picnic with Homer limping along beside me.

'Homer, my poor dear!' Annette exclaims, jumping up and dropping her arms around the wolfhound's neck.

'Some terrier attacked him,' I explain. 'There was nothing I could do.'

'We ought to be getting home,' says Sean. 'We'll walk him back to the car, see how bad it is.' At the word 'walk', Homer's limp miraculously disappears.

'Let the children hang on to the blanket,' Annette says. 'I'll pick it up when I next see you, Sadie.'

Sean and Annette take their leave and walk away arm-in-arm. Michael rounds up the kids to take them up to the kiosk to buy them ice creams. 'How about you, Helen?' he asks. 'Sadie?'

'No, thanks,' Helen says, her eyes following Sean and Annette as they stroll up the hill. 'Don't you think there's something rather obscene about couples in their thirties and forties who carry on behaving like teenagers in public?'

'I think it's wonderful that they feel so comfortable with each other,' I say. 'Do I detect a note of envy?' Helen doesn't respond. 'Would you really want Michael to suck your toes and call you "my honeybunch" in front of everyone?'

'Of course not.'

I suspect that Helen isn't telling the truth, that she would like Michael to be more like Sean – more romantic, but less embarrassing.

'Annette and Sean didn't contribute much to the

119

picnic, did they?' Helen goes on. 'A cheap bottle of wine and crisps from a multi-pack.'

'Sean's always been tight, but Annette was very generous before the baby business arose,' I say in my sister's defence. 'It must be a real struggle to find the thousands of pounds needed for private fertility treatment. I thought you'd understand.'

'I suppose I ought to be more sympathetic,' Helen says, softening slightly. 'I can't imagine my life without Charlotte.'

'Nor mine without the twins.' I go on to tell Helen about finding Dan in the bushes with Wendy, and then, when Michael returns with the children, all sticky because the ice creams melted before they could walk back, I lie down in the sun until my face is ablaze. If Dan can find himself a new lover, then so can I . . .

Chapter Seven

Gareth's weather forecast turns out to be no more accurate than those of the weekend weathermen. A depression sweeps in from the Atlantic sooner than expected, and I find myself on Monday morning, lying on my mattress with the twins' blue plastic paddling-pool liner across the top. I've tried moving the mattress to a dry area, but there is more than one drip. However, I look on the bright side. For all the Meldrews of this world, like Dan and Michael, the ceiling hasn't caved in yet.

Gareth is late. He said he'd be here at nine, and it's already nine thirty. I expect his wife has made some excuse to keep him at home. Envy and spite knife my heart. How I hate that woman. I peer out through the grimy front-room window. The main pane is cracked and held together with plastic tape, another problem that I missed. I don't know how. It's glaringly obvious, like the spot that has appeared overnight at the side of my nose. I don't miss the pick-up that's jolting over the speed hump outside the house though.

He's here. No, he isn't. The pick-up disappears up

the road then reappears a few minutes later at the other end, and parks outside next door. My heart misses a beat. It's definitely Gareth. I am at the door before he can knock.

'Hi, Sadie.' I watch him scramble over the paving slabs that crowd the front garden to reach me. He's wearing a royal-blue rugby shirt and black jeans.

'I could get rid of this rubble for you for twenty quid,' he says. 'I know someone who needs some hard-core.'

'Hardcore? That's for the patio.' I try to sound outraged, rather than insanely pleased to see him. 'You found the house all right?'

'I guessed it was this one from the state of the exterior. You said it was called *St Ives*, but there's no sign.'

Stupid me. 'I changed its name.'

'I like it.' He grins. '*Sod 'em all*. It describes how I feel sometimes when I have clients chasing me up to repoint a wall, or move a window a couple of centimetres. Don't let it worry you, Sadie. I'm perfectly competent, but people have such unreasonable expectations nowadays.' Gareth pauses. 'Can I come in?'

'Yes, yes.' I hang on to the door jamb to keep myself upright as he holds my gaze with those gorgeous eyes of his. His eyes pick up some of the colour from his rugby shirt, which appears from the number of tears in it to have been ripped by more than one leftback in its time.

I wish I'd made a little more effort with my appearance, but I wanted to appear professional. I'm wearing a pair of leggings so old that they bag at the knees, and a sweatshirt. I've brushed my hair, and applied plenty of mascara and lippy. (Lorna says it's not cool to call it lipstick. It's like referring to shades as sunglasses which I still do, but only in private.)

'Just a minute.' Gareth squats down on the front step, unlaces his boots and slips them off to reveal a pair of bright green socks with a red devil motif. It's a thoughtful gesture, but unnecessary, considering the state of the house. 'I'm ready,' he says. 'Show me to your bedroom.'

'I beg your pardon?' I press myself against the wall as Gareth brushes past me into the hall.

'Your bedroom. You said you had water coming into your bedroom.'

'So I did.' I follow Gareth upstairs, watching the curves of his buttocks tighten and relax beneath his close-fitting jeans. The fabric has that textured look, like moleskin, that cries out to be stroked, and it takes remarkable effort for me to keep my hands to myself.

'You've got your work cut out to get this straight while you're living here at the same time,' Gareth begins as we reach the main bedroom. 'This place has lots of potential though. In fact,' he adds, 'I wish I'd bought it myself.'

His eyes sweep the room, and I realise that my nightie is still on the floor where I stepped out of it first thing this morning, and it isn't a slinky nightie, but a tent of brushed cotton with blue sheep leaping across it. My duvet is covered with an assortment of items that I would prefer Gareth not to have seen: a pair of dirty, flesh-coloured, hold-your-belly-in knickers lying gusset up and inside out; a clump of cat hair; a smear of Sam's toothpaste; a tube of pile-shrinking cream without its top; stray strands of used dental floss, and a paddling-pool liner. Mine is a bed to rival Tracey Emin's.

I slide past Gareth, and point out the patches on the ceiling in an attempt to distract him from the muddle that I have created. He steps over my make-up and hairdryer that are on the floor, and pushes aside with his toe Topsy's wig, and the box containing the vibrator that Helen bought for me for my birthday. I wait while he deliberates. The rain slashes at the window, and seeps through my ceiling, forming three or four steadily dripping leaks.

'You're getting wet,' Gareth observes.

Wet? How does he know? His smile broadens to a mischievous grin.

'You're standing under a drip.'

Blushing, I take a step to one side.

'What you need,' he begins, moving closer, 'what you really need is a new roof.'

'Can't you just patch it up?'

'If you want my opinion . . .' he breathes seductively.

'Yes?' I find myself breathing back as I gaze into his teasing eyes.

'I think it's best to go all the way, don't you?'

'It's very tempting,' I murmur. My heart is beating like a hammer-drill, and my bra suddenly seems two cup sizes too small for my breasts. 'It's very tempting,' I repeat, 'to cut corners to save money.'

'If you don't have a new roof, a surveyor will pick

up on it straight away and that could knock thousands off your asking price when you come to sell it. You did say you were doing this up to sell?'

'That's right.'

'In that case, I imagine you want this work done fairly quickly,' he says.

All I am imagining now is Gareth throwing me down on the mattress and ravishing me. I'm not wearing knickers, not because I don't normally wear them, but because I couldn't find a clean pair this morning. I haven't plumbed the washing machine in yet. Note my confidence. *I* am going to do it.

'Sadie?'

'Yes?'

'I thought you'd gone into a trance. Can self-employed magic operatives do that, hypnotise themselves as well as other people?' Gareth is very close to me. His lips are parted slightly. His eyes flash an invitation to a kiss. Fortunately, a picture of a meal for two flashes up in front of my eyes just in time. Whatever spell Gareth has cast is broken and I step back towards the door to make my escape onto the landing. Even if Gareth wasn't married, this would all be too much too soon. In spite of my attempts to behave like an outrageous bohemian, I have only ever slept with Dan, and it took him two years to persuade me that that was what I wanted to do.

I show Gareth into the kitchen downstairs.

'It smells damp,' he comments, wrinkling his nose, but all I can smell is the heady scent of mint toothpaste and shower gel. Gareth strolls across – I say strolls, but it's barely two of his paces from one end of the kitchen to the other – to inspect the wall beside the back door.

'What do you think?' I ask.

Gareth turns to me, stroking his chin. 'I've got a mate in demolition.'

'It's falling down, isn't it?' I panic. Will the insurance cover structural collapse if we haven't had a proper survey? How long will it take to rebuild?

'Sadie, I'm joking.'

'It isn't funny.' I take a deep breath. 'You nearly gave me a heart attack.'

'I'm sorry,' he chuckles, 'but your face was a picture. All I need to do in here is make some repairs to the damp-proof course.'

'One more thing. I – we, that's me and Helen, my business partner – would like an estimate for taking the wall out between the kitchen and dining room.'

'That shouldn't be a problem. It isn't a supporting wall,' Gareth says as I prop myself against it. My knees are weak and trembly with both lust and relief, in spite of the fact that I had three Shredded Wheat for breakfast.

'I'll fetch my ladder.' Gareth brings a ladder in from the back of the pick-up and squeezes up through the trapdoor into the loft. After a few minutes, he declares that some of the timbers need replacing. It's a big job. He gives me a ball-park figure. It is a lot of dosh, more than I was expecting, and I shall have to run it past Helen.

'Would you like a drink? Coffee? Tea?' I try to recall what else there might be in the house, but there's only

Lorna's strawberry milkshake and a blackcurrant Fruit Shoot.

'I have to go.' He glances at his watch. 'I've got a job to finish down the road in Tolworth by the end of the week. I'll be back tonight with a written estimate, and while I'm here, I'll patch that roof up with a piece of tarpaulin until I can do the work properly.'

'Thanks, Gareth.'

'Anything to keep you warm in your bed . . .'

What does he mean by that, I wonder when he's gone. I am unsure that I want Gareth to come back, putting temptation in my way, because it appears, and I hope it isn't just wishful thinking on my part, that he is just like Dan, a married man groping for quick thrills without commitment. Perhaps I'm being a little unfair here. I might have led him on just a teensy-weensy bit. That's just like me: when I get on my high horse, I dismount very quickly. I find I can't ride a high horse for very long.

I wander back upstairs to tidy my room. I pick the vibrator up from the floor and open the box. It wouldn't be any use at all, nowhere nearly big enough to match Gareth if the size of his feet are anything to go by, and a vibrator doesn't have eyes or lips or emotions, and I don't know whether it would work in the rain. I told Helen to take it back, but she looked so disappointed that I didn't appreciate her gift that I backpedalled and said I'd keep it. I haven't used it at all, but the batteries came in handy.

I drop the vibrator onto the duvet and try, but fail, to satisfy my frustrated desires by stripping the wallpaper in the smallest of the three bedrooms. At five o'clock I am still stripping. At least, that is what I am supposed to be doing. Helen is here, and we're taking a break. Helen is sitting on Topsy's Director's chair, and I am sitting cross-legged on a cushion that I crotcheted when I was pregnant with the twins.

'I think I should meet this builder before we make any firm decision to take him on. It's a lot of money.' Helen plucks aimlessly at one finger of the pink Marigold gloves she is wearing. 'I don't suppose he'll turn up again anyway. You know what builders are like.'

'I don't actually. I've never had one.'

Helen smirks.

'Don't tell me that you have!'

Just as Helen is about to tell me exactly how many builders she's had, Lorna and Charlotte interrupt us.

'We need string, chicks, hairspray and yellow card,' Lorna announces.

'We're doing a *Blue Peter* make,' says Charlotte, pushing Lorna aside. All those activities that Helen takes her to are doing wonders for her social skills – if I could afford them, I'd send Lorna to make her a bit more pushy. 'Those are the ingredients we need.'

'Ingredients?' says Helen, arching one eyebrow. 'Don't you mean materials?'

'We need punnets as well,' says Charlotte, ignoring her.

'Is that all?' I remark. When I was a kid, you could make everything that Valerie Singleton suggested with nothing more than brown paper and sticky-backed plastic.

'We've found some tissue paper, twigs and paint,' says Lorna, slipping in front of Charlotte again.

'She pushed me,' Charlotte exclaims, shoving Lorna back.

'That's enough,' Helen warns. 'I have string at home.'

'That's no good, is it?' says Charlotte. She pouts like a temperamental ballerina.

'Can't you paint some card yellow?' I suggest.

'The instructions say that we must use yellow card,' says Lorna, who is a stickler for precision.

'I suppose they say you must have real live chicks as well.'

'Oh, don't be silly, Mum,' says Lorna.

'That would be nice,' says Charlotte hopefully.

'You'll have to improvise,' I say. 'Now, hop it.'

'When is it tea-time?' says Sam, pushing in between the girls. 'I'm starving.'

'What is for tea?' asks Lorna.

'I don't know, do I?'

'You must do,' she says. 'You're our mother.'

I dig about in the freezer in the kitchen.

'Microwaved pizza and chips?' I offer.

'Again?' groans Lorna.

'Could I have some?' asks Charlotte.

'Is that all right, Helen? Would you like to stay for tea as well?'

'No, thanks,' she says. 'I'll eat with Michael later.'

There's a knock at the door. There's another task for us to find room for in our schedule, to install a working doorbell.

'Chuck those in for us, will you?' I throw the pizza

129

box at Helen, and dash for the door. I yank it open. My heart sinks. It isn't Gareth.

'Good evening,' I say, at a bit of a loss, to the elderly man who stands on my doorstep, dressed in a grey flasher mac. 'Can I help you?'

'I'm from next door, number thirteen,' he says, pointing with his stick.

'Nice to meet you,' I say, assuming that he's popped round to welcome me to the neighbourhood.

'I'm not here to make polite conversation.'

'Oh?'

'I noticed in passing that you've removed the sign with your house name.' The man pauses. 'I hope you're going to replace it.'

'I already have.' I point to the new sign in the window.

He peers towards it, squinting through his tortoise-shell-rimmed glasses, then turns back to me.

'That isn't in keeping with the character of the rest of the street, is it? I can't abide newcomers who walk in, thinking they own the place.'

'I do own the place, so I'll do what I bloody well like,' I interrupt. 'Goodbye!' I slam the door in his face and return to the kitchen, stealing a chip from Lorna's plate.

'Who was that?' Helen asks.

'The man from next door, establishing neighbourly relations.'

'How kind of him to drop round. What's he like?' I can almost see Helen's eyes glazing over as she pictures the perfect man for me, available and living right next door.

'He isn't someone you'd want to borrow a cup of sugar from,' I respond. 'I think I'd rather have Ozzy Osbourne as a neighbour.'

Feeling just a little guilty that I've been rude to an elderly person, I head for the third bedroom with Helen to strip more wallpaper, leaving the children to eat choc-ices in the kitchen.

'Did you like the colours on the mood-board for this room?' Helen asks, resting her scraper on the floor.

'The shades of beige?'

'Magnolia is so versatile. It goes with anything.'

'I'd prefer something unusual, something a little off the wall, like warm terracotta, and Mediterranean blue.'

'*Llamedos* might be a beautiful name, Sadie,' Helen smiles, 'but it doesn't suit the house. A Spanish theme isn't a good look for a terraced house in the middle of suburbia.'

Spanish? I study the scuffed remains of magenta nail polish on my fingernails, trying not to chuckle.

'What's so funny?'

'Nothing.' I clear my throat. 'How's Tom? It was kind of him to entertain Sam at the picnic yesterday.'

'I keep thinking how terrible it is that Tom's been driven out of university because he disagreed with his Professor.'

'I can't believe that he left university over a few snails. Do you think there's something else? Girlfriend trouble?'

'Some girl has been ringing him up, claiming she's his girlfriend, but he won't speak to her. I wish he would talk to his friends. It would be best for Tom to make up his own mind about going back to university rather than have Michael forcing him into his car and driving him there.'

'Tom's a grown man. He doesn't have to do what Michael says any more.'

'We'll see.' Helen smiles. 'I don't understand why you're so twitchy, Sadie. Your builder isn't going to turn up.'

'I'm not twitchy,' I insist, just before discovering that I've kicked over a bucket full of sludge. I use my scraper to steer as much of the sludge of old paper and paste as possible back into the bucket. 'Gareth won't have forgotten.'

'I expect he's gone home to his wife,' says Helen. 'If I was his wife, and he's as gorgeous as you say he is, I wouldn't let him out of my sight. Talking of which, I'd better be going home to see what Michael's been up to. He promised he'd be back in time to tuck Charlotte into bed tonight.'

'Is everything all right between you two?'

'I don't know. I expect it's the time of year. By the middle of May most people are looking forward to the summer, but Michael's worrying about the price of gazebos, and whether he's ordered too many cushion pads for his plastic recliners. Last year he had to buy extra of those digging dogs' rear ends to cope with demand.'

'You couldn't get me a new paddling pool on the cheap, could you?' I ask, following Helen downstairs to the hall. 'Alvin's clawed holes in the old liner that I've had on the bed.'

A vehicle pulls up outside. I recognise the particular throb of the engine. It has to be Gareth. I beat Helen to the door, and let him in.

'Don't worry about taking your boots off,' I say. 'Come in and meet my friend and business partner.'

Helen takes one look at him, and turns white through her Clarins foundation. She's met him before, hasn't she? She's already shared more than I care to imagine with Gareth, while I've been imagining that he might want to share his body, if not his soul, with *me*. I am gutted. How is Gareth ever going to fancy someone like me, if he prefers the tall, lean type like Helen?

'Gareth?' Helen says sharply. If looks could kill, Gareth would be dead.

'Hi, Helen. It is Helen, isn't it? I never forget a . . .' Gareth hesitates. I thought he was going to add 'an arse' or 'a tit', but he continues, 'How long is it since I last saw you?'

'Have you brought that estimate?' Helen asks, ignoring his question.

Gareth pulls a piece of paper from his jeans pocket and hands it over to me, but I can't concentrate. There are too many questions that I have to ask Helen. How long did she and Gareth go out together? Was it serious? Were they in love?

'It's what we agreed this morning,' Gareth says, pointing to the estimate.

'We haven't agreed anything yet,' Helen interrupts.

'Don't hang about if you want me,' Gareth says. 'I have three other jobs lined up that I could start on Monday.'

'I'll let you know first thing tomorrow,' I say quickly.

Gareth smiles. 'My phone number's at the top.'

'Thanks for dropping by.'

'It's a pleasure. It's . . . er . . . great to meet you again, Helen.'

Helen mutters something under her breath, indicating that the feeling isn't mutual. At the same time, Lorna comes running into the hall, clutching the *Blue Peter* make, a shared effort, I assume. It looks like a barn owl's breakfast – an assembly of contorted cotton-wool chicks in the bottom of a tomato punnet.

'Sam's wrecked our make,' Charlotte wails from behind.

'I haven't!' yells Sam from behind her.

'He has,' says Lorna. 'He threw the chicks on the floor and stamped on them, and now look at them!'

'Sam? Get your fingers out of your ears, and listen to me.' To my surprise, he does as I ask. 'The girls won't let you join in if you keep wrecking their things.'

'I wrecked their things because they wouldn't let me join in. You always blame everything on me. You never listen to my side of the story.' In front of Helen, and Gareth, and the girls, Sam sticks his middle finger up at me.

'That's a swear, isn't it, Mummy?' Lorna says, wide-eyed.

'You know very well what it is,' I say. 'There's no need to look quite so appalled.' I start to wonder if the girls have been winding Sam up to get him into trouble, and in consequence I resolve to be more gentle with him than I would have been. 'Lorna and Charlotte, you go and stick the heads back on your chicks. I'm sure you can salvage some of them,' I add as Charlotte opens her mouth to argue with me. 'Sam,' I call through to the kitchen where he has taken refuge. 'We'll have a little chat later.'

'Nice kids,' Gareth comments.

'Charlotte is mine,' says Helen, 'and the twins belong to Sadie.' There is a malicious edge to her voice. If Gareth wasn't married, then I guess the presence of the twins, especially Sam, would be enough to put him off me.

'Sadie's told me all about her children,' Gareth says.

Have I? I'm sure I haven't. He winks at me, making my stomach lurch. When I can tear my eyes away from his face, I realise that Helen is scowling. Why is she being such a cow? She usually has a good laugh about her ex-boyfriends. She roadtested them all like cars, giving them points for performance, style, reliability and optional extras.

'You will let me know tomorrow?' Gareth says.

'I promise.' I shut the door behind him and rush back to join Helen, who has retreated to the kitchen where Sam is sitting on the floor with Alvin. 'You do know him then?'

'Know him? I was practically engaged to him once.'

Maybe it's my expression, but Helen softens the blow of that revelation a little by adding, 'It was a long time ago, and Gareth was a complete bastard.'

'Why? What did he do to you?'

'I was supposed to be meeting him in the pub one night, and he left a message at the bar saying that he'd had to cancel because he wasn't feeling well. On the way home, I saw him helping his ex out of his car. She had her ankle in plaster. Gareth said he cancelled our date because she needed a lift back from the hospital, so I asked him why he had lied about it, and he said he'd lied because he knew I'd be angry with him.' Helen chews her lip. 'How could I trust him after that?'

'He must have changed since then,' I suggest hopefully. 'He's married now.'

'People don't change just because they get married, do they?'

I don't point out that this is exactly what Helen did when she married Michael, making an instant transformation from shameless hussy to modest wife.

'You didn't mention Gareth before. Is he one of the three ex-lovers?'

'We went out together for two whole months.'

'That's hardly long enough to constitute an engagement.'

'I considered going on the Pill for him.'

'That's a real sign of going steady.' I'm being ironic here, but Helen doesn't notice. 'What was he like?'

'Same as he is now.'

'I meant in bed.'

'He was fantastic.' Helen's eyes focus on a point somewhere outside the window. 'Ten out of ten in all categories in the roadtest, apart from reliability. He had the biggest—'

'I don't think I want to know, after all,' I interrupt. 'Why do you hate him so much?'

'Because I really, really wanted him, and he didn't want me,' she says bitterly.

'Did you ever see him again?'

'Once, a few years later, when I took great pleasure in telling him that I was engaged to Michael.' A shadow crosses Helen's eyes. 'Actually, it wasn't a pleasure at all. I don't know who suffered most, me or Gareth. You see, Sadie, I might have married Gareth Bryant if things hadn't worked out the way that they did.'

'Do you regret marrying Michael then?' I ask, keeping my voice down in case the children are listening.

'Of course not.' Helen twists the wedding ring on her finger then looks up. 'Okay, I don't approve of everything he does, making business decisions without consulting me first, and spending more time than I'd like him to down at the Golf Club, but you can't have everything. I don't know why you're so upset about finding out that Gareth and I used to be an item, Sadie,' Helen continues. 'It's ancient history. We're not the same people.' She corrects herself. 'At least, *I'm* not. Gareth's still a Neanderthal.'

Later, after Helen and Charlotte have gone home, Sam and Lorna come running downstairs in their pyjamas.

'Mum, Lorna wants to ask you something,' Sam says.

'Why aren't you upstairs cleaning your teeth like I asked you to?'

'I've done them,' he says, baring his molars with a loud, 'Aaah!'

'I can't smell toothpaste.'

'He hasn't done them, Mum,' Lorna cuts in.

Sam's face reddens. He makes a grab for Lorna's arm. She squeals with mock agony.

'You're hurting me!'

'I'm not touching you . . .'

'That's enough!' I bellow. 'It's eight o'clock, far too late to be fighting.'

'Lorna started it,' Sam says, folding his arms and sticking his lower lip out. 'She says I haven't cleaned my teeth, but she hasn't done hers either.'

'Enough!' It's at times like these when it's particularly stressful being a single parent. Good guy, or bad guy? Which role should I choose? I watch the twins' wary faces. Making peace before bedtime is far more appealing than starting a fight. 'What is it you wanted to ask me?'

'Lorna wants a big half-brother like Tom,' Sam says.

'I'm afraid that's impossible.'

'She'll have to make do with just me,' Sam says, his face breaking into a grin.

'Isn't one brother enough for you, Lorna?' I say, turning to her.

'Charlotte says that Tom gives her piggybacks,' she says mournfully, 'and he gives her sweets.'

'I'll share my sweets with you,' says Sam, patting Lorna on the shoulder.

'Thanks, Sam,' she beams. 'Race you upstairs!' she adds, taking him by surprise and giving herself a headstart. Sam thunders after her. I hear them yelling at each other, and laughing as they fight for the toothpaste – the worst of enemies, and the best of friends.

Chapter Eight

'We can't do it without one,' I mutter through the hair-slide between my lips. Charlotte is waiting in Helen's car, and Helen is standing outside my front door at eight forty-five on Monday morning. It's her turn to do the school run. 'We need a builder, Helen.'

'What you need, Sadie, is a bloody good—'

I flash her a warning glance, as I continue plaiting Lorna's ponytail.

'I really think we should have found someone other than Gareth,' Helen goes on.

'Why are you all dressed up today, Mum?' Lorna interrupts.

'I'm not.'

'You are,' Helen agrees.

'Not particularly,' I say, tugging at the hem of my shortest and tightest black skirt.

'Is that new lippy?' says Lorna.

'Just some old stuff I found at the bottom of my make-up bag.'

'You haven't taken mine from my Barbie Set again, have you?'

'No.' I spit the hairslide into the palm of my hand, and turn away quickly to hide a guilty look. I haven't taken Lorna's lippy this time, but I did borrow a smear of her lipgloss.

'Hurry up, Mum,' Lorna grumbles. 'I don't want to be late. We're doing fractions in Numeracy.'

'Sam, have you put your shoes on yet?' I yell up the stairs as I've seen no sign of my son since breakfast.

'Sam's picking his verruca instead of getting ready for school,' Lorna informs me.

'Stop telling tales. Sam, get down here at once!' With the hairslide I catch the stray hairs from Lorna's fringe that she's growing out at the moment and tweak them unnecessarily hard.

'Ouch!' Lorna squeals.

'Having your ears pierced hurts a lot more than that,' Helen cuts in.

'*Sam!*'

'We should have three estimates from different builders. We should have references, and guarantees that all work will be backed by insurance,' Helen tries again.

'That seems a bit over the top,' I grumble.

'You don't know Gareth like I do. We've already made a mistake not having a survey done, and now we're intending to employ some cowboy builder just because you've taken a fancy to him. Gareth's completely unreliable.'

'You're basing your opinion on what you know of

140

his love-life, not on how good he is as a builder.' I refuse to allow Helen to put her peace of mind before our profit. 'That isn't what successful property developers do. They choose the best professional for each job.'

'What makes you believe that Gareth qualifies as a skilled craftsman? Is he a member of the Federation of Master Builders?'

'I don't know. I didn't ask him.' I waver for a moment. 'It's a gut instinct.'

'I think it has more to do with your basic instincts than your gut.' Helen throws me a challenging look. 'When Gareth walks out leaving us with half a roof and a hole in the wall, you can sort it out, Sadie. Don't say I didn't warn you.'

'It's five to nine,' Lorna whines. 'We're supposed to be at school by now.'

'I can't find my shoes,' Sam says from halfway down the stairs.

'You'll have to wear your trainers.'

'We're not allowed to wear trainers to school,' says Lorna. Suddenly, she bursts out laughing. 'Sam, you've got your shoes in your hand.'

Sam isn't sure whether to laugh or not. In the end he settles for laughing at Lorna's expense, insisting that he's tricked her, knowing all along that he was carrying his shoes. I bundle him out of the door, telling him he'll have to put them on in Helen's car as they are already late.

Gareth is late too. I return to picking wallpaper off the walls in the third bedroom. There are four layers of paper, the last of which is so intimately adhered to the underlying wall that the plaster comes away with it. It takes ages to make any impression. Everything is taking longer than I expected, but I guess we'll be able to speed things up if Gareth starts. Helen's pessimism is wearing off on me. What I mean is, when Gareth starts.

He arrives at twenty past nine.

'Hi, Sadie,' he says softly.

'Gareth?' I close my mouth as he steps forwards into the hall and picks out a curl of wallpaper from my hair in an intimate gesture that sets my pulse racing.

'I see you've been at it already this morning,' he grins.

'You've lost me.'

'Stripping wallpaper.' He hesitates. 'You seem surprised to see me. Did you think I wouldn't turn up?' He frowns. 'What's Helen been saying? Is she happy about me working here?'

'Shouldn't she be?' I probe.

'No, no reason I can think of,' he says a little too quickly.

'She thought you'd gone into the Army.'

'I did for a while, but I was discharged. There was a question over my fitness.'

'Really?' I am surprised. Gareth is the fittest man I've ever met.

'My back gave out. Don't worry, it doesn't hinder me in any way,' he smiles. 'I get the odd twinge now and then, and have to take a couple of painkillers. Anyway, the Army probably did me a favour. I worked as a brickie in Central London, and joined a friend's firm to learn about other aspects of the building trade, before I set up on my own. I'd hate the discipline of a nine-to-five job. I like to come and go as I please.'

'What about you and Helen?'

'We went out together a few times, that's all. It was nothing serious.'

Anyone would think that Gareth is talking about a different affair altogether. Can two people's perceptions of what happened really be so extreme, I wonder. 'Would you like a drink?' I offer. 'Coffee? Tea?'

'Anything as long as it's warm and wet.'

'That's me, that's me,' I want to shout, as Gareth asks for tea with milk and three sugars. He gets to work straight away, stripping down to his vest, donning a hard hat and collecting a sledgehammer from his pick-up to attack the wall between the dining room and kitchen.

'You see, Gareth isn't a cowboy,' I tell Helen when she returns from the school run. 'He came fully equipped. He's even wearing a helmet.'

'Not all cowboys wear ten-gallon hats,' she says sourly, as we stand watching him from the dining-room door. 'Nor do they all keep their guns in their holsters, if you get my meaning. Watch him, Sadie.'

'I am watching him.'

The muscles in Gareth's broad shoulders tighten as he lifts the hammer and smashes it against the wall. The rhythmic beat of the hammer is broken intermittently by the hollow sound of shattering bricks. The back of Gareth's neck is flushed and shiny with sweat. His vest has become damp and clings to his torso. If I close my eyes, very briefly, because this sight is too good to miss, I can smell the aphrodisiac scents of musk and brick dust.

'I wish you weren't so critical of him, Helen. Can't you forgive and forget something that happened so many years ago?'

'I'm trying to protect you. When I suggested you found yourself a new man, I didn't mean one like Gareth.'

'He is gorgeous though.'

'I suppose he is,' Helen murmurs grudgingly.

'It's not like we're doing anything wrong by looking.'

'I wouldn't mind touching, if I wasn't married,' says Helen, loosening up. We giggle out loud, and Gareth turns and looks through the swirling clouds of dust, his eyes narrowed.

'How big do you want it?' he says, pointing to the hole that he's made. He's teasing and messing about again, not at all like I imagine a married man should. I wonder if all men are like this when they are at work, or if it is just builders who behave like sex-starved rabbits.

Two hours later when the dining room is full of rubble, and dust has settled on just about every surface in the house, Gareth announces that he's taking a break. He goes out, and doesn't return until Tuesday lunchtime. Luckily, Helen is out having her highlights done on Tuesday morning. Not that I'm expecting anything to happen. Nothing can because Gareth is married and I don't do married men and, if I keep repeating this to myself, I might just begin to believe it.

'Helen and I have to have this property on the market by November,' I observe when Gareth is standing in the kitchen at midday with a cup of tea.

'You did tell me about your deadline. Don't worry, Sadie. There's plenty of time. I'll be finished and out of your way within a month or two.'

'A month?' I splutter into my tea. 'As long as that?'

'There's been some trouble with that job I told you about in Tolworth. It's not my fault. It's down to one of the sub-contractors, the electrician. I call him The Prince of Darkness.' Gareth grins and my heart melts, which is unfortunate because I promised Helen that I'd rip him off a strip, and hold him hostage by stealing the keys to his pick-up until he'd put in some hours. 'I'd better get on with some work now that I'm here,' he says, leaving his mug on the draining board. 'The forecast is for rain, so I'll tack some tarpaulin up in your loft to make a temporary repair.'

It is fantastic. The tarpaulin goes up. Some rubble from the dividing wall gets loaded into a wheelbarrow which is left in the middle of the dining room, and then Gareth's mobile rings from the worktop in the kitchen where he's left it.

'I'll get it for you.' I grab the phone and answer it.

'Gareth, I want you here now!' comes a female voice.

'This isn't Gareth. Who's speaking?'

'He knows who I am. Tell him to get himself down here this minute or he's finished.' I can tell from the unsuppressed fury in this woman's voice that she has a passionate, demanding nature. 'I knew from the start that he was a rogue.'

145

'I'll hand you over,' I suggest, but Gareth is at my side with his finger on his lips and shaking his head. 'He's just popped out. I'll get him to call you back, shall I?'

A baby wails in the background. The phone goes dead.

'Saved by the battery,' says Gareth, taking the phone from me.

'I wouldn't like to be in your shoes when you get home.'

'It's work,' he sighs. 'It's that job I told you about.'

'Tolworth?'

'That's the one.' Gareth pauses. 'Sadie, I've got to nip out to buy some materials for finishing off your archway here. I'll be back later.'

I wish I'd asked Gareth what the concept of 'later' means to him. On Friday he doesn't turn up at all for the third day running. Helen and I are no further forward since we can't agree on a colour for the third bedroom now that we've finished stripping it.

'It's no use skulking around out there,' Helen calls.

'At least I'm doing something useful,' I call back from where I am snipping at the brambles that are invading our back garden through the gaps in number thirteen's shiplap fence.

'What exactly are you implying?' Helen emerges from the back door with a tea-towel thrown over her shoulder. 'I've been doing your washing up. What have you been up to? Recycling the twins' dirty breakfast bowls?'

'Probably.' I squeeze my secateurs. A length of bramble drops to the ground.

Helen walks up to the clothes-line, a piece of blue cord tied between the drainpipe outside the back door and the old pear tree that almost fills the rear lawn. She runs one finger along the cord, and screws up her face.

'That needs a good clean too.' She fetches a bowl of steaming bubbles and starts to wash the clothes-line. 'I didn't tell you before because I didn't want you having time to make up excuses for backing out, but I've arranged a date with John for you.'

'Please, tell me you're joking.'

'He seems very pleasant on the phone. Intelligent. Charismatic.'

'So was Hannibal Lecter.'

Helen ignores me. 'I've sorted through your clothes-rail upstairs and laid a couple of outfits that might be suitable on your duvet. All you have to do is change, put on some slap, and meet him at eight o'clock in the Royal Oak. He'll be carrying an orange gerbera.'

'How over the top! How old-fashioned! Gerberas are so passé.'

'Don't look at me like that. I've done you a favour. It'll cheer you up.' She smiles. 'You don't have to sleep with him, you know. It is just a date.'

'When did you say you'd arranged this for?'

'Tonight. Please, Sadie, John's been on his own since his divorce, just like you have. Don't let him down.'

'It's no good playing on my sympathy. I'm not going out with a man because I feel sorry for him.'

'Listen, I'm going to look a right idiot if I have to ring John back to cancel. You said you wanted to start meeting men again.'

'All right, I did.'

'It's Gareth, isn't it?' Helen probes.

'It has nothing to do with Gareth.'

'Prove it.' Helen wrings out her cloth and shakes it. 'Go out with John tonight.'

'What will we talk about?'

'I don't know, do I? Your work? Hobbies?' She pegs the cloth to the clothes-line. 'John says he's into motor-bikes and home computing.'

'I don't know anything about them.'

'Dan's into computers, isn't he? You can ask him when he comes to pick the twins up for the weekend.'

At seven, Dan comes round for the twins. He's wearing a Fatface sweatshirt and a pair of Merrell sandals. They make him look like a middle-aged surfie, and very not Dan.

'Are you okay?' I invite him into the sitting room, offering him the cushion to sit on while I take the Director's chair.

'Never felt better,' he yawns. 'I've just done a weights session down at the gym. I ran into Sean. He said to tell you that he and Annette will drop round to see you some time this weekend. That's something to look forward to, isn't it?'

I think that Dan really means this, but I find I can't read him like I used to.

'I shan't be sitting in all weekend waiting for them,' I say. 'I have things to do, people to see.'

Dan raises his eyebrows in disbelief, then frowns as though he has remembered something.

'Don't tell me – you're meeting that boy you were

with in the park. That's ridiculous, Sadie. He must be half your age.'

'Not him. That was Tom, Helen's stepson. You last saw him when he was about twelve. No, I'm meeting a man with a gerbera.'

'You're pulling my leg?'

'I wish I was.' When I tackle Dan about whether he has a new job or not yet, he is evasive. He's evasive about the new girlfriend too.

'Why did you lie to me about seeing someone?' I ask. 'Are you ashamed of her? Embarrassed?'

'I didn't want to hurt your feelings, Sadie. I didn't know how you'd react.'

Dan's sickening thoughtfulness makes me want to say something rude that might undermine our attempts at conducting a grown-up relationship for the sake of the twins. I send them upstairs.

'What for, Mum?' Sam moans.

'Go and find your toothbrushes.'

'I've already packed mine,' says Lorna in her most insufferable voice. She sounds so much like Dan sometimes.

'Go and help Sam find his,' I suggest.

'Perhaps we should have two toothbrushes,' Sam says. 'We could keep one here and one at Dad's.'

'I've already packed Sam's,' says Lorna.

'Go and find the toothpaste then.'

'I have,' she says.

'Just go away then. I'm trying to have a private conversation with your father. Go on, hop it!' Lorna giggles, and follows Sam trying to hop up the stairs. 'Don't earwig like you did last time.'

'Wendy lives next door. We met while she was putting up some shelves. She drilled her way into my bedroom – literally – and we've been together ever since.' Dan smiles smugly as if he's apologising for being so damned irresistible, which he isn't. I didn't marry him for his looks and, if I married him for his scintillating personality, I was duped. Actually, I'm being mean. Dan is a good father. He *was* a good husband.

'This is great, isn't it, you and me talking civilly to each other,' Dan says.

'Bloody marvellous,' I say.

'Are you going to Glastonbury this year?'

'I'm too busy with the house, and anyway, I'm not paying one hundred quid for a ticket. How about you?'

'Wendy wants to take me body-surfing in Cornwall.'

'Wendy's Dad's girlfriend,' Sam interrupts from the top of the stairs. 'I saw them kissing the last time we stayed the weekend.'

'When?' blusters Dan.

'I couldn't sleep, and I heard voices, and funny noises, and when I went to investigate, I saw you snogging this woman.' Sam sticks his fingers down his throat as if to make himself sick. 'I've heard you talking to her on the phone. Dad calls her Wendy-pops,' he goes on, turning to me.

'Wendy-pops? How sweet.'

Lorna flies headlong down the stairs, eyes wide with alarm, and flings herself at Dan. He lifts her up, and she wraps her arms around his neck and her legs around his waist.

'I don't want another mummy,' she sobs.

'Neither do I,' adds Sam. 'I couldn't stand having two mums going on at me. I couldn't bear it.'

Dan manages to convince the twins that having a second natural mother is biologically impossible, and that he has no intention of introducing a stepmother into their lives. Lorna stops crying. Sam begins to wonder if he has been too hasty in condemning the idea of an extra mother.

'Kyle at school has a stepmother, and she's just bought him a go-kart,' he says.

'Will you pay for me to have my ears pierced?' Lorna shouts with glee. 'Please, Dad.'

'I suppose I'm in for another arm-twisting over the weekend,' Dan sighs.

I smile, but don't suggest that his life would be easier if he just said yes.

I don't tell the twins that I'm meeting a man with a gerbera. The only person who knows, apart from Dan, is Helen who has rung me four times already this evening to make sure I am still going. Maybe John will turn out to be my kind of man. I apply a second sweep of mascara as I get ready. Motorbikes and home computing? Maybe not.

There are two men at the bar when I arrive. One is tall, moderately attractive, and without a gerbera. The other is cuddly, and white-faced like a panda, but there the resemblance ends. He has a sheen of sweat across his forehead, and he's dressed in a black Goretex motorbike jacket and trousers. When I observe the orange gerbera that's wilting in his fat hand, my instinct is to run, but my phone rings, stalling me. I answer. It's Helen. Again.

'You haven't copped out yet? Please tell me you haven't.'

'I'm here, aren't I?'

'Have you seen him? What's he like?'

'You might remember that I once said that appearances don't matter . . . I've changed my mind.'

'Sadie, give him a chance.'

'Okay, okay.' How do I feel? Disappointed that he doesn't match up to Gareth? Relieved?

'Call me back straight away if he gets too hot to handle.'

I cut Helen off and approach the man at the bar. 'You must be John.'

'Hello.' He hands me the flower. 'For you, Sadie. Can I get you a drink?'

'A white wine, thanks.' I sit myself down at an empty table while he orders. He joins me, bringing the drinks, plus a whiff of Imperial Leather soap and onions.

'I thought I was going to be late. I was reformatting my hard disc, and I didn't notice the time.'

For once I am at a loss to know what to say.

'Have you got a PC?' he asks.

I shake my head.

'Pity. We could have networked them. If you had one. Which you haven't.' He gives a nervous chuckle, and takes a sip of his beer which leaves a frothy tide-line on his upper lip. I force a smile. I can feel sweat trickling between my breasts. 'I could build you one if you like.' John is gazing at my breasts as he is speaking.

He starts patting his jacket-pockets one by one – there are at least six – then he turns them out, throwing coins, chewing-gum wrappers and a small spray-bottle of mouthwash onto the table, all the time keeping his eyes fixed on my décolletage.

'I've lost my bike keys,' he mutters.

I want to tell him that he won't find them down my cleavage, but I bite my tongue. I grab my phone and bag, and stand up.

'Listen,' I say. 'I'm sure you're a lovely guy, but—'

'You're not leaving already?'

'I'm really sorry. I made a mistake. I don't do blind dates.' I head home, still clasping the gerbera. I suppose I should have given it back, but it's a wonderful colour, much more vibrant than any of the samples that I splashed on the walls in the third bedroom today. Inspiration strikes. Never mind finding myself a man. I've found the perfect colour for the bedroom.

I call Helen.

'Don't tell me, you're going back to his place,' she says.

'It's over,' I explain. 'He wasn't my type.'

I walk home with thoughts of the weekend stretching out in front of me. When I was married I was desperate to have a few days on my own, and now I hate it when the twins are away.

The following evening, after I have spent the day in Homebase with the gerbera and a paint colour-mixing machine, I try to make solitude seem more attractive by reminiscing over my brief encounter with John. I slip into Topsy's dungarees and hoop, and press the red sponge ball onto my nose. I try crimping Topsy's wig with Lorna's crimper for a different look, then I put eggs on to boil in the kitchen, timing ten minutes with the pink pig, twist-and-ping timer. As the timer goes off, there is a knock at the front door.

Annette and Sean are on the doorstep, holding out a bottle of Appletise and a bunch of freesias. Homer pushes past them, and starts rogering my leg.

'Get that dog off me!' I yell as I try to keep myself upright in the face of an amorous Wolfhound. Don't get me wrong, I like dogs, but there is a limit to my affection. 'Isn't it time he went to the vet?'

Sean pulls him away.

'It must be those dungarees of yours, Sadie,' says Annette. 'He doesn't do it to anyone else.'

'He's just randy,' says Sean proudly.

'I'd say he was confused.'

'He thinks you're a Yellow Labrador.' Sean drags Homer into the front room, and sits him on the floor.

'You don't mind us dropping in, do you?' says Annette, following them.

'Of course not. I can't wait to show you around the house.'

'I thought Topsy was retiring. Mrs Oaten insisted that your advert be taken down from the noticeboard at school.' Annette looks around the room. 'This is very nice. We've got almost the same wallpaper at home.'

'This is going,' I say. 'Helen and I want to give the place a much more contemporary feel.'

'Where are the twins?'

'It's Dan's weekend.'

'I told you so, Sean. I said Sadie would be wanting some company.'

'And you were right, darling. Can I smell cooking?' Sean adds hopefully.

'I'm doing hardboiled eggs so that Topsy can practise a new magic trick. She has a few engagements left, and I want her to go out with a bang.'

'You couldn't spare a couple, could you?' says Sean. 'I could murder an egg sandwich.'

'He's been in the gym all day,' says Annette.

My sister accompanies me into the kitchen where I make Sean a sandwich and pour all of us a mug of Appletise.

'Thanks for the flowers,' I say.

'I'm sorry, I should have bought you a vase to put them in,' says Annette when I tell her she'll have to use a mug.

'No need to apologise.'

'I'm sorry, I don't realise I'm doing it.'

'You're doing it again.'

'Sorry . . .' Annette's lips curve into a small smile.

'How is IT going?' I ask tentatively.

'Sean and I have just started our last attempt at ICSI,' Annette tells me, referring to Intra Cytoplasmic Spermatozoan Injection, her last-resort option for fertility treatment.

'After that, if I can't have a baby,' she continues, 'I'm going to have a horse and keep it in a livery stable at the end of the A3.' Her mouth is turned down at the corners. Her eyes glitter with tears. Her desire to conceive is like a malignant cancer that's taken over her life. 'I used to dream that my kids would be running around with yours, but it looks as though by the time I have any – if I ever do – yours will be having kids of their own.'

I put my arm around her shoulders. 'Remember what I said about helping you. I can donate eggs. I'll be a surrogate if that's what it takes.' I make the offer again, half-hoping she'll say yes, half-hoping the answer will be no.

'You'd never give up a baby that you had carried,' Annette says tautly.

'I could if I knew from the beginning that it was yours.' I'm not sure I could, but I could force myself if I knew it would make Annette happy. I wouldn't sleep with Sean, of course. It would have to be done in the best possible taste with soft music, and a syringe.

'Thanks, Sis.' Annette pauses. 'I'm on the drugs again. Sean had to stick a needle in my bum this morning. I can hardly sit down for the bruise, so maybe it's a good thing that this is our last try.'

'I hope it all goes well,' I say hopelessly. I wish Topsy could wave her wand and conjure up a pregnancy for them.

On our return from the kitchen, I offer Annette the Director's chair. Sean is on the cushion which leaves me with the floor. Homer lies slobbering at Sean's feet, distracted from his male urges by the scent of food. Sean has switched the telly on, and is flicking between BBC1 and ITV1.

'You'll never sell this house if it doesn't have Sky,' he grumbles.

'We don't all watch the telly all day,' I point out, 'especially when we're entertaining guests.'

Sean turns the volume up a notch so that I can hardly hear what Annette is trying to tell me.

'The picnic in the park was such fun,' says Annette. 'Michael told me that it's his fiftieth birthday this year. He looks amazing for fifty.'

'Who wouldn't if they had all the money Michael has?' Sean cuts in. 'Mind you, I shouldn't think that his BMI is up to much.'

'His what?' I ask.

'Body Mass Index.' Sean lifts his T-shirt at the waist, and examines his six-pack. 'I reckon Michael carries a far greater proportion of body fat than I do.'

'He's invited us to his party,' says Annette.

'I didn't know he was having a party.'

'He says that Helen's planning a surprise party,' says Annette.

'Is she?' This news is certainly a surprise to me – and to Helen, I suspect.

'This picture's rubbish,' Sean says, flicking channels again.

'I'm going to buy an aerial for the loft.'

'You need a smoke alarm too,' says Sean. 'I don't suppose this place has one, has it?'

'I'm hardly going to be here long enough to worry.'

'Long enough to die,' he says dramatically. 'I'll come and fit one for you some time. If you give me the cash, I'll even pick one up for you to save you the bother.'

'That's great, thanks.' I find that I am losing the will to live at the thought of spending another evening sitting here listening to Annette going over and over the subject of IT while Sean drills holes in my ceilings. I always try to be supportive, but eventually compassion fatigue sets in, and I end up feeling almost as depressed as Annette – which is no help to her at all. I fetch my purse from my handbag where I have left it slung over the banister at the bottom of the stairs, and hand over my last twenty-pound note.

'We'd better go,' says Annette. 'I wish we didn't have to leave you all on your own.'

'I'm not alone,' I insist. 'I have Alvin.' I glance towards the door to the dining room, behind which lies the arch that Gareth has made, and some of his tools. And I have my dreams.

Chapter Nine

Whenever someone knocks at the door, I assume that it's Gareth. So far today though, the man from number thirteen, who I have christened The Neighbour From Hell, has knocked to complain about the rowdy party I held last night – actually, it was just me dancing to Kylie while Alvin looked on – and Dan for me to let the twins in. Helen knocks too, much later when the twins are in bed, and I have set up the video and opened a bottle of wine.

'Are you spying on me?'

'I'm making sure you're all right.' Helen peers around the door to the front room. 'I take it that you're not still working.'

'I'm watching a dirty video.'

'Sadie, what's come over you?' Helen comes in and stands right in front of the telly with her hands on her hips. From where I sit on the Director's chair, I can just see the goings-on on the screen between her knees. 'What on earth is this?'

'Some kind of DIY fetishist's fantasy, I think.'

'Masturbation, you mean?'

I can't help giggling. 'I thought you were so open-minded, Helen,' I snort.

'Who makes this kind of smut?'

'It's a practical guide to ceramic tiling, running time approximately thirty minutes.'

'He has nice hands, whoever he is.'

'Wine?'

'Please.'

'Sit your bum down then,' I say, giving up the Director's chair.

'I had to get out of the house for a while,' Helen sighs as she kicks off her pink mules and stretches her long legs out in front of her.

'So you didn't come here out of the goodness of your heart, after all?'

'I thought we could talk. You sounded very down on the phone last night. John didn't turn out as well as he made himself out to be—'

'Just like every other man I've ever met,' I interrupt.

'I'll help you find someone. You do need help, Sadie. I don't want you choosing the wrong kind of man.' Helen prods me in the ribs. 'Your eyes are glazing over.'

'It's the video.'

'You can't fool me. You're thinking about Gareth. Well, don't! You're wasting your time. We won't see him again.'

'He's left his wheelbarrow here,' I protest.

'He won't bother coming back to fetch a wheelbarrow,' says Helen. 'I doubt very much that it belonged to him in the first place.'

'Are you accusing Gareth of being a thief as well as a libertine?' I find that the more Helen denigrates Gareth, the more I want to stick up for him, just as I stick up for Sam in the face of Miss Watson's accusations.

'I want you to realise that Gareth is far from being the prince that you magic up for yourself in Topsy's fairytales. I'm not trying to poison you or anyone else against him because I want revenge for how he treated me. I'm looking out for you because you're my best friend.'

'Thanks, Helen,' I say caustically.

'Perhaps those fair hands on the screen belong to Brad Pitt,' says Helen, changing the subject. She starts talking about the concept of downdating which means you go out and find a partner who is less attractive than you are.

'Apparently, goodlooking men like Brad have enormous egos that demand constant attention from their partners.'

'I'd rather take on the challenge of keeping Brad happy than someone like David Brent from *The Office*. I shouldn't think that Brad's ego is any larger or more demanding than Michael's is at the moment.'

The television screen goes black, and the video player whirrs to a stop.

'Michael's snappy with me and Charlotte, and it's all because of Tom,' Helen continues. 'He was so proud when Tom got a place at university – he's the first member of his family to go into higher education. He even came to terms with the fact that Tom wasn't doing what he considers to be a proper degree like Medicine or Law. Now it looks as if Tom isn't going to get a degree at all.'

'Isn't he moving out yet?'

'He's moved himself in. Sonya, this girlfriend of his, who isn't his girlfriend, is always ringing him up, and I've heard Tom picking up the receiver and saying he'll ring her back to save her the phone bill. That's my phone. That's my bloody phone bill. And his trainers stink to high heaven, and he doesn't do anything to help out. He doesn't have a clue how to stack a dishwasher.'

'The novelty of being stepmother to Tom is beginning to wear off then?'

'I'm quite happy to be his stepmother, but from a distance, preferably of no less than fifty miles.'

'Tom could work for us on the development,' I suggest, because the more I look at our project, the more I realise what a challenge we've taken on. We're going to need all the help we can get.

'He isn't staying,' Helen insists. 'Michael's right – Tom has to go back to university. A degree in Conservation and the Environment is better than no degree at all.'

'Do you think it would be a good idea to arrange a surprise party for Michael's fiftieth?' I don't mention that it is Michael who has cleverly put the idea into Helen's head via myself and Annette.

'What on earth would I want to do that for?' Helen thinks for a moment. 'I suppose it would cheer him up. Actually, that's a brilliant idea.' She downs a glass of wine and refills mine. I fetch a second bottle from the kitchen while Helen collects a brochure from her car. I try to refill her glass, but she won't let me.

'I'm driving home tonight,' she says. 'Now, what do you think of this?' She opens the brochure at a page she's marked with one of Charlotte's pink hair ribbons.

'If you're trying to get me drunk so you can have the kitchen you want, it won't work. We've agreed to change the doors on the units that are already there.'

'Everyone knows that a new kitchen pays for itself.'

I go as far as admitting that the granite and natural wood finish kitchen with brushed steel appliances in the picture is out of this world, but it's also out of keeping with the house. I'd prefer something more traditional with a bit of melamine to brighten it up.

'I spoke to the salesman at the showroom,' Helen goes on. 'He said that the waiting time from ordering to delivery was four months on a bespoke designer kitchen like this, but he could do it for me in three, if I put a deposit down by the end of tomorrow.'

'What about our budget?'

'We're well over what you planned originally with the unforeseen building work, so what difference is the price of a quality kitchen going to make?'

'It'll wipe out our profit,' I wail.

'You're beginning to sound like Michael, worrying about his margins all the time.'

'I thought we were in this purely to make as much money as we can in as short a time as possible.'

'It isn't just about money. I don't want to do a tacky

make-over with tarted-up secondhand furniture and MDF. I want to make a statement.'

Helen is adamant, and so am I. I start to wonder if friendship and property developing are as incompatible as a hangover and family life.

The next morning I feel fine, lying flat on my back and focusing on the mould on the ceiling that shimmers as it advances and recedes in rhythm with the waves of nausea that threaten to overwhelm me. This is ridiculous. How many times have I promised myself that I'd never have a hangover again?

'Mum, Mum!'

The mattress rocks beneath me as Sam and Lorna jump up and down on it, and bring me the worst news that a person suffering from the after-effects of alcohol intoxication could wish to hear.

'Mum,' says Sam, 'Alvin's been sick on my duvet.'

There's only one thing for it. I confess to feeling a little under the weather, grit my teeth, and get up to face the day. It isn't so bad. I find that cleaning up gerbera-coloured sick (I wondered where that flower had gone) reminds me of my adventure into colour-mixing, and that I forgot to show the result to Helen last night.

'What do you want for breakfast, Mum?' asks Lorna when I am emptying the bucket down the kitchen sink.

'Nothing, thanks. What's come over you?'

'I'm being helpful.' She isn't concentrating on what she is doing, and Cheerios are pouring out of the box she's holding, and spilling over the rim of the bowl.

'Lorna! That isn't being helpful, is it?' I snatch the

box, and stuff handfuls of loose Cheerios back inside it. I must have shouted too loud. Lorna's face crumples and she bursts into tears.

'She *is* trying,' says Sam protectively.

'She certainly is,' I huff. 'I have enough on my plate without having to clear up after you two.'

'I hate this house,' Lorna wails. 'I hate living here.'

My heart melts.

'You don't mean that . . .' I drop my arms around her and give her a hug, and realise for the first time how selfish I have been in forcing the twins to live in this dark, dirty house that will never be our home. 'We won't be here for ever, my fairy.'

Lorna starts sobbing again. 'That's just it, Mum. The Tooth Fairy doesn't know where we live any more. What will happen when my next tooth falls out?'

'Sam, will you get your breakfast ready,' I say before Sam can make his usual comment on the non-existence of the tooth fairy which will only make Lorna more upset. I push my daughter's hair back from where it has stuck to her face with a mixture of snot and tears. 'There's bound to be a tooth fairy here.' I show her to the window overlooking the back garden. 'You see that pear tree? It makes a perfect home for a tooth fairy.'

Lorna stops crying, and gives a loud sniff. 'Can I leave her some Cheerios?'

'Go on then.'

I watch Lorna take three Cheerios out to the pear tree, and place them carefully along a branch. When she returns indoors for her breakfast, she is smiling again.

I can't face breakfast myself. All that I can force down is a coffee and a packet of cheese and onion crisps.

Helen calls to say that she can't possibly do the school run because she's going into Kingston to put a deposit on the kitchen as we agreed last night. Did we? I find that I can't remember . . . She reminds me that we are partners and, as I chose the builder, she should be allowed to choose the kitchen. She makes this sound so fair and reasonable that I agree, and head off to school, risking meeting one of the Big Guns of the PTA. Caroline, the biggest gun of all, both physically and in her position at the top of the PTA organisation, a mafia of the bitchiest and bossiest mothers, accosts me at the school gate.

'Sadie! It is Sadie, isn't it? Helen's told me how keen you are to do Topsy for us at the school fête.'

'Has she? Topsy's fully booked for June.'

'The fête's in July this year.'

'That's a shame. Topsy will be retired by then.'

'Helen says that you're keeping Topsy available for special occasions like the school fête. She says that she herself is too busy working to volunteer to do the *Guess the Number of Smarties* stall this year, but she feels sure that you'd want to help out for a couple of hours, selling balloons to raise funds for new PE mats.'

I want to kill Helen, but I remember that Caroline is particularly skilled at twisting what people say to her into what she wants to hear, and Helen probably said nothing of the sort.

'Did Helen mention that I'm working full-time too?'

'Lorna will be disappointed if her mum's not at the fête,' Caroline persists. 'We have such fun with face-painting and a bouncy castle.'

'Please, Mum.' I look down at Lorna's face, still pinched from crying, and I relent.

'That's very public-spirited of you, Sadie,' says Caroline. 'I'll put you down for the whole afternoon on the first Saturday in July. Don't forget. You know how maddening it is when someone lets you down.'

'Yes, I do. I know exactly how frustrating that is,' I say, wondering if Gareth will turn up at the development today.

When I return home, or to work as I should probably call it during the daytime, I find that the dust has settled on my falling-out with Helen over the plans for the kitchen, and on the kitchen worktops.

'The new kitchen will be here in three months,' Helen says, cleaning up before she makes coffee. 'Have you seen this?'

The words SNOG and FART are written in the dust.

'That has to be Sam.'

'I thought you said he couldn't spell.'

'That's Miss Watson's opinion.' I loosen the belt on my jeans. I am swelling with pride at Sam's achievements, and the gas created in my stomach by fermenting cheese and onion crisps. 'Gareth hasn't turned up?'

'I hate to say "I told you so".' Helen shrugs.

'No, you don't,' I snort. 'You're loving it.'

'I'm not. I want this to work out as much as you do, but we have to face facts. Gareth always was impossible to pin down.'

167

What do I feel? Relief that Gareth hasn't turned up this morning because I look like a shredded dishrag? Utter devastation that he hasn't when I survey the wreckage he has left in his wake? When I look at the ragged hole that leads into the dining room, and the rubble, and Gareth's wheelbarrow, I want to cry.

'I'll ring him,' I decide.

'I don't suppose he'll answer.'

'I'm sure he has a good reason for being late.'

'He isn't late. He isn't coming. For goodness sake, Sadie, why don't you ever listen when someone's trying to help you?'

I try dialling Gareth's number but there is no answer, just his gravelly voice asking me to leave a message.

'I won't leave a message. I don't want to sound too desperate.'

'We *are* desperate. We've got less than six months to make this place habitable,' Helen moans. 'Are you all right, Sadie? You've gone very quiet.'

'I've got a thumping headache.'

'Thank goodness for that. For a minute, I thought you were dead.'

'It isn't funny. You haven't got any painkillers with you, have you?'

'I thought you didn't believe in painkillers?'

'I don't unless I'm in pain, which I am now.' The pain in my heart is more intense than the ache in my head. I misjudged Gareth. I assumed that he was a straightforward and honest man, but it seems that I was wrong.

'We'd better get on with what we can until we find another builder,' says Helen. 'Coffee?'

'You don't have to ask.' I recall that I haven't shown Helen the paint that I had mixed at the weekend. I show her, and promptly wish that I hadn't. We come to a tense agreement that we will look for an alternative colour to gerbera to paint the third bedroom, and start stripping wallpaper in the front room downstairs with the radio on. 'Our House' by Madness is playing as Gareth parks his pick-up outside the development, and strolls up to the door.

'He's back!' I throw down my scraper, run my sticky fingers through my hair, and dash into the hall to let him in.

'Hi, Sadie,' he grins.

'You're late,' Helen says coldly from over my shoulder.

'I didn't think you'd miss me,' he says. 'I'm flattered.'

'Where have you been?' Helen asks.

'I've had one or two things to sort out.'

'What things?'

'Woman trouble.'

'You're fired,' says Helen dramatically.

'You owe me for that hole,' says Gareth, pointing towards the dining-room door.

'We owe you nothing. You're hopelessly unreliable, and unprofessional. Look at the mess you've left us with all week.' It's driven Helen mad. She's been itching to clear it up.

'I'm here now, and I'll clear all the rubble away.' His

eyes settle on mine. The heat in his gaze melts any resolve that I had to give him a piece of my mind. 'I promise.'

'You could have rung to let us know when you were coming back,' is the best that I can manage.

'I did.' Gareth frowns. 'I tried the number you gave me. It's unobtainable.'

'You're lying,' Helen snaps. 'I've rung Sadie hundreds of times in the last week.' She isn't exaggerating much – she used to ring me almost as often when I lived across the road from her. She would lift a corner of her net curtains to wave at me when we were on the phone to each other. She's taken the nets down since we decided to become property developers, and put up voile drapes instead.

Gareth takes a piece of paper out of his pocket and reads out the number that I gave him.

It's very familiar, more familiar to me than my new one. I beat my brow with the end of my fist. It's confession time.

'That's my old number. I must have given you the wrong one.'

'You idiot, Sadie!' Helen turns on me. 'You're impossible.'

'I'm sorry.'

'I assumed that you'd try to get in touch with me,' Gareth says.

'I did, but I didn't leave a message. Your phone was switched off every time I rang.'

'I was up at the hospital. You can't use mobile phones in the wards in case they interfere with the heart monitors.'

Heart monitors? If I were attached to one right now, the trace would be all over the place as I picture Gareth at his wife's bedside, holding her hand as she takes her last breath. I support Gareth during a respectable period of mourning, like five days, give him emotional first aid and then . . . I'm a bitch, aren't I? I deserve to die.

'You'll give me another chance then?' says Gareth. 'I should have tried to drop round to see you, but I was busy.'

'Sadie?' Helen looks at me. I look at her.

'It'll take ages to find another builder. Look how difficult it was to find this one.'

'All right,' she sighs. 'We'll give you one more chance, but if you let us down again, you're off the job.'

Gareth smiles. 'I'll move this rubble out of your way.' He disappears into the dining room. Helen and I return to the front room. 'Oh, and I could do with some cash up front for materials,' he calls out. 'Five hundred?'

'When?'

'Monday will do.'

'No problem,' I say brightly. My bank balance has been incredibly healthy since Michael paid in Helen's share of the development costs.

'I can't remember Michael giving up a day at work for my sake,' Helen whispers. 'Maybe I've been too hard on Gareth. He obviously loves his wife very much, taking all this time off to be with her.'

'You've changed your tune.'

Helen stares at me. 'Oh Sadie, for once in your life take some advice from me – don't interfere in Gareth's marriage. You'll only make yourself look ridiculous.'

'It's what you did to Michael and Suzanna.' I watch Helen's face redden. Tiny crows' feet appear at the corners of her eyes.

'It wasn't,' she pouts.

'Was.' My irritation evaporates at the thought that we are sniping at each other, just like Annette and I used to when I was about ten. 'Now you're learning what it would be like to have a sister,' I smile.

Helen starts laughing. 'In that case, I wouldn't want one.' She glances at her watch. 'Coffee?'

'I'll make it,' I offer quickly. 'It's my turn.' It occurs to me as the kettle is boiling in the kitchen that we haven't got a project manager on the development. I appoint myself, pour water on three coffees, and deliver one to Gareth via the hole in the wall.

'Have you got a plan for the building work?' I ask him. 'Only it all seems a bit haphazard.' Bob the Builder, who Sam used to watch avidly, seems much more organised than Gareth is, but that's probably because Bob has Wendy to help him.

'I have a plan, Sadie,' he murmurs as he takes the mug from me, brushing dust onto my hands and looking deep into my eyes. 'And I'm working on it right now . . .'

My stomach does a double somersault, and a back-flip.

'Where's that coffee?' Helen calls from the front room.

'I'm just asking Gareth if he'll give us a third opinion on the paint,' I call back. 'Would you mind?' I ask him. We join Helen in the front room. I pick up the smallest of the containers that I had mixed up, place it in the middle of the floor and open it with a flourish. 'Da da!'

'What is that colour?' says Gareth.

'It's revolting, isn't it?' Helen shudders.

'It is orange gerbera. It's warm, bright and gorgeous. What do you think?' I wish I hadn't asked because Helen just happens to mention that the paint colour was inspired by the flower that my hot date gave me this weekend.

'Why did you have to mention John?' I whisper once Gareth has returned to his wheelbarrow in the dining room.

'No reason,' she shrugs.

'You made one date sound like going steady, when I hardly said more than two words to him.'

'It was something to say.' Helen twists her gold chain tight around her neck, half-strangling herself, which is what I'd quite like to do to her after that comment of hers. 'For goodness sake, what does it matter? Gareth isn't interested in you or what you were doing at the weekend.'

He was interested in me until Helen mentioned John. When I collect his coffee mug, he is very quiet.

'How's it going?' I ask brightly.

'Not bad.' He tosses a brick into the wheelbarrow. As the clang dies away I find myself wondering why the clanger that Helen dropped should affect Gareth so badly if I don't mean anything to him. I wonder why I am unlucky in love. I wonder if Gareth can be all that good at rugby when the next brick that he throws misses the wheelbarrow, and ends up back on the floor.

At three Helen leaves for the school run to collect the twins and Charlotte and take them all swimming so that I can keep working.

'Don't do anything I wouldn't do,' she says as she slams the door behind her, leaving me and Gareth alone in the house. We are in different rooms, yet I am painfully aware of his presence: the odd knock and thud from beyond the wall, the rattle and squeak of the wheelbarrow as he pushes it out through the hall to the front garden, the clattering sound as he tips the contents out onto the heap of rubble that he has already made. For a while the house falls silent, and I wonder if he's abandoned the development again already.

I creep up to the window and look out. Gareth is squatting on a paving slab, stroking Alvin while he talks on his mobile. He looks up towards the window. I smile and give him a wave. He waves back. Five minutes later, his head appears around the door to the front room.

'Sadie, we need to discuss the lining for the arch,' he says.

I follow him into the dining room, our feet scrunching across scattered fragments of plaster.

'What kind of finish do you want?'

I glance down at the floor. At my feet is a large chisel. I pick it up and wrap my fist around its smooth, knobbed handle. There's Gareth talking about finishing when he hasn't even started on what I'd really like him to do for me.

'Pine? Ash?' Gareth continues.

'I hadn't thought about that yet,' I say stiffly because

I am not inclined to forgive him for being more concerned that I have a boyfriend than he is that he has a wife.

'I expect Helen has an opinion on it,' he grins. 'She always was terribly opinionated.'

'Did you go out together for very long?' I ask.

'Hasn't she told you all about it?'

'There are two sides to every story.'

'There isn't much to tell. I suppose you'd describe what we had as a casual fling. I'd forgotten all about it until I ran into her the other night.'

'Helen told me that you were practically engaged.' I shouldn't have broken Helen's confidence, I know, but I am still smarting after her references to John, and Gareth is very close to me, with streaks of sweat and dust across his cheeks, and I am imagining what it would be like to take him outside in the rain, strip off his dirty clothes, and let him shag me senseless.

'I'm not renowned for my sense of commitment,' he begins, 'but I never raised the subject of marriage, or love with Helen. We had two months together, for goodness sake, not two years.' He pauses. 'I'm not sure I've ever been out with a woman for as long as two years.'

'You have been engaged though?'

'Not to Helen.' He clears his throat. 'Can I relieve you of that chisel, only what you're doing with it is driving me mad.' Gareth moves close enough to reach out and take the chisel from my hand. 'This boyfriend of yours . . .'

'John isn't, wasn't and never will be my boyfriend,'

I say vehemently. 'He was someone that Helen set me up with.'

'So you won't be seeing him again.' I can hear the relief in Gareth's voice. I can also hear the roughening catch of his breathing. I can see the shape of the chisel handle that he has slipped into his trouser-pocket, or is it the handle of another heavy-duty tool? I step back, pressing myself against the wall.

'Sadie?' Gareth murmurs.

'Coffee? Tea?'

'No more. I've drunk enough tea to sink a clipper. I won't be able to sleep for the caffeine. Not that I'll be able to sleep anyway for thinking about you . . .'

'Me?' I squeak, forcing myself to look up into his eyes. His pupils are dark and dilated. Sea-green irises flash with lust.

'Beech,' I say quickly. 'We'll have beech for the arch.'

'I don't understand you. One minute you come across all hot and up for it, the next . . .' His voice tails off. 'I'd really like to kiss you.'

'I c-can't,' I stutter.

'It isn't that difficult, is it? All you have to do,' he slips one hand around my shoulders and tilts his face towards mine, 'is relax.'

I pull away roughly. I want to so much that it hurts.

Gareth frowns. 'I thought this is what you wanted. Look how you picked me up in Waitrose.'

My skin tingles with desire laced with suspicion. 'Is that why you agreed to do the work here at short notice, because you thought you'd get laid?' My ire rises. 'Listen to me, Gareth Bryant, you won't get laid here.

You're a married man. I don't do married men!'

'I'm not married.'

'That's what they all say.' I turn away, thinking of my father and his denials, and of Dan. 'That first time we met, you were on your way to your wedding.'

'I didn't go through with it.'

'Oh?' My heart skips a beat.

'It was something you, or Topsy, said about love that made me realise that marrying Alison would be a terrible mistake, not just for me, but for her, so I cancelled the wedding at the door to the Register Office.'

'That took some guts, didn't it?'

'It was one of the worst things I've ever had to do.'

I want to jump up and down and screech with joy, but I keep my dignity, remembering Gareth's excuse for not turning up last week. Woman trouble. If there isn't a Mrs Bryant, then which other woman is it?

I feel the weight of Gareth's hand burning into my shoulder. 'Doesn't knowing that I'm not married make any difference?'

'What about your girlfriend?' I mumble. 'You said you had woman trouble. You've been on the phone to someone for half the afternoon.'

'Five minutes,' Gareth chuckles. 'I think you'll find that I'm entitled to a break now and then.' His hand slides down my arm, his fingers brushing bare skin where the sleeve of my T-shirt stops. I turn to face him. 'I have no wife. I have no girlfriend.'

I start to open my mouth.

'Before you ask,' Gareth says, 'I have no ties to any ex-girlfriends either. I was speaking to my mum. She hasn't been well. She relies on me, you see. My dad died when I was fifteen, and my sister lives abroad.'

'I'm sorry . . .'

'Mum's back at home now. I live with her, although it isn't something that a man of my age wants to brag about – that he's had to move back in with his mother. Once I cancelled the wedding I was obliged to settle all the bills for the dresses, cake, reception, car, flowers, honeymoon in the Seychelles . . . Alison decided she'd pay my share of the mortgage on the house that we bought together, so I had nowhere else to go.' His hands have found the soft curves at my waist. 'Can I kiss you now?'

I gaze into his eyes, lift my arms, and slide my hands up around his neck.

Our lips touch. His tongue probes my mouth, and I wish in a momentary panic that I hadn't eaten those cheese and onion crisps this morning, but it doesn't matter. Nothing matters. Gareth doesn't belong to anyone after all.

I taste sweet tea on the insides of his cheeks, graze my tongue on the jagged edges of his teeth, run my hands through his hair. The shudders that rack my body have nothing to do with the passing train, and everything to do with the way that Gareth crushes my softness against his hard length, matching heartbeat to heartbeat, and breath to breath. This is no tentative teenage snog. This is a grown-up, going-all-the-way encounter. Gareth is going to shag me.

My body stiffens slightly. The contact between Gareth's tool and my belly softens in response, and his lips leave mine.

'Do you want me to stop?' Gareth growls, pressing his mouth to my cheek. 'Only if you do, you have to say so now. I want you, but if you're not ready . . .'

'I'm not sure . . .'

'How can I persuade you?'

Gareth's fingers that were digging into my buttocks, are tangling in my hair, caressing the side of my neck. Gareth is like a puppetmaster, pulling strings that seem to be knotted to my nipples, and a place that I'd forgotten about between my legs. His lips find mine again. Am I persuaded? I close my eyes . . .

'Bye!' calls Helen from the hall. 'I won't stop!'

'Mum! Mum! We're home!' The twins come running into the kitchen, turn and find me and Gareth in an intimate embrace.

With a groan of frustration, Gareth tears himself away, and we stand facing the twins like a pair of sheepish teenagers caught out by their parents. Inwardly, I curse myself for giving Helen a key so she can come and go at the development as she pleases.

'Mum, why are you eating the builder?' says Lorna, her eyes wide with disbelief.

'She isn't eating him. She's snogging him,' says Sam, throwing down his rucksack and swimming bag into the rubble. 'That's disgusting.'

'Actually, it's rather nice,' says Gareth at the same time as I deny any improper conduct.

'Is there anything else to eat apart from the builder?' Sam asks. 'I'm starving.'

'Get that grin off your face, young man. You can have an apple or a banana.'

'We always have a biscuit,' says Lorna.

'So much for healthy eating. Go on then.' They head straight for the biscuit tin beside the draining board. I turn to Gareth and mouth, 'I'm sorry,' and he smiles ruefully and mouths back, 'Another time.' I don't think the twins saw anything. There wasn't anything much to see.

'Can I have a drink of water?' asks Lorna.

'Yes.'

'I can't reach the glasses.'

'So? What do you say?'

'Will you get one down for me?'

'And?' It isn't glamorous being a mother unless you're Madonna or Catherine Zeta Jones. Every so often I realise that the twins have managed to force me into a life of domestic slavery without me knowing it.

'Please,' says Lorna, grudgingly.

'Just remember that I'm not your servant,' I grumble as I take a glass down, and hand it to her.

'Can I have orange squash, *pleeease*?' says Sam.

'Of course you can.' I am delighted that he's asked me nicely for once. I pour Sam's drink and, once I've handed it over, he skips off to the front room to watch the telly for a while, leaving his rucksack on the floor. I am in a benevolent mood because of Gareth, so I don't hassle him to unpack it. You can't have everything, can you?

'Can I have the key to the back door?' says Lorna. 'I want to see if the Tooth Fairy has taken the Cheerios.'

'There isn't a key. You can let yourself out,' I reply, hoping that the birds have taken the Cheerios because I forgot to remove them myself.

'I'll go,' says Gareth. 'I can see you're busy. I'll be back tomorrow morning though.' He pinches my bum. 'I promise.'

Gareth is coming back. He fancies me. The Cheerios have disappeared into the Tooth Fairy's store cupboard, according to Lorna. For the rest of the day I am walking not on rubble, dust, or bare splintery floorboards, but on air – until I unpack Sam's rucksack. As well as a crumpled sweatshirt, half a sticky Penguin, three escaped grapes, a lunchbox with a recently broken hinge, and three Top Trumps cards, there is a note from Miss Watson, dated several days ago, requesting that Dan and I make an appointment to see her urgently. No wonder Sam's been acting so polite with me!

I find him in the bath, emptying half a bottle of Lynx shower gel on his hair. Lynx is the brand he chose for showering after swimming – he's eight going on eighteen. I blame the power of advertising.

'Sam! What have you been doing this time? I'll kill you if you've been hurting Harry.'

'You always say that,' he says, 'and I'm still alive, aren't I?' He pronounces 'aren't' without the t.

'Don't you answer me back like that. What have you done?'

Sam closes his eyes tight, and massages his head, sending foam and bubbles streaming down his face.

'Harry was cheating at football. He said I was offside when I wasn't. I should have had a goal.'

'What did you do?'

'I kicked Harry instead of the ball.'

'Sam!'

'Mum, can you pass me a towel?' Sam grimaces. 'I can't open my eyes.'

'Serves you right.'

'But it stings,' he sobs. His shoulders start to shake. They are so small and bony that I relent and hand him a towel, and help him wipe his face. 'It was an accident, Mum,' he says.

'How do I know that you're telling the truth when you lie to me?'

'I don't lie.'

'You do.'

'I only lie sometimes, and I'm not lying now.'

I search his face for clues that he is telling the truth. I believe him this time. I do. As I go back downstairs, I wonder if Sam and I have made a breakthrough today. Gareth and I have, but I messed it up with my uncertainty which was pretty appalling for an outrageous bohemian like me. And if that hasn't put Gareth off, the twins turning up like that just as I'd decided that I could let myself go, must have done. There is only so much frustration a red-blooded male can take. Come to think of it, there's only so much a red-blooded female can take as well.

If he comes back tomorrow, I shall say yes, yes, yes . . .

Chapter Ten

'Where's Helen?' is the first thing that Gareth says when he arrives the following morning at nine on the dot.

'She's gone shopping,' I tell him, absorbing the fact that Gareth's wearing his blue rugby shirt again, but this time the shirt is unironed.

Gareth smiles. My heart flips.

'The twins?'

'At school.' I pause, hugging a load of soggy clothes that I've just pulled out of the washing machine to my chest. 'Tea?'

'Later,' Gareth murmurs, extricating the washing from my arms and dumping it on the banister rail at the bottom of the stairs. He takes my hand. 'Shall we go upstairs?'

'You're starting the roof already?' I ask, half-afraid, half-shuddering with excitement.

'I'm starting something else, I hope.' He pauses. 'If you want to . . . You weren't sure yesterday.'

'It isn't something I do – jump into bed with a man I hardly know.'

'I can be patient, Sadie.' He squeezes my hand. 'I admit that I haven't always behaved as well as I should have done, but I'm not a complete bastard.'

Gareth wants me. He'll wait for me. My mind races. How does an outrageous bohemian behave in this situation? Helen wouldn't hold back. Her record, she says, is three minutes from meeting to mating, and how long have I known this man? Five, six days? Oh hell, I've held out long enough, haven't I? I've known since Gareth kissed me that this was going to happen. I tidied my bedroom this morning, changed the sheets and piled Topsy's clothes and my vibrator beneath a spare duvet cover in the corner of the room. I even slipped on a pair of clean, high-leg knickers.

I hold Gareth's hungry gaze. 'It'll have to be quick. I don't know what time Helen's coming back.'

'Forget Helen,' he murmurs as he guides me upstairs to the bedroom. He releases my hand and pulls the curtains closed. 'Come here.' He rests his hands on the curves of my waist, and pulls me close. We kiss. I close my eyes. It is as if someone has knocked the floor out from beneath my feet, and I am plummeting out of control.

'I'm not sure I can remember how to do this.'

'It's like riding a bike,' says Gareth.

I don't think it is, I muse, as he slips my top over my head. My breasts bounce free from my bra. 'Gareth?'

I am answered by a grunt and a sniffly moan. He reminds me, very briefly, of a baby tapir rooting for its mother's nipple that I once saw on a programme about a wildlife park. Except in this case, it's Gareth searching for mine – and oh, he's found it! I tug at his shirt, slide my hands beneath and maul his broad chest, catching my fingers in the coarse curls of his body hair. He kisses me again. I make a grab for the buckle of his belt at his waist, unfasten it, and grope for the button beneath. The metal teeth of his fly are cool to the touch, but the flesh beneath is hot and hard.

'Steady!' Gareth's hand is on my wrist. He reaches his free hand to his pocket and pulls out a packet of condoms, and in the time it takes to unroll a Durex Fetherlite, Gareth is on top of me, thrusting to cross the threshold and enter my front door, so to speak, and I can hear someone crying out. It's me, and I'm coming, and I'm definitely not faking it.

'Oh, Sadie . . .' Gareth shudders to his climax and lies gasping with his face pressed into the pillow beside me. I stroke the side of his neck. There is a small mole I hadn't noticed before in the depression above his collarbone.

'That was magic,' he whispers hoarsely, turning to me.

Suddenly, I want to cry.

'Are you all right?' Gareth asks worriedly. 'Have I hurt you?'

'No.' I rub a tear from my eye and force a smile. 'It's just a stray eyelash.'

Gareth smiles back.

I am happy. I'm relieved too. Neither of us has found my lack of practice in the lovemaking department to be a problem. It's a natural process, isn't it, more like falling *off* a bike than riding one? I run my fingers through my tangled hair. Who could have imagined that a week ago I'd have had sex by ten on a Tuesday morning with the man of my dreams?

I turn and snuggle into Gareth's body, guzzling the warmth of intimacy like a neglected pot-plant soaks up water. Gareth runs his hand down the curve of my waist, and dives down to cup my buttock. What do I feel? Joy that Gareth and I are together? Regret, and sheer terror that he might leave me? I try to push him away with my feet against his shins, my palms against his chest.

'Shouldn't you be laying some bricks?'

'Laying the lady of the house is far more exciting,' he says, nibbling at my earlobe. 'Are you free tonight?'

I am just about to invite him over for dinner when I remember the twins.

'Not tonight. The children will be here.'

Gareth's face falls.

'I'd like to get to know them one day,' he says, 'but I understand if you think it's too soon.' He rubs my nose with his, then kisses me softly.

'Lorna and Sam will be staying with their dad this weekend,' I say. 'How about Saturday evening?' I want to suggest Friday night, Saturday morning and afternoon as possibilities too, but I try to play it cool.

'I've arranged to meet a couple of my rugby friends for a drink early on Saturday evening, but I can come round afterwards, say about eight? I'll take you out for dinner.'

'No, I'll cook,' I insist. I haven't cooked anything more elaborate than microwave pizza and chips, and the odd rasher of bacon for weeks. 'It'll make a change. Just turn up when you're ready.'

Gareth kisses me again. 'What about Helen? What will she think?'

'She's been trying to find me a boyfriend anyway, not that you have to be a steady boyfriend. You don't have to be a boyfriend at all, if you don't want to.' I realise that I am making myself sound desperate. Me and my big mouth.

Gareth raises himself on one elbow. 'We'd better get dressed.'

I can't move. My muscles don't work any more.

When Gareth stands up, I notice that he's still wearing his socks: scarlet ones that match the sex flush that has flared across his chest. They would make an ordinary man appear ridiculous, but Gareth has more than enough sex appeal to distract attention from them.

'Sadie,' he hisses, 'will you hurry up and get dressed, unless you want Helen to find out what we've been up to?' He pauses. 'You gave me the impression you wanted this kept quiet.'

I am torn. I don't want to be classified as a desperate divorcée who jumps into bed with all and sundry, and I need time to convince myself that I'm not dreaming, that Gareth really did make love to me, yet I am bursting to tell someone. I sit up reluctantly. Maybe Gareth is right. What happened is between us, and Helen doesn't need to know just yet.

Helen almost discovers what we have been up to straight away. She arrives at the house seconds after I have brushed my hair, and Gareth has tied the laces on his boots. It's true what Helen says, by the way, about men with big feet . . .

'What's he been doing in your bedroom?' Helen asks as I race downstairs to intercept her, while Gareth flushes the evidence of our coupling down the toilet.

'Who?'

'Gareth, silly. I saw him pulling back the curtains.'

'Oh, that? He's been looking at the ceiling.' It's almost true, isn't it? He's been lying on his back on the mattress beside me.

'You should have come into Kingston with me for the early summer sales. What do you think?' She slinks up and down the hall like a drunken supermodel, showing off a pair of bootleg jeans.

'I think that your new clothes are going to get dirty and spoiled.'

'I had to have something to wear. I've put it on expenses.' She hesitates, staring at me. 'What on earth have you been doing?'

I rub my inflamed cheeks.

'I told you not to use that piles cream on your face.' Helen witters on, and I am only half-listening as I try to recall everything about Gareth making love to me, every caress, every murmur, every nuance of his behaviour that might indicate that the episode meant more than a quick shag to him. 'Are you sure you're all right, Sadie, only you've just agreed to use soft cream in the third bedroom?'

'I haven't!'

'You have.'

'Haven't!'

'No, you haven't,' Helen laughs.

'Nice try though.' I hear water running in the bathroom, then Gareth trudges downstairs, greets Helen and retires to the new open-plan dining area to line the arch. I start to pick up my washing from the banister rail.

'Don't hang that out just yet. I've brought something to show you.' Helen goes out to the car and returns with a stack of magazines. My heart sinks.

'Not more *House Beautiful*?' I follow her into the back garden. 'Or is it *Garden Answers*?'

'Try again.' Helen lays the magazines out on the ground in a semicircle. 'Look at that!' she exclaims, opening the last one and pointing to a rather fetching photo of a female nude, unravaged by pregnancy or childbirth. Her firm, cellulite-free legs are spread in front of her and her painted fingernails point towards a triangle of coiffured pubic hair. Her expression is blank, as if she is merely a mannequin, demonstrating basic gynaecological anatomy.

'How rude.' I turn the pages. They are hardly thumbed. 'Ooh, look – I didn't know you could do things like that.'

Helen looks at me pityingly.

'All right, if I did know, I've forgotten. Whose are they? Michael's?'

'No way. He knows I'd kill him if I found him with a stash of porno magazines. They were under Tom's bed.'

'Aren't you making a fuss over nothing? I mean, they're pretty harmless.'

'Anyone else could have found them – Charlotte, Sam, Lorna.'

'But they wouldn't have been rooting around under Tom's bed, would they, you nosy cow!'

Helen flushes. 'It isn't Tom's bed. It belongs to me and Michael.' She straightens. 'If you must know, I was looking for the source of the pong that Tom seems to have moved in with him. He's always in the shower, using all the hot water, yet he still stinks. It's a fishy kind of smell.'

'What do you expect?' I say. 'Tom is a Kipper Kid, after all.'

'What do you mean by that?'

'A Kid in his Parents' Pockets Eroding Retirement Savings.' I suppose I shouldn't be surprised that Helen doesn't find this amusing, when Tom is spending money on top-shelf literature that she thinks should be used to provide for Charlotte's future.

'I couldn't understand it until I checked his room,' she goes on. 'It's his trainers. They're disgusting. I've washed them in the machine, and flooded them with a whole canister of Odor-Eaters Foot and Shoe Spray, and I'm praying that it's done the trick.' Helen gathers the magazines up in an untidy heap. 'Have you got any matches?'

We set Tom's magazines alight, and stand and watch the flames consume pages and pages of naked flesh and pubic hair.

'When *is* Tom moving out?' I ask.

'He isn't,' says Helen sharply. 'He says he's dropped out of university, and he's aiming to be the next Big

Thing in the music business. He brought my hair-dresser's daughter home the other day.'

'What's she like?'

'I don't know. Tom won't let me meet her. He takes her straight up to his bedroom.'

'What about Sonya, the girl from the university?'

'She phones every day, but what am I supposed to say? Tom's upstairs getting it on with my hairdresser's daughter?'

'Is he? I mean, are they?'

'I think so . . . I am pretty sure that they are.'

'Haven't you listened at the door?'

'No, of course not!' Helen pauses. 'That boy has far too much time on his hands.'

'Why don't you ask Tom to come and take a look at this jungle here? I asked him before if he'd like to help, but he didn't seem interested.'

'I'll tell him to drop by sometime – if I see him. He gets up after midday, goes out and often doesn't return until after midnight. I dread to think what he's getting up to. Why are sons so much trouble?'

Why indeed, I echo as I head off for my appointment with Miss Watson to talk to her about Sam. Dan can't come. He has a job interview. I wish him luck with it. He wishes me luck with Miss Watson.

'Thanks for coming, Mrs Keith,' says Miss Watson. 'Sam has explained how busy you are.' She pauses. 'There was another incident with Harry.'

'Sam told me.'

'Did he?'

'It was an accident, and I believe him.'

Miss Watson looks at me through narrowed eyes. Without her glasses on, I'm not sure that she can see me.

'I shall have another word with Harry,' she says, biting her lip. She props her glasses on the bridge of her nose, picks up an exercise book and hands it to me. 'I thought you might like to see Sam's handwriting while you're here.'

I stare at the pages.

my mum is all ways nackered from striping worl payper

'What's the problem?' I ask defensively. 'It's very good for Sam.'

'I'm very pleased with his recent efforts, although he still can't spell "wall",' says Miss Watson, smiling. 'I'd like you to consider some kind of reward scheme for him. Like all children, Sam responds much better to praise and encouragement than punishment and persecution.'

I am about to tell her where she can stick her advice, but I remember Helen's accusation that I never listen when someone is trying to help me.

Miss Watson dismisses me, and I leave the school feeling as if I have just had a lecture on Child Management. I'm not grateful to be persecuted for my inconsistent parenting, but I should be. I'm beginning to see where I have been going wrong with Sam, being too hard on him one minute, and too soft the next, which makes him behave inconsistently in turn. When I arrive home I realise that my housekeeping abilities are no better than my parenting skills – that wet washing is still draped over the banister rail at the bottom of the stairs.

*   *   *

During the rest of the week, I can't eat or sleep, partly because of Sam, mainly because of Gareth. I lurk around the development waiting for Gareth to pinch my bum, or give me a quick snog, but Helen is always about, fussing around with her mood-boards and swatches of curtain material and, as it's my turn to do the school runs, Gareth and I are never alone.

On Friday, Gareth leaves the house at noon. Helen leaves at three, but not before asking me what my plans are for the weekend.

'I'll get on with some work here, I suppose.'

'Don't work too hard, will you?'

'I'll try not to,' I say in the martyred voice of a lonely divorcée. I put on my gloomiest face, which I fear I've overdone, since Helen goes all sympathetic on me.

'I don't like to think of you here all on your own. Come round tomorrow night. Michael will be at the Golf Club.'

'No, thanks. I'm going to have a quiet night in doing my nails.'

'You can do them tonight.'

'I've just remembered that Sean and Annette said they'd call in. Sean's going to fit a smoke alarm.'

'Can't you put them off?'

'Annette will want to talk about her ICSI cycle.'

Helen smiles. 'You're a saint, Sadie Keith.'

Am I? I picture Gareth on his back, and me riding him with my head and arms thrown behind me, and my boobs thrust out in front like the pictures in Tom's magazines, not down to my knees which is where they tend to settle now if I'm not wearing a bra. A saint? Hardly.

Saints don't skive, and on Saturday morning, when the twins are at Dan's, I am prowling the first floor in Bentalls in Kingston, looking for lingerie, instead of working on the development. Forget the packs of seven pairs of plain pants, one for each day of the week. Show me the individual creations of wispy white lace, or scarlet netting.

I find that I can't decide between the soft plum satin, or the raspberry and cream, so I take both pairs along with matching basques, to the changing room. I strip and slip into the satin, and I'm practising my seductive moves in the mirror, when I hear a familiar voice from the cubicle next door. It's Helen, asking the lingerie assistant for a larger size.

I step out of my cubicle, and stick my head around her curtain. 'Hiya!'

Helen grabs her T-shirt off the hook on the wall, and clasps it to her naked breasts. 'Sadie? What are you doing here?'

'Same as you, I expect.'

'You can't be shopping for your husband, or a lover, because you haven't got one.'

I ignore that leading comment. 'What's this about a larger size? Are you putting on weight?'

'Of course not,' Helen frowns. 'Some of the ranges in this department are cut much smaller than average, that's all.'

'Really?' I arch one eyebrow.

'Really!'

'Can I come in?'

Helen nods.

'What do you think?' I give her a clumsy twirl.

'You look like you're auditioning for a part in *Chicago*.' She smiles. 'I think it's hideous, completely over the top.'

'I love it,' I say, pressing my boobs up and together with the flats of my hands.

'I suppose it doesn't matter, since no one's ever going to see you in your underwear again at the rate that you turn down perfectly reasonable dates.'

'It was just one,' I argue, as I start trying to wriggle out of the satin basque.

'Oh? Excuse me,' says the shop assistant, opening the curtain to find the two of us behind it. She hands Helen an almost invisible string with a spangling diamanté strap at the back, before making a hasty retreat.

'I thought you hated wearing strings?'

'I do, but I made a deal with Michael over going into partnership with you.' She pauses, and stares at me through narrowed eyes. 'There's nothing you'd like to tell me about, is there, Sadie?'

'Not at all. Like houses, women need good foundations, especially when they're built like I am. All I am doing, Helen, is looking for some new knickers. It's no big deal.' I turn my back to her. 'Would you mind letting me out of this basque?'

Helen fiddles with the catches down my back. 'You're going to have to buy this one,' she giggles. 'You're trapped.'

'Don't make me laugh,' I warn. 'I might split it, it's so tight.'

It is too late. We are both hysterical. By the time that Helen finally releases me from the grip of the satin basque, overheated and aching with laughter, I've decided that I have to have it.

When I leave Bentalls, it strikes me that I've spent over a hundred and fifty quid from our budget for the new roof to make myself feel like a million dollars, so I make some urgent economies, buying a simple dinner of fresh pasta and sauce, some Parmesan cheese that Sam says comes from picking verrucas, a frozen chocolate gateau, and a bottle of mid-price Zinfandel.

As I pay at the till in Marks & Spencer, I find myself wishing that we hadn't called the cat Alvin, because it reminds me of the TV finance expert Alvin Hall, and I picture him waving his finger at me and telling me off for spending money that I haven't got. I feel slightly nauseous, until recalling Dan's new surfie clothes and contact lenses puts me on the road to a complete recovery.

Back at home in the evening, I throw a blouse and a flirty, floaty skirt on over the top of the plum satin ensemble. At eight, I light a tealight in the front room, drop some ylang ylang oil onto fresh water in the top of the burner, open the wine, and wait. At eight fifteen, I begin to prowl to and fro across the bare boards, while Alvin squints at me from where he is curled up on the Director's chair.

At eight thirty, Annette and Sean turn up with Homer.

'Hi,' says Sean, holding out a plastic bag from B&Q. 'I've come to fix your smoke alarm.'

'It isn't terribly convenient. You should have rung. I don't sit here indoors on my own all the time, you know.'

They look at me as if I have just declared the definitive existence of aliens.

'This won't take long,' says Sean.

'Okay.' I try not to sound too ungrateful. Sean might be mean with his money, but he makes up for it by being generous with his time. 'Come on in.' Sean heads for the kitchen. Annette and I settle in the front room. My sister scoops Alvin up from the chair and sits down with him on her lap, but when Alvin sees Homer, he scarpers. I continue pacing up and down, stepping over Homer where he lies sprawled across the floor, each time I cross the room.

Where the hell is Gareth? He said he was meeting his rugby friends, but I can't help picturing him in the arms of a woman more alluring and voluptuous than me. I am being silly. Being more alluring is easily achievable. Being more voluptuous would make her clinically obese.

'I can't bear it,' Annette begins.

In my anguish, I have forgotten that my sister is suffering too.

'We're waiting to see if we have any embryos,' she goes on.

'Oh, Annette.' I drop my hands around her shoulders to give her a hug, but she pushes me away. The only physical contact she craves is with a baby, her own baby. I don't know what I can say to console her.

'How's Sean coping?'

197

'He's wonderful, so supportive. I couldn't wish for a better man.'

'Uhuh?' I say, noncommittally. That's one of the duties of a sister, to demonstrate unconditional approval of your sibling's choice of partner, even if you harbour secret reservations about his subhuman social skills. Sean does have his good points, though. Annette, who has inherited some of our mother's depressive tendencies, chose an adoring and biddable husband.

'Does Mum know you're having another attempt at ICSI?' I ask.

'Yes,' says Annette. 'She phoned this morning. Hasn't she been in touch with you?'

'I was out. If she did try me, she didn't leave a message.'

Since her divorce, our mother Belinda has made up for lost time with a series of boyfriends. At the moment, she is on holiday in Venice with some Italian guy she met in Solihull. He's called Roberto Castello and he's five foot nothing, and I can't help thinking she might not be so smitten if he was called Bob Castle, and didn't own a chain of beauty salons.

'She asked after you and the twins,' Annette says, 'and I told her that you'd set yourself up as a property developer.'

'What did she say to that?' Mum knew we were moving, but I haven't talked to her properly for ages. I gaze at Annette, wondering if she is going to lie on our mother's behalf, but she doesn't.

'She said that it had to be better than making your living as a clown.'

'She approves then?' I'm being ironic here – our mother never approves of anything I do. Annette has always been her golden girl, but how can I be jealous of Annette any longer when I have the one thing for which she yearns, but cannot have? As I rack my brain cell for something else to talk about that won't revisit the painful subject of babies, there is a terrific crash from upstairs.

'The roof's falling in!' I scream over the sound of Homer barking. 'Let's get out of here'

'Sadie,' yells Sean from the kitchen, 'someone's broken in upstairs. Let me go.'

'It might be the cat,' I call after him as he heads upstairs, carrying one of Gareth's hammers.

'It's a bloody big cat.'

Homer keeps barking. I can hear Sean's heavy tread overhead, and the sound of groaning. I recognise that groaning.

'Stop! Don't hurt him!' I dash upstairs after Sean. Annette follows, holding Homer back by the collar.

'There's a man in your bedroom,' says Sean when I arrive, gasping for breath. Sean is standing beside Gareth who appears to have fallen in through the window; he has caught one leg on the sill. 'Try burgling an empty house next time, mate.'

'My foot's stuck,' Gareth says through gritted teeth. 'Help me.'

'It's all right, Sean. This is a friend of mine,' I explain. A breeze wafts the hem of the curtain across the upright of a steel ladder that I can see outside the open window. 'Gareth, what on earth do you think you're doing?'

'Bringing some romance into your life.'

Sean unhooks Gareth's trouser leg from the sill. Gareth drags himself upright, pulls a flower from his pocket, and sticks it between his teeth. It's a single pink rose, and I bet I know where it came from.

'You're pissed,' I observe.

Gareth grabs the rose, and hands it to me with a drunken flourish. 'I had a couple of pints in the pub.' He slips one arm around my back, and looks Annette and Sean up and down. 'Aren't you going to introduce me?'

'This is my sister Annette and her husband, Sean.'

'And this is Homer, our dog,' Annette cuts in.

'Sean is installing a smoke alarm for me.'

'What kind of a ladder do you call that?' says Sean, looking out of the window. 'I have a professional interest in ladders.'

'So do I,' says Gareth. 'I'm Sadie's builder.' What Annette and Sean don't seem to realise is that he is my builder in both a personal and professional capacity, because they hang about chatting for hours.

'I was beginning to think they'd never leave,' I say, when they finally push off home, 'and I was beginning to think that you'd never turn up.'

Gareth reaches for my hand. I turn away.

'What's wrong?' he asks.

'Where did you get to earlier?'

'I told you I was meeting some old friends for a few drinks.'

'Why do you smell like a curried chicken?'

'Because we stopped for a tandoori before we went

our separate ways.' Gareth is frowning. 'Sadie, I don't understand. You said you didn't mind what time I turned up.' His hand is on my shoulder.

It's true. That's what I said, but what I imagined, of course, was that I was so irresistible that Gareth would drop his friends and come round early.

'I mind you turning up completely sozzled, with one of The Neighbour From Hell's roses between your teeth.'

'The who?'

'The man who lives at number thirteen. You haven't met him yet. He counts those blooms every evening. I've seen him.'

'You can't be serious.'

'I am. Deadly.'

'I'll make this up to you.' Gareth's voice is soft, persuasive. 'I'll protect you from The Neighbour From Hell . . .' His hands slip down my back, and my stomach turns in the best possible way. I lead Gareth upstairs, taking the burner and tealight with me: light from a naked flame is remarkably sympathetic to cellulite.

Gareth undresses me slowly, releasing my ample flesh from the restraint of the basque, and sliding my satin knickers down my hips.

'You are one gorgeous woman, Sadie Keith,' he murmurs. 'I'm going to make love to you all night long,' and he does so with the rhythmic accompaniment of a squeaking floorboard.

Helen says that she can judge a man's character by observing his behaviour after sex. Some, according to Helen, roll over and snore. Some dash off to the bathroom to clean up. Some arrange for counselling. Gareth is none of those. He is attentive and, from the stirring I can feel between his thighs as I lie in his arms, ready to go again.

'I expect you go around seducing susceptible women all the time.'

'I don't force myself on anyone, if that's what you mean.' Gareth rubs my nose with his. 'I haven't slept with anyone since Alison. I don't jump into bed with everyone who chases me into Waitrose.'

'Oh?' I try to smile. 'I've only ever – you know – with Dan, my husband, when he was my husband.'

'You don't have to tell me,' Gareth says. 'I'm not interested in history. It's now that's important to me.'

Why not the future, I want to ask, but I don't dare in case Gareth tells me something that I don't want to hear.

'Having said that,' he adds, 'I'd like to keep you here on this mattress for ever . . .'

'And I'd like you to make love to me naked in the rain.'

'The forecast is for unbroken sunshine,' Gareth grins, 'but as soon as it rains, I'm more than willing to try it.'

'Gareth?' My voice, for once, comes out as a whisper. He reaches out his hand to take mine, raises it to his lips and presses his mouth to my knuckles.

'You're looking serious, Sadie, quite out of character.'

'I was thinking about the twins, and how they'll react to you and me.' I watch Gareth's face. 'You said you wanted to get to know them . . .'

'And you decided that it was too soon to tell them

about us. You're right. I've seen what happens to kids when their mum brings a new boyfriend home. At first they're resentful, then, just as they've got to know and like him, the relationship breaks down and they never see him again.' Gareth pauses. 'It's what happened to my nephews, my sister's children, until my sister remarried and settled in New Zealand. The boys love their stepdad, but they went through some difficult times before he turned up.'

'So what are you trying to say?'

'I suppose I'm saying that it'll take *me* some time to get used to the idea that we're like we are.'

'Together?'

Gareth nods.

My heart sinks.

'Now you think I've been taking advantage,' he says sharply. 'It isn't like that.'

'It seems like that to me,' I say in what I hope is a devil-may-care tone.

'I'm sorry, Sadie, I don't like rushing into things.'

'You were in enough of a rush to get into my bed.' I correct myself. 'Onto my mattress.'

'I couldn't help it . . .'

I pull the duvet up around my breasts. Gareth tugs it back. He moves his face close to mine until I can feel his breath on my lips. They burn as if I have pressed them against an ice-pop straight from the freezer. My breasts ache for Gareth's touch. Liquid heat forms a slick between my legs. I want him all over again.

Just as our lips touch, the cat lands on Gareth's back, peers over his shoulder, and jumps off again.

'Nosy sod,' Gareth chuckles as he reaches out and aims one of his boots at Alvin. It misses, and Alvin stalks away with his tail in the air, curved like a question mark, a reminder of the questions I should be asking myself. Gareth is my property – for now. Do I own him outright or, with his cavalier attitude towards meeting me tonight and his apparent lack of desire for commitment, have I only just started paying the mortgage?

Later I lie beside Gareth while he sleeps and the mattress vibrates beneath us. At first, I imagine that there's been a derailment at the end of the garden, but the noise turns out to have more to do with Gareth. He snores like a train. I wake in the morning, hardly rested, and lie curled against Gareth's warm body with my fingers tangled in the hairs on his chest.

'Morning, Sadie.' A hand slips between my thighs. My belly crumples. 'What's for breakfast?'

'Me.'

We make love, then eat a breakfast of eggs on toast and coffee outside in the wilderness of the back garden, with Gareth pottering about in his hipster pants. Something rustles in the undergrowth in front of the tumbledown shiplap fence between us and number thirteen. Is it a bird, or a rat? No, The Neighbour From Hell is peering through a gap that he's made with a pair of secateurs.

Not only does he accuse me of stealing one of his prized roses, but when I was cutting the brambles the other day, I also snipped off the fruiting shoots of his tayberry bushes. I don't know why he's so precious about roses and tayberries when his house needs new windows and some roof-tiles replacing. Although at first glance, I assumed from the fact that the front garden had been turned into a parking space, that number thirteen had been reasonably well-maintained, I have since noticed that it needs almost as much care and attention as our house. Having had my say, and him having had his, The Neighbour From Hell returns to his pruning, and Gareth and I retreat indoors with me complaining about next door's verbal incontinence.

'I expect you're the only person he'll speak to today,' Gareth says.

Gareth's comment hits me like a fist in the chest. What must I sound like, slagging off a lonely old man? I turn away, my cheeks hot with shame, and make a silent resolution to try to mend fences with The Neighbour From Hell, maybe even offer to replace the shiplap boundary between our houses.

Gareth goes upstairs to dress. When he comes back down, he has his boots on.

'I promised my mother I'd take her out for Sunday lunch.'

A picture of Gareth's mother flashes through my mind, a woman in her sixties or seventies, with a dowager's hump and a halo of thinning white hair. I imagine conversation about her recent outings to the hospital, the state of her arteries, and the price of PoliGrip.

'Mum misses the company,' Gareth goes on. 'That's one of the reasons I moved in with her. She asked – no, begged – me to stay with her for a while. She gives me board and lodging, and I drive her about in her car. She isn't allowed to drive at the moment, you see.'

I nod. It isn't surprising that an old woman with a heart condition has had her licence taken away.

'You'd better get some clothes on if you're coming with me,' Gareth says.

'Me? Your mother? Lunch? We've only just had breakfast.'

'I'm still hungry.' He walks over to me, puts his arms around me and pulls me against him so that I can feel the evidence of his hunger against my belly.

'You have an enormous appetite, Gareth Bryant,' I smile.

'Well, are you coming with us?'

I glance past Gareth's shoulder at the peeling wallpaper in the hall. Meeting Gareth's mother? So soon?

'Next time, maybe,' says Gareth, picking up on my hesitation. 'I don't know what made me ask in the first place. I mean, you don't know *me* very well yet. You'd hardly want to meet my mum before I've even taken you out on a proper date.' As he kisses me, I realise that it's too late to change my mind. 'I don't know if you're free the Saturday after next?'

'Possibly,' I say, slowly to give the appearance that I am running through a mental diary stuffed with exciting appointments.

'It's the Rugby Club's Black Velvet event. Are you interested?'

'Oh yes, thanks.'

'You can come and see the last match of the season too. That's next weekend.'

'Okay.' I am aware that I am responding slightly less enthusiastically. I doubt that even Joan Collins could make herself look glamorous, standing on the touchline or whatever the edge of a rugby pitch is called.

After promising that he'll be back on Tuesday morning – he's taking his mother to the hospital for what he hopes will be her final check-up tomorrow – Gareth leaves me stripping the wallpaper in the hall, and wondering how he would have introduced me to his mother. As a client? A friend? Anything but his lover, I suspect, considering his reaction to my idea of telling the twins about us. Yet he's asked me out. I am confused. Is Gareth looking for a brief fling that lasts as long as he's working on the development, or a longterm relationship?

When I am alone, I tend to think too deeply, but I am not alone for long today. Dan drops the twins off at four. Lorna rushes in and gives me the biggest hug ever. Sam skirts past me, and makes his way to the kitchen.

'Anything to eat, Mum?' he says. 'I'm starving.'

'I'll find something in a minute.' I turn to Dan. 'Is everything all right?'

'Fine,' he says, looking me up and down.

'Is there something wrong with me?' I ask.

'You look different. Have you changed your hair, or had one of those lip-enhancing treatments?'

Is Dan trying to say that I have a trout pout? I respond with a smile. He doesn't realise that I just got laid. 'How did the interview go the other day? I forgot to ask.'

'They offered me a part-time, temporary contract,' Dan says. 'I'll pay some money into your account as soon as I can.'

'Regular payments?'

'I'll do my best.'

'You'd better.'

'I don't see how you can claim poverty now when you've had the lion's share of the money from the house *and* Michael's contribution to the development.'

'You have no idea how much it costs to pay for materials and contractors.' And fancy underwear, I think to myself.

'Talking of contractors, Lorna informs me that you've had a builder in.'

'Oh yes,' I say as nonchalantly as I can.

'I'd better be going,' Dan says. 'Tell the twins I'll be in touch during the week.'

'Guess what, Mum,' says Lorna, jumping up and down once Dan has gone. 'Dad says I can have my ears pierced.'

'Are you sure? He didn't mention it.'

'He said I could be the one to tell you.' Lorna is grinning. One of her upper teeth has broken through the gum at the weekend. 'Can we go now, before he changes his mind?'

'The shops are closed now. We'll go tomorrow, after school.'

'Oh?' she wheedles.

'Don't go on at me like you did at your dad.'

'Please . . .'

'I can do it at home with a pin if you like,' I suggest.

'No, thanks. Charlotte says it's the worst pain in the world.'

'Charlotte hasn't had her ears pierced. She has no idea.'

'Wendy has no idea about what kinds of food me and Sam like. Did you know that she's a vegan? We had to have muesli with soya milk, and lentil casserole.'

'She's moved in with your dad, hasn't she?' When I dropped the twins off at Dan's on Friday, I didn't miss the fact that the clothes-horse in the kitchen was draped with several sets of Lycra micro-vests and shorts. 'Did you and Sam have to sleep downstairs?'

'No,' says Lorna. 'We slept upstairs as usual. Dad and Wendy slept on one of those blow-up campbeds, but they weren't very comfortable because Vinnie – that's Wendy's dog – popped it in the middle of the night.'

'He died?'

'He attacked the campbed. Dad had to mend the puncture the next day. He said that Vinnie would have to go, and Wendy told Vinnie off for letting her down.'

'Literally, I suppose,' I say, grinning.

'What?' says Lorna.

'Nothing. It doesn't matter.'

'Can we have this for tea?' Sam butts in. He's standing in the doorway to the kitchen, holding up a pack of fresh pasta, the one that I was going to cook for Gareth last night.

'Let me find a saucepan.' I bustle past, giggling to myself.

'What did you do all weekend, Mum?' says Lorna. 'Who came to see you?'

'No one.'

'Why have you got two glasses out then? And two bowls, and two plates, and two knives and two forks?'

'I had a friend round for a meal.'

'Helen?'

I don't confirm or deny this. Without waiting for me, Sam has put the pasta, packet and all, into the microwave. All hell breaks loose. The packet catches fire, the microwave starts breathing smoke, Sean's smoke alarm fires off with a hideous, earsplitting series of bleeps and, whether by coincidence or as a consequence, the electricity goes off.

I try ringing Gareth, but he's not answering his mobile. Where is he? Who is he with? Did he really take his mother out to lunch? I don't know. I am powerless, in more ways than one.

Chapter Eleven

What is the World Record for the number of people you can squeeze inside a Mini Cooper? We have six, and a guitar – a real one, not the electric kind. Tom refuses to leave it behind. Either he is afraid that Michael will destroy it as some kind of revenge for him refusing to go back to university, or he hopes to meet a talent scout for a record label while we are out and about.

Charlotte is in the front with the guitar across her knees. Tom and I are in the back with Lorna on my lap, and Sam on Tom's. I know it's inadvisable and illegal, but we're not going far. Tom is folded up beside me, pressed against the passenger door, trying to put some distance between our bodies, which is difficult when I freely admit that my bum spreads across more than one seat.

I don't want to go out this morning because of Gareth, but I've left a key under one of the paving slabs, so he can make his way into the house to start work before we get back. If he can't find it, he can always break in. He knows how to. I've left him three messages on his

211

mobile as well, asking him if he'll get in touch with his electrician friend to see if he'll take a look at my fusebox.

'Mum, what's that smell?' asks Lorna. In the reflection from the rearview mirror, I can see that she's screwing up her face.

'Petrol?' I say tentatively.

'Egg sandwiches,' says Charlotte.

'Someone's done a fart!'

'Sam!'

Helen leans forward, bracelets chinking on her slim, tanned forearm, as she puts her foot down and lurches into the traffic on the main road. Her hair is scraped back in a Croydon face-lift which isn't Helen's usual style. Tom remains silent. Even the vapours from three different car air fresheners fail to overpower the smell of old trainers.

'I know, it's Mum,' says Sam.

'I washed this morning,' I protest.

'We haven't got any hot water.'

'You can wash in cold. Hang on a mo.' I grab Sam's chin and turn his face towards me. 'You didn't wash your face.'

'Did.'

'What's this then?' I press the side of his mouth with my thumb.

'Nothing.'

'Looks like chocolate milkshake to me.' I find a tissue screwed up in the bottom of my sleeve, spit on it, and wipe.

'That's disgusting,' he says. 'You're giving me your germs, Mum.'

'Next time, wash your face when I tell you to then.'
I let him go. 'We haven't had any electricity at the
development since Sunday night, Helen.'

'We had to have candles in every room,' says Lorna.
'It was brilliant.'

'Hardly,' I say. 'I couldn't see a thing.'

'Helen, did Mum light the candles when you came
round for dinner with her at the weekend?' says Lorna.

'Me? No, I was at home with Charlotte and Michael.'

'Mum said you had a meal with her, so that she
wasn't lonely.' Lorna cricks her neck round to look at
me, and stabs my left boob with a bony elbow. She is
bony all over. It's like having a three-and-a-half-stone
toast-rack upside down on your lap.

'Mum,' she frowns, 'you lied.'

'I didn't lie. I didn't say anything. You assumed that
I had dinner with someone, and that that someone was
Helen. I didn't have anyone round for dinner. I may
not have had any dinner at all.'

'I don't suppose you were hungry,' Lorna cuts in.
'Mum's been too busy eating the builder,' she
announces.

'She's what?' Helen stalls the car.

'We saw her last week.'

'Oh, Lorna,' Sam groans, 'Mum was snogging him.'

'It looked more like eating to me. She had her—'

'Don't!' I interrupt. 'Don't go there.'

'I've told Miss Watson,' says Sam. 'I wrote it in my
journal.'

'What did she say?' Lorna asks.

'Her eyebrows disappeared up under her hair, and

213

then she told me I'd spelled "builder" wrong, and made me go and copy it out again from my word book.'

'What's going on, Sadie?' Helen asks in a low voice as she restarts the engine.

I choose to remain silent, inhibited by the presence of Tom and the children, and the expression of horror on Helen's face. I half-expect her to put me out of the car as well, when we reach the school gates to drop the children off, but she lets me stay, flashing me disapproving glances in the rearview mirror now and then, while Tom talks remarkably lucidly for someone I had assumed had the verbal skills of a two year old, about his ideas for the garden on the way to the garden centre.

'What we need are feature plants and decorative ornaments,' he says. 'I'm visualising a series of layered lawns and a terrazzo terrace.'

'You haven't seen the garden yet,' says Helen. 'You can have a lawn or a terrace, not both.'

'If it's that cramped, we need mirrors and small plants to give the impression of space.'

'Did you do any work at university?' Helen asks. 'Only you seem to have been watching too many garden-makeover programmes on daytime TV.'

'In spite of what my father says, daytime TV will turn out to be of far more use to me than higher education,' Tom counters.

We turn into the car park. *Organic compost, 3 for 2* is chalked on a blackboard leaning against the base of an urn. The urn is filled with tumbling red and white petunias which remind me of Topsy. I miss her.

'We should have one of those,' says Helen, reversing at high speed into a parking space.

'Not bedding plants,' I point out as we jolt to a stop. 'They'll be dead by November when we come to sell the house.'

'I didn't mean the plants. I meant the urn for your ashes, Sadie Keith.'

'I've upset you then?'

Tom is opening the car door.

'When were you going to tell me?'

Suddenly, Tom unfolds himself, jumps out and dances like a demon around the car park, clutching his calf. 'Aye, aye, aye!'

Helen and I follow. 'What's wrong?' Helen yells after him.

'I've got cramp,' Tom yells back.

'Wiggle your foot about,' Helen says crossly. 'Stop making such a bloody fuss, and go and look for some inspiration for the garden.' She grabs my arm. 'You and I are going to have a little chat.' She waits until Tom has disappeared down the Hebes aisle in the outdoor plant section, before she drags me into the coffee-shop and parks me at a table beneath the dripping fronds of a tropical fern.

'I'll get the coffees,' she snaps. 'You stay right there.'

'Am I forgiven?' I ask, eyeing the slices of carrot cake that she brings back from the counter with two large café lattes.

'If you tell me that what happened between you and Gareth was just a snog, and it's never going to happen again,' she says, taking a sip from her mug.

215

'I slept with him.'

Helen chokes on her coffee. I thought she was impossible to shock, but she sits silent for a while, her lips pursed in thought. 'Sadie, you've done this on the rebound to spite Dan for not telling you about his new lover.'

'I haven't. It's nothing to do with Dan. I like Gareth.' I pause. 'Don't tell me you can't see why.'

'Are you an item then?'

'I suppose so. I hope so.' I tell Helen how Gareth climbed through my window with a rose between his teeth, but I omit the facts that he was both late, and drunk, and that he didn't pay for the rose. I tell her about the event at the Rugby Club.

'Who's to say that he won't let you down?'

'He won't,' I insist, wondering if I have done things the wrong way round, sleeping with Gareth before getting to know him properly.

'Quick. Duck.' Helen leans one hand on my shoulder, pressing me down so that my chin is crushed against the table-top. The woman behind the counter gives us a funny look. 'It's Tom. No, it's all right. He's gone now. He was pushing a trolley right past the window.'

'Shouldn't we let him know where we are? He might be looking for us.'

'Let him look,' says Helen. 'He's driving me mad.'

'You liked him last week.'

'He's always under my feet. I can't relax. If he'd just go back to university, Michael, Charlotte and I could get on with our lives and be a normal family again. Tom's a strange boy.'

I suppose there is something odd about Tom. He has an intensity about him that is quite scary. When we finally wrench ourselves away from a second slice of carrot cake that beckons from the counter, he has assembled a trolley full of blue ceramic pots, a yucca plant, three bags of organic, peat-free compost, a chiming toadstool, a box of solar lights and a statue of a Greek god which bears more than a passing resemblance to Justin Timberlake.

There are plants too. I check the labels. £9.99 and up.

'That's grass, isn't it?' I point out gently. 'We're not spending what's left of our budget on grass.'

'It's *Stipa tenuissima*. It adds movement to a garden.'

'It looks like grass to me. What do you think, Helen?'

'Put it back, Tom,' she sighs. 'And the rest.'

'Can I keep the statue? You said you wanted something sculptural.'

'I was talking about a theme for the garden – clean lines, sharply defined horizontals and verticals, not statues. Who's been planting these ridiculous ideas in your head? Alan Titchmarsh?'

'I thought that gardening was about vacuuming lawns and pruning hedges,' he says excitedly. 'I didn't realise until I came here that it could be so challenging. I won't have to sacrifice my principles – I can see an environmentally friendly garden that attracts all kinds of butterflies and bees. Think tall grasses, and wildflowers.'

'Think again!' says Helen.

We persuade Tom to put the toadstool and solar lights back, but he insists on keeping the statue.

'It's really edgy,' he keeps saying, 'and if you can't appreciate it, I'll buy it myself.'

We let him have it in the end. I guess he inherits his lack of taste from his father.

On the way home I admire Helen's idea for the design of the garden. 'You sounded so professional.'

'I haven't a clue,' she says. 'I made it up.' She parks in the space outside the development where Gareth's pick-up should be, and looks at me with her 'told you so' expression.

'I expect Gareth's picking up some bits and pieces from B&Q,' I say quietly, 'or he's still trying to get hold of an electrician.'

'Or he's abandoned the job now that he's had his fun,' Helen adds.

Smarting, I slide out of the passenger seat and slam the door so hard that the car rocks.

'There's no need to take your angst out on my car,' Helen grumbles.

I am not angsting, I tell myself as I help Tom wrestle Justin Timberlake through the front door. I am all screwed up like the pieces of tissue paper that Lorna has unloaded from her school bag and left in a heap at the bottom of the stairs instead of throwing them in the bin. Is it asking too much for Gareth to call me to let me know why he hasn't turned up today? If Helen is right, he could at least ring to tell me he isn't coming back at all . . .

I make grapefruit squash instead of coffee because of the lack of electricity, then show Tom into the garden, while Helen assembles her mood-boards for the bathroom.

'It's dark, isn't it?' Tom mutters, by which I think he means 'it's cool' since it's most definitely daylight. 'Challenging . . .'

'Have you ever done any gardening before?'

He shakes his head.

'It's pretty straightforward. You'll be fine.'

'Is it all right if I stay here for a while, and catch some rays?' he asks.

'Go ahead.'

'Helen and Dad are driving me mad at home, going on at me all the time, as if they own the place.' He pauses, his brow furrowed, then adds, 'Which they do, of course.' His expression remains without a trace of humour, just like Helen's when she reminds me that I am supposed to be picking the twins up from school this afternoon.

'Charlotte has French Club. I'll pick her up later.' French is Charlotte's latest after-school activity – Helen says that it's useful to have someone in the family who can speak French at the hypermarket check-outs in Calais. 'I'm off home to put a white vinegar wash through my dishwasher. I can't get on with anything here until the structural work is done, and for that we need a builder – which you, Sadie, haven't got.'

I deep-breathe my way through the pain that stabs at my heart. I did have a builder. At least, I thought I did. I don't need Helen to remind me of that in such a callous way. I don't need her to add to my uncertainty.

'You could knock the tiles off the bathroom walls,' I suggest lightly.

'I couldn't possibly,' Helen says. 'I'd have to move

219

all your stuff into the bedrooms, and you'd have to wait until you get your electricity back to hoover up the dust. I knew it was a mistake you living here while we're trying to develop the property. You couldn't keep an empty room tidy, and Lorna leaves her Polly Pocket toys all over the place.'

'Sam leaves his Meccano lying around too,' I point out, my hackles rising in my daughter's defence.

'That's to be expected – Sam's a boy. You can train girls to be organised,' says Helen. 'Charlotte would never dream of leaving her pens and pencils out after she's used them, not that she has much time to make a muddle. Did I tell you that she's been picked for the gymnastics squad?'

'You must have done. It isn't something you'd forget to tell me.'

Helen stares at me. 'There's no need to be narky with me because you're angry with Gareth. Go on. You'd better get down to school. I'll lock up.'

I collect my keys from where I left them on the kitchen worktop and go to find the twins, remembering my promise to Lorna.

'Where are we going?' says Sam when we drive the wrong way home.

'To have my ears pierced,' says Lorna smugly.

'I want to go straight home,' moans Sam.

'Well, you can't,' I snap. 'There's no one there.'

I glance towards Lorna, her face aglow with excitement.

'I'm going to have my ear pierced then,' says Sam. 'This one.' He clasps his left earlobe.

'You are not.'

'Daddy didn't say anything to you about having *your* ears pierced,' says Lorna.

'Did.'

'Didn't. You weren't even there when we were talking about it.'

I park in the Malden Centre car park, and take Lorna to one of the salons on the High Street. Cheryl, a glamorous blonde whose skin appears to have been veneered and polished with every product that is on show in the window, introduces herself. She shows Lorna the range of earrings on offer. Lorna isn't impressed. She really wants gold hoops like Beyoncé's, but in the end, Cheryl persuades her to settle for a pair of blue enamelled butterflies backed with gold.

'I'll have a plain stud,' says Sam.

'You can't,' I protest.

Sam sets his mouth in a determined line, and I try the more subtle approach. 'I don't know why you're so keen. It hurts.'

'Does it?' says Lorna quickly.

'You know it hurts. Dad's told you. I've told you.'

'Is it worse than a wasp sting?' asks Sam.

'Much worse.'

Sam gloats. Lorna squirms.

'It's like giving birth,' I add.

'It isn't that bad,' Cheryl cuts in, apparently unhappy at the possibility of losing a customer.

'I don't suppose you've had any children.'

'No, I haven't,' she says.

'I had two at once.' I try to compare memories of

those labour pains with the pain that I'm labouring to control whenever something reminds me of Gareth: the sight of a Waitrose carrier bag, or a white pick-up, and the plaintive bleating of my mobile which turns out to have received two text messages – one from Helen inviting me and the twins to have a bath at her house, and one from Sean asking me if I'll drop in to see Annette later today.

'There's really nothing to worry about, Lorna,' says Cheryl. 'I have a magic spray that makes your skin go cold so that you can't feel a thing. First of all though, we must decide exactly where you want the holes.' She draws a dot on each of Lorna's earlobes to mark the site of the piercing.

'Can't you do it without making holes?' asks Lorna in a wobbly voice.

'I'm afraid not.'

'Have you changed your mind?' I ask Lorna.

She shakes her head, and Cheryl goes ahead. 'Hold your mum's hand.'

Lorna's fingers tighten around mine until mine are white, and as Cheryl pierces the first ear, she lets out a bloodcurdling scream.

'There, look at that,' soothes Cheryl. 'That's one done.'

'One? Is that all?'

'One more stab, and it'll all be over,' says Cheryl.

'I'm n-not letting you d-do it again,' stutters Lorna. 'No way.'

'You'll look silly with one earring,' I point out.

'You'll look like a boy,' swaggers Sam.

In the end, brute force not vanity wins out. I pin Lorna to the chair, and Cheryl pierces the other ear. Lorna's tears don't last long. Walking back to the car, she tries to catch sight of her reflection in every shop window.

'All we have to do now is keep those ears clean so that they don't go septic,' I tell her.

'What's septic?'

'Harry at school had a septic finger,' says Sam. 'He stuck a pintack in it and all this green stuff came out.'

Lorna's hand goes clammy in mine, and I wonder for a moment if she's going to faint, but she recovers quickly as we walk past McDonald's.

'Do you think that as I've been so good having my ears pierced, and Sam has been so good watching me, that we could eat out, Mum?'

'No,' I say firmly. 'It was your choice to get your ears done, and I've run out of money.' I've taken to paying for everything in cash. After the Tesco débâcle, I'm a little wary of credit cards.

'If we can't eat out, can we go to Dad's on the way home and show him Lorna's earrings?' says Sam.

'If you want to.'

'Daddy will be down at the gym,' says Lorna.

'We'll drive over there and see.'

'But I'm really hungry and I want my tea,' Lorna continues.

'I thought you'd be desperate to show those earrings off. Come on, we won't stop for more than five minutes, and when we get home, it'll take me two minutes to make a cheese and pickle sandwich.'

'We had cheese and pickle sandwiches for lunch,'

sighs Sam. 'We've had pizza and chips, or sandwiches almost every day since we moved into the new house, which isn't a new house at all, but a very old, smelly one. Can't we have sausages?'

'We were going to have sausages yesterday,' says Lorna, 'but Daddy burned them.'

'Real sausages? Meat ones?' I ask. 'I thought Wendy was a vegan.'

'He cooked them while she was out.' Lorna falls silent in the car. Every so often I catch sight of her raising her fingers to her ears, and wincing.

Outside Dan's, I stop and park. His car is on the drive, with what looks like a motorbike parked under a tarpaulin behind it. I suppose it must belong to Wendy, although I imagined her taking off to Newquay in a Campervan. How does she carry a dog and a surfboard on a motorbike?

Sam runs up and knocks on the door. Lorna follows behind me. There is barking and swearing, and a couple of minutes later Dan opens the door.

'Is it safe to come in?' I ask.

'Vinnie's upstairs in the bedroom,' says Dan. 'It isn't a good time,' he adds, frowning.

'Lorna wants to show you her earrings,' I begin, inviting myself into the house where Washboard Wendy is curled up on a new sofa bed, looking pale and tightlipped. Is it down to the lack of iron in her diet, or have she and Dan had a row?

'What earrings?' says Dan.

'You said she could have her ears pierced.' I turn to Lorna, but she's disappeared.

'She's gone back out to the car,' says Sam smugly.

'I'm not surprised. I didn't say anything of the sort, Sadie,' says Dan. His face reddens. 'You know how I feel about piercings.'

If I didn't before, I do once Dan has finished his tirade on the subject, and so does Wendy, who is sitting upright now, fiddling with the jewel in her bellybutton. Unhygienic? Tacky? Unnatural adornments worn by tarts and whores? Dan will have some grovelling to do later . . .

'This episode just goes to prove that Lorna is her mother's daughter,' he finishes.

I'm glad. I wouldn't want her to be anybody else's. Secretly, I'm so proud of my rebel daughter's subversive plot that I can't bring myself to tell her off for lying to me. It shows that Lorna does have a spark about her after all.

When we return to *Llamedos* I find that there is no sign of Gareth, or the electrician. Even worse, I discover that I have run out of cheese. No problem. I touch up my mascara and round up the twins who are having a game of Battleships together.

'We're off to see Auntie Annette.'

'Great,' says Sam, performing a karate chop on his arm. 'We can play in Homer's kennel.'

If Sam thinks he's going to wind me up, he's wrong. I don't mind if he wants to play in Homer's kennel, because there is no risk of him catching worms, or distemper, or any other dog disease for that matter. Homer has never slept in it, having decided that the foot of Sean and Annette's bed is far more comfortable.

'Is it about Auntie Annette's test-tube baby?' asks Lorna.

'Won't it come out looking like Tom did when he got stuck in a drainpipe in *Tom and Jerry*?' says Sam.

'I don't want either of you mentioning the subject of babies while we're over there because it upsets Annette.'

Unfortunately, my sister is already upset when we arrive at her house. 'I suppose Sean sent you?' she says, keeping the chain on the door.

'He thought you might like some company while he was on duty.'

'He thought wrong.'

'Can we come in?'

'It's up to you.' Annette opens the door and lets us in. The children go out to play in Homer's kennel. Homer mooches around the kitchen while I try to cook the tea that I've cadged from Annette in her oven which is one step up from cooking on an open fire. Annette sits, resting her elbows on the painted table that's shoved up against one wall of cracked blue and white tiles. The décor isn't merely tired. It's exhausted. Think *Mrs Beeton's Household Management* as opposed to Nigella's *How To Be A Domestic Goddess*.

There's a pair of white baby socks in the middle of the table. Annette snatches them away, but it's too late. I've already seen them.

'You're not?'

'No.' Annette bites at her lip.

'Those are the socks I gave you on your hen night. You kept them all this time?' They were an innocent joke of a gift, like the wind-up willy and the rolling pin for use against errant husbands. I didn't realise then how hurtful the sight of a pair of socks would turn out to be.

Annette fingers them for a moment, then swivels round and drops them into the swingbin.

'After all those injections and trips to the clinic, we ended up without a single embryo.' She looks up with tears in her eyes. 'Sean says I have to accept that there will be no baby, and get on with my life, which isn't fair. You'd have thought he'd give it one last chance after all that we've been through.'

'I imagine that's why he wants to call it a day with the fertility treatment,' I say quietly. 'I don't think he's being unreasonable. It must be as painful to him as it is to you each time it doesn't work. I think he's been a real hero.'

'He's mean-spirited and a coward,' says Annette. 'He says that he can't bear to inject me any more because he hurts me, and when I said I didn't mind because it was only a little prick and not very often, he said, well, he'd guessed that was what I thought of him, and stormed off to work.'

'He was upset,' I say soothingly. 'Listen, Annette, if having a baby was that important to Sean, he'd have left you a long time ago. He wants to be with *you*. He adores you.'

'The feeling isn't mutual,' Annette sniffs. 'At the moment, I wouldn't care if I never set eyes on him again.'

'You don't mean that. You're just saying it because you're under so much pressure.' I am trying to be helpful. This is the first time I've heard Annette utter anything but glowing praise for her wonderful husband. 'We all feel like that sometimes, but it passes.'

'I'd like to believe you, Sadie, but you're hardly an expert in relationships. You and Dan got divorced, and now you're seeing some drunk who falls in through your bedroom window in the middle of the night . . .'

'That's enough,' I warn her. The smell of toasted breadcrumbs drifts from the front of the grill, along with a swirl of smoke.

'I'll admit that I can see the attraction – Gareth's a charming rogue.' Annette smiles wistfully. 'He reminds me of Dad.'

'Are you trying to tell me that I'm looking for a father figure, because I'm not,' I say emphatically.

'I meant that my first impression of Gareth is that he's a man who doesn't take life seriously, that he's more important to you than you are to him.'

Taking the manky rag that masquerades as both kitchen towel and oven glove, I grab the tray of singed fish fingers out from under the grill, and drop it onto the draining board. 'You sound just like Helen. She doesn't like Gareth either.' My eyes water. A tear drops, and sizzles on the tray.

'Oh Sadie, I'm so sorry. I was only making conversation.' Annette stands up and moves up behind me. I can feel the pressure of her hand rubbing back and forth across my back. 'I didn't mean to upset you. I don't know Gareth like you do.' She pauses. 'You've been so kind and supportive and yet, when you find yourself a wonderful new partner, all I do is snipe. I'm really, really sorry – there I go apologising again. It's just that I can't help myself. You've always had everything that I wanted.'

'*Me?*' I turn to her, surprised. 'But you're the clever one. You're the one with all the qualifications.'

'When has an in-depth knowledge of the amoeba's locomotor system ever been relevant to my daily life? Has anyone asked me to translate the line *Julia puella est* since O-levels?'

'You've lost me.'

'It's Latin for "Julia is a girl". So what!' Annette's lip trembles, and her face contorts before she regains control of her emotions.

'Mum was so proud of you,' I remind her. 'I had to struggle to pass my Cycling Proficiency Test, let alone school exams. I was so envious of you.'

Annette frowns. 'But I was jealous of you ... Still am, in a way.'

'Why? Mum always loved you more than she loved me.'

'Granny Louisa more than made up for that. She always preferred your company to mine.'

Granny Louisa was my maternal grandmother. When she died three years ago, I was devastated. She was my role model, the life and soul of the family, the person I believe my mother would have been if she hadn't suffered from depression throughout most of her married life. Annette and I often stayed with her. I still hear her voice in my ear, when Topsy is facing a particularly critical audience. 'Sadie,' she says, 'if I managed to walk seven miles to have all my teeth pulled out without anaesthetic, and walked back home again, then you can face up to a few insolent kiddies. Go for it, girl!'

'Granny Louisa always called you "the pretty one", not me,' I counter. 'You've always been so slim.'

'Skinny,' says Annette, rolling up her sleeve. 'Look at my elbows – they're so bony that no one could ever give me a cuddle without complaining that I was hurting them.'

Like Lorna, I think guiltily, promising myself not to refer to her spiky bones ever again in case it should give her a complex like Annette's.

'You have a lovely figure,' Annette goes on, 'and you can do the one thing that I can't – have babies – and you didn't have just one baby, you had two at the same time.'

So, nothing's changed, is my initial reaction. We are back on the subject of IT. However, I am wrong.

'Sean's right,' Annette sighs. 'I must let go of the past and concentrate on the future, and so must you. I can't wait to meet Gareth again.'

'Don't hold your breath,' I advise, and then I confess that he hasn't been in contact with me since Sunday, that he didn't turn up for work. The fish fingers grow cold, and I have to reheat and rehydrate them on a plate over a saucepan of boiling water. (Annette doesn't believe in microwaves.)

Annette calls the twins in from Homer's kennel for tea. I hassle them, telling them to eat up quickly because we have to go home.

'Do we have to go back to that house, Mum?' Lorna complains.

'I hate it,' says Sam. 'The rooms are even more dusty than yours, Auntie Annette.'

'Sam!' I warn.

'The telly doesn't work,' says Lorna. 'There's no electricity, and no hot water.'

'Oh, you poor things,' says Annette. 'You can have a bath here tonight. You can too, Sadie, although you'll have to share the twins' bathwater, or wait for the immersion heater to warm up again.'

I am torn. Do I stay to enjoy the relative comforts of Annette and Sean's house, or do I dash back to the development and curl up under my duvet, watching the flame from a candle flicker and die, like my hope that Gareth might fall through my window and make mad, passionate love to me all night long? I choose a bath.

Chapter Twelve

Dream or nightmare? I can hear the low rumble of men's voices downstairs, yet my alarm reads 7.00 a.m. I pull my dressing-gown on over my leaping sheep nightie, and wander downstairs. My heart quickens. Gareth is in the hall.

'Hiya, Sadie.' He turns towards the understairs cupboard. 'Allow me to introduce you to Craig Donkins, spark.'

A man's hand waves from the cupboard. The fingers are long and lean, the nails stained with nicotine.

'How did you get in? I didn't leave the key out all night.'

'The twins were trying to get the television to work,' says Gareth. 'Sam let me in.'

'How long do you think it'll take to get the electricity reconnected?' I ask, pulling the belt of my dressing-gown tight round my middle and running my fingers frantically through my hair.

'How long is a piece of fuse wire?' is the man's rejoinder.

'Can you fix it straight away?'

'Oh, no. This'll take some time.'

And money, inevitably, as it turns out. Three hundred quid for starters.

'Let me get dressed,' I suggest, 'then I'll come down and make some coffee.'

'You can't,' says Gareth. He grins, at which a massive surge of electricity rushes between us. I can't help thinking that, if we could harness some of this power, there'd be no need for us to be connected to the National Grid. 'My mum sent me out with a flask of tea as well as my packed lunch this morning – I can pour you a mug if you like.'

I dress, rinse my face in cold water and slap on some lippy before joining Gareth in the kitchen to drink tea. I lean against the fridge and nudge at a loose piece of brick on the floor with my slippered toe.

'So, where did you get to yesterday?' I say more harshly than I intend.

Gareth frowns from the shadows. 'I'm putting myself out for you, Sadie,' he begins.

'Oh, is that how it is?' I say sarkily. 'If finding time to share my bed is such a trial –'

'I'm talking about work,' Gareth interrupts sharply. 'I'm putting myself out fitting this job in between the others.'

'What others?'

'I'm trying to run three or four jobs at once.'

'You didn't make that clear when Helen and I took you on.'

'I was economical with the truth. I can't afford to turn work away.'

'So where were you?'

'I still have a couple of sub-contractors finishing off at Tolworth. Craig's one of them, but I persuaded him to drop by to help you out.'

'Thanks,' I say grudgingly.

Gareth drains his mug and rinses it out under the kitchen tap.

'What you've really been asking me is not where I've been, but who I've been with,' he says softly. 'Why do you assume I've been seeing some other woman?' He slips his arm around my shoulders. 'Is that why you and Dan got divorced? Because he was unfaithful?'

'We split up because he kept staying out late without a word of explanation.' As I say it, I realise how pathetic it sounds. 'I was jealous, but Dan gave me good reason to be,' I add.

'I'm not Dan though, and believe me, Sadie, you're more than enough woman for me.' Gareth smiles. 'That's supposed to be a compliment.' He kisses me with the gentlest pressure on the lips. 'I'm off then. There's nothing I can do here until you're reconnected.'

'Where are you going now?' I blurt out.

'Tolworth. Teresa, my client, isn't happy with the plumbing in the new shower room. She says the radiator is three inches too far over.'

'Silly woman,' I say, relieved. 'I don't suppose it matters. Three inches is nothing.' And I think of Gareth's eight, or more.

'It is when you can't close the shower-room door,' Gareth chuckles. 'Teresa's nice enough, but she's incredibly fussy about the smallest detail. I've spent hours poring over lay-out diagrams with her.'

'What's she got that I haven't?'

Gareth looks at me, one eyebrow raised. 'Four kids under five, washed-out blonde hair, a flat chest, and a weasel of a husband. Oh, and money to burn.'

I can't help feeling that he's saying that because he knows that it's what I want to hear, apart from the money, of course, contrasting Teresa's wealth with my poverty which is becoming more extreme with each trip that Helen and I make to B&Q.

This morning, after Gareth has left, we drive there to keep out of Craig's way. We left him taking a fag break in the front room – I had the foresight to hide the Director's chair so that he couldn't make himself too comfortable. Somehow, Helen and I end up sharing sticky Danish pastries upstairs in Tudor Williams.

'Have you found an outfit for the Rugby Club do?' Helen asks.

'I thought I'd get away with my flirty skirt and black jacket.'

'Very sensible not to buy anything new, in case Gareth changes his mind. What story has he spun you for not working at the development today?'

I explain. Helen isn't happy.

'Do you know what I'd do if I were you?' she says grimly. 'I'd follow him to Tolworth.'

'No, I couldn't. Helen, you can be so underhand.'

'Gareth needn't know if you – if we – are discreet. We could have a look at the extension at the same time as checking out this Teresa woman, something we ought to have done before we hired him.'

I refuse to spy on Gareth, but I do check my bank balance at the cash machine across the road. It isn't looking good. I couldn't afford a new outfit for the Rugby Club event even if I'd planned to, and the purchases I make before we collect the children from school and head back to Helen's are meagre – a bag of grapes for Sam's lunchbox and half a pound of cheese. On the way in the car, I can hear Charlotte and Lorna plotting to steal the grapes for the Teddy Bear Café they're going to set up in Helen's sitting room.

'Charlotte, you can't play until you've done your homework,' says Helen.

'I've got a headache.'

'In that case, you must go to bed. You can't afford to miss the audition for the ballet concert next week.'

'But Daddy promised he'd be home early tonight.'

'Yes, it's a pity that you'll be asleep when he gets in,' Helen observes.

'My headache isn't that bad.' Charlotte blinks a couple of times. 'In fact, it's better.'

Helen winks at me as she turns into the drive outside her house.

'We have to make a model of a skeleton with moving joints tonight,' Sam pipes up. 'All of us.'

'Sometimes I think the teachers expect more of the parents than the pupils,' Helen says scathingly. 'I'll have to go through my cupboards.'

'I'm sure you'll find a few skeletons in those,' I tease.

Once we're indoors, Helen finds some card and pipe

cleaners, and sits the children down in the kitchen to make skeletons. Correction. *We* make skeletons: human ones for Charlotte and Lorna, and a dinosaur for Sam. The children slope off to play before Helen cooks tea.

'I won't put anything in for you, Sadie,' she says. 'I suppose you'll be eating with Gareth later.'

My stomach growls, but I don't respond. I realise I have no idea what Gareth's plans are for the evening.

'If you want a bath, there's plenty of hot water,' she continues.

'I'd prefer a quick shower if that's all right.'

Helen's face tightens. 'Michael keeps the ensuite bathroom for our exclusive use,' she says. 'He doesn't like the idea of anyone else using his shower.'

I am disappointed. I was looking forward to trying it out – as apparently it has a steam unit, lights and a choice of sound effects – whale music, birdsong or waterfall. Instead, Helen shows me to the bathroom.

'I know where I'm going,' I point out as she walks in ahead of me, switches on the extractor fan and turns on the taps.

'There's a clean towel on the rail,' she says, 'and if you wouldn't mind rinsing the bath out when you've finished.' She pulls out a cloth, and bottles of Cif and Mr Muscle Bathroom Spray from the unit under the sink, and forces them into my arms. 'Oh, and watch the floor – the slightest drop of water marks the laminate.'

I spend more time cleaning the bath than bathing in it, and when I return downstairs, the children have almost finished their tea. Sam has eaten everything.

Charlotte and Lorna are pushing broccoli around their plates.

'Can I leave the table?' Sam asks.

'Not until Charlotte and Lorna have finished,' says Helen.

Charlotte sits stubbornly staring at her plate while Lorna puts the tip of a broccoli floret into her mouth, and gags.

'Eat up, both of you,' Helen niggles.

My mother used to niggle at me and Annette. Annette knuckled down like Charlotte while I rebelled against the notion that success is more important than happiness.

'Go on, Sam, you can go,' Helen says eventually.

'*Olé, olé, olé,*' Sam chants with a gloating edge to his voice as he runs out of the kitchen.

'I've finished too.' Charlotte jumps down, her plate clear.

I am trying to work out how Charlotte made her broccoli disappear, when I realise that she's transferred it to Lorna's plate with admirable sleight of hand.

'Mum!' Lorna wails, just as Michael calls through from the hall, 'I'm home, darling!'

While Helen is distracted, I grab the broccoli and stuff it down. It's cold, and tasteless – Helen doesn't use salt in her cooking because she worries about Michael's blood pressure. Lorna grins at me, and skips off.

Helen turns from greeting Michael. While she's taking three glasses out of the cupboard beside the walk-in fridge, Charlotte clambers onto a chair and throws herself into Michael's arms, squealing like a baby.

'How's my girl?' says Michael, smiling. 'What've you been up to today?'

'Nothing much.'

'Oh come on, Charlotte,' Helen says encouragingly. 'You've been to school, helped make skeletons, and eaten all your tea, even your greens.'

'Didn't you have a spelling test?' Michael asks.

Charlotte whispers into Michael's ear.

'Six out of ten – that's pretty good.' He gives her a squeeze, and lets her slip down to the floor. 'I never got more than three out of ten for spelling.'

'Did you really?' Charlotte says, wide-eyed.

'You'll have to try harder if you want to go to university like Tom,' Michael goes on.

'A lot harder,' says Helen.

'We can't all be brilliant at everything,' I interrupt, trying to protect Charlotte. I can recall exactly what it feels like when six out of ten isn't good enough for a pushy parent – my mother, in my case.

'Hi, Sadie,' Michael grins. 'Champagne?'

'What are we celebrating?'

'My next million,' Michael says. 'You've got something caught on your teeth.'

'Broccoli,' says Helen disapprovingly. 'I can't believe you ate that to let Lorna off the hook, Sadie, when you're the only person I know who thought that the Take Five campaign was a pop group. The nearest you get to a vegetable or fruit is the orange juice you mix with your vodka.'

'And strawberry-flavoured Chewitts,' I add.

'Don't you want to hear my news?' Michael cuts in.

'Of course, Mikey,' says Helen.

'You are looking at the man who has bought up the next six-months' entire world production of Glowie Balls.' Michael hands Helen a bottle of champagne, then delves into his jacket-pockets, pulling out a ball the size of a tennis ball.

'Sam and Lorna can have one each – I've got some more in the car. These things are going to take off like wildfire. Go on.'

'Are they?' Helen sniffs as I take the ball and examine it.

'Who's going to want to buy a grey rubber ball?'

'Bounce it,' says Michael.

'Not in the house!' Helen cuts in quickly, but it's too late. The Glowie Ball is bouncing across the kitchen floor, its core glowing spaceship blue.

'You see? They come in all different colours,' says Michael, catching the ball. 'I tell you, these'll be the next Beyblades, or Top Trumps cards.'

My mobile rings, interrupting any further discussion on playground toys. I snatch it out of the bag that I've left on the kitchen worktop, and answer. 'Gareth?'

'Hiya, Sadie,' he says. 'I dropped back into the house to see you. I thought you'd like to know that Craig's fixed your electric,' he continues as I kick myself for not being there.

I tell Helen and Michael. The Prince of Darkness said, 'Let there be light,' and lo and behold there was light – which is great because it also means that we have power and I can catch up with my washing. He's also left a huge bill – Gareth warned me how much – and an estimate for rewiring the whole house.

'How much?' says Michael. It may be my imagination, but he goes slightly pale when I tell him. 'It's a good thing I'm not relying on you two to make my fortune out of that development of yours.' He nips upstairs and returns with a cheque for the full amount of the bill in my name. 'That,' he says, 'is a drop in the ocean compared with the banker's draft I arranged today.'

I take it, fold it and tuck it into my purse. I can see that outfit for the Rugby Club event – something long, clingy and sparkling . . .

'Thanks for offering to do this,' I say, looking up from where I'm ironing my new dress on a towel on the floor, when Helen turns up to babysit the twins on the evening of the Rugby Club event.

'I didn't,' she says, smiling. 'You said you'd never speak to me again if I didn't come over tonight. Why couldn't Dan have the twins this weekend?'

'He'd promised to take Wendy to see *Jerry Springer the Opera* to make up for what he said about people with body piercings.'

'A terrible penance indeed,' Helen grins. 'Are Sam and Lorna in bed yet?'

'They're in the garden, building a jungle camp with the branches Tom's lopped off the pear tree. That's his sole achievement so far. He says that gardening helps him think, but that's all he does out there.'

'He should be thinking about going back to university.'

'Perhaps he is.' I fiddle with the iron, and take a sip of vodka. 'Are you sure Michael's not overstretching himself with buying all those Glowie Balls? He wasn't too keen on financing your share of the rewiring costs.'

'It isn't because he hasn't got enough cash. He's worried about your ability to manage it,' Helen says. 'Michael's been bankrupt before – before me. He lost everything – his home, girlfriend, reputation ... He wouldn't risk going through that again.'

'I suppose not.'

'You've just poured vodka into the steam compartment of your iron,' Helen points out. 'You're daydreaming about lover-boy again.'

I don't deny it. I was picturing Gareth as I saw him playing rugby last weekend. He ran up to me after scoring the winning try, spat out his mouthguard and grinned. He had a small cut above his left eye that had been taped with crosses, and a support bandage wrapped around his knee. He smelled of an arousing, earthy mixture of crushed grass and sweat, and for the rest of the day I was a slave to his pheromones.

I unplug the iron and pick up the dress just as there's a knock on the door.

'You get that, Helen!' I run upstairs to dress. Lippy? Magenta or scarlet? Scarlet. Definitely.

'Hurry up, Sadie,' Gareth calls. 'The cab's waiting.'

'Cab?' I brush a little more shimmer across my cheeks, slip into my heels and head downstairs to the front room where Gareth is waiting, dressed in black tie. He looks me up and down, and up again, his eyes darkening with what I hope is desire.

'You look amazing,' he breathes.

I feel amazing, and so I should. I deposited Michael's cheque into my account and paid Craig for reconnecting us. I gave Gareth the up-front payment he asked for and then went shopping for the dress. There isn't enough money left for the rewiring, but Craig is on holiday at Butlins for the next two weeks.

'This is for you.' Gareth steps forwards and hands me a single red rose, its stem wrapped in cellophane.

Helen snatches it. 'I'll put it in water. Now, off you go. I'll say goodnight to the twins for you.'

'Thanks for this, Helen. I really appreciate it,' says Gareth.

'Think of me sitting here watching *Celebrity Stars in Their Eyes* and endless repeats of *Friends*.'

'We won't,' Gareth grins.

Helen gives a grudging smile back. 'I'll see you later.'

It turns out that Martine, the wife of Gareth's friend Rob, is grudging with her smiles too. Martine is wearing a dress that's remarkably similar to mine, yet her husband's eyes linger on my cleavage, not hers. Martine scowls at him, and taps her tiger-print purse with curved, talon-like fingernails.

'This is Niall, and his wife Kate.' Gareth continues with the introductions when we arrive at the Rugby Club. Niall smiles. His boyish looks remind me of James Nesbitt. Kate, who's shorter and rounder than I am, ducks forwards and kisses the air at my left cheek.

'Gareth's told us so much about you,' she says, immediately putting me at ease.

I wish my conversation was as sharp and sparkling

as the Bucks Fizz in my glass, but I remind myself that when I try to make an impression I can overdo it. Helen says that I end up sounding more like a certain overblown magic operative than myself.

'Wine?' asks the waiter when we are sitting down to dinner.

'Please.' Gareth winks at me. 'I think it's too late to worry about the consequences of mixing drinks. Black Velvet – champagne and Guinness – is one of those situations where the rule of not mixing grape and grain doesn't stand up.'

'I wonder if anyone will be left standing up at the end of the evening at the rate they're going,' I observe.

'Speak – or should that be shout – for yourself,' sneers Martine, who's sitting opposite.

In normal circumstances, I'd have a go back, but Gareth has his hand on my thigh, squeezing it in what I assume is a warning not to embarrass him by stirring up trouble.

After dinner and speeches, Martine and Kate disappear without waiting for me. I find my way to the Ladies and lock myself in a cubicle, listening to the sound of running water and voices outside.

'I don't know what he sees in her – big tits and an even bigger mouth, I suppose. She's louder than a psychedelic T-shirt and drinks like a fish. He'll leave her, you'll see. He's too fond of his freedom.'

'I shouldn't let Gareth hear you say that. He seems very fond of her.'

Gareth? I flush the loo and throw the door open.

'That wouldn't be my Gareth you're talking about, would it?'

Kate turns, blushing. Martine falls silent, throws a tissue in the bin and stalks out.

'Sorry about that,' Kate says. 'Alison . . .'

'Gareth's ex-fiancée?' I ask.

'She's Martine's cousin. They're very close. Martine had to deal with the fall-out when Gareth jilted Alison on what was supposed to be their wedding day.' Kate sighs. 'Not only that, Martine's riled because you're wearing the same dress as her, and it suits you better because you have a bust. No, really, you look fantastic. Don't worry about it,' Kate continues while I wash my hands. 'In my opinion, Gareth had a lucky escape. Alison wanted him to stop playing rugby and seeing his friends.'

'How long have you known him?'

'I've known Gareth since I met Niall ten years ago. He was best man at our wedding, the only one of Niall's friends that I could rely on to get him to the church on time, and remember to bring the rings. And he rushed me to the hospital when I was giving birth to our first child, Ben. Ben was premature, and Niall was away. Gareth was fantastic. I couldn't have done it without him. He was there at the birth, along with my mum and sister. There was quite a scrum in the delivery room.'

I wonder for a moment if I am mistaken, if this is really my Gareth whom Kate is talking about. 'He didn't tell me.'

'I'm not surprised. Gareth doesn't brag. He's a real gentleman. So is Niall, of course.' Kate pauses. 'Are you all right?'

'I'm slightly sozzled.'

She laughs. 'Not too sozzled to dance, I hope?'

When Kate and I arrive back, the tables have been pushed against the walls and the dancing is in full swing. Gareth offers me his arm and we trip across the dance-floor together. Who cares that Gareth's disco is more of a shuffle, that my jive is more roll than rock? The slow dances suit us better. Gareth takes me in his arms with one hand around my waist, the other buried in my hair at the nape of my neck. His breath is hot against my cheek.

'You didn't tell me you helped deliver Kate's baby.'

'I didn't do very much,' Gareth protests softly. 'Kate did the hard work. I held her hand while the midwife, a rugby-playing cattleman from Australia, looked after the birth.' He pauses. 'I hear you had a bit of a ruck with Martine. I'm sorry about that. I should have warned you.'

'It doesn't matter,' I want to say, but Gareth smothers my mouth with a kiss that lasts three and a half tracks when, by mutual agreement, we head for home.

'I'd have had the twins for a sleepover if I'd known you were going to stay out all night,' Helen complains when we let ourselves into *Llamedos*. Then she gives us both a welcoming smile, suggesting that she is coming to terms with the fact that Gareth and I are lovers.

'It's only two o'clock,' I observe.

'We're very grateful,' Gareth adds.

'The twins didn't want to go to bed,' Helen tells me.

Gareth and I don't have the same problem. As soon

as Helen leaves, we retire upstairs. While Gareth strips off, I stare out of the window.

'Aren't you coming to bed?'

'I'm watching for clouds across the moon . . .'

'You have quite a way with words, Sadie,' Gareth says softly. I smile to myself. He thinks I'm being poetic, but I'm actually looking for rain.

After we have made love, Gareth falls asleep and I lie by his side, listening to him snoring. Someone stirs. One of the twins? I leap up before they can come in and try snuggling into my bed.

'What's up?'

'Mummy,' Lorna calls nervously.

I go and see her in the bedroom. 'What's wrong?'

'There's a pig in the house.'

'A what?'

'A pig. Can't you hear it?'

I try to hold in my own snort of laughter. 'It's Alvin – he's asleep on my duvet.'

'He isn't. He's sleeping on Sam's pillow. Look.'

'It must be The Neighbour From Hell,' I say. 'He snores so loudly that we can hear him on the other side of the wall.'

Lorna seems reassured.

'Go to sleep now.' She lets me kiss her on the forehead as she drifts back to sleep, and I return to lie cuddled up against Gareth, jolting the mattress as I wriggle back underneath the duvet. Gareth's breathing stops. So does mine as I recall phone-ins to media medics on the subject of sleep apnoea and the potential for sudden death. I lean across so that my right ear is close to Gareth's face, straining to hear the slightest sign of life. Just as I am about to leap up and call for an ambulance, a vibrating sound like the one that my washing-machine makes on full spin, explodes from the back of Gareth's throat.

I try rolling him onto his side, but he rolls back. I try pinching his nostrils, but nothing works to stop him snoring. I sit back, infuriated. How is it that this man can drive me wild with both desire and irritation? I am amazed by the unexpected violence of my emotions. It must be love.

There's unrequited love – the rushes of lust that Helen feels for Jude Law, for example – there's Müller love, which I imagine is much the same except that it can be satisfied merely by consuming a yoghurt, and there's maternal love which consumes much of my time and energy.

'Mum, look up here! Mum!'

When I open my eyes to the harsh light of morning, I find that Sam is laughing and waving his Glowie Ball at me out of a hole in the ceiling. Am I hallucinating? I scrape my furred tongue across the sharp edges of my upper teeth, and try to focus.

'What do you think you're doing?'

'Gareth sent me up here to check the tarpaulin after the rain last night.'

'Get down at once.' I scramble out of bed and head for the landing where Gareth is standing at the foot of a ladder that goes up into the loft. 'I'll hold you responsible if Sam falls and breaks his neck, or the roof comes down on him,' I snap.

'He'll be fine, Sadie,' Gareth soothes.

'You don't know Sam like I do. He managed to break his arm running up a slide last year.'

I push between Gareth and the ladder, and start climbing. It's a sight to cure the worst of hangovers – my son is standing straddled across two supports, and holding onto one of the crossbeams in the roof that I know for a fact are riddled with rot. My heart starts beating in my mouth. 'Get down this minute, Sam!'

Something creaks. Sam's face contorts. 'I can't,' he wails.

'You've panicked him now,' Gareth grumbles. 'Here, let me help him down.'

I hesitate.

'Trust me,' he adds.

I move aside, and let Gareth onto the ladder from where he talks Sam down, distracting him from his and my fears of falling through what remains of the ceiling into the bedroom below with conversation about Michael's new toy. Of course, once Sam's back down, he's all swagger, and Gareth acts as if nothing has happened. Sam aims a couple of high kicks in Gareth's direction. Gareth takes Sam by surprise, tackling him, and grappling him to the floor.

I am trying to give Gareth my opinion of his behaviour over Sam's giggly attempts to persuade Gareth to let him go, when Lorna interrupts, coming upstairs with Gareth's mobile in her hand.

'Gareth, it's your girlfriend.'

'My girlfriend's right here.'

'Not Mum,' Lorna says. 'No way.'

Gareth's smile fades in the face of Lorna's scowl. He looks to me for confirmation, but I'm still furious with him for putting Sam's life in danger.

'Who is it?' I ask coolly.

Gareth releases Sam and takes the phone. 'I'd better find out, hadn't I?' He stands up and strolls into the bedroom, shutting the door behind him.

'Who is it?' I tackle Lorna. 'Did she say she was Gareth's girlfriend?' Lorna bites her lip in sullen silence so that I can hear the fierce timbre of Gareth's voice next door. 'Well, did she?'

Lorna shakes her head. Her lip trembles and she bursts into tears.

'Oh, Lorna.' I pull her close and hug her against my belly. 'What's the matter?'

'I don't want you to be Gareth's girlfriend,' she sobs. 'I hate Gareth.'

'You'll like him when you get to know him.'

'I won't!' Lorna stamps her foot. 'I know I won't.'

'This is about Dad, isn't it?' I pause. 'Listen, Lorna, it's time you realised that me and your dad will never get back together. We're friends, that's all.' I am about to remind her that Wendy is living with Dan now, when the bedroom door flies open.

'I've got to go,' says Gareth, tipping his head to one side in apology.

'I was going to cook a brunch,' I say, disappointed.

'I'll have to miss out, I'm afraid, thanks to the rain last night. Teresa says that the flat roof on the extension's leaking.'

'Can't she stick a bucket under it, or ask her husband

251

to tack some tarpaulin up like you've done here? It is Sunday.'

'Her husband's on a business trip.'

'What about my roof? When are you going to start on that?' Am I overreacting again? Am I being greedy, wanting to spend the rest of the day with Gareth after we had such a wonderful night together?

'I'll see you later,' Gareth says, kissing me softly on the lips. I watch him go from the bedroom window, then turn to find that he's left his mobile on the mattress. I bury it under the duvet. Out of sight, out of mind. Or is it?

Gareth's definition of later is clearly different from mine. At nine in the evening, after I've turned down an invitation to tea at Helen's in case he turns up, there's still no sign of him. Helen's suggestion that I follow him and find out what he's getting up to, and who with, keeps running through my mind. I dig out his phone and dial up the Call Register. Before I know it, I'm speaking to Teresa.

'How did you get my number?' she asks, her voice heavy with suspicion.

'Your builder said to call you, to ask if you'd mind showing me around your extension.'

'Gareth said that, did he?'

'I'm thinking of having some work done ...' The phone keeps slipping in my hand. I shouldn't be snooping like this.

'Mr Bryant wouldn't be my first choice, but if you want to have a look, you're welcome.'

When Teresa shows me round the extension the

following morning, after Gareth still hasn't turned up back at *Llamedos*, I understand why she keeps calling him back. She points out the line of the original foundations that had to be filled in and re-dug by order of the Building Inspector because they didn't follow the plans, the water damage to the new carpet, and the temporary repair to the flat roof that Gareth's coming back to renew completely at some later date.

'I told him this week, but I shan't hold my breath.'

If the extension isn't as I imagined it would be, Teresa isn't either. There's nothing washed-out about her blonde locks, as Gareth suggested. She's taller than me, younger than me, and she carries a toddler with a grubby, tear-streaked face on her hip.

'Gareth's a nice enough man, but he's a useless builder,' Teresa says. 'Sometimes he turns up to work when he says he's going to. Sometimes he doesn't. Next time we want more room for the kids, we're going to move, not extend. It's too much hassle.' She frowns suddenly. 'What exactly are you here for? It isn't about the extension, is it?'

I can't deny it.

'You're the girlfriend he keeps going on about. You want to know if I'm sleeping with Gareth Bryant.' She starts to laugh, making it quite clear that she isn't, and never would. 'I thought there was something odd about this visit. Even Gareth wouldn't be so thick as to recommend my house as his showhome.'

I beg her not to mention it, and give her one of Topsy's cards when I leave, offering her a generous discount. I feel deeply ashamed that I ever imagined that Gareth was involved with the woman from Tolworth in anything but a professional capacity. However, a niggling doubt remains. If he isn't with her, where is he?

Chapter Thirteen

Excuses, excuses. That Sunday, after Gareth finished patching Teresa's roof, he went back to his mum's where he ate the roast she'd saved him, and fell asleep during the ITV *Weekend News*. He was late the following day because he overslept, not gaining full consciousness until the lunchtime episode of *Neighbours*.

Gareth's still making excuses two weeks later when The Prince of Darkness returns to rewire the house, lifting floorboards all over the place, drilling conduits down the walls in the third bedroom which ruins Helen's paintwork, and leaving his fag ends stubbed out in the sink. Gareth says he can't possibly start on the roof because he's discovered that the plaster in the kitchen has to come off, and one of the exterior walls is in such a state that he'll have to rebuild it. I try to dissuade him from making any further structural alterations, partly because we're short of cash, and partly because of the state of the brickwork on Teresa's extension. I daren't tell Helen that I've seen evidence of his slipshod work, or she'd have him off the job immediately. I also daren't tell Gareth that I've been spying on him. I hope Teresa isn't anything like me, that she's the kind of woman who can keep her mouth shut.

The kitchen wall comes down in a shower of dust. The cooker is disconnected, the electricity is off more than it's on, and I have to cook on a camping stove in the front room. It's the middle of July, and the weather is warm and dry, and I'm beginning to think that I'd prefer to live in a tent in the back garden.

It's hot at the school fête. I am melting beneath Topsy's wig and make-up, even taking advantage of the shade of the verandah outside one of the classrooms. I've told the story of the snoring prince who falls asleep for one hundred years, until the princess, dressed as a clown, wakes him with a kiss so that they can live happily ever after. I've performed the trick with the eggs, marred only by Sam's contribution that the eggs I use are hardboiled so that there is no risk of them smashing and making a mess on the playground. By four thirty, I have run out of modelling balloons, and energy.

Helen strolls up, holding two Magnums. She unwraps one just as she would for Charlotte and hands it to me.

'I can manage that myself, you know,' I grumble. 'I'm not a kid.'

'You behave like one sometimes,' Helen smiles. 'Aren't you going to say thank you?'

In spite of my mood, I can't help chuckling with her. Helen was going to spend the day working on the development, but she's ended up looking after the twins and Charlotte who insisted on accompanying Topsy to the fête. Dan couldn't have the children as I'd originally planned – he's gone to Newquay with Wendy for a dirty weekend.

'I wish John had turned out all right,' Helen goes on.

'I couldn't have gone out with John. It would have been like shopping in B'Wise when you're yearning for Jaeger.' I turn to her. 'I wish you didn't hate Gareth so much.'

'I don't hate him. I just don't want him to hurt you like he hurt me, that's all.'

'You almost sound jealous.'

'Well, when you're talking to him all the time, it makes me feel left out, as if you don't want to know me any more.'

'That's ridiculous, and you know it.'

'And I don't understand why you took Lorna to have her ears pierced. Charlotte's going on and on at me to let her have hers done.'

'Well, why won't you?'

'Because Michael and I think it's tarty.' Helen bends forward to pick up a wrapper she has dropped, revealing the diamanté strand of a string above the hipster cut of her jeans – a double standard, perhaps? I feel a sudden pang of envy and anxiety. Everyone fancies Helen. Why should Gareth be any different, especially when she flaunts her underwear like this? Gareth has hit my vulnerable spot, and my G spot – although I read in the paper the other day that there isn't such a thing, which is odd, because I could have sworn that Gareth has found it.

'Talking of Lorna's earrings, did you hear anything more from the school?' Helen asks.

According to the letter that came home from the Head, studs should be plain, and stuck down with tape for PE, games and in the playground. When I scribbled a note back, pointing out that this would encourage airless, sticky conditions that would result in infection and harm to my child, I received a second letter, saying that parents shouldn't allow children to have their ears pierced. I wrote back, complaining that the school was treating Lorna like a child. Back came a third letter, shorn of all the usual attempts at tact and politeness, reading *Lorna is a child!*

I shake my head.

'At least Sam's happier now,' I say. 'He came home with a sticker for being the only one in his class who knew what an assassin was.'

'I'm not surprised,' Helen says, pointing towards the lawn on the far side of the playground. 'He's assassinating Harry as we speak.'

'Sam!' I bellow. Sam has Harry in a headlock, and won't let go. Harry is kicking at Sam's shins. I waddle across in Topsy's dungarees. *'Sam!'* He looks up, instantly lets go of Harry, and grabs my Magnum.

'Thanks, Mum,' he grins, as he backs off from Harry's raised fists.

'It isn't for you,' I say, trying to snatch the Magnum back. 'It's mine, you little toe-rag. What the hell do you think you're doing, scrapping with Harry like that?'

Sam's face falls.

'We're not fighting,' Harry pipes up. 'We're playing. Sam is Jackie Chan, and I'm his *emeny.*'

'You always do this to me, Mum.' Sam shoves the Magnum back into my hand. 'You never listen to me. You never give me anything.'

'I do!'

Sam's lip wobbles, then stiffens. 'You and Dad never wanted me.'

I can hardly believe my ears. 'Of course we do. We love you!'

'You don't love me as much as you love Lorna!' Sam stamps his foot and storms off across the field with Harry trailing after him. I am about to follow, but Helen stays me with a hand on my shoulder.

'Leave him,' she says quietly. 'I'll have a chat with him later. Come back to the verandah and sit down.'

I walk slowly back, aware of people staring at me: Miss Watson, clutching a pink teddy from the Tombola stall; Caroline, holding a cash-box. I drop the sticky remains of the Magnum into the bin beside the classroom door, and sit down.

'I didn't know Sam felt like that,' I mutter from the depths of my humiliation. 'I didn't realise he was quite so sensitive. Helen, what have I done to him?'

'It isn't so much what you've done to him,' she says, 'it's Sam's *perception* of what you have done to him that's the problem.' She looks out towards the lawn. There's no sign of my son. 'I'll go and find him. Don't worry, Sadie. You and Sam will be fine.'

I do worry. I worry too when I'm carrying Topsy's boxes back to the car with Caroline at my heels. I am walking very fast, almost running, but Caroline's sports trainers outpace my Doc Martens, and she draws level.

Uh-oh, she's going to co-opt me onto the PTA committee, or the mums' team for Sports Day.

'Sadie . . . Didn't you hear me?'

'No, I must have some wax build-up, or something.'

'Have you tried Hopi ear candles? They're brilliant at drawing out impurities.' Caroline smiles. 'I wanted to invite Sam to tea one day next week. Harry would love it.'

Having built myself up to say, 'No,' to Caroline, I suddenly find it difficult to say, 'Yes.'

'Well?'

'Y-y-yes,' I stammer. 'Thanks.'

'By the way, don't think I'm poking my nose in, but I wouldn't let Sam play with that Glowie Ball if I were you. I heard on the radio the other day that some poor boy's ball exploded, releasing some toxic chemical, and he's in hospital with facial burns.'

On our journey home in my car, I ask Helen if she's heard the story of the ruptured Glowie Ball.

'It's just sour grapes on Caroline's part,' says Helen. 'She's made it up. Michael certainly hasn't mentioned it, and he'd be the first to know.'

'Mum thinks we didn't notice that Gareth stayed overnight at our house again,' Sam interrupts. 'We heard his pick-up drive off at seven o'clock.'

'He isn't her boyfriend though,' Lorna chips in. 'I've told Dad that he's just a friend.'

Will Lorna ever accept that Gareth is part of our lives, I wonder? When I went into the twins' room to raid their piggybanks for cash to buy bread, I found Topsy's collapsible wand on Lorna's bed along with a handmade book of *Spells for the Removal of Unwanted Persons*. At first, I thought she was getting her own back on Sam for putting a sign up on their bedroom door, reading *No Girls Aloud*, but I fear that it has more to do with getting rid of Gareth.

Back at her house, Helen invites us in for tea and a piece of the chocolate cake she bought at the fête.

'Do you know who made it?' I ask, eyeing it dubiously as she hands out slices to the children.

'Marks & Spencer,' she smiles, offering me a plate. 'I saw Caroline taking it out of its wrapper. It's quite safe, just like a Glowie Ball. Michael wouldn't let Charlotte play with toys that might be dangerous.'

Helen and I sit in the conservatory where we can keep an eye on the children playing in the garden. I'm sweltering in Topsy's dungarees in spite of the fan.

'I'm expecting The Prince of Darkness to present me with the bill for the rewiring,' I say. 'Would you mind asking Michael for the money?'

'I thought you were handling our finances.'

I don't deny it. I don't tell Helen that there isn't much finance left to handle. I've reached the limit of my overdraft, and the bank is reluctant to extend it.

'Why can't *you* ask him?' Helen goes on.

'I'm not taking my clothes off and flouncing about in skimpy knickers for your husband. That's your department.'

'I wouldn't be any good anyway,' Helen says gloomily. 'It isn't true what they say, that the more sex you have the more you want it. Michael's losing enthusiasm. It's as if all the exotic massage oils and erotic films have dulled his senses.'

'Perhaps you should try approaching him in a winter coat, gloves and balaclava if all that flesh is putting him off.'

'It's nothing to do with me,' Helen says quickly. 'I look after myself. It's Michael. He keeps complaining that he's tired all the time.'

'Perhaps he's depressed.'

'Michael's planning to have the shop in the High Street refurbished. The first shipment of Glowie Balls has sold out. What's he got to be depressed about, apart from Tom?'

'Talking of Tom, would you have a word with him too? It's time that he made a proper start on the garden. I'm fed up with seeing Justin Timberlake lying flat on his back in the middle of my lawn.'

'Some people would think it was their birthday . . .'

It *is* my birthday later in the month, and I've invited Helen and Michael, Annette and Sean, and Gareth, of course, to celebrate with a drink in the pub. Gareth came over to *Llamedos* this morning to wish me a Happy Birthday before he shot off without a word to say where he was going. He left me a present, a necklace from Argos – I checked the price in the catalogue, not because I wished to insure it, but because I wanted to see how much I'm worth to him.

After tea, I drop the children at Dan's for the night.

'You don't have to stop, Mum,' says Sam.

'I want a word with your father.'

'You're not going to argue with him again, are you?' says Lorna.

'Probably.' I find myself carrying Sam's football and Lorna's Sand Art set up to the door. I ring the bell, triggering a sad, electronic version of 'When the Saints Go Marching In'.

Dan opens the door. The twins run upstairs with their rucksacks.

'Thanks for having the twins, Dan,' I say. 'I'm sorry if you had to be home early from work.'

'I've taken a sickie,' he says tightly. His eyes look tired behind his glasses.

'Can you afford to do that? I mean, you haven't paid any money into my account this month. I was relying on it to feed the twins, and Sam needs new school shoes.' I turn the emotional screw. 'They're so battered that he's going to get teased at school.'

'I've got a twenty – that's all I have left,' says Dan, handing it over to me.

'I'll have to go to Shoefayre rather than Clarks then.'

'Hold on a minute. I might have some change in the pot.' He searches through the jam jar of change in which he keeps coins for the car park. 'Here you are,' he says. 'Three pounds in tens, twos and ones. The twins told me that you've been having trouble sticking to your budget for the development, because Helen's ordered a kitchen that's going to make the house look like the inside of the Starship *Enterprise*.'

'There's been more expense since.' I pause. 'Go on, tell me that you told me so.'

'I'm not saying anything.'

'Are you all right?'

Dan shakes his head. 'I suppose you're going to find out sooner or later, but Wendy dumped me at the weekend.'

'Dan, I'm sorry.'

'Yeah, go on, it's your turn to have a good gloat.'

'I'm not gloating. What happened?'

'She met someone in Newquay, a champion surfer with a tan and blond ringlets.' Dan hesitates as if he's deciding how much he wants to tell me. 'It was going wrong anyway. That damned dog of hers refused to let me into bed with her.'

'Any chance of a quick coffee?'

Dan makes me a cup of the cheapest instant. I sip at it, then let it grow cold as I talk about what Sam said about feeling unwanted and unloved. I assume that Dan is trying to be helpful when he points out that Sam inherits his disposition from me, his mother.

'He's insecure in his relationships with other people,' Dan continues. 'He demands constant attention and reassurance. He's also very jealous. I wouldn't mind betting that some of this latest outburst is down to the fact that you paid for Lorna to have her ears pierced, but you didn't buy him anything.'

'I never wanted to treat the twins in exactly the same way.' I strain my larynx, trying to keep my voice down. 'I've always wanted them to feel free to express their individuality.'

'You've succeeded in that aim, Sadie.' Dan leans towards me. 'All you need to do now is convince Sam that you treat him and Lorna fairly and equitably. Don't ask me how you do that. I'm not in my most innovative mood at the moment.'

I stay longer than I intended. I was supposed to be at the pub at eight. It's ten past nine. I say goodnight to the twins, but they are too busy doing Sand Art all over Dan's bedroom carpet to take much notice of me.

'Did you ever buy yourself a vacuum cleaner?' I ask, twiddling with Gareth's necklace.

Dan shakes his head ruefully.

'I would lend you mine, but it's being repaired. The engineer gave me a Network Rail kind of excuse. He said I was using it on the wrong kind of dust. Apparently, plaster dust blocks its micro-filters and jams the motor.'

'In that case, I wouldn't risk using it on sand,' says Dan. He smiles for the first time this evening. 'What kind of dust can you use it on?'

'House mites and dander.'

'You've been spending too much time listening to Helen talk about the science of housework.' Dan pauses. 'Happy Birthday, by the way. Go on, Sadie. It'll be last orders by the time you get down to the Royal Oak.'

I swap the car for an umbrella back at *Llamedos* as the rain is still falling, slanting past the streetlights and forming puddles across the pavement. I jog along the High Street with water splashing up my ankles. Making love in the rain is definitely a possibility tonight, but when I arrive at the pub, Gareth draws me aside without a smile, without a kiss. His hand is clenched around an empty pint glass.

'Where were you?' he says.

'I had to drop the twins off at Dan's.'

'You're very late.'

'Dan's girlfriend has left him. He was a bit down. I couldn't leave him on his own.'

'So you left me standing here on my own at your birthday celebration, while you nursed your ex-husband's broken heart.'

'We're still friends. You can't be with someone for sixteen years, and suddenly have no feelings for them. I don't mean those kind of feelings, not the ones I have for you,' I add quickly. 'Look, I'm sorry. What more can I say?'

'It's all very well saying that you're sorry, but you're always running off to help someone. If it isn't your sister, it's your ex-husband. You surround yourself with needy people. Even Topsy demands your attention. What about me, Sadie? What about us?'

'You can't talk, Gareth. Yes, I have obligations, but at least I don't go out getting sozzled when I'm supposed to be seeing you.'

'I've been slightly pissed once.'

'You don't turn up when you say you're going to. You're always letting me down.'

'If you're talking about the other weekend, I went out for a few drinks with Rob and Niall. It was late. I crashed at Niall and Kate's, that's all, whereas you've been up to goodness knows what with your ex-husband.'

'Dan's the father of my children! I still worry about him for their sake, that's all.'

'One more thing . . .' There's something in his expression that sends a chill down my spine. Gareth looks towards the table where my friends are sitting, then back to me. 'It can wait.'

'We'd better join the others,' I suggest, once Gareth has bought me a white wine spritzer. (I am determined to pace myself tonight – I fear that I'm going to need a clear head later.) We pull stools up and elbow our way in to sit at the table with Helen, Michael, Annette and Sean. Their glasses are empty.

'Drinks, anyone?' Gareth asks.

'It's Sean's round,' Michael says. 'Sit down, Gareth.'

'Happy Birthday, Sadie.' Helen hands me a present. 'How does it feel to be forty?'

'Don't remind me.' I rip at the silver wrapping paper. 'A cordless electric screwdriver! Thanks so much.'

'You don't have to say that it's all you ever wanted,' Helen smiles. 'Mikey thought you'd find it useful.'

'There's a cheque too for the rewiring,' says Michael. 'What happened to the other money that I gave you?'

'I had to pay Gareth.'

'Oh? I want to see a receipt from the electrician this time. I want receipts for everything. You are keeping a record of your business expenses?'

'I've bought a cash book.' Michael doesn't have to know that I haven't written anything in it yet.

Michael leans towards me, keeping his voice low. 'Just remember, Sadie, that I'm not a limitless resource. To be a success in business, you have to keep a tight rein on the finances.'

'You haven't been to the development recently, Michael. I thought you'd want to see how your investment was coming on.'

'Helen keeps putting me off, don't you?' he says, turning to her. 'I can't understand why it isn't finished already, with all the hours you're putting in.'

'It's hard work,' says Helen.

'How do you know?' Gareth banters. 'You never do any.'

'I do!'

'I see Sadie grafting, and you sitting around with brochures and cups of coffee.' Gareth's thigh presses against mine.

'I couldn't do this without Helen,' I say.

'Thank you for your support, Sadie.' Helen changes the subject. 'Did you know it's Mikey's birthday next month?'

'Hey, don't tell everyone.' Michael gives her a dig in the ribs, and shrugs with mock embarrassment.

'I couldn't believe it when you told me you were going to be fifty. I thought you were nearer forty,' Annette giggles. 'We do all get an invite to your party?'

'Yes – everyone's invited,' says Michael.

'*I* was planning your birthday celebration,' Helen interrupts. 'It was supposed to be a surprise.'

'It isn't now,' says Gareth.

'I thought . . .' Helen begins. Then: 'No, it doesn't matter. You're all very welcome. Tom can help me out with the cooking. He isn't doing much gardening at the development – it's time he did something to justify his existence.'

'He's still living with you then?' says Annette. 'I imagined he'd have taken off somewhere exotic to work on a conservation project for the summer, or at least found a bar job to earn some money for the next academic year.'

'I'd made a hundred grand by the time I was Tom's age, and signed the lease on my first shop,' says Michael.

'Tom thinks he's going to make his fortune writing and singing songs,' says Helen. 'On the rare occasion that he isn't asleep in his pit of a room, or splattering my kitchen with cooking oil, he's strumming that guitar of his and scribbling lyrics on the back of his lecture notes.'

'You have to admit that my son has a good ear for music,' says Michael. 'He's like me. He could turn his hand to almost anything.'

'You can't sing,' observes Helen. 'In your version of "Rock DJ" in the shower this morning you sounded more like Kylie than Robbie.'

'I chose the wrong song,' Michael shrugs. 'Anyway, if Tom decides that he isn't going back to uni, as he calls it, I can see him being a success in the music business. More drinks?' Michael adds, looking pointedly at Sean who remains very quiet. 'It's your round, isn't it?'

Sean picks up his glass and drains the last drop of lager that has collected in the bottom. 'What's everybody having?'

It is quite a round: tequila slammers for me and Helen, a pint of bitter for Gareth, and a large single malt whisky for Michael, a packet of crisps of each flavour because we can't decide which ones we prefer, three packets of roasted peanuts, and a bowl of chips. Sean is moving on to orange juice and lemonade since he is driving home. I'm not sure what Annette is having.

Michael pushes his way out to help Sean at the bar, but Sean returns without the order. Michael waits with the tray of drinks on the bar at his elbow, and the barman stands, tapping his pen impatiently against the till.

'Annette, darling, have you brought your purse?' Sean asks. 'I've forgotten my wallet.'

As Annette scrabbles about in her clutch bag, that prickling sensation flares across my chest. She pulls out a card. 'That's for the library. And this one's for the AA. I've lost my credit card.'

'Lost it? Where?'

'I don't know, do I?' Annette bites her lip. 'I'll have to notify the bank.'

Annette might lose her way quite often, but it isn't like her to lose something as important as a credit card. I'm beginning to wonder if she's discovering that it isn't so easy to put IT behind her and move on as she planned.

'Are you sure you haven't got any cash on you, Sean?' she asks.

'Twenty p for emergencies – phone calls, the loos at Victoria station, that kind of thing, though I usually try to hang on until I'm on the train.'

'Twenty p won't be enough, will it?' groans Annette.

'No, it's more like twenty quid,' Sean says. 'I can't recall a round of drinks costing anywhere near that much the last time we paid for one.'

'That's because we've had a few years of inflation since,' Helen mutters.

Gareth starts to put his hand to his pocket. I give him a nudge, and shake my head.

'Let me deal with it,' Annette says eventually. Sean sits down while Annette goes up to the bar. I don't know exactly what she says, but Michael pays, and Annette brings the tray back to our table.

'Crisis over,' she says smoothly. 'I said that we'll pay Michael back,' she tells Sean. She serves the drinks, then perches on Sean's knee. Michael sits down, runs his hand through his hair and winks at Helen.

'That'll teach me to order the most expensive malt, won't it?' he grins.

'I don't suppose it will,' says Helen crossly.

The wall lights opposite me begin to drift across my vision, or is it me who is drifting – it may be the effect of three tequila slammers on an empty stomach.

Gareth gives me a nudge. 'Wake up, Sadie.'

I sit up. Blink. Try to show an interest in Michael's talk of the refurbishment of one of his shops, and the price of ceramic lighthouses.

'Perhaps you should go home,' Gareth continues.

'You haven't been here very long,' says Michael, who is one of those people who measures the success of an evening on the length of time you stay out.

'Yes, I'm sorry I was late.' I stand up on shaky knees.

'So was Gareth,' says Helen, stroking the back of Michael's neck in a gesture of possession.

'Was he? I didn't know.'

'You wouldn't, would you? You arrived after him.' Helen gazes at Gareth, challenging him. 'He wouldn't say what he'd been up to, or with whom.'

I turn to Gareth, who gives an almost imperceptible shrug, then back to Helen. How dare she insinuate that

Gareth has been up to anything with anyone but me? How dare she nurture the seedlings of doubt and suspicion that are already rooted in my mind? I find myself standing up, my fists clenching and unclenching at my sides.

'What are you trying to prove? You can't wait to find a reason to break me and Gareth up, can you? Just because you're still carrying a grudge against him for something that happened years ago.'

Michael is looking at me. Everyone is looking at me. You could hear a dart drop.

'You didn't tell me you used to know Gareth,' Michael says quietly.

'It didn't seem important,' says Helen.

'She says she was practically engaged to him.' The words explode from my lips. Maybe it's down to my repressed anger at Helen disapproving of my relationship with Gareth. Maybe it's down to the stress of the development, and the cost of that kitchen.

Helen is frowning at me and shaking her head, but Michael's got the gist. If he were a knife-thrower, and Helen his assistant, she'd be pinned to the board with multiple blades.

Michael's face is the same colour as Annette's port and lemon when he turns to Helen. 'Is this true?' The muscle in his cheek tautens and relaxes, and Sean and Annette lean forward, awaiting Helen's answer. I can't bear it. I shouldn't have said anything.

'Er, excuse me.' I run to the Ladies and hide in a cubicle for a while. When I emerge, Helen is waiting for me.

'Sadie, you've really dropped me in it.'

'I didn't realise. I didn't know. I should have known,' I blurt out. 'When you told me that you'd told Michael that you'd had three ex-lovers, I guess Gareth wasn't one of them. Why didn't you make it clear?'

'I thought you knew.' Helen chews her lip. 'I thought you bloody well knew.'

'One more won't make all that much difference then, in the scheme of things?'

'Gareth makes all the difference. If I've missed Gareth out, Michael will be wondering who else I've conveniently forgotten. What's more, Gareth mattered to me.' I hear a sob catch in her throat. 'I loved Gareth.'

'I'm sorry. I'm so sorry.'

'It's too late for that.' Helen splashes her face at the sink, dries it roughly on a paper towel and storms out.

'Where are you going?'

'Home!' she yells back.

When I return to the table, Michael has gone too. Annette looks at me.

'Well done, Sis,' she says. 'I was having such a great evening . . .'

'In that case, you should get out more.'

'It's time we were going anyway,' says Sean. 'Homer will be waiting for us. It's time for his evening Bonio.'

We say goodnight at the entrance to the pub and head in opposite directions – Annette and Sean to the car park, Gareth and I towards the High Street. I reach for Gareth's hand, but he hides it in his pocket.

'Is there something wrong?' I ask. A rhetorical question – I know very well that there is.

273

'I believe you have something to tell me, Sadie,' he says, stopping under a streetlamp in the rain. 'Like why you've been following me.' He pauses. 'I know you went to Tolworth to speak to Teresa.'

I mutter something about how I understand that he's embarrassed about the quality of his work, especially considering the finish that Helen and I are expecting for our development, but it's no good.

'Yes, we're on first-name terms, but nothing more intimate than that,' Gareth continues.

'How did you find out?' I bluster. 'Teresa said she wouldn't say anything.'

Gareth pulls Topsy's card from his pocket. 'You left this.' The muscle in his cheek tightens. 'How could you?'

A horn beeps alongside us. Annette waves from her and Sean's Daewoo. 'Do you want a lift?' she calls.

'No,' I call back, as Gareth yells, 'Yes,' and pushes me towards the car.

'Aren't you coming too?' I turn to him. 'Oh Gareth, this is our first row.'

'And our last. I was beginning to think that we had something special, but if you can't trust me, Sadie, then what's the point . . . ?' His voice trails off. I am in tears.

'I'm so sorry.' Why did Helen plant the idea of going to see the woman from Tolworth in my head? I blame it all on her, although the blame lies entirely with me for going along with it.

'Save it,' Gareth growls. 'You didn't have to bother. I finished the Tolworth job today. I went to replace the last piece of flashing on the roof. I shan't be setting foot in that place ever again. It was the job from hell – everything went wrong.'

'Please come with me.'

He shakes his head and folds his arms. I climb in and stare back through the rain that pours down the rear windscreen until I can't see Gareth any more. I think of Helen at home trying to explain herself to Michael. Me and my big mouth. How much damage have I caused to my relationships with Gareth and Helen? Is it too late to make emergency repairs?

Chapter Fourteen

Apologising doesn't come easily to me, even when I know that I'm in the wrong, but I don't have a chance to mend bridges with Gareth because he's already on his way across the Forth Road Bridge. The next morning, on my return from the school run, Helen tells me that he's phoned to say that he's en route to Scotland.

Everything – the sander that Helen's running along the skirting board in the front room, the television, the traffic outside – stops. I can't hear anything. I can't see anything except Helen's face swimming in a sea of black. I can't feel anything except a dull ache in my chest.

'Did he say anything about me?'

'He said to let you know he'll be back in two or three weeks. You know what this means?'

'It means that it's over between us – Gareth couldn't have made it more clear.'

'Well, I hate to say it, but I told you so.' Helen's hand is on my shoulder. 'We're going to have to find another builder. I'm not waiting for him to come back and mess us about again. We have our deadline to keep.'

I don't care any more. Our careers are in a state of arrested development, so to speak, and my heart is derelict. Annette's heart is derelict too.

'Gareth might come back. He didn't *say* he wasn't coming back?' Annette tries to console me when we meet the following weekend for a stroll in the park with Homer.

'Gareth's gone, just as I realised that it didn't matter that he wasn't the best builder or the most reliable time-keeper in the world. I loved him anyway.'

'I'm very sorry,' says Annette.

'Did you find your credit card?' I say, changing the subject before the tears that are welling up in my eyes can spill over.

'Yes,' she replies. 'I'd left it at the check-out in Tesco. Luckily, someone handed it in to Customer Services. I was so embarrassed at the pub the other night. I thought I'd nagged at Sean enough about not forgetting his wallet.' She pauses. 'I must be losing my touch.'

I follow her gaze towards the city skyline.

'I've been offered a promotion to Deputy Head,' she says quietly.

'Congratulations,' I say tentatively as she doesn't seem terribly excited about the prospect of taking a step up the career ladder.

'I'd give up teaching like a shot if I had a baby. I hate work. I hate seeing the mums collecting their children from the school gates. If they're not pregnant, they're pushing prams or carrying babies in car-seats . . .' Annette turns to me. 'How can I come to terms with not having a baby when I see them everywhere I go?'

'Give it time,' I say, but I know I don't sound at all convincing.

'It's easier for Sean. He's disappointed, but it doesn't eat away at him like it does me.' Annette clears her throat. 'Have you heard from Mum?'

'She did ring me to boast about how she and Roberto are going to sell up and settle in Italy, how they're going to buy a farmhouse and grow olives and—'

'She's over the moon,' Annette cuts in. 'Can't you try to be pleased for her, Sadie?'

It's difficult. Mum disapproved of my divorce. She said I should have waited until the twins were older, and I said, 'Like you did, you mean,' and she got cross and said that she hadn't had a choice because she didn't have the means to support us as a single parent.

'You didn't tell her about Gareth, did you, Sis?'

Annette shakes her head.

I am relieved. I couldn't bear to be weighed down by my mother's disappointment on top of my own.

On the first day of the school summer holidays, I am at Helen's, sitting with her in the conservatory. Yes, I know we should be working at *Llamedos*, but The Prince of Darkness is back. The light turned out not to be eternal, in spite of the rewiring. Craig claims that Gareth is helping his mate, Jim the roofer, renew the roof on Jim's brother's pub.

The children are playing in the paddling pool in the garden, putting the hose at the top of the slide on Charlotte's climbing frame to make it more slippery. I can't bear to watch.

'How are you and Michael?' I ask Helen tentatively.

'We've been better,' she says. We are interrupted by pigeon droppings spattering across the glazed roof above. Helen gets up, runs out through the double doors and down the garden, clapping her hands and shooing. The people next door keep racing pigeons in their shed. Helen hates them, and the pigeons.

'I'm really sorry about the other night,' I start again when she returns.

'Oh,' she shrugs, 'we could survive much worse than my so-called friend shooting her mouth off. I'm going to make sure that Michael has the best birthday he's ever had to make it up to him. I've traced one of his oldest friends through the internet.'

'I don't suppose I'm invited?'

'You're like a Molotov cocktail at a social gathering, Sadie, but yes, you are.'

So that's me been told and, I think, forgiven. I turn to the newspaper open on the wicker table. A photo catches my eye beneath the headline *Dog on the Crest of a Wave*.

It's Wendy, clutching Vinnie who's wearing shades, to her chest.

Vinnie, four-year-old terrier, joins league of superdogs, performing a radical backhand vertical re-entry at the National Surfing Championships in Newquay. 'He's a rising star,' says his agent, Aiden 'Rip-tide' Davis, 'and open to offers of sponsorship.'

I show Helen the picture of Dan's ex, and she's just saying that she can understand why Wendy left Dan for Aiden when there's a fracas of splashing and shouting from outside. Charlotte and Lorna are tugging at each other's swimming costumes.

'What is your problem?' I yell as they come running in, dripping muddy water over Helen's ceramic tiles.

'Charlotte says my ear's gone septic, Mum. Has it?' Lorna is on the verge of tears.

I lift the lobe and examine both sides. 'It's fine.'

'Charlotte says it's going to drop off.'

'No, it isn't. Now go and make up.'

'*She*,' says Charlotte, meaning Lorna, 'said nasty things about me.'

'What kinds of things?' says Helen.

'She said I was minging because I haven't got my ears pierced.' She stamps her foot. 'And we're playing mums and dads, and Lorna doesn't want to be the baby any more.'

'I want to be the ex,' Lorna nods.

'What's an ex?' Helen asks.

'We're playing mums and dads and the ex-tra girl-friend.'

Helen winks at me, and smiles. I bite my lip. They are all so serious. Lighten up, you're only eight, I want to say.

'Should we explain?' Helen asks me. I can't. I am giggling too much, the first time since Gareth walked out of my life. When I am able to speak, the girls have rejoined Sam in the garden. Sam seems happier since I offered him the equivalent of Lorna's ear-piercing in cash, and promised him that I'd stop yelling at him all the time. Dan was right in a way. Sam's relationship with Lorna is like mine was with my sister. Annette was the dutiful elder sibling, and I didn't get a look in, what with her being superhuman at everything. The only way I could get noticed was if I did something bad, and then bad wasn't good enough, and only really bad would do.

'Is Tom still in bed?' I ask.

'Doubtless,' says Helen. 'You should see the state of my faux-fur throw.'

Before I can ask why, the phone rings. Helen answers.

'Hi, darling,' she says brightly. 'You want to speak to Sadie? She's here.' She hands the phone to me. 'It's Michael. He has a favour to ask.'

How can I refuse after what I said about Helen and Gareth? I find myself agreeing to be Topsy at the re-opening of one of Michael's shops, the one in New Malden High Street, in six weeks' time for a cut-price fee.

'I'll have Annette's number from you too,' Michael adds. 'I'm going to ask her and Sean if they'll drop in as well.'

'You do realise that Sean won't buy anything?'

'It doesn't matter,' Michael says. 'The more people there are in the shop, the more passers-by will want to join them.'

I hand the phone back to Helen.

'I thought Topsy had retired,' she smiles, 'but thanks for agreeing to do that for Michael.'

'Topsy's returning to work part-time, not because she's bored, but she needs the money. *I* need the money. Dan pays a few quid into my account now and then, but it isn't anywhere near enough. I had to ring the

Building Society last week to arrange a payment holiday for the mortgage on my share of the house.'

'Did they agree?'

'I said that if they didn't, I'd have to default on July's payment anyway, so they agreed to extend the terms. Their money's safe – it won't be long before we can sell up and I can pay them off.'

'We are still on target to make a profit?' Helen enquires. 'Michael asked me about it the other day. I don't know why he's worrying about money – he can't get enough of those Glowie Balls, and if the weather carries on like this, he'll make a fortune out of the hand-held fans that he's ordered.'

The weather is fantastic – hotter than the Costa Brava according to the Met Office – and Michael has had to restock his shops with fans, of both the hand-held and freestanding varieties. However, all this sunshine drains my energy. Gareth texts me twice, asking me to ring him, but I don't. What's the point when he's drinking pints of bitter in a loch-side beer garden by day, and curling up with a Carol Smillie lookalike at night?

Helen and I persuade two builders to assess the property and give us estimates to finish the work, but one won't countenance finishing off anything that another builder has started, and the other can't start until the end of September. Work stops. The house is in such a mess that it's all too easy to say that we'll go round to Helen's for a splash in her paddling pool, or slip off to the park for ice creams, while Helen and I reassure each other that we'll still have three months in which to finish the development once the children go back to school. There's plenty of time.

A mixed outlook for tomorrow. That is the gist of what the weatherman said last night in his lowest, most tantalising, 'I may have a surprise for you' voice. And there's a belt of rain spreading south. Black clouds are building on the horizon, just in time for Michael's birthday barbecue.

Sam and Lorna are ready, Lorna jumping up and down with excitement, and Sam moaning that he doesn't want to go.

'If I have to go, I'm taking my football *and* my Glowie Ball,' he grumbles.

'You know Helen doesn't like you playing football in her garden.'

'Perhaps I could stay behind,' says Sam.

'You can't.' I put my foot down rather hard on a stray nail, and it is some time before I can recover my composure to say any more than 'Damn and bother it,' or words to that effect. 'You're coming with me. Helen wants this to be the best party ever.' I pick up Michael's present and a bottle of wine. 'Now, let's go.'

We arrive at Helen's a mere half an hour later than I said we would, and before Annette and Sean turn up. Helen shows us through the conservatory to the garden.

'Still no sign of the cowboy builder?' teases Michael as he flicks the switch on a new gas barbecue.

'At least if some cowboy should turn up, you have somewhere for him to hitch his horse,' I say stiffly, pointing to the palisade fencing.

Michael's mouth is smiling, but his eyes are not. He considers the fence to be the height of good taste, and I guess he feels the same about the new gold watch that flashes on his wrist. Or perhaps it isn't the implicit criticism of the fence that's bothering him . . .

'Sadie, allow me to introduce you to our other guests,' he says, taking my arm and steering me towards two couples who are huddled together on the edge of the decking. 'This is Kitty and her husband Alexander.'

'Pleased to meet you,' I say. (It's true what the experts say on the telly about human behaviour – an adult lies on average three times a day.)

'And this is Maggie and Pete. They're all friends from the Golf Club.'

Both couples are in their late forties or early fifties. Alexander and Pete nod vaguely towards me before returning to a conversation they had already begun. Kitty bares a set of immaculate white teeth. Maggie bears an air of mild surprise.

'Sadie's a friend of the family. She's Helen's partner in the development I told you about, Pete. Perhaps you could give her some advice sometime.' Michael turns back to me and smiles condescendingly. 'Pete's involved in a multi-million refurbishment in the City.'

'He doesn't get his hands dirty any more,' Maggie says.

'I don't either,' I say. 'Helen and I employ contractors to do the work.'

'Oh really?' Maggie arches one eyebrow – it moves stiffly as if the muscles beneath have been poisoned by an overdose of Botox. 'Kitty and I are in fashion together.'

I don't know what to say. Kitty's wearing a red polka-dot blouse and skirt, and a cardigan in navy crepe. Think Berketex, not Bella Freud.

'We run a consultation service, advising women how to make the most of themselves,' Kitty explains, handing me a card.

'For example,' Maggie goes on, 'if you must wear a fuchsia-pink top, you should carry the colour through to the lower body, not cut yourself in half with a dark skirt.'

I am just about to comment on Maggie's high hairline, and ask her if she can recommend her plastic surgeon when Michael catches my elbow. 'This way, Sadie.' He quickly steers me on to the second and last group of partygoers – the B list, I suspect, since once we are introduced, Michael makes a hasty return to the first.

There's Clare, Helen's hairdresser, a bubbly woman in her early thirties. Her own locks are short, ragged and multicoloured as if she's plucked the hairs from a sample card of dyes and glued them onto her head. Her daughter Alice, who stands arranging the straps on her bra and two vest tops, wears the face of a seventeen year old who's been condemned to a life of eternal boredom. There's also a mystery guest whose presence Michael fails to acknowledge.

'So, what line of work are you in, Clifford?' Clare asks him.

I try to guess before he replies. He looks as if he's about sixty. His forehead and the end of his nose are shiny and glowing with sunburn. His gut spills over a pair of tight white trousers.

'I front a rock 'n' roll band,' he says, patting his forehead dry with a grey handkerchief. 'We play the clubs in Magaluf during the high season.' He coughs, takes a cigarette out of a packet he keeps in the breast-pocket of a yellow short-sleeved shirt, and puts it between his lips. 'Helen asked me not to smoke in front of the kids, so I won't light up.'

'How do you know Michael and Helen?' I ask.

'I was Mick's best mate at school,' Clifford says. 'I hadn't heard from him for years, until Helen contacted me out of the blue on one of those reunification websites, inviting me to this do.'

'Oh?'

Clare kicks a loose stone towards the border with her toe.

'Sometimes I do Elvis,' Clifford begins, gyrating his hips a few paces down the lawn. 'Sometimes I do me, meself – if you know what I mean.'

I leave Clifford to Clare, calling Lorna over to give Michael his present, breaking up a conversation about who will be the new chairman of the Golf Club.

'Happy Birthday, Michael,' Lorna says.

'Thank you very much.' He tears the paper off. 'Ah, balls. You can never have too many balls when you're a golfer, even one with a low handicap like mine.' He glances over my shoulder. 'Sadie, here's your sister with her handicap.' He grins as if he's made a joke, but I don't find it particularly funny.

'You mean Sean?'

'He is a bit of an idiot, isn't he? He hops around with one foot permanently in his mouth.'

'A bit like Sadie,' Helen comments, moving through to welcome them.

Annette looks different, quite stunning. She's had her hair cut short, and run through with red highlights, and she's wearing a low-cut cream vest and a long khaki skirt. Sean is behind her, hauling on Homer's collar.

'Thanks for inviting us to the party.' Annette smiles and hands over a bottle of wine.

'Why did they have to bring along that dog of theirs?' Helen mutters to me when I go inside with her to help her fetch the drinks. 'They haven't even brought Michael a birthday present.' She stabs a corkscrew into the top of a bottle of wine and twists it furiously. 'I'm surprised that Sean's let Annette spend money on having her hair done.'

'She looks great,' I point out.

Helen's shoulders relax slightly. 'I suppose so,' she says grudgingly. 'For her age,' she adds.

'Talking of age, Clifford can't possibly be Michael's old schoolfriend, can he?'

'Oh yes, he's aged ungracefully.' Helen lowers her voice. 'I wish I'd never invited him. Michael's furious with me. He told me to get Clare to keep him out of Alexander and Pete's way. It turns out that Michael and Clifford fell out over a girl not long after they left school, and never spoke again.'

'Why did Clifford accept your invitation then?'

'I don't know, do I? Why do people go to school reunions?'

'Is that Michael's cake?' I ask, catching sight of a sponge decorated with tiny golfing figures and a ring of gold candles. 'Did you make it?'

'Of course I didn't. I haven't had time. With the work I've been doing at the development, and looking after Charlotte, I haven't had time to wash my floors, let alone make a cake.'

'Cheer up, Helen.'

'I want this party to be a success.'

'It will be.'

It isn't only Helen who is trying to make up with Michael. Tom is too. He takes over operating the barbecue, and the chiminea, in which he's slow-roasting a chicken. He's wandering from one complex marinade to another on the table outside, checking them, tasting them, adding more ingredients: a splash of Tabasco, a pinch of salt, a sprinkling of hot spice.

One or two pigeons home in above us, leaving sizzles of poop on the barbie, which doesn't seem particularly hygienic to me. That's the trouble with barbecues. You can never be sure you're not going to go home with food poisoning. The meat's raw in the middle and burned on the outside, and you wonder how you can find an excuse to pop down the road for chips without appearing ungrateful. I have to say though, as we sit at the hardwood table that matches the decking, that Tom does a better job than most.

'Lovely food, Tom,' I say.

'Thanks,' he mutters.

I'm not the only one who appreciates it. Annette is tucking in as if she hasn't eaten for several weeks. When Michael tops up her glass, she giggles. She seems very drunk, but I know for a fact that she's drinking lemonade because I drank out of her glass by mistake.

'Are you and Helen going on holiday this year?' she asks Michael.

'We haven't booked anything yet,' he says. 'It's this development. Helen doesn't seem able to tear herself away. We might have a winter holiday on the profit Helen and Sadie are going to make.' He's bluffing, of course. He doesn't believe there'll be any profit now that Gareth's gone.

The golfing couples suggest a couple of ideas – a cruise on the *Queen Mary 2*, and a safari combined with ten nights on the Gold Coast.

'Where would you recommend, Annette?' Michael asks. 'You're the expert.'

'I wouldn't rely on Annette to get us anywhere,' Helen cuts in.

'How about Cyprus,' suggests Annette, ignoring her, 'where Aphrodite, Goddess of Love, emerged naked from the waves?'

'Sounds good to me,' says Michael. 'What do you think of Grenadine?'

'Don't you mean Grenada, the Spice Island?' says Annette. 'Sean and I are dreaming of Kos.'

'Isn't that a lettuce?' I say, trying to lighten things up.

'You can't go far wrong with Magaluf,' Clifford interrupts.

'I'll bet you stay in all the best places,' Michael says.

'I get to sleep in the tour bus with the rest of the lads. Hey, do you remember when we borrowed that tent off your dad, Mick, and we stayed at that farm on the coast? Where was it?'

'Can't recall,' says Michael.

'Weymouth. That was it – summer of seventy-three. We filched a couple of firkins of scrumpy, and you had the farmer's daughter in the haybarn. Her dad chased us off with a shotgun.'

There is a deafening silence. Now I know why people go to reunions – to embarrass former acquaintances.

'I suppose your holiday plans depend on the progress of your fertility treatments,' Helen says eventually, turning to Annette.

I flash Helen a warning glance. I thought I'd told her. I *have* told her.

'I suppose it does,' Annette says, smiling sweetly.

'Actually, we've given up trying for a baby,' says Sean, putting his plate down and resting his hands on his thighs. 'We've exhausted every avenue.'

'There were a couple more,' says Annette. 'You said –'

'I know what I said, what we agreed,' Sean interrupts. 'Adoption is a no no. I don't want busybodies from Social Services poking through my private life.'

'I think we should cut the cake,' says Helen, standing up from the table. I help her light the candles in the kitchen before she carries the cake outside, singing 'Happy Birthday' out of tune. Michael blows out the candles. Helen relights them for the children to have a go, then we all sing 'Happy Birthday' again. Helen stands close to Michael, her face bearing a fixed smile, reminding me of Geri Halliwell singing to Prince Charles. Helen doesn't realise how lucky she is – I shan't be singing 'Happy Birthday' to Gareth when he's fifty.

'Where are you off to?' I call to Sam as he runs off

back to where he has been making a small mound of grass pullings in the corner of the lawn.

'Nowhere,' he says. 'I'm bored. I've had more fun at the dentist.'

'What are you doing to Helen's lawn?'

'I'm making a buggery.'

Michael sniggers.

'What's that, Sam?' says Annette.

'We're doing Minibeasts at school. I'm making a trap for them.' He grins suddenly. 'I've already found a snail.'

'Good man. I'll have that,' says Michael, jumping up. 'I can't abide snails. Look what they've done to Helen's marigolds this year.'

Sam fetches the snail on a leaf, and hands the whole thing over to Michael. Michael takes the salt cellar off the table and tips salt over the snail, which tries to retreat, too late, into its shell. At this, Tom, who I thought was such a quiet boy, goes ballistic.

'You bastard!' he shouts. 'You rotten bloody bastard!'

Sam stares, wide-eyed, as Tom steps up close to Michael and aims a punch at his nose. Michael ducks and, being the shorter of the two, gives Tom a swift uppercut with his left, which catches him hard on the chin. Sean and Michael's golf buddies are up on their feet too, Sean grabbing Michael from behind and catching his wrists, Alexander putting Tom in an armlock, while Pete gets in the way.

'That's enough,' Sean growls.

Michael shakes Sean off and inspects his new watch for damage. Cautiously, Alexander releases Tom and brushes down his shirt.

Why does Tom react so violently towards his father, I wonder? Is this about a snail, or Michael disapproving of Tom's choice of degree course, or Michael abandoning Tom when he left Suzanna for Helen?

'Let's calm down, shall we?' Sean suggests. 'Tom, it's your father's birthday.'

'He's no father of mine,' Tom snaps.

'You can stick your baked bananas, you ungrateful little sod,' Michael snaps back. 'You can take your present back too – I've had three "Nifty at Fifty" golfing ties already today.'

Annette's scream of horror breaks the tension. 'Sean, why didn't you remind me? We haven't given Michael his birthday present. It's on the fence-post over there.'

Sean fetches a small package and hands it to Annette, who stands up and hands it to Michael, as if they're indulging in a game of Pass the Parcel. Michael gives her the briefest of kisses on the cheek in exchange. Annette blushes the colour of her highlights as he opens the present to find a mug with the words *Diamond Geezer* splashed across it.

The Diamond Geezer in question does his best to sound suitably grateful. He pours champagne into his new mug, and peace is restored. Clare and her daughter and the golfing couples take their leave. Clifford remains sprawled on his back in a deckchair asleep, his flabby jowls vibrating as he snores. Charlotte and Lorna are playing on the climbing frame. Homer is quietly eating a piece of steak from the barbecue. Sam is trampling the bedding plants for Minibeasts. I wander over to talk to Tom, who is sitting on the bench at the end of the garden in the shadow of the conifer hedge, singing ballads to the accompaniment of his guitar.

'I've always wanted to play the guitar,' I announce. 'I'd like to play slowhand blues like Eric Clapton.'

'I'm planning to audition for the next series of *Pop Idol*.' Tom strums a couple of mournful chords. 'What do you think?'

'Who would you like me to be?' I ask, choked up. 'Foxy or Simon Cowell?' It doesn't matter. Tom's music brings tears to my eyes. 'Did you write those songs yourself?'

Tom nods, and turns back to his guitar. His compositions evoke the pain of love and loss, of being uncertain and alone, emotions that I didn't experience until my break-up with Dan . . . and again now, with Gareth. I leave Tom to it. He's completely spoiled my afternoon, dredging up memories of the not-so-distant past.

Sean is regaling Helen with tales of daring fire rescues which I have heard many times before. I don't know where Annette or Michael are. I excuse myself, and nip inside for a glass of water. As I leave the kitchen, I run into Annette coming down the stairs.

'Where have you been?'

'Looking for the bathroom,' she says, straightening her ruckled skirt.

'The cloakroom's just here.' I point at it.

'You know me. I can't find my way anywhere.'

'Have you seen Michael around?'

'No, I expect he's counting his balls.' Annette grins. 'That's what golfers do, isn't it?'

'Annette!'

'You know, Sadie, just lately you've quite lost your va va voom.' My sister takes my arm and leads me back into the conservatory. She seems to know exactly where she's going now. 'Oh, don't look at me like that. I've made a positive decision to put IT into perspective and try to enjoy life, instead of moping around like some chronic depressive who's forgotten to take her Prozac. It's what you wanted for me, isn't it?' She stares at me. 'I don't understand you. You said you wanted me to be happy. Well, I am.'

'Happy, or manic?'

'I want you to be happy too,' Annette continues, ignoring me. 'Have you heard anything from Gareth?'

I shake my head.

'You and Gareth seemed so right for each other,' she sighs. 'Lorna had even planned how she was going to be bridesmaid at your wedding.'

'I didn't think she liked Gareth that much.'

'She wouldn't care who the bridegroom was. She just wants that princess dress, Sadie. It's every little girl's dream.'

'I'm too old for dreams,' I say glumly.

'I thought you were feeling better,' Annette says. 'You're not dressed head to toe in black today.'

'Only because all my black tops are in the wash.' I can hear footsteps trotting down the stairs beyond. Michael? What's he been up to? My mind begins to run riot. Recovering from a quick assignation with Annette? Surely not.

I reassure myself that Michael would never risk damaging his reputation as a ladies' man by sleeping with someone older than his wife. I am about to step outside with Annette when Michael calls me back.

'Sadie!' he hisses. 'I need a word. *Now!*'

'What is it?'

Michael's face is as white as the icing on his birthday cake. 'Promise you won't breathe a word to Helen.'

'How can I promise that? I'm hopeless at keeping secrets.'

'I know, but it isn't really a secret,' Michael wheedles. 'I don't want to worry her.'

'You're worrying me.'

'It's about the Glowie Balls. I've had a Prohibition notice from the Under Secretary of State for Competition, Consumers and Markets, and a visit from Trading Standards. The Balls have been banned.' He hesitates. 'I thought you should know – I'd hate anything to happen to Sam and Lorna.'

'Why can't we tell Helen?'

'I've paid for twenty thousand crates, each containing a hundred boxes which hold five Glowie Balls each. Work it out!'

'You know I'm no good at maths.'

'I've spent hundreds of thousands of pounds on a product that I can't sell.'

'Can't you send them back?'

'That's what I'm trying to find out. In the meantime, keep your mouth shut!' For Michael, the health of his bank balance is a matter of pride, which is why he doesn't want anyone to know, least of all Helen and his Golf Club friends, when it's a little under the weather. For me, it's a matter of life and death. In spite of my urgent attempts at resuscitation with injections of Michael's cash, my own bank balance remains moribund. I shall have to insist that Dan contributes more than the odd ten or twenty quid here and there for the twins' upkeep.

Outside, giant grey clouds, like the slugs Sam is collecting for his bug-house, as Annette has persuaded him to call it, slip along the horizon, and I push my financial difficulties to the back of my mind. When the first drops of rain fall, I leave with the twins, just as Sean is asking if he can take a doggy bag home for Homer, who is relieving himself in the middle of Helen's Busy Lizzies.

Back at the development, I find water leaking through one corner of Gareth's tarpaulin. It's a typical botch-job, a sign that I shouldn't take him back as my builder, let alone my lover – if he should ever return.

Chapter Fifteen

It is easier to part a fool from his money than confiscate a Glowie Ball from my son. Talking of fools and money, I manage to negotiate a discount from Craig on the basis that if he'd rewired the house properly in the first place, we wouldn't have had to call him back. Lorna gives her Glowie Ball up immediately, saying that it's rubbish anyway. Sam escapes with his in his coat-pocket when Helen calls to pick the twins up for school, because the phone rings, distracting me. It's some distraction. It's Gareth . . .

'Hiya, Sadie,' he says. 'I'm at Gretna Green.'

My mind leaps to the inevitable conclusion – that he's met some woman on his extended holiday in Scotland and married her.

'You could have had the decency to let me know—'

'I *am* letting you know – that's why I'm ringing. I'll be back in to see you tonight.'

'To work?'

'I was hoping we could kiss and make up. I've had time to think. I shouldn't have walked away on your birthday, Sadie,' he says softly. 'I'm sorry . . . but I was so angry with you for doubting me.'

'It turns out that I was right,' I say hotly. There's a man's voice in the background, the slamming of a van door. 'Does your new wife know that you're planning to rekindle our romance?'

'Wife?'

'Why else would you be in Gretna Green?'

'I'm at Gretna Green Services, off the M6.' I can hear the laughter in Gareth's voice. 'I've got to go – my burger's getting cold. I'll see you as soon as I can.'

'I'll have to speak to Helen.' The line goes dead. I clutch the receiver to my breast. What does this mean? If Gareth is prepared to forgive me for suspecting him of having an affair with Teresa, shouldn't I be prepared to forgive him his absence?

Helen disagrees.

'If it wasn't for our deadline, I'd give him the sack.'

'He works hard when he is here,' I say loyally. 'He's always on the job.'

'Yes, the wrong one.'

I admit that Gareth did spend rather a lot of time with me, studying the grain of the bedroom floor-boards.

'You're not considering getting back with him, are you?' Helen nags. 'He didn't try to get in touch once while he was away.'

'He did text me a couple of times.'

'You can't sustain a relationship on text alone.'

What Helen says makes perfect sense, but all sense flies out of my head when Gareth strolls through into the kitchen several hours later, after she has gone home. He looks fitter than ever, and his face bears a healthy tan, along with a few tell-tale midge bites.

'I missed you,' he says, and my stomach turns over.

'Would you like to stay for tea? I'm doing chicken and chips for me and the twins.' Gareth is welcome to my share – I couldn't eat a thing.

'I'll stay if you've got ketchup,' Gareth grins. He moves towards me. I raise my oven-gloved hands and back away.

'Why didn't you ring me? Why did you have to dash off to Scotland out of the blue?'

'Because I'm a selfish, thoughtless member of the male species.'

'I wouldn't care so much if it was just me,' I point out. 'The twins are part of my life whether you like it or not, and you've let them down too – Sam, at least.'

'I'm sorry,' Gareth says, the smile disappearing from his face. 'I didn't think.'

'Obviously not.' My voice chokes up. 'I thought you'd gone for good.'

'I'll never do it again, I promise. I'll give you an advance list of my engagements – people, places and times, if that'll make you happy.' He reaches his arms towards me. 'Being away from you made me realise that what we have is too good to give up.'

How can I resist his seductive words? We hug and kiss until the oven-timer buzzes, bringing the twins from the front room where they've been watching *SpongeBob SquarePants*. If they're surprised to see Gareth, they don't say so.

'Can I help with the roof tomorrow?' Sam asks when we sit down to eat in the dining area, perching on a selection of steps, chairs and stools with our food on our laps.

'I'm afraid I won't be starting on the roof for a while longer,' Gareth says, turning to me.

I'm pretty annoyed, but Helen will be furious.

'Jim, the roofer, fell off a ladder and broke his leg while we were in Scotland. He's going to be out of action for a few weeks, but we'll get it done as soon as we can. Where are you off to, Sadie?'

'To check the weather forecast.' According to Teletext there's a 40 per cent chance of rain, which is a disaster from the fantasy fulfilment angle, but the TV weatherman is more optimistic, and outside the sky is unusually dark. My heart beats faster. I can smell rain.

After tea, I put the twins to bed. They both fall asleep as soon as their heads touch the pillows, allowing me to extricate the Glowie Ball from Sam's grasp and remove it outside to the wheelie bin. Gareth is filling the kettle when I return.

'What on earth do you think you're doing?'

'Making you a cup of tea.'

'I thought we'd go outside.'

'Isn't it raining?' frowns Gareth.

'You're an outdoor kind of man.' I flutter my eyelashes.

'I prefer to spend my spare time indoors when it's tipping it down.'

I remove the kettle from Gareth's hand and place it on the draining board. Gazing up into his eyes, I begin stripping his clothes off, rolling the stretchy material of his vest up over his torso. Gareth puts his arms up and leans his head forward. I pull the vest over his shoulders, over his head, kissing him at the same time, devouring his lips, his mouth, his tongue . . .

'Is it my birthday today?' Gareth says gruffly, as I toss his vest to the floor and turn my attention to unzipping his fly. I slip his shorts and boxers down over the hard muscle of his buttocks.

'You'll soon warm up,' I observe as his whole body shudders at my touch.

'Oh, I'm not cold, especially when you do that!' Suddenly, Gareth hauls me close, slides his hand up the front of my T-shirt and unclips my bra. I kick off my flipflops and wriggle out of my skirt, and Gareth deals with the rest.

He grabs me about the bum and lifts me onto the draining-board. I don't know how he does it – and I don't care. I have my arms around his neck. I can smell his scent of talc, and tomato ketchup. I can feel the stubble on his chin grazing my cheek. My heart pounds. My blood surges. Gareth forces my legs apart, and his tool is about to engage when the sound of rain pattering against the kitchen window impinges on what's left of my consciousness.

I close my knees sharpish, and summon all my reserves to resist. 'No!'

Gareth's face falls. 'Don't you want me?'

'Outside!' I slip off the draining-board, take Gareth's hand and lead him towards the back door.

'What if someone sees us?' he says.

'No excuses. You promised we'd make love naked in the rain. If we don't do it now, who knows how long we'll have to wait for another anticyclone?'

Gareth bursts out laughing. 'And I was worrying that you fancied the weatherman.'

We dash outside, tripping over the buckets and tubs that Tom has left lying around on the bare earth that is supposed to form a base for the crazy-paving patio. Gareth is glancing all around him, and I wonder if he's having second thoughts, but it turns out that he's looking for a secluded spot that is conducive to lovemaking. There is no scented bower of dripping roses, no soft bed of leaves, so we make do with me standing on a stack of paving slabs and pressed back against the wall beside the kitchen window. It doesn't matter. It's fantastic. Me and Gareth. The heat of Gareth's body. The shocking sting of the rain. Gareth inside me. The rain hammering down faster and faster with each rhythmic thrust until I am oblivious to the jagged bricks grazing my skin.

I love the rain. I love Gareth. I can hold back my feelings no longer. As my body bucks against his, I open my mouth and yell at the top of my voice, 'I love you . . . !'

Gareth responds with a series of groans, then rests his head on my shoulder until he catches his breath enough to be able to speak.

'Sadie,' he says, 'you're gorgeous.'

Gareth saying that I'm gorgeous isn't the same as saying that he's in love with me, is it, I muse as we drip our way indoors. Gareth is limping, holding his left buttock as he makes tea.

'Are you all right?'

'I've got a touch of sciatica,' he says, reminding me that we aren't a pair of teenagers. We retire to bed with a cup of tea, another sign of age, I suppose. I lie on my back with my hands up behind my head. It's a deliberate manoeuvre – when I'm on my back, by some miracle my belly almost disappears. Unfortunately, my boobs do too – I look as if I have an extra-large fried egg in each armpit. Gareth pulls the duvet down and strokes my body, almost unconsciously it seems, like I do with Alvin.

Does it matter that Gareth doesn't love me? I can live with that as long as he isn't in love with anyone else, but how do I know? When he's away at nights, he says he's at his mother's. When he's late, he says he's meeting his rugby mates. When he isn't here during the working day, he says he's troubleshooting at one of the other jobs he took on at the same time. How can I keep a closer eye on him?

I recall Annette's comments about Lorna wanting a bridesmaid's dress. I wonder. I shall never marry again, but moving in? There's an idea.

'Why don't you move in with us?' I suggest.

Gareth's brow furrows. He doesn't want to, does he? He doesn't want to be tied down. He doesn't want me.

'It would be rather convenient,' he begins.

'Convenient?' I'm asking because I want to be with you, I don't say. I want to fall asleep in your arms, and wake up with your breath warm against my cheek.

'That isn't the response you wanted, is it?' Gareth pauses. 'I'm sorry, Sadie. I'm no good at the hearts and flowers, and small talk.'

'At romance, you mean?'

'Yeah, that.' His fingers trace the contour of my collar-bone. 'I'd like to move in, if that's what you want.'

'What about your mother? Won't you have to have a word with her first?'

'I'll speak to her when we collect my things. It'll be better if I don't give her too much time to list her objections.'

'I didn't think you'd be such a mummy's boy.'

'She's on her own. I'm all she has left.' Gareth cuddles up to me. Within seconds, he is snoring, whereas I lie awake worrying about what the twins will say when I tell them in the morning.

'Lorna and Sam, I have something important to say,' I announce at breakfast-time.

'Have you seen my Glowie Ball?' Sam interrupts. 'I had it last night, and now it's gone.'

'Gareth is coming to live with us.'

'Okay,' says Sam. 'Is there a packet of Cheerios some-where? I've gone off cornflakes.'

'So it's all right?'

'Fine,' says Sam, emerging from the cupboard, spilling Cheerios in a trail across the floor to the worktop. 'I don't suppose he'll want to stay long.'

'He can't stay here.' Lorna's face flushes with fury. 'You're only doing this to get back at Dad.'

'Who says so?'

'Dad did.'

'How? No one knew Gareth was moving in until last night, and that includes Gareth himself.'

'Dad warned us that this would happen. I don't

want Gareth living with us. He isn't anything to do with our family.'

'He's my boyfriend.'

'I don't care.' Lorna storms out into the back garden. 'I don't want Gareth here.'

I am torn, shredded right through, like the mustard curtain that dangles from the rail above the kitchen window. I should have asked the twins before I invited Gareth to move in, but I thought they were both used to him. I thought Lorna wouldn't mind. What about Gareth's mother Kath, I wonder as I help Sam search for his Glowie Ball, afraid to tell him that I've thrown it away. Will she object too? When we drive off to Kath's house the next day – me, Gareth and the twins in the Peugeot – I can't help feeling a little apprehensive.

'Stop worrying, Sadie,' says Gareth as we follow the twins up the steps to Kath's house. 'My old mum will adore you,' and, once more, I picture a dowager with glasses on a string around her neck, and a hump. The reality is somewhat different. A woman wearing jeans and a pale blue roll-neck sweater, who looks more like she should be Gareth's sister than his mother, opens the door and introduces herself as Kath.

It is as if she has been waiting for us. In fact, she *has* been waiting for us, I think, letting my eyes sweep over the stack of crates and cardboard boxes in the hall that are crammed with clothes, CDs and books. She has coffee on. I can smell it, percolating through notes of cinnamon and apple pie.

'You're late as usual,' she says, greeting Gareth with a hug before turning to me and the twins. I realise that my attempt at reading character from the handwriting on the shopping list Gareth was carrying when I chased him into Waitrose was pretty inaccurate. Pessimistic? A control freak? Kath is neither of these. She's warm and down to earth, just like her son.

'I can't tell you what a weight this is off my mind,' she says. 'I've been trying to tell him, in the most tactful way of course, that he can't stay here for ever, and now it's done for me. I am very grateful, Sadie.' As if to show her gratitude, she gives the twins a fiver each, which goes down very well, especially with Lorna who had to be dragged out with us, kicking and screaming.

'I thought you liked having me here, Mum,' says Gareth.

'I do. I did. It was wonderful to start with,' she says, 'but after a while . . .'

'I got on your nerves,' Gareth interrupts.

'I'm like you. Sometimes, I need my own space. I like to wake up when I'm ready, not when some clumsy builder son of mine brings me tea at seven in the morning.'

'I thought you liked it.'

'I do, occasionally.'

'What about doing your shopping?'

'I can take the bus. I enjoy taking the bus. It's a great way to meet people.' She looks at me. 'I'm used to travelling on public transport since I lost my licence for that silly oversight of mine.'

'Oversight?'

'I had one too many gins one afternoon, and was arrested for performing an illegal manoeuvre at the

Robin Hood roundabout. Serves me right.' She offers us coffee. Gareth asks if we can take her out to lunch. She declines.

'I've invited Desmond here to celebrate his retirement – he used to drive the K1 bus into Kingston.' She smiles. 'It'll be nice to be able to invite him back without worrying that Gareth is going to turn up at any minute. Don't look so shocked, Gareth. I don't see why I should live the life of a celibate because I'm on the wrong side of sixty.'

'But your heart?' says Gareth.

'I'm fine. Yes, it gave me a scare when I had to go into hospital for those tests, but the doctors have given me the all clear. Now, if you'd just load this up as quickly as possible, I need to wash my hair.'

'Is this all you have?' I ask as we carry boxes down the steps to the car.

'I travel light,' Gareth says.

'I'm being sarcastic. How do you think we'll fit all that in the car, let alone the house?' I peer down, cross-eyed, at the top of the box I'm carrying. 'What's in these things anyway?'

'That's my train set,' Gareth confesses.

My jaw drops.

'It's all right, Sadie,' he chuckles. 'I haven't got an anorak to go with it.'

'Why don't you get rid of it if you don't play with it any more?' I tease.

'It brings back happy memories,' Gareth says more seriously.

'It's the one Gareth had for his twelfth birthday,'

Kath informs me. 'He used to spend hours planning layouts with his dad.'

Before I can apologise for my flippant remark about the train set, Gareth says, 'I thought Sam might like to help me set it up sometime once we've finished the house.'

My throat tightens as I picture Gareth and Sam building a railway together like a father and his son. If I thought I couldn't possibly fall more deeply in love with Gareth, I was wrong . . .

We manage to force Gareth's belongings into the boot, and on the way home, Gareth starts singing along to Van Morrison's 'Brown-eyed Girl' on the radio. He gazes out of the window. His mind is elsewhere, and it needles me.

'Can't we have the Sugababes tape?' Lorna whines.

'No, you can't! We're almost home.' I run my hand along Gareth's thigh and give it a squeeze. 'What are you thinking about?' I ask.

'Nothing,' he says.

'She had brown eyes, didn't she?'

'Who?'

'Alison, your ex-fiancée.'

Gareth frowns. 'Alison . . . ? Yes, she did,' he says eventually. 'I'd forgotten. How did you know?'

'I guessed.' I pause. 'I bet you don't know what colour mine are.'

'Of course I do,' he says, staring at me as I drive. 'They're like woodsmoke.'

If that's meant to be a compliment, I don't take it as one. I stamp my foot on the accelerator and send the car off too fast, jerking Gareth forwards in the passenger seat.

'I didn't start this conversation,' he reminds me.

'Well, you shouldn't have looked all wistful when you were singing about brown eyes.'

'It's a song, Sadie. I can't change the words. Specially as "woodsmoke-eyed girl" doesn't fit.' He's joking, but it rankles. I know it's ridiculous when it's me Gareth's moving in with, but I don't like the way that the name of someone who's supposed to be an ex lingered on his tongue.

No sooner has Gareth settled his feet under the table (metaphorically speaking, since we still don't have a table) and his boxes in the hall, than there is a knock on the front door and Tom appears, carrying his guitar over his shoulder and a rucksack on his back.

'Hi, Sadie.' He runs one hand through his long, limp hair. 'Everything's gone a bit like, you know, heavy.'

'You mean you've been kicked out.'

'Is there any chance of board and lodging?' he asks apologetically.

I think for a moment. It would be a help to Helen if Tom was living here, instead of causing trouble between her and Michael, and perhaps she could persuade Michael to contribute towards Tom's keep: anything to ease my cashflow problems. I feel sorry for Tom too. Helen blames him for anything and everything that goes wrong in her household. He could probably do with a break.

'I might have a vacancy,' I say, smiling, 'if you agree

to do all the cooking as well as getting on with the garden, which I notice isn't coming along very well.'

'It'll be much easier if I'm on site,' Tom says. 'Helen's been trying to get me out for ages. She's been leaving a video of *The Beach* lying around in the hope I'll watch it and be attracted by the drugtaking culture to go off to Thailand for a while.' He pauses. 'Are you sure this is all right?'

Of course I am. I move Tom into the third bedroom. Lorna is miffed because she's had her eye on it since Helen and I finished decorating it in a compromise colour of apricot white. Gareth is unhappy about Tom staying too.

'What's he doing here?' he complains later.

'I said he could stay for a while. He's fallen out with Michael.'

'I was looking forward to it being just us two. You know, romantic dinners and all that.' I open my mouth to object – not to the idea of romantic dinners, but to Gareth's suggestion that there are just two of us to consider – but he pre-empts me by continuing, 'At least the twins are tucked up in bed by eight o'clock so we can have the rest of the evenings to ourselves.'

'I hate to disillusion you, but Sam's often still up practising karate chops on the landing at nine, and Lorna comes down at least three or four times after I've kissed her goodnight.'

'Why?' Gareth looks appalled.

'All kinds of reasons – she's having a bad dream, she's forgotten to warm her Beddy Bear up in the microwave, she wants a drink, or just a cuddle.' I pat

Gareth on the bum. 'You'll get used to it.' At least I hope he will. 'Tom won't be any trouble,' I add.

Famous last words. There are queues for the bathroom, and Gareth and I have about as much privacy as Michael Douglas and Catherine Zeta Jones had at their wedding, but there is a buzz about the house. I love it. Sam loves it. Tom is like a big brother, someone to play football with, and to teach him the guitar. Lorna loves the idea of Tom living here because she can lord it over Charlotte. Dare I hope that she's beginning to accept that Gareth is part of our lives? I've noticed that she included him when she counted out the cutlery for tea, and the choc ices for afters.

And Gareth? I love seeing his razor in the bathroom, the shavings of stubbly hairs in the sink and the smudges of building sand on his towel. I can't wait to tell Helen that he's moved in, but when I phone her, she's out. I assume that Michael has roped her in to helping with the last-minute touches to the newly refurbished shop, which opens tomorrow. Topsy is going to do a bit of juggling – she can just about keep three balls in the air at the same time. Four is impossible. It's like me trying to juggle the roles of mother, lover, property developer and magic operative. At midnight, I am hardboiling the last few eggs from the fridge for Topsy's latest trick. I leave them in a bowl on the hob to cool down. In the morning, they have disappeared. Someone other than Topsy has magicked them away, and I bet I know who.

I burst into Tom's room without knocking. 'What happened to my eggs?'

Tom's head appears from underneath his duvet. 'I

313

had a snack,' he admits eventually. 'I didn't think anyone would mind.'

'I mind. Go and buy me some more.'

'Now?' he groans.

'Now,' I confirm. 'There's a container in Topsy's box of props. Put them in there.' I hesitate before I leave his room. 'What's that smell?'

'My skanky trainers,' Tom says sheepishly.

I pick them up from the heap of clothes on the floor, wondering if I should have worn gloves, open the window and put them out on the sill.

'I need those,' Tom protests.

'You bring them in when you're ready to put them on,' I say. 'I am not letting those shoes back in my house. Is that clear?'

When I return downstairs, Gareth is already putting his boots on. 'Where are *you* going?' I say irritably.

'Tolworth.'

'I thought you'd finished there ages ago.'

'So did I.'

'What's the problem?'

'That rain we had the other night . . .'

My skin tingles at the thought. I run my fingers down the side of Gareth's cheek.

'You said that you'd fixed Teresa's roof.'

'She says her gutters aren't draining into the down-pipes on the extension.'

'What about my gutters? What about my roof? My new kitchen? My bathroom?'

'I'll get on with them as soon as I can. I promise, Sadie . . .'

I sigh inwardly. It isn't all Gareth's fault. We're still waiting for the plasterer to deal with the kitchen walls before Gareth can put the kitchen in. The kitchen is here, stacked up in our way in the dining area.

'Are you going to drop into Michael's shop this morning?' I ask.

'Sorry, Sadie, I'm too busy. I'm sure Topsy'll be a hit though.'

I watch Gareth go. The Neighbour From Hell accosts him briefly as he gets into the pick-up, and I find myself wishing that I could lip-read.

While Tom goes out for eggs, and Sam and Lorna rifle through Topsy's props, I dress and apply my make-up. Today, I draw a tear below my left eye – our dead-line for finishing the development is slipping away further into the future.

Michael is doing better in business than me and Helen, judging by the appearance of his shop. It is filled with those must-have items that end up in the back of the cupboard, or in the bin – the contoured foot-spas, battery-powered salt grinders that cost less than the batteries to put inside them, and boxes of Sing-a-long Christmas lights with a choice of a static or pulsing display, accompanied by traditional music or Rock 'n' Roll. I am tempted by the lights, and a Festive Tin Fireguard, but Christmas is still fourteen weeks away.

When I arrive with the twins, Michael is putting up a banner across the front of the shop, and Helen is organising the tills. I squeeze Topsy and her hoop between the handpainted porcelain woodland fairies and all-

315

surface dusters, finding a space where she can perform. Sam drops the bag of balloons he was carrying for me at my feet, and wanders outside to talk to Michael.

'I'll help you,' says Lorna. 'Charlotte will too,' she adds, as Charlotte turns up from the back of the shop with plastic tumblers for the wine that Michael has arranged in order to lure potential customers inside. I give the girls a modelling balloon each to blow up. Charlotte insists on having a second one, so that she can make a pair of earrings which we attach to her head by tying them on to her hair with pieces of ribbon. Sam turns up too, but he doesn't want a balloon. He wants a replacement Glowie Ball. When I explain, out of Helen's earshot, that there are no more Glowie Balls, he decides that he'll have one of the disc guns that Michael has on display instead.

'Please, Mum.'

'I'll see . . .'

Helen leaves the tills and joins me.

'This is going to be a very long day,' she complains.

I can't wait any longer to tell her. 'Gareth moved in this weekend.'

Helen puts on her disapproving face. 'Don't come crying to me when he moves out again.'

'Can't you be pleased for me?'

'Oh, all right,' she says grudgingly. 'If he makes you happy . . .'

'I don't want to spend the rest of my life on my own.'

'Sometimes that seems like an attractive proposition,' Helen sighs. 'Michael checked my credit-card statement – the one he knows about – the other day.

I'd swear he's been taking lessons in tightfistedness from Sean.' She brightens slightly. 'I'm sure things will get better between us now that Tom's moved out. Michael's hoping that he's hitched his way back to university.'

'Tom's moved in with me.'

'Really? You must be nuts, Sadie. You know what trouble I've had with that boy.'

'He didn't have anywhere else to go.'

'The ungrateful brat has a place in a hall of residence at university, a room that's been paid for, and is now standing empty.'

'Tom's hardly a brat,' I observe. 'He's eighteen. He has to make up his own mind what he wants to do. I admire him for standing up for himself.'

'He isn't standing up for himself, is he, not with you taking him in and offering him work?'

'I thought you might ask Michael to release the next tranche of cash for the development?'

'Me? What next tranche? He's paid out all we asked for in the beginning, and more.'

'What about the contingency fund?'

'There never was a contingency fund. You said we wouldn't need one.'

'Well, I ought to pay Tom for the gardening.'

'You mean, you want Michael to pay Tom, so that Tom can pay you for his keep?'

'Please, Helen, I'm really short this month.'

'You'll have to ask Michael yourself. Whenever I mention money at the moment, he flies off the handle.'

'What about *Llamedos*?' It doesn't sound as if

Michael's sorted out the return of the banned Glowie Balls, and without his money, I'm in trouble. If I keep defaulting on the mortgage payments, I'll be in danger of losing the house altogether.

'Helen! Give us a hand, will you?' Michael calls from outside.

'I'm on my way!'

A pair of elderly ladies drift in at nine thirty to drink wine, and drift off again, only to return later with friends, so that by eleven the shop is crammed with tipsy pensioners. Topsy is slightly tipsy too.

'Keep some of the wine back,' Michael tells me and Helen. 'Don't let them have more than three cups each. Now, please will you go out on the street and persuade some mums and tots to come in and watch Topsy – perhaps they'll buy more than a few clothes-pegs and tea-towels.'

I perform for a pale, harassed-looking mother and her two toddlers, who are not particularly interested until I start the egg in a bag routine. I show them the pouch, casting a warning glance towards Sam who is watching from beside me with the girls. The pouch is empty. Abracadabra, and there's an egg inside it. Charlotte begs to be the one who takes it out for Topsy. In dives her hand. Scrunch. Out comes the dripping remains of a raw egg.

'Sadie, you're making a mess!' shrieks Helen, at which the toddlers burst into tears. Lorna consoles them with a balloon while Helen cleans up Charlotte and the floor, and Sam jumps about, laughing.

'Someone played a trick on Topsy,' he chuckles.

'It was Tom,' I seethe. 'He ate Topsy's eggs last night, and forgot to boil the ones he replaced them with, or maybe I forgot to tell him to boil them before he put them in with Topsy's props.' I'm not sure why Helen is so upset about a broken egg. She looks about as tearful as the toddlers who are leaving the shop with their mother. 'At least you've got plenty of cheap cleaning materials to hand.' I look up. Annette's here. She's talking to Michael at the tills, quite animatedly if they're merely discussing the price of the candles that she's holding.

'Michael's having an affair,' Helen says glumly.

'Whatever makes you think that?'

'The way he's behaving, how he runs off and hides when he makes phone calls, his lack of interest in the bedroom.'

I realise that Michael has a way with women – look how easily he chats to Annette – but he doesn't come across as the unfaithful type. 'There must be another explanation,' I say, trying to reassure Helen.

'How can there be?' She pauses. 'He denies it, of course.'

'Helen, I'm sorry.'

'I really didn't think he'd do this to me,' she sniffs. 'I'll find out the truth, and when I do, I'll kill him.'

Annette wends her way along the aisle, stepping over boxes that have spewed out their contents of sports socks and tinsel, to interrupt our conversation.

'Michael says to ask if there's any wine left?' she says breezily. There is, and I pour cups for Annette, Helen, Michael and me, and we drink a toast to the shop's future.

'What did you buy, Annette?' I peer into my sister's

bag and try to sound excited about a set of aromatherapy candles which are on special offer. 'Very nice.'

'Michael let me have them for free.'

'Mikey, you didn't?' Helen flashes him a look.

'Let's call it a gift to thank Annette for turning up this morning,' Michael says smoothly. 'She didn't have to waste the last day of the school holidays here.'

'I've rather enjoyed myself,' Annette says, her cheeks colouring slightly.

'Strange woman,' Helen mutters into my ear.

When Annette has gone, Michael tries to justify his charitable gesture.

'That sister of yours can be very pushy when she wants something, Sadie.'

'So can I. As you're giving stuff away, I'd like one of those disc guns for Sam and a packet of those butterfly hairclips for Lorna.'

Michael looks towards Helen.

'I suppose so,' she says reluctantly.

Helen might be annoyed at Michael's generosity, but Sam is delighted.

'Thanks, Mum,' he says when I give him the disc gun on the way back home.

'It's for keeping your mouth shut while Topsy was working today. Don't tell me that I never give you anything.'

'Hey, Mum, is that our bathroom?' Lorna says when I park outside the house.

'What's it doing in the garden?' asks Sam.

'That's exactly what I'm going to find out,' I say, slamming the car door behind me.

I tackle Gareth, who's sitting in the Director's chair with a can of lager open at his feet.

'Why did you have to take the bathroom out today?'

'Calm down, Sadie. I was back early. I thought you'd be pleased – it has to come out sometime.'

'I was looking forward to a long soak in the bath.'

'Well, it's done now. The water's back on so you can wash in the kitchen sink. There's a bucket in the bathroom for everything else, and a curtain across the doorway – I had to take the door off to get the bath out.'

'When will you have the new suite plumbed in?'

'Two days.' Gareth smiles. 'Long enough to put pressure on Tom to move back in with Helen and Michael, I hope. He didn't get up till three, and then he spent the rest of the afternoon pottering about in the garden. When I asked him what he was doing, he said he was meditating. Meditating might be good for Tom's state of mind, but watching him do it really winds me up. You haven't persuaded Michael to contribute to Tom's food and lodging yet, have you, only I might feel better about him being here if he was paying his way.'

I shake my head, but Sam makes further discussion impossible. Accompanied by space-age sound effects and blinking lights, he shoots at Gareth with the disc gun. Foam discs come flying out at great speed and bounce off him, the walls and the telly . . . Gareth jumps up, wrestles the gun away from him, and shoots him back. Giggling, Lorna runs into the line of fire, grabs a handful of discs that head her way, and races out through the kitchen and into the back garden.

'Lorna!' Sam yells. 'Mum, she's nicked my discs.'

'I'll get them. Take that and keep me covered,' Gareth says, handing the gun back to Sam. Gareth chases after Lorna. Sam follows Gareth, and I tag along behind Sam. Lorna stands beside the old pear tree, waving the discs.

'Can't catch me,' she teases.

'Want to bet?' Gareth laughs, and lunges towards her.

'Mum!' Lorna throws the discs towards me. Sam tries to intercept them, but he's too late. I sweep them up and hold them above my head.

'Don't move,' Sam warns, 'or I'll shoot.' He nods towards Gareth who runs in and grapples with me.

'I give in,' I shriek, flinging the discs in all directions. 'Take me prisoner. Do what you will with me.'

'That's some invitation,' Gareth chuckles as he pulls me close, then kisses me full on the lips. When I can finally tear myself away, I find that the twins are searching around the garden for missing discs instead of making rude comments about how sick kissing is, as they usually do.

'Will you help us, Gareth?' Sam calls.

'Please . . .' adds Lorna.

'Of course,' Gareth says.

'I shouldn't be too quick to assist,' I warn him. 'They'll make you their slave.'

'It'll take some of the burden off you,' he says with a grin.

I smile to myself. He'll learn.

Once the twins are in bed, Gareth tells me that The Neighbour From Hell threatened to report to the police any further lewd behaviour that he might see whilst enjoying the view from the rear of his house, in spite of the fact that Gareth offered to replace his shiplap fence.

'We'd better behave lewdly upstairs then,' I suggest.

'Not this evening,' Gareth says. 'I'm meeting Niall and Rob. Their wives have given them special dispensation to enjoy a Saturday night out.'

'I haven't given you special dispensation.'

'You're not my wife.' He kisses me hard on the lips. 'I'll see you later.'

Later? I spend the evening studying Tom's drawings for the garden while he strums his guitar. At midnight, I call Gareth's mobile. Someone answers it – I think it's Rob – and gives an incoherent explanation of where Gareth is. In the background, someone else, another male voice, says, 'Ooh, she's checking up on you . . .' and then the phone goes dead. When I ring back, it's been switched off. It's still switched off the following morning.

I'm trying to prepare breakfast around the boxes that contain the new kitchen units, while Sam complains about the splinters in his feet and Lorna moans about the bathroom arrangements. In desperation, I decide to seek comfort at Dan's. It isn't Dan, but Wendy who answers the door.

'I thought you were in Newquay?' I stammer, as I watch her arrange a scarlet kimono, embroidered with fire-breathing dragons, over a set of paw-print pyjama shorties.

'Wendy-pops, who is it at this time of the morning?'

Dan appears behind her, rubbing his eyes. 'Sadie, what are you doing here?'

'I wouldn't have come if I'd known.'

'You'd better come in,' Wendy says. 'I'll leave you to it, Dan.' She kisses him. He kisses her back, pulling her into full body contact. It's strange. I thought I'd be devastated to see him being intimate with another woman, but I don't mind at all. I'm pleased for him – and just a little embarrassed.

'Can I use your toilet, Dad?' Lorna interrupts, pushing past. 'I'm busting.'

'We have no bathroom, and she refuses to use the bucket,' I explain.

'I'll see you at the gym, darling,' Dan says, pinching Wendy's bottom before she runs next door to her house.

Dan and I chat over coffee while the twins are in the bath.

'Wendy's working extra hours to pay off the bills she ran up while she was in Newquay,' Dan says. 'Listen, Sadie, I know I said I'd pay some money into your account, but can I leave it for a month or so? I'm a bit short.' He hesitates. 'I don't earn nearly as much as I used to, whereas you'll soon be raking it in.'

'Actually, I'm brassic.' I bury my head in my hands. 'All that money I had from the sale of the house, I've spent it – and more. I can't even afford to pay off the minimum amounts on my credit card any more.' I look up again.

Dan is frowning. 'What are you going to do?'

'Go to Bingo? Play the Lottery? Take up religion and pray for a miracle?'

'I would suggest that I moved somewhere smaller, but I don't think that's possible,' Dan says, 'unless I move in with Wendy. I'll ask her, then I can pay you the equivalent of the rent. It's for the twins though, not the development.' He scratches his cheek. 'The things people do for money . . . That surfer Wendy met thought he'd cash in on the dog. He wasn't interested in Wendy at all.'

'Where is Vinnie?'

'Wendy's left him with her mum. It just goes to show how much she loves me, giving up her dog like that.'

'Who's to say she isn't going to run off with the next pretty boy she meets?'

'You're such a cynic, Sadie. I trust Wendy. Relationships are built on trust.'

'I can't trust Gareth,' I blurt out, my eyes pricking with tears.

'You'll drive him away, if you feel like that,' says Dan. 'When Wendy left me, I learned exactly how painful it is to find out that the love of your life is having an affair. I know how you felt when we broke up.'

'You didn't have an affair.'

Dan stands up and looks out of the window, then turns back and looks me straight in the eyes.

'You did!' I gasp.

'With someone at work. I could say that your possessiveness drove me to it, but it was my choice.'

'You lied to me. You made me believe it was all my fault that our marriage failed.' All the anger and hurt that I thought I'd worked through after the divorce comes flooding back.

'I'm sorry, Sadie.'

'Sorry? Is that all you can say? I've been floundering in a mire of guilt for allowing our family to break up while you pretended you had nothing to do with it. How could you?'

'Shh,' Dan warns. 'These walls are like cardboard.'

'I think it's better that Wendy hears us so she knows what you're really like!'

'I was thinking of the twins,' Dan says, glancing towards the ceiling. 'Isn't it too late to be apportioning blame?' he goes on quietly.

I bite my lip. It's true. We've both moved on, yet I am afraid that even if I can let it go, the fact that Dan lied to me for so long will niggle at me, like one of those splinters in Sam's feet.

'I'd love to see you happily settled with Gareth,' Dan says. 'Sam likes him, and now Lorna's mellowing towards him. She told me that he whizzed her up and down the road in his wheelbarrow. She says that he makes you laugh . . .'

It's true. However, after four days without a bathroom, nothing that Gareth says or does can make me laugh any more.

'You'll have it back tomorrow,' Gareth promises when I get home. 'Why don't you go round to Helen's for a while and have a soak in her bath, like she suggested?'

Why not? She's out shopping. Michael's playing golf. I keep a spare key to their house for emergencies.

'Will you come, Gareth?'

'It's a tempting offer, but the lady of the house will

be livid with me if I haven't finished connecting the taps by tonight,' he says ruefully, 'especially as she has a deadline to keep.' He lowers his voice. 'I saw the letter from the Building Society among all your other bills and final demands today.'

'They're threatening to repossess this place.'

'Does Helen know how bad it is?'

I shake my head.

'Don't you think you should tell her? You are supposed to be partners.' Gareth tries again. 'She can ask Michael to help you out. You can pay him back when you sell up.'

'Michael says he's paid in more than enough already.'

'I've got some savings.'

'I'm supposed to be paying you.'

'You can settle up when you've sold the house. Please, Sadie, I'd like to help.'

'If you're sure . . .' I leave for Helen's light of step, in spite of the fact that I've put on half a stone over the summer. I knew something would turn up. Michael turns up too, as I'm standing in his shower, clearing my sinuses with the steam unit on full and listening to the booming repertoire of a whale voice choir. I realise as I emerge dripping and red-faced that it isn't a good time to ask him for more money, but he isn't as angry as I expected him to be. I whisk my clothes up from the floor in the bedroom and clutch them to my body. Michael sits on the bed and yanks at his tie, loosening it from his collar.

'Helen said you'd be playing golf.'

'I'm resting my shoulder – I wrenched it last time I

played.' He then decides to tell me the truth. 'Actually, I'm waiting for a call from my agent in China about returning a consignment of Glowie Balls. I'm pretty confident that I'll get my money back soon.'

Confident enough to write me another cheque? Like a worn-out Glowie Ball, Michael seems to have lost some of his shine. I notice too that he's still wearing his outdoor shoes.

'Look, I'll go as soon as I've dressed and cleaned your shower.'

'No, don't bother. Helen will only clean it again before she uses it.' Michael changes the subject. 'How's that son of mine?'

'Eating me out of house and home.'

'You'd better send him out to work then, or kick him out altogether.'

'I couldn't do that. Tom isn't that much of a trial to live with.' If I say it often enough, I might begin to believe it.

Chapter Sixteen

If Topsy did possess the kind of magic powers that Lorna believes she has, they wouldn't be powerful enough to evict Tom from *Llamedos*. It would take something stronger, like voodoo.

After six weeks of his dirty socks and stinking trainers, I decide to take action, even if he is finally making inroads into the gardening. If Tom doesn't move out soon, Gareth will. On the Friday just before the October half-term, I leave the twins with Gareth after school and drop in at Helen's with Charlotte. My plan is to attempt to reconcile Tom with Helen and Michael so that he moves back in with them.

Helen has been waiting in all day for the courier from *Next*.

'Hello, darling,' she says, taking Charlotte's schoolbag at the door. 'How was your day?' She opens the schoolbag and pulls out a lunchbox. 'You've left your roll again.'

'I hate ham rolls. Can't I have strawberry jam instead?'

'Of course not.'

'Lorna does.'

Helen looks at me.

'I ran out of cheese and pickle.'

'It's a pity that the school doesn't enforce some consistency in their policy on healthy eating,' Helen says. 'Have they started the auditions for the Christmas play yet?'

'No, Mum,' Charlotte says, 'and I'm not going to be in it this year, so there.'

'But it's your ambition to go on the stage,' Helen protests. 'I thought you wanted to be a dancer or an actress.'

'Oh, I want to be on the stage,' says Charlotte. 'When I'm older I'm going to be a clown like Topsy.'

'Not if I can help it,' Helen mutters as her daughter skips off upstairs.

'What happened to her plan to be a world-class swimmer?' I ask.

'Charlotte still enjoys her swimming, but I'm trying to steer her more towards the performing arts.' Helen pauses. 'Don't look at me like that, Sadie. I'm not expecting her to win an Oscar. I just want her to have the opportunities that I didn't. I don't want Charlotte ending up like me, and you. Talking of careers, being at home today has made me realise that I need a break,' she continues. 'I am entitled to holidays, aren't I? I haven't had a day off since we started this project.'

You have, I want to say. You've had loads of time off. You don't know what work is.

However, Helen does look rough. If she's been

applying anything to the bags under her eyes, I'd recommend that she insists on having a full refund.

'I never have time to clean my own place. Just look at it.' Helen appears to have thrown herself into clearing up. The air reeks of Pledge and Mr Muscle, and there are heaps of black bin-liners in the hall. 'I didn't have time to do my usual springclean. When I agreed to help you do up that house, you told me that all it needed was some cosmetic work. I thought we'd have it ready to dress by now.'

'We will soon.'

'You've said that so many times that I don't believe you any more.'

I follow Helen into the kitchen.

'Open the wine. It's in the rack there,' she says, pointing. 'Corkscrew's in the drawer.' She hacks at ham and tears at fresh basil with the ferocity of an electric shredder, and chucks it all into a saucepan with some sundried tomatoes.

'Helen, I'd like to arrange for Tom to have a chat with you and Michael.'

'I wonder why that could be?'

I can tell from her tone of voice that I'm not going to get anywhere. I slench back a glass of wine. 'What are you cooking?'

'Pasta. Do you want to try some?'

'I don't want to eat Michael's dinner.'

'Michael's gone,' Helen says abruptly.

'What do you mean "gone"? Has Michael moved out?'

Helen bursts into tears.

'Why? When?' I reach my arm around her shoulder. 'What happened?'

'I accused him of having an affair.' She grabs for the nearest cloth, which turns out to be a duster, and sneezes. 'The bastard didn't deny it. The double bastard!' She sneezes again. 'I shall never forgive him. Never!'

'Where's he gone?'

'He's sleeping in the flat above the shop in the High Street – he'll find out just how comfortable those cheap easy-fold sun-loungers really are.'

'Michael seems to have been under some stress recently,' I suggest, recalling his problems with the Glowie Balls. 'Perhaps he's having a breakdown of some kind.'

'No, he's just being an idiot. It turns out that he was blacklisted by the Golf Club for abusing a green.'

'He did what?'

'He lost his temper after hitting three balls into the rough. He pulled the flag out of the eighteenth hole and snapped it in two, then cut up the turf with his club.' Helen bites her lip. 'He didn't tell me straight away – he said he was too ashamed, and worried that I'd feel as if I'd lost my status in the community. I said how could I be sorry that I was no longer a golf widow, and he got really angry.'

'Have you told Charlotte?'

'I'll tell her when I'm ready. She thinks her dad's on a business trip.'

'If you want to talk, just call me,' I offer. 'It's the least I can do after all that you did for me when Dan left.'

* * *

I try to help Helen over the next couple of weeks, as much as she'll let me. I worry about her being alone at home, and do all that I can to encourage her to spend more time at the development. I don't give rein to my suspicions that Annette might have something to do with her marital break-up. I still don't understand what my sister and Michael were doing upstairs at Michael's party. Nor do I enlighten Helen as to the state of the finances. I don't tell her that we're at risk of losing the house altogether, that we'll be left in considerable debt, not profit, if that should happen.

We are nowhere nearly finished. Each little job that you imagine will take half an hour, ends up taking half a day. Helen seems to find some consolation in chatting to Gareth, which I wouldn't mind so much if Gareth ever finished anything off.

'Aren't you supposed to be putting the mirror up in the bathroom, Helen?' I interrupt when I find her and Gareth gossiping over coffee in the kitchen.

'I tore my nail on the wrapping, and I came down here to see if I could borrow some of your varnish.' Helen bends down to pick up a stray Cheerio from the floor, revealing that spangling diamanté string of hers. 'You haven't got any clear, have you?'

'You can have magenta, plum or black.'

Helen disappears with the magenta varnish from my handbag, and I am left with Gareth, whistling 'Brown-eyed Girl' as he returns to installing the kitchen sink.

'Were you and Helen talking about me?' I ask.

'Why do you always jump to that conclusion, Sadie? That you're so interesting that everyone must be talking about you?' There is an edge to Gareth's voice. Don't go there, I hear a voice inside me say, but when have I ever heeded a warning?

'Are you hiding something from me? You both went very quiet when you realised I was here.'

'Did we?' Gareth puts his pencil behind his ear, and turns to me.

'Keep those dusty hands off me,' I squeal as he drops them onto my shoulders and plants a kiss on my forehead in a friendly, non-sexual way which only makes me more paranoid.

'Helen was talking about Michael,' he says quietly. 'She's very cut-up and confused, and lonely.'

'She doesn't have to be on her own,' I observe. 'She's declined my invitation to drop in for a drink with Annette and Sean on Saturday.'

'Leave it with me,' says Gareth. 'I'll see if I can persuade her.'

But even Gareth's considerable charm fails to convince Helen to join us. On the Saturday afternoon she phones to confirm that she's staying at home. Dan phones too, to tell me he can't have the twins overnight.

'You couldn't have them last night either,' I moan. Dan's last-minute announcement that he couldn't have the twins ruined Gareth's plans for a romantic dinner for two. I'd imagined that Gareth would be annoyed, but he sat the twins down in front of the video of *Finding Nemo*, and served up Spanish omelette and crusty bread. 'They'll be so disappointed,' I continue.

'Couldn't you ask Tom to babysit?' Dan asks.

'No, it's your responsibility – you're their father. I

shan't be happy if you're ducking out of your commitments to our children because of Wendy.'

'It's work,' Dan tells me. 'This job is more demanding than I thought it would be. Please tell the twins that I'll make it up to them. Please, Sadie . . .' His voice sounds strained. I imagine him all alone in an office with a network of computers, their screens flashing with error messages, and begin to feel some compassion. 'I'll have them next weekend.'

'Okay,' I sigh.

The twins don't mind not seeing Dan as much as I thought they would. On Saturday, at tea-time, they plot to stay up until midnight, but they are both asleep before Annette and Sean arrive.

Sean holds out two bottles of organic elderflower wine. 'I found them in our understairs cupboard – Annette won them in a tombola in the summer. I wouldn't like them to go to waste.'

'Thanks very much,' I say, but my sarcasm is wasted on Sean. Homer rushes in, filling the hallway and whipping my legs with his tail. He thrusts his wet muzzle up my skirt and into my crotch, almost lifting me off the floor. 'Get off, dog.' I tap him on the head with the bottle in a reflex action. Homer yelps and ducks back. Sean doesn't notice.

'You have a long way to go with the roof,' he comments.

'I haven't started it yet,' says Gareth. 'Jim, my roofing mate, isn't available at the moment, and anyway, these women are always finding me other jobs to do. Come through. Have a lager.' The men disappear into the front room. Tom is in the kitchen. I take Annette aside.

'Jim's had his plaster cast removed, but he has to have physiotherapy before he can go up a ladder again,' I explain. I lower my voice. 'Tell me, is there anything going on between you and Michael?'

'Michael?' Annette laughs. 'He confided in me, that's all. And before you ask, I can't tell you what it was about. I promised.' She fixes me with an unwavering gaze. Reassured, I lead on through to the kitchen.

'Tom's about to make a start on dinner.'

'We haven't got any food left,' says Tom.

'That's the problem with developing property,' I say. 'No time to go to the supermarket. No money either. There are some eggs in the fridge.'

'The date on the eggs,' says Tom, shuffling about barefoot, and in tatty old shorts and no T-shirt. 'Is that when they were laid, or when they're supposed to be eaten by?'

'It doesn't matter too much as long as they've been kept in the fridge. They'll be fine if you cook them properly. Tom, can you do something different with them? I'm sick of omelette and scrambled eggs.'

'How about a soufflé?'

'That's a bit seventies, isn't it?'

'It sounds great,' says Annette. 'There is a way to tell if eggs are fresh by floating them in a bowl of water. If they float they're off, if they sink they're okay – or is it the other way round?'

Tom soon has eggs bobbing about in a paint kettle. He lifts them out one by one, breaks them into a bowl, and whisks them together. He laces the eggs with parsley, and salt and pepper, before transferring the mixture to another dish. He puts it in the oven, and we wait, chatting about Tom's plans for a water feature.

'Are you sure those eggs were all right?' I ask, pouring myself a second glass of elderflower wine, on the assumption that the more I drink, the better it might taste. 'What's that smell?'

'It isn't my trainers, because they're on the windowsill outside my room where you told me to leave them,' Tom says defensively.

'It isn't Homer either.' Annette pauses. 'You know, I feel as if I haven't eaten a decent meal for weeks.'

'I fear you may have to wait a while longer,' I say.

'How long has it been in the oven?' Tom asks. 'I've forgotten to set the timer.'

'I don't know. Forty, fifty minutes?'

'It should've been twenty.' Tom yanks open the oven door and grabs for the bowl through a swirl of smoke.

'What happened to the smoke alarm?' Sean demands, coming into the kitchen via the finished arch.

'Never mind the smoke alarm,' I grumble. 'What about our dinner?'

Sean reaches up and presses the button on the alarm. 'The batteries aren't working.' He flips the cover off. 'There *are* no batteries. Sadie!'

'It kept going off,' I protest. 'I took them out.'

'That's the whole point of having a smoke alarm.'

Meanwhile, as Sean gives me a lecture on fire safety, Tom inspects his cooking. With the corner of a tea-towel held over his face, he approaches me with the blackened disc.

'What's that?' I ask. 'A frisbee?'

'You could patent that as a dental-health product for dogs,' Annette chips in, 'as long as you could persuade a dog to chew it. Homer would turn his nose up at that.'

'Shall we try?' I suggest.

Tom throws it to the floor. Homer ignores it. Gareth goes out to fetch a takeaway. Sean goes with him, apologising in advance that he's left his wallet in his locker at work. On the way home, Sean makes Gareth stop for beer, and batteries. He stands watching me put the latter into the smoke alarm before we eat.

'We ran into Dan at the pizza place,' Sean says.

'Dan hates pizzas,' I say, frowning.

'People's tastes change,' says Annette. 'Is he comfort eating? Has that girlfriend of his left him again?'

'I doubt it. Dan's moved in with her. Lorna says that he's doing all her housework and cooking. Apparently, Wendy calls him her Peter Pan.' I change the subject. 'What do you think of the house?'

'You won't want to sell it once you've finished it,' says Annette.

It's true. With all the sweat and soul we've put into it, the house is beginning to feel like home.

'I like the kitchen worktops,' Sean comments, a string of mozzarella dangling from his chin. 'You'd never guess that was melamine.'

'That's because it's polished granite,' I observe crossly. 'Can't you recognise quality when you see it?' I can. I am sitting beside Gareth who exudes quality. I shift my chair, one of the stainless steel ones that Helen

338

chose to match the new table which arrived this week, closer to his. I am wearing a pair of old jeans with a hole in the knee. Gareth slips one finger into the hole and caresses my skin. A shiver runs down my spine. Tom keeps his eyes averted. Alvin, tempted by the scent of beef and pepperoni, turns up and jumps onto the table. He stands with his front paws on Sean's plate and headbutts his face. Alvin has grown sleek and fat, and I wonder if he might have to go onto the Atkins rather than the Katkins diet.

As soon as dinner is over, Sean and Annette leave with Homer, because Annette says she has to mark twenty assignments on *How to Read an Ordnance Survey Map* by Monday. She looks exhausted. She seems very together, though. She and Tom talked conservation and snails, and the sight of eggs didn't appear to trigger any thoughts of IT. She didn't mention her ovaries once.

Gareth and I retire for the night. We talk for a while. I drop the subject of Helen's diamanté string into the conversation.

'I could hardly miss it, could I, the way she's been flashing it about.' Gareth looks at me. 'That wasn't what I was supposed to say, was it?'

'You were supposed to say that you only have eyes for me.'

Gareth kisses me softly on the lips. Within minutes, he is snoring and I can't sleep. At midnight, someone starts knocking at the front door.

'Who the hell is that at this time of night?' I stamp up and down the bedroom, hoping to wake Gareth so he can see who it is, but he keeps on snoring and I have to go downstairs. I open the door and shine a torch straight into the eyes of a striking young woman who reminds me of Cameron Diaz.

'I'm looking for Tom,' she says. Her voice is strong, but a fragility lies behind her eyes, suggesting someone at the end of her tether.

'I'm not sure he's here.'

'His parents gave me the address. *Llamedos*.'

'What is it you want to see him about? Are you pregnant?'

'It isn't anything like that . . .'

'You'd better come in.' I usher her into the front room and offer her the Director's chair. 'Wait there.'

Tom isn't asleep. He's staring at the flickering screen on Gareth's portable TV that he's appropriated for his room since I banned him from watching *Hollyoaks* in front of the children.

'Tom, Sonya's here to see you.' I have to repeat this twice before Tom responds.

'Tell her to piss off,' he hisses, his voice stricken with what sounds like sheer panic.

'She's missed the last train home. I can't let her spend the night on New Malden station. Listen, Tom, why don't you speak to her? If you get whatever's troubling you out in the open, you'll be able to deal with it and get on with your life rather than vegetating here.' I bend down, pick up a handful of items of the clothing that's built up into a heap to rival the Cairngorms, and chuck it at him.

'Sadie!'

'Get down there and get talking!'

I creep about on the landing, hoping to hear what Tom does talk about, but all I can hear are low whispers, then raised voices, then slamming doors, and Tom running outside. I charge downstairs to console Sonya who is sitting on the Director's chair, sobbing.

'I insisted on knowing, but now that I do know, I wish I hadn't. Tom and I are finished. He says I'm beautiful, and perfect, but he doesn't love me and never will. I don't know what's wrong with me,' she cries.

'There's nothing wrong with you. It's Tom. If he can't see how gorgeous and devoted you are, coming all this way—'

'We'd been going out together for three months and three days when Tom left uni without telling me,' Sonya bursts out. 'I can't bear to think that he's given up his chance of a degree because of me.'

'I thought it was because of the snails,' I say gently.

'Snails? Oh no! Tom persuaded the Professor that any students who objected to carrying out the experiments that involved killing snails could use last year's results. Do you think Tom will change his mind about me and him?'

Sonya has lovely eyes – irresistible to most men, I should imagine – but Tom's not most men, is he?

'I don't think so.' It has become clear to me that Tom is running away not from something in his life, but from himself – which, of course, is impossible.

'He's ruined my life.'

'That's rubbish. In a while, you'll be able to put this episode down to experience and move on.' I wrap Sonya in a blanket, and we drink Baileys by candlelight until I feel sozzled enough to wander back upstairs to Gareth who is still snoring. I lie down, curl up against his back and close my eyes.

'Mum, Mum.' Lorna is crying in her bedroom. I crawl out of bed to find her.

'I dreamed my ear fell off. It hasn't fallen off, has it? Where is it?' She is still half-asleep, her eyes wide open and unseeing. 'It's gone. Where's it gone?'

'Hush, my fairy. It's still here,' I soothe, hugging her close.

'I want to sleep in your bed,' she sobs.

'I'm sorry, but you can't. You're too old.' In the end I sleep in Lorna's bed, crushed against the wall. I imagine that I was more comfortable than Tom was, because in the morning I find him asleep in the garden wrapped in a couple of dustsheets at Justin Timberlake's feet. I grab his shoulder and give him a little shake.

'Sonya's gone,' I whisper.

Tom rubs his eyes. 'How did you manage to get rid of her? If Sonya was a mollusc, she'd be a bloody limpet. She wanted to spend every minute in my company.'

'That sounds perfectly reasonable to me for a girl who's in love.'

'I'm not in love with her. I like her, and I'm flattered that she asked me out, but I couldn't love her back, and then I couldn't bear to tell her because I knew she'd be hurt, so I ran away.'

'Someone else will come along. Another girl?' I say challengingly.

'Girls don't normally take any notice of me.'

'Maybe you don't notice when they do.'

Tom isn't the only one who is glad that Sonya has gone. I would have been envious of the way that I imagine Gareth would have looked at Sonya if she'd stayed.

There, I've admitted it. Ever since Annette learned to tie her shoelaces and read *The Hums of Pooh* all the way through before I did, I've been racked with jealousy. Am I going to let it poison my relationship with Gareth? Am I really going to let it drive us apart?

Chapter Seventeen

No fireworks. That's what I promise myself. If Gareth spends more time chatting to Helen than me, or takes off to meet Niall, or Rob, or his mother, I shall remain calm and rational. I shall burn essential oil of lavender, and start reprogramming my mind with a Paul McKenna self-help book.

'Annette's just phoned to say that she and Sean can't come to the party tonight,' I tell Gareth when he comes downstairs straight from the shower, with his hair dripping wet and a towel around his middle. 'It's something to do with Homer being scared of loud bangs. Annette and Sean are staying in to play his CD to him.'

'What's Homer's taste in albums?' says Gareth. 'Kate Bush's *Hounds of Love*? Snoop Doggy Dogg's *Doggystyle*? The Baha Men's *Who Let The Dogs Out*?' He chuckles at his own joke.

'It's a recording of firework noises to help Homer overcome his phobia. They're trying a pheromone diffuser, but it isn't working yet.'

Gareth pinches a tiger prawn out of one of Tom's

marinades on the kitchen worktop. I sent Tom down the road for pasta and bolognese sauce this afternoon, and he came back with a tray of tiger prawns, rice noodles, root ginger and coriander which must have cost a fortune. I asked him for the change, but there wasn't any. He spent the last tenner on saké.

'If I'd known we were eating Oriental, I'd have nipped into Michael's shop and picked up some rice bowls and chopsticks,' I observe. 'I'll go now. There's still time.'

'The shop's closed.'

'Michael keeps it open till six thirty.'

'No, it's closed. Boarded up. Didn't Helen mention it? Michael's run out of money. He's been banned from trading. The liquidator's taken possession of his shops.'

'When did Helen tell you? When you were supposed to be working?'

'We *were* working. We put the curtain pole up in the front bedroom. I drilled the holes, Helen held the pole. I screwed—'

'You did what?' I interrupt.

'Does it matter who did what?' Gareth stares at me, his eyes narrowed. 'Do I detect a touch of paranoia? You have nothing to be jealous of, Sadie, nothing at all.'

'I'm sorry.' I am sorry, but the green-eyed monster which lurks deep inside me like a pot of play slime, is slithering towards the surface and threatening to erupt like something out of *Alien*. I know that I resolved not to, but I can't help wondering if Gareth is lying to me. Dan lied to me for years, until I almost came to believe him. I shan't make the same mistake again.

'I've been grafting all day, and you haven't even mentioned the kitchen,' Gareth says accusingly. 'The units are finished, apart from the handles, and the new cooker's connected.'

'I'm sorry,' I repeat. I look around, forcing myself to examine our surroundings. Helen was right. It *is* a beautiful kitchen. Its sleek lines and gleaming surfaces distract from the odd flaw in Gareth's workmanship: an off-centred handle; a slight mismatch between two unit doors; a surfeit of filler between the back of the worktop and the wall.

'Well? What do you think?'

'It looks fantastic. Thanks, Gareth.' I fling my arms around his neck, kiss his cheek, his lips . . . 'Shall we slip upstairs for a while?'

'I must get dressed,' he says quietly. 'Helen will be here soon.'

Helen again? Helen is single and vulnerable. So what? When I was in her position, the last thing I wanted was another man. I have questions for Helen, but I can't speak to her when she arrives at the development for the firework party because of the children. We stand out in the back garden, wrapped up in hats and scarves, clutching mugs of mulled wine.

Gareth has fixed a Catherine Wheel to the new fence that Tom has erected between us and The Neighbour From Hell. When he lights the fuse it sparks into life, and spins first one way and then the other, before whirling in burning circles of colour like the thoughts that are whirling around my brain.

Why did Helen tell Gareth, not me?

Gareth and Tom line up rockets in beer bottles. The children wave unlit sparklers. Helen has decided, in the interests of safety, that we will hold them once they are alight.

'It'll be more fun for us,' she whispers as the acrid scent of smoke drifts across the patio. Tom has arranged the paving slabs, but not concreted them in, and I find my kitten heels catching in the gaps.

There is a brief silence then the hissing of a series of rockets taking off in sequence, before they explode, spreading showers of spangling stars that slowly fall and fade out across the sky. Like a love affair, I think, looking towards Gareth. Perhaps I've had too much mulled wine already . . .

'Watch out!' yells Gareth. 'Stand back!'

There is a problem with one of the rockets. The bottle has fallen over and it's aiming straight for Justin Timberlake. The light dies, comes back, and Tom is crouching among a constellation of sputtering stars, holding Justin above his head – singed, but intact.

The Neighbour From Hell waves furiously from his kitchen window. I wave back.

'Silly old sod,' I remark to Helen, 'making a fuss about a little bit of noise.'

It is quieter now. All I can hear are the soft popping expulsions of pink and green lights from a giant Roman candle, yet it deceives me, going off like an artillery gun at the end. My ears are still ringing when we go back inside to sample Tom's party food.

The children are most put out when they discover that there are no jacket potato halves with their flesh pricked

up into hedgehog spikes, or mini-bonfire cakes smoth-
ered in chocolate vermicelli. Charlotte confides in me as
she picks out a couple of tiger prawns for her plate.

'My mum and dad have been divorced for four weeks
now,' she says quietly.

My heart melts. 'They're not divorced, Charlotte.'
Her face crumples and I give her a hug. 'Nothing's
decided yet.'

'Can I come and live with you?'

'I'm sorry, but the best I can offer you is a sleepover.'

Charlotte opens her mouth to protest, but shuts it
again as Helen approaches to suggest that she tries the
rice noodles with ketchup, if she doesn't like tiger
prawns. Charlotte takes a spring roll instead, and joins
the twins at the table in the dining area.

'We should have paid for someone other than Gareth
to fit the kitchen,' Helen says, stroking the granite
worktop.

'Shh,' I warn, not wanting to hurt Gareth's feelings.
'It looks fabulous. As you said yourself, it'll be a real
selling point.'

'But look at this.' Helen slides one of the drawers
out and forces it back in with great effort. 'And I'm
sure that cornice is crooked.'

'Just like your curtain pole,' I bite back.

Helen frowns.

'I'll show you.' I grab the spirit level from the
cupboard under the stairs, and take it up to the bedroom
to demonstrate, standing precariously on a set of steps.
I am right. The bubble rolls just left of centre. 'I don't
suppose you bothered to check it.'

'It doesn't show,' she says.

'It does to me.' I glance towards the door. No one is listening. 'Why didn't you tell me that Michael's gone bankrupt?'

'He hasn't. His company's gone into liquidation. There is a difference.' Helen glares at me. 'What you really want to know is why I told Gareth, not you?'

'Well, yes, actually.'

'It slipped out.' Helen pauses and smiles a predatory smile. I've seen her flash her teeth like that when she goes into the garage to buy tokens for the car wash. The man behind the counter is charming, and reminds her of Ben Affleck. 'Gareth is so easy to talk to. He seems to understand what I'm going through at the moment.'

'You've changed your tune.'

'I know. I didn't want to like him after what he did to me, but when I look back, I realise it was partly my fault. I made my reputation as the girl who couldn't say no, which isn't fair, because none of the men I approached ever said no either.'

'But why? What's the point when one man is so clearly like another?'

Helen latches onto the bitterness in my voice. 'So Gareth's halo is beginning to slip?'

'At least it isn't around his knees, like your knickers.'

Helen's lip wobbles. 'That's a mean thing to say.'

'You're not going to try to tell me that you slept with all those blokes because you didn't get enough approval and love from your parents?'

'Of course not. I craved excitement and variety. I

wanted to be different. Later, I realised that I was like everyone else after all, and I wanted to get married and have kids, and Michael came along . . .' Helen bursts into tears '. . . and now he's gone.' She pushes me away as I try to console her. I think of her confiding in Gareth, and I wonder about her motives, conscious or not. I should be pleased that my best friend is getting on so well with my boyfriend. It's what I wanted, isn't it?

'How's Michael? Have you seen him?'

'I've seen him all right. He came round this afternoon to explain that he moved out as he was too ashamed to admit that he'd lost the business because he'd made a mistake. He says there wasn't anyone else involved. He wasn't having an affair.'

'Do you believe him?'

'I don't know,' Helen sighs. 'He begged me to forgive him for keeping me in the dark about the fact that those Glowie Balls had been banned, and he couldn't get the money back.'

'He told me about the Glowie Balls,' I confess. 'I needed more cash for the development, and Michael said I couldn't have it. I didn't mention it to you because I thought something would turn up, and it did. Gareth—'

'Him!' Helen interrupts, her cheeks flushed with fury. 'You mean, you've let *Gareth* bail us out! We're supposed to be doing this together, you and me, and now you've sold out to him.'

'It's the only way I could see to keep the development,' I say quietly. 'Gareth isn't buying into our partnership. It's more of a loan.'

'It's *our* project.' Helen glares at me. 'You're supposed to consult with me before you go making any rash decisions. What if Gareth suddenly decides he wants his money back tomorrow?'

'I don't have to pay him back until we sell the house.'

'I hope he doesn't change his mind.' Helen falls silent for a moment. 'Everything's such a mess . . .'

'That curtain pole doesn't look so bad after all,' I say, trying to cheer her up.

'Sadie! Helen!' Gareth calls up the stairs. 'Are you coming down for something else to eat?'

Helen follows me slowly downstairs.

'Chocolate? A glass of mulled wine?' Gareth offers.

Helen and I both decline.

'Are you two on detox?' Gareth smiles.

I shake my head. My stomach is churning and it isn't the effect of Tom's exotic marinades.

'It's time Charlotte and I went home.' Helen collects her coat and leaves with Charlotte. Tom goes out too, and the twins grumble all the way to bed. Gareth and I remain, clearing up the kitchen. Gareth dries the last of the plates that won't fit in the dishwasher and throws the tea-towel down on the worktop. He moves behind me as I stack the plates away and wraps his arms around my belly. I lean back against him, turning my head slightly so that I can hear the regular pounding of his heartbeat. We've been together – on and off – for over six months, and I've never been so happy. In fact, I'm beginning to change my mind about not marrying again . . .

'We'll have to start looking for another house to live in soon,' I say, 'and next year, we'll go on holiday – the four of us.'

'Hold on, Sadie,' Gareth says quietly.

'If you don't want the twins to come with us, I'm sure Dan and Wendy will have them.' I keep my reservations to myself about letting Lorna spend too much time in Wendy's company, being indoctrinated in the benefits of a vegan lifestyle when she is so easily influenced.

'It isn't that. You're going too fast.'

'I'm planning our future.'

'I've told you before. I don't like to be tied down.'

'Not even to me?'

'I don't know. I'm enjoying being as we are, taking one day at a time.' Gareth pauses. 'In my experience, as soon as you start having expectations of the happily ever after, something goes wrong. You start questioning if you're doing the right thing. You kill the passion and spontaneity with analysis and doubt.'

'What about Niall and Kate?'

'For every Niall and Kate, there's a Rob and Martine, forever threatening each other with divorce.'

'I didn't know.'

'Rob said that Martine was on the phone to the solicitor the day after the Rugby Club do, asking if she could sue for divorce because he'd been glancing lecherously at other women,' Gareth goes on. 'I don't want to be rushed into anything, Sadie. Do you understand?'

The flame of hope that was burning in my breast for a sign of commitment, and everlasting commitment at that, from Gareth, sputters and fades like the light from a spent firework. My jealousy wells up instead. It's always there, no matter how hard I try to suppress it, making me question my relationships and spoiling my happiness. Not once has Gareth told me that he loves me. Why is that?

'It's Helen, isn't it? You've always fancied her.'

'It has nothing to do with Helen. It's me.'

I don't know whether it's down to my natural stubbornness, but when Dan said he didn't love me any more, I felt that I loved him more than ever. It is the same with Gareth.

Two weeks later, we are still together. There is one week until our deadline runs out. The kitchen is almost complete. The roof is still covered with more tarpaulin than tiles because Jim walked out when Gareth told him that I couldn't pay him until the house was sold. To be more precise, he limped out on his gammy leg, since he started back at work before his physiotherapist gave him the all clear.

Helen comes wandering in this morning, her shoes covered with leaves.

'You're late.' I hand her a paintbrush. 'We can't afford to waste a minute. This place goes on the market next week.'

'Sadie, we can't finish it in a week. There's still too much to do. I've made a list – there's woodwork to gloss, furniture to assemble, carpets to fit, and the roof! We can't start dressing any of the rooms because you've got too many people living here. And no, you can't come and stay at mine. Michael and I are in delicate negotiations, and I don't want half of the population of New Malden listening in.'

'Have you let him move back in?'

'Not yet – he's staying in a B & B – but we are talking. I'm talking sense and he's talking rubbish as usual. Although he's convinced me that he was having a mid-life crisis, not an affair, when he left, I'm not sure that I want him back.'

'What about Charlotte?' I ask.

'She misses him, of course,' Helen sighs. 'I suppose that Michael and I need to make a decision about our future and stick to it.'

'How are you managing for money?'

'Our house is secure because the last business was set up as a limited company, and Michael still has one or two small deals going on here and there. He can still trade as an individual. I told him I'm happy as long as we can still afford for Charlotte to keep up all her activities and pay Clare to do my highlights. All this stress is turning my hair quite grey.'

I think of poor Dan and the fifty quid he's managed to scrape together to buy the twins new winter coats this month.

'What about the Golf Club? Can Michael afford to pay his fine for damaging the green, and renew his membership?'

'He'll have to stick to pitch and putt for a while.' Helen hands the paintbrush back to me. 'Coffee?'

I glance at the bare plaster wall we're supposed to be sizing before we paint. It's a long job. What difference will half an hour make? What are deadlines for, if not to be missed?

A week after our deadline passes, I find myself in one of the local DIY stores in the screws and fixings aisle. I've offered to shop for some bits and pieces for Gareth at the same time as collecting the flocking machine that I've ordered. I had to get out. Tom's presence is already driving me mad, even though he's not up yet. He's left a chip pan filled with oil and greasy potato pieces on the new hob, and there weren't enough bowls for cereal this morning because he's stashed the rest away in his room.

The garden is beautiful, but it's costing a fortune. We had The Prince of Darkness back to fix up a cable for Tom's water feature, a small pond adjacent to the completed crazy-paved patio. Justin Timberlake stands in splendid isolation on a rock in the middle, among some tatty brown reeds.

I digress. I am looking at screws. Size 8. Brass, steel, roundheaded, crossthreaded? How should I know which type to choose? I take out my mobile and dial the house. The answerphone cuts in. No, I don't want to leave a message.

'Do you desire any assistance, madam?' asks a whiskery chap in a brown overall who is lurking about the shelves.

'I'm looking for a screw.'

'You've come to the right man,' he says, gazing at my cleavage. 'Double hardened? Low friction coating? Self countersinking? That'll give you a nice flush finish, if you know what I mean.'

I think I have one already. That prickling feeling is breaking out across my chest. I turn away and try phoning home again. Tom must still be unconscious, and Gareth refuses to answer because he says it's always for me: credit management companies offering to consolidate my loans, or the Building Society enquiring how I'm going to pay the next instalment of my mortgage and catch up on the arrears. The credit-card company have stopped calling since I paid off the minimum monthly amount with the money Dan gave me for the twins' coats – they'll have to squeeze into their old ones until the January Sales.

I collect the flocking machine, and three packets of different kinds of screws in the hope that one of them fulfils Gareth's requirements, along with several other items that are on offer. The transparent toilet seat, run through with barbed wire, and the turquoise, seashell-shaped soap dish will complement my design for the bathroom, if not Helen's. Mine has a beach-hut theme. Helen's is cool and minimal.

I try Helen's mobile. It's switched off. Normally, I'd assume that she's watching *This Morning*, but those screws glint from the bottom of my trolley, putting ideas into my head. Gareth and Helen? Surely not. Except that Helen's gorgeous, and she used to have a thing with Gareth, and she's vulnerable with all the worry over Michael and their finances. I whizz the trolley to the check-outs and pay with cash that I borrowed from Gareth. I'm shaking so much that I can hardly drive home. I park behind Gareth's pick-up outside the development, and take the shopping up to the front door, looking and listening for clues.

There's no evidence that some lurid drama of illicit passion is unfolding inside – no steam rising out of the open windows, no shuddering of the foundations, no creaking floorboards. The telly is on very loud. I can hear Fern Britton chattering on about a competition to design and make the best chocolate bra – I suppose that it satisfies a generation brought up on *Blue Peter* makes. I relax slightly. Gareth and Helen? If I was being silly, imagining that Gareth was calling from Gretna Green to say he'd got married, I'm being ridiculous now.

I slip the key in the lock and push the door open. My mouth goes dry and my heart starts pounding. How do I know where they are? I just do.

I creep straight upstairs. The door to the third bedroom is closed. The bathroom door is open – the lid on the toilet seat, I notice in passing, is up. The second bedroom door is ajar, with a trail of pyjamas strewn across the floor. The main bedroom door is open a crack.

I can hear voices – Gareth's low chuckle and Helen's breathless protest.

'Oh Gareth, please don't. It's too much. I can't bear it.'

Neither can I. I kick the door open. They are laughing, lying in a sprawling embrace on my mattress. A pain racks my chest, as if Gareth has thrown one of his bricks at me, crushing my ribs, and my dreams for the future. I wonder if I am about to have a heart attack, which would serve them both right ... Very briefly, I picture three funerals: my own, with the black horse from

Lloyds Bank pulling a purple hearse, and the cremation of two dismembered bodies cast into the fiery depths of Hell.

Gareth sees me before Helen does. He leaps up from the bed.

'Er, S-Sadie,' he stammers. 'Did you get those screws?'

'While you were screwing Helen?' I want to break down and cry, but I can't in front of them. 'How could you?'

'It isn't like that. We weren't, you know . . .' Gareth straightens his vest and tucks it into the waistband of his trousers. Helen sits on the edge of the mattress, with her long legs stretched out in front of her, her face flushed and her hair messed up. She tugs out her scrunchie and twists her hair back up into a ponytail.

'We were just messing around. Helen said, "Wouldn't it be a laugh to bounce on the mattress," so we did, and we fell down, and she was ticklish, and you came in.' Gareth pauses for breath. 'Sadie, I was cheering her up.'

'How very charitable of you!'

'We weren't doing anything,' he insists.

'Oh, shut up!'

'I'll leave you two to it,' says Helen, getting up from the mattress.

I wait until she has left the room. 'Gareth . . .' My voice falters. 'How could you?'

'Nothing happened.' He pulls at his hair in exasperation, a theatrical gesture that only compounds his guilt.

'What am I supposed to think when I find you snuggled up with my best friend? You were *in* our bed!'

'*On* our bed,' says Gareth. 'There is a difference.' He drops his arms around me but I push him away, assaulted by the mixed scents of his aftershave and Helen's perfume on his skin. 'Okay, I shouldn't have done it,' he tries again.

'So, you're admitting it now?'

'I admit that I should have realised what conclusion someone who's as insecure and jealous as you are would jump to, if you saw us messing about,' says Gareth. 'Why can't you trust me? Is it because you don't really want me, because you don't love me like I love you? It's true, Sadie,' Gareth goes on hoarsely. 'I love you.'

Love? How long have I been waiting to hear that word? Now that I've heard it, it is too late.

'If you really loved me, you would have said so before. You're only saying it because you're guilty as hell of sleeping with my best friend. You've wanted her all along. That's the real reason you moved in with me, isn't it?'

'You're being ridiculous,' Gareth says coldly.

'I'm not.'

'For goodness sake, Sadie, go and talk to Helen. Perhaps you'll listen to her.' Gareth heads towards the door, but I block his way.

'Where do you think you're off to?'

'Back on the roof, if you want it finished.'

I let Gareth go, and return downstairs to tackle Helen who is standing at the front-room window, chewing her nails. In the background, Philip Schofield is introducing a feature on choosing spectacles. I fear that it's too late for me to book an eye-test. If I'd bought a pair of glasses when Gareth started work at the development, I might have been able to see what's been going on under my nose all this time.

I ask Helen the same questions as I asked Gareth. She doesn't say that she and Gareth did have sex, but she doesn't say that they didn't.

'You can believe whatever you like,' Helen taunts, with a sly smile that irritates the hell out of me.

'I suppose you wanted to sleep with him for old times' sake.'

Helen shrugs.

'Helen, how could you? Your husband moved out so you had to sneak back and shag my boyfriend to make yourself feel better.' I swallow back tears, and tell myself to toughen up. 'I didn't realise it before, but you're the kind of woman who thinks she's only something if she has a man. Well, you're mistaken. You are nothing!'

Helen picks up her car keys from the windowsill and heads for the door. I can't believe she isn't stopping to argue her case.

'Where are you going? There's work to be done!'

'I'm going home,' Helen snaps. 'I've had enough of this bloody development, of men, of you!'

Sick at heart, I watch her go. She shoots her car with the key, then slides into the driver's seat without looking back. Behind me, I hear Gareth's footsteps. I turn towards him.

'She'll be back, Sadie,' Gareth says. 'Helen can't keep away.'

'From the development, or from you?'

'From you, of course,' he says, eyebrows raised. 'There's never a dull moment when you're around. Helen won't want to miss anything.' Gareth holds out the packets of screws that I've just bought. 'I hate to tell you this, but these are the wrong ones.'

I stare at him. His eyelids flicker, a sure sign of guilt, yet laughter threatens to break through the stern tone of his voice, a cover for his betrayal, perhaps. Does he really believe he can get away with shagging my best friend right under my nose? I snatch the screws and throw them at him, yelling at him to pack his things and go.

'I never want to see you again!'

Gareth's face pales. He has an angry mark flaring across his temple where one of the packets of screws hit its target.

'Helen told me all that I need to know,' I continue.

'What did she say?'

'She didn't have to say anything. Her expression told it all. You betrayed me, Gareth.'

'You believe Helen over me? You can't.'

'Why should she lie?'

'Because she's jealous of our relationship. She always has been.'

'Well, she needn't be any more because it's over. Finished.'

Gareth thinks for a moment. 'What about the twins?'

'I'm still here for them, aren't I?'

'What about the development?'

'I'll get another builder, one who knows what he's

doing. Helen was right. You're unreliable, and bloody hopeless in every department.'

Gareth opens his mouth to protest once more, but I cut him short. 'Just go!' I open the front door and wait on the steps until Gareth has cleared out most of his tools and personal belongings. I don't care that it's freezing, and that The Neighbour From Hell is staring at me from his window. Helen and Gareth have gone. The bitch and the bastard. I don't need them. I don't need either of them.

As I watch Gareth's pick-up disappearing around the corner at the end of the road, biting back tears, a tatty old trainer whizzes past my left ear and lands on the ground a couple of feet away. Tom shouts down from his bedroom window, 'Are you okay?'

I find that I don't know. I can't feel anything. My fingers, my toes, my heart – they're all numb. Tom, dressed in nothing but a duvet, drags me back inside. He sits me on the Director's chair and pours me a mugful of whisky.

'It's my dad's Lagavulin,' he explains. 'He bought it to impress his friends at the Golf Club. I stole it when I was mad with him and Helen.'

I slug it down, and choke on sharp accents of peat and heather. A burning sensation crawls down my gullet, and I wonder if I'm getting an ulcer.

'I think you're supposed to sip it,' says Tom, patting me on the back. He returns upstairs to dress, then cooks up a fried brunch with chips. I can't eat. I can't think straight. It's all I can do to remember that I'll have to collect the twins later – I assume that Helen won't be in the mood to do the school run.

In the meantime, I watch Tom in the garden, planting out winter pansies.

'I'm going out tonight,' he says.

'You don't have to keep out of my way.'

'I'm meeting a special friend.'

'A boyfriend?'

Tom nods.

'I guessed a long time ago, although the fact that you were seeing the hairdresser's daughter confused me for a while.'

'I wasn't seeing Alice as such,' says Tom. 'We talked a lot. She helped me.'

'And the magazines that Helen found under your bed?'

'I had to be sure.'

'You ought to talk to your dad,' I suggest.

'What, tell him I'm gay, you mean?'

'It's no big deal.'

'It is for me. Dad'll kill me.'

'Your dad has no right to make a judgement on your sexuality.' It seems such a waste seeing Tom, one of the few men I know who has a brain, kicking about with no real purpose. Yes, I'm being bitter and shrewish – I have good reason. 'Have you thought any more about going back to university?'

'I think about it all the time,' Tom sighs. 'I just can't decide what I want to do with my life.'

Does this mean that Tom will soon be moving out? Being uncertain about his future must be an improvement on being adamant that he wasn't going back to university.

Don't get me wrong. I like Tom, but I don't like his

vices which, even for an outrageous bohemian like me, are extreme: collecting mould in dirty mugs, arranging used plasters along the top of the bath, and the worst – hoarding urine samples in lemonade bottles. I realise that there's often a queue for the bathroom, but he could at least throw them away discreetly rather than leave them under his bed.

I collect the twins at three, and am so busy trying to avoid Helen at the school gates that I step backwards into Caroline. As a way of making up for not having invited Harry back for tea in return for the times she invited Sam during the summer, because the development is more like a building site than a home, I find myself agreeing that Topsy will put in an appearance at the school's Christmas disco.

On the way home, the twins talk in stereo, Sam one side, Lorna the other, from the back seat of the car.

'We thought it was Helen's turn to pick us up.'

'I wasn't busy. I thought it would be a nice surprise.'

'Have you been crying? Your eyes are red.'

I grip tight on the steering wheel. 'I suppose I'd better tell you. Gareth has moved out.'

'Why?' says Sam.

'Because we had an argument.'

'I'm always having arguments with Charlotte but we get back together,' says Lorna. 'You'll make it up with him soon, Mum.'

'It wasn't an argument over anything as simple as earrings,' I sigh.

'I like Gareth,' moans Lorna. 'You must make him come back.'

'You didn't like him much before.'

'I do like him. I'll miss him.' Her lip wobbles. 'I'm missing him already.'

When Dan left me I swore I would never trust a man again, then I let Gareth's charm, sense of humour and sea-green eyes seduce me into forgetting my vow. As for Helen, I'm going to have to find some way of working with her until this place is finished. We are bound, like a miserable married couple, by money, contracts and this millstone of a house. I shall never laugh or smile again.

I throw myself into helping with homework, making sandwiches for the next day, and cleaning up the kitchen. All it needs now is tiling and painting, neither of which is beyond my capabilities.

'Mum, are you cooking tea tonight, only Tom isn't here,' says Lorna.

'And I'm starving,' says Sam.

I glance at my watch. No wonder. It's gone eight.

'I'll dial a pizza.'

'Great,' says Sam. 'I wish your boyfriends would leave more often so we could have pizza all the time.'

I ring the Pizza Parlour on the High Street, and we wait.

'When's it going to be here?' moans Sam.

'Soon. Perhaps they're busy tonight.'

An hour later and dinner still hasn't arrived. I'm not bothered, but the twins are hungry.

I phone again and insist on speaking to the manager who apologises and promises to send the pizza round within ten minutes with free garlic bread and ice cream by way of compensation. Exactly ten minutes later, the pizza delivery boy turns up. In the half-light at the door, he turns, keeping his visor down as if he might be disfigured in some way, and therefore reluctant to be seen. There is something vaguely familiar about him.

'It's Dad,' says Sam. 'Hey, Lorna, it's Dad.'

I thought I'd never laugh or smile again, but I am wrong.

'What are you doing here?' I grin. 'Is this some kind of joke?'

Dan flushes as red as a jar of passata. 'That job I took locally,' he mutters.

'You're a delivery boy!' Once I get my giggles under control, I continue, 'You hate pizzas! You used to pick off the pepperoni and jalapenos. Why didn't you tell us?'

'How could I? I want the twins to be proud of me. I want them to hold their heads high, and tell everyone that their dad's a well-paid computer consultant who works in an office in Town. Look at me.'

'At least you can say you have a company vehicle.' I point to the moped that's parked in the place where Gareth usually leaves his pick-up. Gareth. Suddenly I'm not laughing any more.

'It's great to see you, Dad,' says Lorna. '*I'm* proud of you.'

My eyes fill with tears. It has been an emotional day. I cling on to the order that Dan hands over to me, and watch the twins say goodbye to him. The pizza is cold, and the ice cream is warm. Normally, I'd ring and complain, but I don't want to get Dan into any more trouble with his boss. There is already more than enough unhappiness in the world.

Chapter Eighteen

I half-expect Gareth to come knocking at the door, for him to walk in and hold me, but he doesn't, and he wouldn't, would he, after what he did? Helen turns up though. She arrives at the development the following afternoon, by which time I have experimented with the flocking machine on a couple of lampshades, my coffee mug and exposed parts of the sitting-room floor – by default rather than design. The deep red, furred finish is quite pleasing.

Helen isn't impressed. 'I'm no Linda Barker,' she says, 'but that effect is revolting.'

'In that case, I'll flock the kettle. I'll flock the TV. I'll flock everything I can lay my hands on.'

Helen looks at me, down her nose and with spite, as if she's forgotten we were ever friends.

'I don't care, Sadie. You can flock what you like. I want out.'

I stop flocking. 'What did you say?'

'I want out,' she repeats. 'I've had enough of painting walls, of sanding woodwork. I've had enough of working in a pigsty. I've had enough of you!'

'You can't leave. We have a contract.'

'I know, but considering the circumstances, I'm sure you won't mind me dropping out. You seem to be managing perfectly well on your own. You make all the decisions. You don't take any notice of my mood-boards. The only reason you asked me to be your partner is because you couldn't have done it without my money, and if I hadn't forced Michael to invest in this project, he'd never have lost his shops.'

'Helen!' I hadn't foreseen this. Did I really think though, that Helen and I could work here together again as if nothing had happened? 'We've almost finished!'

'We are finished. Our friendship is over, and so is my involvement in this development.'

I am panicking. What am I going to do? Crawl, I think. 'I know I said some horrid things yesterday, but that was in the heat of the moment – and you were getting it on with my boyfriend, so I have every right to be angry with you.'

Helen smiles coldly. 'I don't want to talk about personal affairs,' she says, emphasising the word *affairs*. 'This is business. This place is never going to make us a profit. I want to sell it now and get it over with.'

'If we sell it as it is, unfinished and undressed, we won't maximise our profit, which is what all this work has been about,' I argue.

'I want this house on the market by the New Year at a realistic price so that it sells quickly. I want my money back.' Helen stops abruptly. 'I'm going shopping.'

'You can't leave me here on my own!'

'Watch me!' Helen leaves me in a terrible state, and with a lot of flocked items that don't look quite so fantastic as they did when I first started. I try scraping the fibres off the side of my mug with my thumbnail, but they're glued on fast. I pick up the phone to ring Gareth, but put it down again, and flock it instead.

A week later, when I've almost accepted that Gareth isn't coming back, he rolls up at *Llamedos* at nine thirty on the Monday morning as if nothing has happened. There's no contrite look, no apologetic smile, nothing to suggest that he has been suffering as much as I have.

'Why didn't you come in last week?' I ask, when he drops his toolbox in the hall.

'I thought we both needed some time to cool down.' He tilts his head to one side and smiles the sexiest of smiles. My stomach turns over and my knees tremble, but I steel myself.

'Where have you been staying?'

'I moved back in with my mum – and Desmond.'

'You'd better get back to them then, hadn't you?'

Gareth frowns.

'You can't walk out, stay out of touch for a week then waltz back as if nothing happened,' I continue.

'How many times do I have to tell you that nothing *did* happen?' Gareth's voice grows husky as he adds, 'I've missed you . . . I've missed watching the weather forecasts for rain. I've missed your laughter. I've missed having you in my bed . . .'

Gareth's words find their way to my heart, but that's

what he intends, isn't it? He wants to make me feel that this was all my fault, that I drove him into Helen's arms with my insane jealousy. He wants me to take him back without a second thought. *Nothing happened.* Just what Dan used to say. My last relationship festered with mistrust for far too long and then, as I was beginning to accept that the split with Dan was all my fault, I found out that I had been right all along, that he had been unfaithful. I am *not* going to let history repeat itself, no matter how persuasive, how charming, Gareth is.

'Don't you feel anything for me?' Gareth asks.

'I hate you.'

He gazes at me, pursing his lips. 'I wish I knew what I was supposed to have done. I thought you'd have cleared it all up with Helen by now. Where is she, by the way?'

'She's left the development, thanks to you and your wandering hands.'

He reaches those wandering hands out to me, as if to touch my shoulders, then retreats as if thinking better of it.

'How are the twins?'

'What do you care?'

'More than you realise, I think,' Gareth says quietly. 'I wasn't unfaithful, but I can see that you don't believe me.' His voice cuts to a sob. He takes a deep breath and starts again. 'You've had some preconceived idea of my sense of honour and commitment since we first met. You've never wanted to believe that I could be faithful to you.' He leans towards me. 'Why is that?'

he whispers. 'What are you scared of, Sadie?'

A shiver runs down my spine. If Gareth kisses me, I won't be able to resist him. I half-close my eyes. Is he going to kiss me? A draught of icy air whisks around my ankles. Gareth has opened the door. He picks up his toolbox, and turns on his heels.

'I'm off.'

'You haven't finished the work . . . the roof . . .'

'So what?'

'I'll pay you.'

'I know you will, Sadie. I've never doubted you.'

'When I've sold the house.'

'Yeah, whatever. I'll fetch the rest of my stuff this afternoon. See you around.' Gareth fixes his mouth in a grim straight line and walks out.

Who do I believe? Gareth or Helen? Why should Gareth lie? Because he regrets sleeping with my best friend and wants me back? Why should Helen lie? Why would she lead me to believe that she did sleep with Gareth if she didn't? What did I see that morning when I returned home from shopping for those screws? What did I *really* see?

Although Helen has made it clear that she isn't returning to the development, I find it difficult to avoid her. I run into her at school, and at swimming. Charlotte wasn't put up into the next swimming class this term, much to Helen's chagrin. I believe that she's finally shelved any plans she had for the 2016 Olympics, and has decided that Charlotte should really concentrate on her ballet, muscular calves being more attractive on a girl than over-developed shoulders. Sam has gone up to the next class, and Lorna, to my amazement, has ascended to the dizzy heights of a Child Beginner Plus, which means that Charlotte and the twins swim at different times on the same day.

Having managed to dodge Helen in the changing rooms, I catch sight of her in the viewing area where she's drinking coffee with Michael. Has she seen me? I'm not sure, but Michael has.

He calls me and Sam over. 'Come and join us, Sadie.'

Sam sits down. He knows that Helen and I have fallen out, but he doesn't understand why. Immediately, he starts chatting to Michael.

'We had to do a survey on our favourite drinks at school,' he says, 'but mine wasn't on the list.'

'What is it then?' says Michael.

'Champagne, of course. I told my teacher, but she wouldn't swap it for orange squash. She wouldn't add it either, because it would spoil the look of our bar chart.'

I keep my eyes fixed on Lorna who is swimming on her back across the pool.

'Lorna's made great strides this term,' Helen comments.

'Don't you mean strokes?'

Helen frowns. I glance from Helen to Michael, and back. I suspect that she's massaging his thigh under the table. What does this mean? Is this a show of solidarity for Charlotte's benefit, or are they really back together? Where is Charlotte?

As if reading my mind, Michael informs me that Charlotte has Drama today – Helen has withdrawn her from swimming lessons.

'I wish *we* didn't have to do swimming,' says Sam.

'I thought you liked swimming,' I say.

'No, me and Lorna hate it. We've always hated it.'

'Why didn't you tell me?'

'Because we didn't want to upset you and Dad. You so wanted us to carry on with swimming lessons that we didn't like to say we didn't like swimming any more.'

'Oh Sam.' I sit silent for a moment. 'You can give up at the end of this term, I promise.'

Michael gets up to buy me a coffee and Sam a Coke, taking Sam with him, which leaves me alone with Helen. I can't bring myself to tell her that Gareth has moved out. I don't want Sam to see me crying in public. He's seen enough of me crying at home.

'I didn't see a *For Sale* board when I drove past the house today,' Helen says.

'There's no point in putting it on the market until the New Year.' I'd like to put it on before so I can pay off my debts, but the weeks before Christmas are a quiet time for estate agents.

'I'll be checking up on you,' Helen goes on. 'In fact, if I don't see that board up by the beginning of January, I won't hesitate to take legal action to get my money back.'

'Helen!' I am on my feet.

'Sit down, Sadie.' Helen tugs on my sleeve, but I refuse to sit down again. 'You're making a scene.'

'Ladies, ladies,' warns Michael, returning with the drinks. 'I wish you two would kiss and make up.' He looks at me. 'If you aren't speaking soon, Sadie, I shall

375

be the one who has to accompany my wife on her marathon Christmas shopping expeditions.'

Christmas? I drag Sam away, Coke in hand. Without Gareth, it isn't going to be much of a Christmas, is it?

Thank goodness for Topsy. I rescue her wig from the understairs cupboard where it has been relegated by mistake to the box of cleaning equipment that Helen assembled for me when we first took over the development. I collect her hoop from the twins' bedroom where Lorna's been playing with it, iron her dungarees and touch up her Doc Martens with silver paint.

When I arrive at school for the Christmas disco with Topsy's box of props, I find myself wondering if it's time Topsy gave up all this voluntary work that she does, and concentrated on finding paid employment. I have to talk my way past the teacher at the main door, because I haven't any money to pay for Sam and Lorna's tickets.

Helen is selling crisps and additive-fuelled soft drinks in the corridor.

'Hiya!' I say, before remembering that we aren't speaking.

'Caroline, the clown's arrived,' Helen calls through to the hall, without looking at me. I gaze towards her, but she keeps her head bowed over her petty cashbox. I guess the fact that Lorna was chosen to be the Angel Gabriel in the school play, and Charlotte was merely an innkeeper's wife hasn't helped.

I head through the doors into the hall where Caroline is helping the DJ set up her music centre and lights. I don't do my turn until halfway through the evening, between 'The Birdie Song' and 'The Conga'.

I do the Magic Colouring Book, the Collapsing Wand, and a variation on the Egg Trick. I don't do eggs any more. I do tennis balls. To fill in the rest of the time, when I'm not centre-stage, I dabble in some face painting, and let the younger children waiting in the queue stroke Ricky.

I catch sight of the twins dancing. Sam is wearing jeans and a waistcoat over a long blue shirt, left untucked. He thinks he looks cool, and so do a gaggle of adoring girls that follow him about. He ignores them, and joins up with Harry and another boy, dancing with enthusiasm and without style, like I used to. Lorna is wearing a sparkly top and skirt, and exposing far too much midriff for my liking. She sways from one foot to the other, gazing dreamily toward the disco lights and mouthing the lyrics to the songs, while Charlotte makes petits jetés and pirouettes across the floor.

On the way home in the car, Sam complains that he misses Gareth. He also tells me that Harry is leaving New Malden in the New Year. 'It took me ages to find a friend,' he moans.

'I expect you'll be able to meet up with him now and then. I don't suppose he's going very far. Where's he moving to?'

'Australia.'

'Oh.' I try to cheer Sam up. 'There'll be other friends. Who was that other boy you were dancing with?'

'Matt, but he's not keen on playing Jackie Chan with me.' He pauses. 'I haven't got any friends – Tom's no good because he stays in bed all day at weekends, and Gareth's gone.'

'I'll be your friend, Sam,' Lorna pipes up.

'That's very kind,' I observe.

'I'll be your friend,' Lorna continues, 'if you let me have all the chocolate coins off the Christmas tree this year.'

'No way,' says Sam.

I try to explain what friendship is.

'It's about having someone to fight with,' Sam interrupts. 'I can't fight with Lorna because she always runs off crying to you, Mum.'

'I don't.'

'You do.'

'That's enough!' I warn. 'Friendship is about sharing and caring, not fighting.'

'You and Helen fight,' Lorna says. 'I've heard you arguing on the phone about the house and money.'

'Helen and I are no longer friends,' I point out gently.

'You'll make up,' Lorna says. 'I'm always making up with Charlotte – we link our little fingers, and sing, "Make up, make up, never ever break up".'

I remember the same ritual from my schooldays. It was easier then. Your best friend nicked one of your Potato Puffs at breaktime, or turned one end of the rope too fast when you were skipping. Helen's betrayal is rather less trivial. I doubt that linking little fingers will be enough to mend our friendship.

Chapter Nineteen

It is Christmas, season of goodwill to all men – except Gareth who has let me down. I miss him. I miss the man I thought he was so much. He waltzes into my dreams, usually dressed in half a morning suit – I shall spare my blushes by not mentioning which half – and brandishing a large screwdriver, a symbol perhaps of my repressed erotic desires.

Enough of Gareth. The house is ready apart from some last-minute touches. I've called in Marcus, the estate agent who ran into my car. He had a good look around, and gave me an excellent percentage to sell it. He pointed out that the roof wasn't quite complete, but I assured him that it would be, as soon as I could find someone to deal with it. He was also a little cautious about the toilet seat, and what he termed the exuberant playfulness of the garden design, but he believes that it will be snapped up very quickly if he advertises it in the New Year. As he said, the buyer can always rip it all out and start again, put their own mark on the property . . .

At dawn on Christmas Day, I am hit on the head by

what turns out to be a weighty pillowcase. While I am recovering from concussion at the same time as emerging from a dazed sleep, I realise that the twins are bouncing on my mattress.

'Mum! Father Christmas has brought us loads of presents. Look!' I have no choice. 'Look, Mum.'

'I am looking.' I can see the weft and weave of the cloth of the pillowcase in the light from the landing.

'Can we open them?'

'Now?' The twins' sing-song voices sound very similar. Their eyes are wide with excitement.

'Please . . .'

'Go on then.' I watch them grab for the first present that comes to hand and rip off the wrapping. 'Have you read the label to see who it's from?'

'It's from you,' says Lorna. 'Thanks, a Double Dance mat.'

'It plugs into the television,' I explain.

'A Hulk bop bag! It's the best present I've ever had in my life,' says Sam, going on to the next present and ripping the paper off that too. Lorna is less enthusiastic. It's her nature.

'Do you know who those presents are from?' I ask, trying to retrieve labels from the crumpled paper strewn across my duvet, 'because you need to know so you can write your thank-you letters.'

'Happy Christmas, Mummy.' Lorna flings her arms around my neck and kisses my cheek. Her breath is warm and scented with fruit pastilles.

'You've opened the sweets Father Christmas left you,' I observe.

'How do you know?'

'Aah, magic.' I wink mysteriously. This is going to be a difficult day for me, but I have to keep everything together for the twins. I won't let them down. In fact, on the basis of Marcus' valuation, I applied for a new credit card so I could put the whole of Christmas on plastic. I shower and dress, and open my presents: a black top that I bought myself from the children, and a cheese-slice with a handle in the shape of a mouse from my mother. On the floor in the corner of my bedroom is the sports holdall I bought for Gareth back in October, still unwrapped. Gareth? I wonder what he is doing this morning and what, or who, he is unwrapping?

Sam is going red in the face trying to blow the Hulk up. You blow it up to 40 inches tall, according to the Argos catalogue, then you knock it down and watch it bounce back. I thought it would allow Sam to relieve some of his pent-up frustrations in a relatively safe manner.

'Let me do it,' I suggest.

'I can do it,' he insists.

I start out in the kitchen while the twins are trashing the dining area. I'm planning to move the table into the sitting room later to give our guests more elbow room. There'll be six of us, counting Tom. Make that eight. When Dan and Wendy call in with presents for the twins, I tell them that they may as well stay for lunch, if they haven't got any other plans.

'Gareth hasn't come back?' says Dan, hovering on the doorstep with Wendy at his side.

I shake my head. Dan knows all about Gareth's betrayal from the twins, and what I told him when he asked me to clear up a few details that they left out.

'Would you like to come in? Both of you?'

'That's very kind of you, Sadie,' Wendy says. 'I was going to take a veggie pasta-bake out of the freezer, but I know that Dan would prefer turkey.'

I show them through to the kitchen, following along behind Wendy in her pink joggers and top. 'I've completed the rest of the work on the development, apart from those few tiles on the roof,' I say. 'Aren't you going to congratulate me?'

'It's looking very different,' Dan says grudgingly. 'If I had the money I'd buy it myself.'

'Dream on.'

'Dreams can come true, Sadie. I can't say too much yet, but I've been offered a job in Town.'

'It isn't anything to do with pizzas, thank goodness,' says Wendy.

'I should hear confirmation of it in the New Year,' Dan continues.

I hope that it comes off this time. I am being sincere. Dan deserves some luck. We all do.

Dan follows me through into the kitchen, and hands over presents to the twins. Wendy watches, arms folded, and I respect her for keeping her distance.

'Thanks, Dad,' says Lorna, unwrapping an art set and paper. 'Why didn't Father Christmas bring it?'

'All right, Princess,' says Dan. 'I ordered it direct from his grotto, and he dropped it at my house by mistake.'

'There's no such thing as Father Christmas,' says Sam. Lorna looks at him as if it's the first she's heard of that possibility. 'Mum says he doesn't bring presents if you don't believe,' Sam goes on, 'but I don't believe and I've got hundreds.'

'I know there's a Father Christmas because I saw him at the end of my bed,' says Lorna.

'It was dark,' says Sam.

'I saw his shadow – he's very fat.'

'That was Mum,' says Sam.

'The sherry and mince pies have gone, and the reindeer have nibbled the end of the carrot,' says Lorna. 'There's the proof.'

'Mum ate it.'

'I can't stand carrots,' I protest.

'A reindeer would eat the whole thing in one gulp, and everyone knows that reindeer can't fly,' Sam goes on.

Lorna flatly refuses to be disillusioned. I give her a hug.

While the twins have been arguing and I have been trying to keep the peace, Dan has pulled the remote-control car that he has given Sam from its box, and is studying the instructions. It's a shiny blue off-roader, jacked up high on its wheels. Dan frowns.

'What's up?' I ask.

'I assumed that it came with batteries.'

I grab the instructions. 'No, look, you need 4 AAs and a PP13.'

'I don't suppose you keep spares anywhere,' says Dan, challenging me. When we were married I used to drive him mad by forgetting to keep the stash of spares topped up.

I go and look. When I return from the cupboard under the stairs empty-handed, Sam's lower lip trembles and his eyes water, but he doesn't cry. My heart twists.

'Didn't you read the box before you wrapped it, Dan? It says quite clearly that batteries are not included.' I realise my mistake too late. Sam is watching me with an air of told-you-so. 'I don't suppose Father Christmas has time to check every single box he delivers,' I continue bravely, in the hope that Lorna has missed my inadvertent confirmation of the non-existence of Father Christmas.

'I thought that's what he had elves for,' says Lorna. 'Maybe he dropped the batteries in the bottom of his sleigh.'

I wonder if I'd manage to get everything right if I had elves to help me.

'There's a battery in the smoke alarm,' I say. 'Sean made me replace it.'

Dan removes the batteries from the smoke alarm and our toothbrushes, and plays with the car, while Wendy rings her mum to check on Vinnie, and I peel potatoes, parsnips and carrots, and ball three different types of melon for the tropical fruit salad I'm making for those who can't stand Christmas pudding. When the doorbell rings – yes, we have a working doorbell now, I fitted it myself – Dan drives the car along the hall to let Sean and Annette in.

Homer lollops through to the kitchen with them, shaking himself and spattering the new units with flecks of wet mud and saliva, before he flops down across the front of the oven. While Sean is already on his knees examining the remote-control car, Annette hands me a bottle of red wine and a carrier bag filled with all kinds of treats – crisps, chocolates and smoked salmon.

'Don't look so surprised, Sadie,' she grins. 'I told Sean that we can afford to treat ourselves occasionally.'

'I heard that, my darling spendthrift of a wife,' Sean says lightly from the hall.

Annette lowers her voice.

'As we're not saving for fertility treatments any more, and I'm starting as Deputy Head next term, we might as well enjoy the money.' She looks me straight in the eyes. 'I've accepted that my chance of having a child is over, Sis. I'll still dream that one day I'll open the front door and find that someone's left me a baby on the step, but I can live with that.'

'And you and Sean?'

'We're fine, closer than ever, in fact.' Annette hesitates. 'It took me a while to realise that I was driving him away with my anger and frustration. It almost broke up our marriage.'

'Did you bring us a present, Auntie Annette?' Lorna interrupts.

'Shh, have some manners,' I say.

'You always say that if you want something, you have to make it clear,' Lorna informs me.

'Don't worry,' says Annette. 'We have brought you presents.'

Lorna is delighted with her camera and Sam's so

excited about his watch that he can't stop jumping up and down on the spot.

'There aren't many people who would invite their ex-husband and his girlfriend over for Christmas dinner,' Annette whispers to me as I continue with the preparation.

'Shh,' I warn as Wendy returns to the kitchen.

'Can I help with anything, Sadie?' Wendy asks. 'Shall I make some drinks?'

'Yes, thanks. There's wine, or vodka.'

'I'm teetotal.'

'Coffee, tea.'

'Not caffeine.'

'There's squash, or water.'

'I don't suppose you have a juicer for making fruit smoothies?' Wendy smiles. 'You haven't. It doesn't matter. Show me where the glasses are, and I'll find out what everyone wants.'

'I'd give you a hand too, Sadie, but I don't want to interfere when you and Wendy seem to have it all under control.' Annette sits down. Wendy sorts out the drinks, and Sean and Dan play with Sam's car while the twins fight over Lorna's new pens.

'It's a pity Mum couldn't be here with us all instead of with Roberto and his family,' Annette says.

'Are you sure?'

'It would have been nice.' Annette pauses. 'Can you smell gas?'

'It's probably Homer.'

'I'm sure I can smell gas,' Annette insists.

I check the hob. Everything's fine as far as I can make

out, although I have to confess that it's taking me and Tom some time to work out how to use the new cooking facilities. I call for Sam to go and wake Tom for Christmas dinner, then I start slicing onions for the stuffing, wishing that Gareth was coming for dinner with us too. I wipe a tear from my eye.

'Onions!' says Sean, coming into the kitchen. 'Why don't you use the extractor hood?'

'The Prince of Darkness is due back to wire it in.'

'The who?'

'The electrician. Oh, it doesn't matter. It's a long story,' and it reminds me of Gareth again, and long after I've cleared up after the onions, I continue crying into the Bisto.

I can hear Tom getting up, and showering overhead. Eventually, he turns up in the kitchen, bringing me a small parcel.

'You shouldn't have.' I open it to find a bottle of perfume from the Body Shop. 'Thanks, Tom.' I spritz some onto my wrist and sniff it. 'It's my favourite. Lorna,' I call, 'bring Tom's present, will you? It's under the tree.' It's a Justin Timberlake CD. Tom says that he is touched.

'When will dinner be ready?' Sean asks, once all the wrapping paper is piled into the bin in the corner of the kitchen. 'You ought to empty that, Sadie,' he adds. 'It's a fire hazard.'

'For goodness sake, Sean,' I grumble, 'can't you take one day off without thinking about work?' I pause. 'Dinner's in half an hour, if everything goes to plan.'

Of course it doesn't, and I'm not ready to dish up

until half past two. It's complicated by the fact that Tom has decided that he doesn't fancy a traditional Christmas dinner, and he's busy peeling and chopping potatoes to cook himself egg and chips. Sean and Dan carry the table into the front room, and Annette sets it with cutlery and crackers.

'I wish you'd come and sit down with us, Sis,' says Annette, returning to the kitchen with Dan.

'The turkey's still in the oven. I don't think it'll walk out unaided unless I've got it totally wrong.'

'Stuff the turkey,' says Dan.

'Is that an order or an expletive?' I remain obstinately on my feet. 'I've forgotten the stuffing. I was going to do onion and lemongrass.'

'Don't worry about that now,' says Annette. 'Let's eat.'

We eat. At least, most of us eat – I'm not hungry, Wendy picks at sprouts and carrots, and Tom's still cooking his dinner – until dribbles of gravy and cranberry sauce festoon the clean white cloth. I didn't have to worry about Wendy's influence on Lorna. Lorna has made up her own mind about veganism. She informs us that it's cruel to kill animals, but she loves meat too much to give it up.

Dan and I reminisce about the twins' earlier Christmases, Sean and Wendy talk about strategies to increase upper body strength, and Annette helps Lorna and Sam with the puzzles that came out of the crackers.

Homer has moved underneath the table where I accidentally make contact with him with my foot. He yelps, and Annette disappears under the table with him to administer comprehensive first aid, which involves a lot of noisy kissing to minimise any post-traumatic stress that I might have inflicted.

'He's all right. His tail isn't broken,' she announces as she emerges once more.

'Fantastic, I've failed to kill the dog,' I mutter, as I gaze at Dan, Sean and Annette, sitting on their bums, looking at me hopefully like chicks in a nest, only nowhere near as cute, waiting for me to feed them. Wendy alone has helped me out. She even persuaded Dan to fetch the butter for his boiled potatoes himself, in spite of the fact that he was feeling the effects of a full work-out at home this morning, including performing a series of abdominal crunches.

Wendy has her arm around Dan's shoulders. Dan's green and gold paper crown is tilted down over one eye, and the necklace of purple pearls that he found in his cracker dangles around his neck. He offered it to Lorna, but she declined, saying she would have liked it if it had been blue. I am sozzled too. My tinsel halo is unravelling, and I no longer care whether I have pudding or not. Like Wendy, Annette hasn't touched a drop of alcohol, and she's excused herself for a while, saying she needs fresh air.

I clear the plates and return to the kitchen. The pudding is steaming in a saucepan on the hob, water seething furiously around it. The icing on the brandy butter sparkles from a dish on the granite worktop. I pour the cream into a jug – it is Christmas, after all.

Tom is draining his chips through a slotted spoon. I snatch one, and drop it on the worktop.

'They're hot,' Tom says, too late.

'Hey, Sadie, what's taking you so long?' Dan calls while I'm inspecting my fingers for burns. It is a chilling flashback to the ghosts of Christmases past when he used to hassle me in exactly the same way, so that he didn't miss *The Wizard of Oz* on the telly.

I lift the basin out of the saucepan, and tip out the pudding. It smells of mixed spice and marmalade. I sent Lorna out earlier into the garden to snip a sprig from one of the ornamental hollies Tom is growing in pots. There are no berries this year. I stick the sprig in the top of the pudding, and prick my finger. I squeeze it. No blood. I am annoyed. I feel that it should bleed. Copiously. To match my mood.

Tom throws the lid back on the chip pan, and carries his dinner into the front room to join the others, while I follow with bowls, cream, brandy butter and serving spoons on a tray, then the fruit salad, or what's left of it after Tom's been sampling the melon balls, and then the pudding to Sam's excited chant of '*Olé, olé, olé!*' I go back, grab the matches and brandy, and shut the kitchen door behind me so that Homer can't sneak in and steal food from the worktops.

I finish the glass of wine that I didn't have time to drink during the main course, before I open the brandy and pour it over the pudding until it fills the rim of the plate. With a Topsy-like flourish, I light a match.

'Prepare to be amazed!' I touch the flame to the top of the pudding. It whips across the surface, making a blue halo in which the sprig of holly crackles and blackens. A tongue of flame licks over the edge of the plate, catching a cracker wrapper and tracking along the tinsel at the base of Lorna's centrepiece for the table, another *Blue Peter*-inspired creation. Within seconds, the tablecloth is alight, and everyone is sitting there watching me as if they expect me to put it out with one great spit.

'Did you say prepare to be ablaze?' Dan slurs.

'You've set the table on fire,' says Sean.

'Great,' I say. 'You noticed?'

'I am a firefighter,' he says coolly. 'That's what I'm paid for.'

'Well, don't just sit there, Sean. Go and fetch a bucket of water, or something.' Sean finally moves those fantastic muscles of his and heads out towards the kitchen while Annette, with unusual presence of mind, tips the twins' glasses of lemonade over the flames. In the background I am vaguely aware of a roaring sound, and choking blue smoke, a slamming door, and Sean bellowing for everyone to get the hell out . . .

'Get everyone out of the house,' Sean orders. 'Quickly.'

I grab the twins' hands, and the rest of the brandy, and run. 'What's happened? Why? What's going on?'

'Chip-pan fire,' Sean yells. *'Get out!'*

In less than a minute, we're lined up on the pavement opposite *Llamedos*.

'Is everyone here?' says Sean, joining us with Homer.

'Where's Alvin?' I panic.

'I saw the cat out in the garden with a piece of turkey just before,' Tom says sheepishly. 'Oh God, I'm sorry, Sadie. I must have left the hob on . . . This is all my fault.'

'It's Mum's fault,' Lorna interrupts. 'How many times has Uncle Sean warned us not to play with matches?'

'No, Lorna, it was me.' Tom looks as if he's about to burst into tears. 'I've ruined the kitchen after all your hard work.'

'Everyone's safe,' I soothe, although I am anything but calm myself. 'That's all that matters.'

'This is so exciting, Mum,' says Sam, jumping up and down as the first fire engine arrives with its siren wailing and lights blazing, then a second. 'I can't wait to go back to school so I can tell Matt.'

The firefighters evacuate the houses on either side, then dive into the development with extinguishers and hoses. The Neighbour From Hell comes straight over with his hands in the pockets of his mac. 'I'd finished watching the Queen's speech, and was having a nap when that lot broke my door in,' he complains, pointing towards the firefighters. 'There's been nothing but trouble since you moved in. This has been an *annus horribilis* for me.'

'And me,' I protest, but my voice comes out weak and small, and I have to sit on the pavement for a minute or two.

'You're in shock,' says Annette, squatting down beside me. 'Have some of that brandy. It'll make you feel better.'

I drink. I offer The Neighbour From Hell a drink too. He accepts on the grounds that it's for medicinal purposes only. Sean fetches several blankets to keep us warm, and counts us for the fifth time.

'Protocol,' he explains.

'Can we go back inside yet?' I ask.

'Not yet,' he says. 'We need to make sure it's safe.' Sean's in his element, liaising with his colleagues and keeping us updated on the progress of the fire. He emerges from the house a couple of times with a sooty face and hands. 'Coming to yours, Sadie, is a busman's holiday.'

'It's lucky we were here, wasn't it?' says Annette. 'Oh Sean, you are such a hero. You saved our lives.'

'Isn't that a little melodramatic?' I suggest. 'Our lives weren't really in any danger.'

'If that chip pan had caught fire in the middle of the night, you'd all be dead,' Sean says comfortingly. 'How many times have I told you to keep a battery in your smoke alarm?'

'We were going to put it back, once Dan had finished playing with Sam's car.'

'Pull the other one, Sadie. If the alarm had been working today, you might have ended up with far less damage than there is.'

'Damage?' I gulp. 'How bad is it?'

'I'd describe it as extensive.'

Sean and Annette make themselves scarce once the Fire Brigade have made the house safe. Dan and Wendy take the twins back to their place for me. Tom and I stay to assess the destruction. My heart sinks. The kitchen is in such a mess that we can't possibly sell the house as it is. The ceiling has come down, and the new units alongside what remains of the hob and oven are destroyed. The hall and the front room have water and smoke damage, and the new hall carpet is smudged with filth from the firefighters' boots. Everything is black.

'I'm so sorry, Sadie,' Tom keeps repeating, but his abject apologies are of no help in retrieving the situation. Even Justin Timberlake is in pieces – one of the firefighters must have kicked him into the pond by accident. Tom rolls up the left sleeve of his sweatshirt, squats down, reaches into the water with his right hand, and raises Justin's head. Tom has tears in his eyes, but I'm not sure whether he's crying a river over Justin's or the development's fate.

'I'll call the insurance company,' I say, trying to console him. 'I'm sure they'll pay up.' At least, I hope that they will. I am at my lowest ebb, in what the people from the Met Office would describe as the deepest depression.

'I suppose you'd like me to move out,' Tom says tentatively. 'I know you've wanted me to leave for some time.'

'I'd rather you stayed now. I don't like the idea of being here alone.'

'Thanks, Sadie.'

'I'd better tell Helen.' I call her from Tom's mobile – mine has been incinerated.

'Are you ringing to wish me a Happy Christmas?' she says coldly.

'Something's happened.'

'What makes you think that I want to hear about your sordid love-life?'

'It's about the development.'

'Don't tell me, you've sold it.'

'It caught fire.'

'When?'

'This afternoon.'

'You're winding me up.'

'I thought you should know.' I hesitate. 'I wanted you to know . . .' I cut Helen off. What's the point? Shivering, I turn to Tom. 'All Helen's interested in is getting her money back.'

'I'm so sorry—'

'That's enough,' I say drearily. 'Go and do something useful.' It's as cold inside as it is outside the house. We can't use the gas or electricity. Tom lights a fire in the fireplace in the front room, and I'm grateful that Helen and I retained at least one of the property's original features. Tom boils water for tea on it and toasts crumpets. Not that I'm hungry. Tom is. He didn't get to finish his dinner.

I pull on a couple of sweaters and sit staring at the charred remains of the Christmas pudding on the table, with Alvin purring on my lap. A car roars up outside. I hear a key slipping into the lock, and the front door opening. I stand up. Helen steps into the sitting room, accompanied by a waft of perfume – *Truth*, I think, from Calvin Klein.

'I had to come and see that you were all right,' she says. 'Where are the twins?'

'They're fine. No one's been hurt.'

'Thank goodness for that. You didn't give me time to ask.'

'I didn't expect you to.'

'Sadie, you're right,' Helen says sharply. 'We aren't

talking, we're no longer friends, therefore I don't care if you're alive or dead.' Her voice softens. 'I do care. I care more than I thought, or wanted to.'

'Oh Helen.' I can't help it. I start blubbing. 'I'm so sorry.'

'What for?' says Helen, putting her arms round me.

'Everything.'

'It was my fault,' Tom pipes up. I'd almost forgotten he was here. He waves a crumpet speared on a fork. 'I left a chip-pan on in the kitchen.'

'I set fire to the table.' I back away from Helen's embrace to pick up a singed paper napkin to blow my nose.

'It *is* a mess!' Helen says, surveying the front room.

'You haven't seen the worst of it yet.'

Helen, although she is as gutted as the kitchen, is optimistic that with the money from the insurers, and some serious work, we can get the property back on the market by the end of January.

'We?' I mumble.

'We'll do it together,' she promises.

'I can't.' I shake my head. 'I can't do this any more. I've had enough.'

'You have to. Come on, Sadie. We can repaint this room and the stairs. Gareth can fit new kitchen units.'

My tears start afresh. 'Gareth's gone.'

'Gone?'

'Gareth was more interested in you than me all along. He came to work on the development, hoping to win you back. You slept with him.' The expression on Helen's face shows that she has no idea what I'm talking about. 'I saw you.'

'You saw what you wanted to see. As soon as anyone so much as looks in Gareth's direction, you assume he must be shagging them. Didn't your divorce teach you anything?'

'Yes – that I'd have to learn how to unblock the sink, catch spiders and change a light bulb pretty quickly.' I choke back a sob. 'You misled me.'

'How would you have felt if you'd been in my shoes?'

I glance down at Helen's high-heeled back boots. 'Superior?' I suggest.

'Try livid and hurt. My marriage was on the rocks, yet all you could do was accuse me of seducing Gareth. I'd have more chance of winning the National Lottery than luring him away from you. Gareth loves you, Sadie.'

I feel stifled, as if Tom has stuffed one of his crumpets down my gullet.

'He said he couldn't imagine life without you.' A shadow crosses Helen's eyes. 'Oh, what a mess I've made! Listen, Sadie, I don't care if you never forgive me, but you must call him.'

'Gareth won't want to work here again.' I am crying again.

'Not for the development – for you, you idiot,' Helen says gently. 'Burning the house down . . .' Her shoulders start to quiver. 'It could only happen to you . . .'

Soon, we are both howling – me with anguish, and Helen with laughter. We are friends again. Helen goes around whistling the tune of 'Relight My Fire', while I find myself humming old Smokey Robinson songs. She tells me that Michael's renting a new shop in the High

Street and hiring a Rolf Harris impersonator to open it, no offence to Topsy, and that Charlotte's given up Drama.

'Charlotte told Michael that she thought she'd be happier if she concentrated on one or two activities at a time,' Helen says. 'She can always go back into acting later,' she adds hopefully.

'She has a few years ahead of her before she has to decide whether or not to take up a place at RADA,' I agree.

'Shall we get started then? We can paint everything with that gerbera paint you have left to save money. We can salvage the granite worktops, but we'll need new units. I'll have a look in MFI. We can ask Gareth to fit them.'

'I'm not going to ask Gareth,' I cut in.

'Sadie, why not?' Helen frowns.

'I just can't.' How can I go crawling back to him and say, 'I'm sorry for accusing you of sleeping with my best friend. I made a mistake.' How can I? I don't call Gareth. I call the insurance company instead.

They send a loss adjuster, a man not much older than Tom, who turns up in a cheap suit with a briefcase, laptop and attitude. I show him through to the front room, and offer him the Director's chair.

'Isn't there anywhere I can work?' he says. 'A table?'

'It was damaged in the fire.' I correct myself. 'In the fires.'

The loss adjuster places his laptop on his knees, and presses a few buttons as I hover at his shoulder. 'Would you like to sit down, Mrs Keith?'

I remain on my feet.

'Just a few routine questions. Date of birth?'

'Do I have to answer that?'

'No,' the loss adjuster says in a way that suggests that it might go against me if I fail to reveal it. 'Occupation?'

Now that he asks, I wonder if I've failed to fulfil my obligations to the insurance company by neglecting to inform them that I am in business as a property developer. To avoid any unpleasantness, I tell him that I'm a housewife and mother.

'You've been doing the property up?'

'It needed a lot of work when I moved in. We'd – I mean I'd – almost finished.' I follow him around as he assesses the extent of the damage.

'How many people are living here?'

'Me, the family and one lodger. Four.'

'Did you notify the insurance company when you took in a lodger for financial gain?'

'Oh, Tom doesn't pay rent. He's more of a visitor.' I pause. 'What do you think? Will you settle on accidental damage?'

'That depends on whether it was an accident, Mrs Keith. As far as we are aware, you're making a claim for two separate incidents that occurred at the same time, in the same house: it suggests arson rather than accident to me, but my line manager might look at your case in a different light. I don't wish to prejudge the claim.'

'You already have.'

'I try to be impartial, but I have to consider your

history. You've already made two claims on your contents policy with us in the past three years.'

'Have I?' A memory that I'd conveniently pushed to the back of my mind resurfaces. Once I did accidentally – maybe a little on purpose – bleach a tatty old carpet because I wanted a new one but couldn't afford it because I'd just had to lay out for the annual insurance premium.

'There was a carpet,' the loss adjuster confirms, 'and a claim for a top-of-the-range camcorder that you lost in Richmond Park. You're either very careless or a liar, Mrs Keith.' He refuses to settle the current claim here and now, but waits until he is safely ensconced back at his office with his manager to back him up.

The company will pay out in full for a new kitchen, and half the redecorating costs of the hall and landing. They will pay out nothing on the contents policy which I took out at the same time as the buildings insurance. The damage to the front room is my responsibility. I can appeal, but they might wish to investigate my previous claims more thoroughly. It reminds me that I never did use the money they paid me to buy a replacement camcorder for the camcorder we never had. They also remind me that they have the right to refuse renewal of the policies next year.

I don't call the Managing Director to make a fuss. I can't, because it's my fault that the company won't pay out in full. I've finally realised that a lot of things are my fault. I'd justified those dodgy claims, telling myself that I was owed something for the premiums that I'd paid in over the years. I was wrong. I was selfish, fraudulent . . .

Because of my lies, I've lost out on any profit I would have made on the development, maybe more than that because I was hoping to use the insurance money to string the Building Society along for a couple more months . . .

I've made mistakes dealing with Sam and his problems, not listening to him when he needed me, not showing him how much I love him . . .

I've lost Gareth because of my paranoia and jealousy . . .

Later the same evening, I turn to the books that I picked up from the library before Christmas: *Hard Times*, *Angela's Ashes*, and *Misery*. I pour myself a glass of wine and wallow.

Chapter Twenty

I can prove that creativity stems from emotional turmoil. Tom has stopped singing his own heart-wrenching ballads since he came out – instead, he strums along to Busted's raucous hits and parodies Dido's mournful compositions – whereas I can't stop making funky artwork for the house.

I'm painting triangular wooden frames with turquoise paint to contrast with the gerbera on the walls in the hall, when Annette turns up with Homer. He wags his tail and drags her indoors by his lead, leaving wet pawmarks on the runner that I've bought to hide the dirty bootprints that the firefighters left on the hessian carpet. Thanks to Homer, I now need something to cover the runner.

'I'm bunking off school,' Annette says, looking around. 'This looks great. You've almost finished.'

'Helen and I have hardly started. The insurers won't pay up for all the repairs, and I can't find anyone to refit the kitchen.'

'Have you tried Gareth?'

I shake my head.

'He hasn't come back then?' Annette says bluntly.

'Why should he? There's nothing for him here.'

'Don't you miss him at all?' Annette stares at me, one eyebrow raised. 'Come on, Sis, you can't fool me.'

'The twins miss him. I feel as though I've let them down – not that it was my fault that Gareth left.'

'Do you remember when Granny Louisa gave us those knitted toys one Christmas?' Annette asks. 'I had the one that you wanted, a pixie with a red hat, and you hacked it to pieces with the kitchen scissors.'

'All right. Maybe it was my fault. I've always been a jealous cow.'

'I never told you, but I was glad you did that because I thought it was hideous, and to make up for it, Granny Louisa made me a handbag with sequins on it instead.' Annette smiles. 'Let's go and sit down. I have some news.'

We settle in the front room, me on the Director's chair, and Annette crosslegged on the floor. She hands over a couple of tins of dog food, the ultimate in generosity. I'm being ironic again. What does she think I'm going to do with them when I haven't got a dog? Make Chappie con Carne for Lorna and Sam?

'Look at these, Sis.' Annette opens her bag and waves two small squares of paper at me.

At first I'm not sure what I'm looking at, until I recall from years past that I had black and white photos like this of the twins.

'You're pregnant! Congratulations!' I should have guessed. Annette can't stop smiling. Her complexion bears the delicate pallor of early pregnancy.

'I bet Sean's over the moon, isn't he?'

'Indeed,' Annette sighs.

'I thought you weren't going to have any more fertility treatment. What happened?'

'The usual,' Annette grins. 'A bottle of wine, a meal and . . . bang! According to our consultant, sperm have to swim the equivalent of travelling from Edinburgh to Paris, and that's without hopping onto Eurostar to cross the Channel, to reach the egg. He said that Sean's couldn't doggypaddle a width of a swimming pool, but one of them made it, and it only takes one.'

'But you and Sean always made out that it was your fault.'

'He asked me to. He said he'd feel less of a man if anyone else found out.'

'And you went along with it?'

'I do love Sean, even if he is a bit of a prat.'

I raise my eyebrows in surprise.

'I know how Sean looks to everyone, but he means well,' Annette continues. 'I wanted us to have AID, Artificial Insemination by Donor, but Sean wouldn't countenance it. He wanted our baby, or no baby at all.' We look again at the smudgy scan photos. 'That's its heart,' says Annette, pointing to a tiny white blot with a dark centre.

'I wish that you'd told me that it was Sean's problem, then I wouldn't have gone on about offering to help you.'

'Actually, you can help me now, Sis. Would you have Homer for a while?'

'What do you mean by "a while?"'

'I can't look after him. Every time I open a tin of that tripe mixture I throw up.'

'Can't Sean feed him?'

'It's difficult with him being on shifts. Please, Sadie. It won't be for ever.'

'All right then.' I have the twins, Gareth – no, not Gareth any more – Tom and Alvin. What difference will one more resident make?

'Thanks.' Annette leaves Homer with me. When I suggest to him that I book him an appearance on *Pet Rescue*, he wags the tip of his tail and gazes at me with mournful eyes. I feed him a cold sausage from the fridge, then settle him down on a rug in the front room before Helen arrives, dressed in jeans, an old sweatshirt and fingerless gloves, and carrying a bucket and a carry-box of various cleaning fluids.

'What's that dog doing here!' she exclaims.

'Sleeping.'

'It can't stay. It reeks of rotting offal. How can we sell this house with that stinking, slobbering, pooping creature here?'

'He'll be going home before we put it on the market,' I say, but Helen will not be calmed until I divert her from the subject of dog hair to the subject of Annette's pregnancy.

'If Sean hadn't kept wearing those tight Lycra shorts and getting himself overheated at the gym, it wouldn't have taken them so long, would it?' she sniffs, unimpressed.

'It may not have anything to do with Sean's shorts,' I begin, but Helen has made up her mind. Tom interrupts any further discussion, walking into the front room with a massive bunch of flowers which he thrusts into my arms.

'For you, Sadie.'

My first thought is that Gareth has sent them. 'There's no note,' I say, rummaging through the cellophane.

'They are from me to you, to say thank you for looking out for me.'

My face falls. I can't help it.

'Don't you like them? I thought everyone liked flowers.'

'I love them, thank you, but you needn't have wasted your money.' I glance down at his feet. New trainers.

'It isn't strictly my money,' Tom explains. 'It's my dad's.'

'You've told him?'

'I used the good news and bad news approach.' Tom looks towards Helen. 'I'm gay, but I've decided to go back to uni.'

'I'll miss you, Tom. You've done a fantastic job here,' I say, picturing the back garden, the blue pots, the bubbling water feature with a central stainless-steel dome to catch and reflect the sun's rays, the giant hedgehog sculpture, hand-wrought in rustic steel, and the solar lanterns that The Neighbour From Hell claims have caused him light-pollution-induced insomnia. All that's missing is one over-arching theme to link Tom's disparate ideas. Tom wants to call it *Contemporary Contemplation with a Touch of the Med*, while Helen's suggested *Municipal Tip*.

'You do like it?' Tom says.

'It's magical,' I say. 'How about *Urban Magic*?' I lean up and kiss his cheek. He smiles. 'Keep in touch.' I don't suppose that he will. He'll be too busy catching up with old friends, and making new ones.

'I've bought a football for Sam, and a pair of earrings for Lorna. Would you give them to the twins for me?'

'Aren't you staying to say goodbye?'

'Dad's running me straight down the M3.' Tom smiles. 'I think he's afraid that I'll change my mind.'

'You're quite right,' Michael cuts in from the doorway. 'Let's get going, Tom.' He nods towards Helen. 'If I'm late back, tell Charlotte that I'll collect her from school tomorrow to make up for it.'

Helen blows him a kiss, but Michael goes one better, moving up close and pressing his lips to hers. I'm not sure what he whispers in her ear before he leaves, but I assume from the fact that it's enough to make her blush, that marital understanding, if not bliss, has been restored.

Once Tom has gone, Helen and I return to the front room to paint over the soot that we tried, but failed, to remove completely from the walls.

'I didn't guess that Tom was gay,' says Helen, wiping paint down her jeans. 'You did, though, didn't you?'

'Yes . . . It's going to take two or three coats to cover this muck.'

'I don't suppose that it matters,' Helen sighs.

'It does. We'll be here for ever.'

'As long as he's happy.'

I become aware that Helen is staring at me. 'Are you listening to me?' she asks.

'I'm tired. Let's pack up,' I suggest wearily. 'I've had enough.'

Helen drops her paintbrush into the paint kettle. 'I'll wrap the brushes in clingfilm so they don't dry out.'

'I was thinking of chucking them in the dustbin. I wasn't talking about packing up for the day. I was talking about packing up for good.'

'Sadie! That isn't like you.'

'I know, but I can't stand it any longer. We're throwing more and more effort at this project, and each time I think it's going to be finished, something happens to delay it. I hate this house. I hate being a property developer!' I start hunting for the phone, finding it under a dustsheet.

'What are you doing?' says Helen, trying to restrain me.

'I'm going to ring Marcus and get him in to value this place as it is.'

'You can't!'

'The house has to go on the market next week anyway. I haven't any choice. We've run out of money.'

Helen's face pales. 'How bad is it, Sadie? I have every right to know.'

'I'm in arrears with the mortgage payments. The Building Society is running out of patience. If we don't sell the house, they'll repossess it, and if they repossess it, I'll never get another mortgage to buy a proper home for me and the twins. I know we'd get more money for it if it was finished, but I can't see any other way out than to sell it straight away.'

'I'll ask Michael for a loan.'

'I don't see why he should risk any more of his money. If I'd been more careful with what he has put into this project, we might not be in quite such a mess.'

'He'd be more than happy to help,' Helen insists.

'I'm sure he'd be delighted to have the opportunity to crow over my failure as a businesswoman.'

'You misjudge him. Michael, of all people, knows what it's like to fail. He might come across as cocky and shallow, flashing his cash about and trying to buy his way into the right social circles, but underneath all that he's a decent man, and he cares deeply about many things.'

'I know . . .'

'He can help you if you let him. The pet shop's monthly turnover is beyond our wildest dreams.'

'Pet shop?'

'Michael did some research on the subject of "Consumers' Attitudes towards their Pets" when he saw how mad Annette and Sean are about that dog of theirs. Sean might be as tight as can be when it comes to spending money on himself, but he's more than willing to spend it on raincoats, toothpaste and special gravy toppings for the dog.'

Helen tries to comfort me, but I won't listen. It isn't just about money. Everywhere I go, I find reminders of Gareth . . .

'I want to get shot of *Llamedos* as soon as possible. It's torture living here. I can't bear it!'

'Sadie! Will you listen to me?'

I take a deep breath, ready to launch myself into another tirade, but something in Helen's expression stops me.

'I've missed coming here every day,' she begins. 'I've missed working with you. Yes, my U-bends are immaculate, and every hair on that Arctic faux-fur throw in the spare bedroom is in its place, but having a clean and tidy house isn't enough for me any more. I need the challenge of an occupation outside the home.' She pauses. 'Oh Sadie, we can't give up now. What will everyone think?'

'I don't care.' I grit my teeth, biting back tears.

Helen finds me a drink, a few drops of Lagavulin that Tom left behind.

'You're scaring me,' she says. 'I've never seen you so defeated and depressed before, even after the divorce.'

'I'm fine,' I mutter.

'Let's get back to work then.'

'I can't.'

'It isn't just the house, is it? It's Gareth.' Helen looks at me. 'You didn't ring him, did you?'

I shake my head. Hot tears pour down my cheeks.

My friend's arms are around my shoulders. 'I'm so sorry that I messed it up for you, Sadie,' she whispers. 'I thought I was doing you a favour, showing you what Gareth was really like, but I was wrong. He's changed. It's all my fault.'

'It's my fault for believing you, not Gareth.' I can't ring him. I didn't trust him. My jealousy drove him away. Why should he want me back when I have no way of proving that it wouldn't happen again? I sniff loudly. Better that it's over now, and I live the rest of my life as a celibate nun.

'I wish I could turn the clock back.' Helen steps back, briefly clasping my hands in hers. 'I must go and collect Charlotte. She has gymnastics after school.'

Dan drops the twins back to the house after school for me. In the kitchen, dishing out snacks and drinks, and brewing tea for me and Dan, I tell them about Tom's departure.

'At least we have Homer instead,' says Lorna, trying to look on the bright side.

'Homer doesn't do gardening.'

'He does,' says Sam. 'He's digging a hole in the lawn.'

'Homer!' I yell.

Lorna fetches him in and takes him upstairs to dress him up as Grandma in *Little Red Riding Hood*. Sam mooches off to watch some telly.

'What did the loss adjuster say about your claim?' Dan asks.

'That they'll pay for the kitchen, not the rest.'

'That's better than a kick in the teeth, isn't it?' he says sarcastically.

'I suppose so.' I watch Dan's face. He can't wait to criticise, can he? Helen's right. I can't let Dan, or anyone else who doubted us, have the satisfaction of saying, 'Told you so'. We can fix this mess. We can complete this project with or without Gareth. 'Give us another two weeks, and Helen and I will have this place on the market.'

Dan hesitates just long enough for me to realise that he doesn't quite believe me. 'That's good news all round then. I've got that new job in Town. I start next Monday.'

'That's fantastic.'

'I'll set up a regular monthly payment into your account.' He passes me a cheque. 'My contribution to Christmas dinner. Don't pretend you don't need it,' he goes on, before I can hand it back. 'Lorna told Wendy that you were feeding her and Sam a vegan diet like hers – baked beans and pizzas without toppings – because you couldn't afford the cheese.'

I'm pleased for Dan, I think later, when the twins have gone to bed and I'm repainting the ceiling in the front room, having scrubbed down the kitchen units that are still intact in the hope that I might be able to salvage them to keep the costs of a replacement down. It niggles me though, that he is happy and I am not.

At about nine, there is a knock on the front door. At first I don't answer it, assuming that The Neighbour From Hell has come to complain about Homer's barking, but the knocking becomes more insistent and the doorbell rings repeatedly, until I can stand it no more.

Grumbling to myself, I make for the door with my Marigolds on, and open it.

'Hiya, Sadie.'

I blink twice, not daring to believe my eyes. It's Gareth, and here I am as fat as a Teletubby, and dressed like a Fimble in a stripy jumper. I feel as if my neckline hasn't seen the light of day for weeks. I hang on to Homer's collar for grim death while he tries to greet Gareth in his most exuberant, slobbery way.

'Just a moment.' I drag Homer into the front room and slam the door on him. He utters a single woof, then goes quiet. 'Come in.' I pause. 'You will come in?'

413

'I'm not stopping long.'

My stomach lurches at the sound of Gareth's voice. He is looking well, a little thinner perhaps. He's wearing a brown cord reefer jacket and jeans, a sharp contrast to my retreat into black. I notice how he wrinkles his nose at the smell of fresh paint as he steps into the hallway, and closes the front door behind him.

'Helen told me you'd had a fire – two fires,' he says, turning to me.

'Helen?' My heart sinks. Exactly how easy was it for Helen to persuade Gareth to drop round tonight? What did it take? A flutter of the eyelashes? A flash of thigh? I tell myself not to be so ridiculous. Helen loves Michael. She isn't interested in Gareth, any more than I am interested in her husband. I'll still kill her though for interfering in my life, sending Gareth round this evening without any warning. If I'd known, I could have swapped my sweaters for a scoop-neck top, swabbed the black varnish off my fingernails and run a brush through my hair.

'Hasn't anyone told you that the general rule of thumb for painting a room is that there should be at least twice the amount of paint on the walls as there is in your hair?' Gareth observes.

I can't help smiling. 'Is this a personal or professional visit?' I have to ask.

'A bit of both,' Gareth admits, tipping his head to one side. 'I've come to see if we can repair the damage.'

'You don't have to . . .' My heart starts to beat with

hope. 'I'm so sorry about . . .' I can hardly speak, my throat is so tight. 'I made a terrible mistake. I know you didn't shag Helen.'

Gareth shrugs.

'I want you back,' I blurt out. 'I've missed you.'

'I've missed you too, but I don't know if getting back with you is what I want.'

'Oh Gareth.' I start to cry.

'What are those? Crocodile tears to make me come back?'

'I can't help it,' I snivel. 'I'm sorry, but I can see it's too late. You don't want me.'

'I didn't say that.' I find myself with his arms held rigidly about me as if he can't bear to touch me, as if I'm repulsive to him. Gareth wipes tears from my cheek with his thumb, but he doesn't kiss me.

'That jealous streak of yours. You always seem so independent and strong, as if you don't need anyone. I wanted you to let me look after you.' His voice grows hoarse. 'I wanted you to trust me.'

'Will you . . .' I stammer, 'c-can you give me another chance?'

'I don't know, Sadie. I don't know if I can.' Gareth clears his throat. 'I'm offering to install the replacement kitchen and finish the roof off, so we'll see how it goes. I've got another job on, so I'll drop in on Saturday and start stripping the old units out.'

'You don't have to.'

'I want to,' he says firmly. 'In spite of Helen's opinion that I'm nothing but a cowboy, I like to see a project through, particularly this one.' I feel his breath against my cheek, the brief touch of his lips, and then he's gone, the door clicking shut behind him.

I sink to the bottom stair and bury my face in my hands. My head throbs. My chest aches. I feel like screaming, like Lorna does when I rip off a plaster that's been covering a graze on her knee for far too long. I go to bed alone, listening for the sound of the rain.

Chapter Twenty-one

If there were Open University courses on Parallel Parking, I'd be the first to enrol. I'm driving along the road to *Llamedos* for the third time, trying to find a parking space that's big enough to pull into without reversing.

'I keep meaning to ask you how much you offered Gareth to come back and fix the kitchen.'

Helen frowns at me. 'There you go again. I didn't offer him anything, apart from the opportunity to get back with you – which he won't, if you don't give him any sign that you want him. You do still want him?'

'Of course I do.'

'There's one,' Helen says quickly.

'One what?'

'A parking space, you idiot. You've missed it now. You'll have to go round the one-way system all over again.'

It's been a long day. It's Sunday and we've been up since five, yet we still didn't arrive early enough at the car-boot sale to bag one of the best pitches near the entrance and the Portaloos. The fact that it was dark when we started out, and freezing too, reminded me that car-booting isn't a great way to make a living.

We sold some of the twins' outgrown clothes, and toys, jigsaw puzzles left over from our craft fair enterprise, and other bits and pieces of junk that I'd collected over the past year. We also sold a flask of tomato soup by mistake. We failed to sell my vibrator, in spite of Helen's enthusiastic sales pitch: one careful lady owner.

I try to park behind Gareth's pick-up outside the development. It takes me three attempts before I hand over to Helen. She reverses the Peugeot into the gap in a single manoeuvre, then gets out, grinning.

'How do you do that?'

'By magic,' she says. 'I see that Gareth's let himself in.'

'I left a key.'

'Relax, Sadie. Stop doing this impression of a Vestal Virgin and vamp yourself up a bit, otherwise Gareth'll assume that you're not interested in him any more.'

'I thought I'd been doing so well.' Look at how I reacted to Gareth's saying he was going off to play rugby, after he'd finished ripping the fire-damaged units out yesterday. 'Should I have asked him what time he was going to be home last night, and who he was going to be with?'

'What you should have done is invited him to drop by afterwards so you could massage his aching muscles.'

'What, with Ibuleve?'

'Something inflammatory, not anti-inflammatory. Something stimulating, like almond oil laced with the sensual fragrances of ylang ylang and patchouli.'

'Do you think so?'

'I know so.' Helen helps me unload the boot of the car. We've bought a few bargains to dress the property, including a blue and white porcelain coffee grinder with plastic attachments, and an antique mirror to hang above the fireplace in the front room to create the illusion of space. We leave them in the hall. Gareth is in the kitchen. Homer is barking in the garden.

'Hi, Gareth,' Helen says, pushing me forwards as if I'm Charlotte about to take a ballet exam. 'Sadie's making us coffee. I'll leave you to it,' she murmurs into my ear before leaving us alone together.

'Er, I'll get that dog in before The Neighbour From Hell contacts the RSPCA.'

'I don't think you'll be having any more trouble from him for a while,' Gareth says. 'He was carried off in an ambulance about an hour ago. I spoke to his daughter who turned up to follow him to the hospital. She says he had a funny turn.'

Helen must have been earwigging. 'Is he coming back?' she says, popping her head around the kitchen door.

'His daughter wants him to go and live with her when he's recovered. She says he needs looking after.'

'That's great,' says Helen. 'We won't have to worry about the Seller's Pack when we put the house on the market. You have to state whether or not you're in dispute with any of your neighbours.'

'We haven't been in dispute with The Neighbour From Hell,' I say. 'He's been in dispute with us.'

'Same difference,' says Helen.

'I think it's sad, losing your independence like that,' I muse.

'It's sad for his daughter,' says Helen.

Personally, I hope that he's happy living with her because I've come to realise that it must have been hell living next door to us. I fetch Homer in anyway, while the kettle comes up to the boil. He greets me as if I have been away for years, not hours. I wish Gareth seemed as pleased to see me.

'How's it going?' I ask him, pouring water into the coffee mugs. I don't really need to ask. He's stripped out the damaged units and tiles. The last wheelbarrow-load stands in the middle of the floor.

'I've finished for today.'

'The new units are arriving on Wednesday.'

'I'm working away this week.' Gareth pauses, staring into my eyes as if he's reading the turmoil behind them. Where? Why? Who with? When are you coming back? I bite my lip, and my tongue. Gareth smiles. 'I'm helping a mate with a job in North London. I can be back here on Saturday.'

So that's it, I think, stirring the coffees furiously. Once Gareth has fitted the kitchen, he'll be off, out of my life for ever. Unless . . . I recall Helen's words. *Be yourself. Show Gareth that you still want him.* However, I can't ask him to stay for tea tonight, because there isn't any, and the twins will soon be back from Dan and Wendy's.

'Perhaps we could do something on Saturday night,' I suggest quietly. 'I'll have Lorna and Sam, but—'

'That's fine with me,' Gareth interrupts, stepping towards me. 'I'll drop by after rugby. We don't have to go out ...' He leans forward and presses his lips onto mine. My heart skips a beat, then another until I think I'm going to faint. I fling my arms around his neck and kiss him back.

'Oh Gareth, I've missed you ...'

The sound of a cough breaks through our breathless fumbling. Reluctantly, Gareth and I separate.

'Where's that coffee?' Helen says brightly. 'It'll be cold by now.'

If it is cold, I don't notice. It is enough to know that Gareth still lusts after me. For now.

The following Friday night, snow is forecast. If it snows, Gareth's rugby match will be cancelled. Never have I prayed so intently for precipitation.

'It's snowing!' yells Sam from the front room on Saturday morning. Lorna takes up his cry, and they charge around the house, shouting, 'It's snowing, it's snowing.'

I open the back door to let Homer out. It's true. Snowflakes spin and bluster from a leaden sky and sting my face. Tom's ornamental hollies are already cloaked in white. The patio is beginning to blend with the lawn.

'Can we go to Richmond Park, Mum?' Sam calls from behind me.

'Please!' says Lorna.

'Not now. I want to be here while Gareth's fitting the kitchen, in case he needs a hand.'

'Later then?' says Sam.

'Oh, for goodness sake, yes, I'll take you to the park later.'

'Promise?' says Lorna.

'I promise.' I am about to clarify my position – that I'm not going if the snow is too deep, or too slushy, or it's too late once Gareth has finished work.

However, it doesn't take Gareth as long as I'd hoped to assemble the units. I hover, watching him snap the last plastic covers onto the screws inside the cupboards, and start packing his tools. He looks up, grinning.

'Anything else you'd like me to do for you?' he asks.

'I'll let you know tonight.'

Gareth runs his hand down my back and cups my buttock, sending delicious shivers up my spine. 'What shall we do now?'

'Mum said she'd take us to the park,' Sam says from behind us.

'You promised,' says Lorna.

'I think you're being set up,' Gareth says, smiling at me.

'Actually, I did promise . . .'

'I'll come with you,' Gareth says. 'This afternoon's match has been postponed.'

I am as excited as Sam and Lorna. Gareth is spending the whole day with us. With me.

I drive us out along the A3 to the Robin Hood Gate entrance to the park, a good decision because the main roads are almost clear. We leave the car, and take Homer out across what appears to be a vast expanse of white desert, dotted with islands of stark, black-limbed trees. The snow has stopped. There is little traffic. The incredible silence is broken only by the twins' shouting and the crunching sound of our footsteps.

Homer sniffs and snorts at the snow, and limps about as it balls up in the fur between his toes. The twins stop to make a snowman. I watch Gareth helping them. He puts his scarf around its neck, and digs for pebbles and twigs to use as a mouth and eyes.

We look like one happy family, but appearances are deceptive. Gareth has given me no indication that he wishes to be a permanent fixture in our lives.

'It's the best snowman we've ever built,' says Lorna, wide-eyed with excitement.

'*Olé, olé, olé!*' Sam scoops up handfuls of snow to throw at Gareth. Gareth throws some back. 'This is so cool,' Sam shrieks.

'Don't you mean cold?' I dig my hands deeper inside my pockets. Gareth comes jogging over.

'Cold?' he says, arching one eyebrow. 'You should let me warm you up.' He wraps his arms around my waist, and kisses me. His mouth is hot. His nose is freezing. The kiss sends heat flooding through my body.

'You are so embarrassing,' says Lorna eventually.

'No one's watching.' I glance across the park. All I can see is a lone dogwalker's footprints heading up the hill away from us.

'We are,' says Lorna. 'And Homer.'

'We'd better get your mum home then, before I cause

any further offence,' Gareth says, grinning. I know what he means – I can feel the evidence of his desire through several extra layers of clothing and coats.

After tea, I send the twins to bed. Fortunately, the excitement of the snow has taken its toll, and they are asleep by eight. I flick the switch on the dishwasher and give Homer his last Bonio before I pack him off to bed too. He sleeps on a beanbag, taking up at least half the dining area. I take a quick look out of the window. More snow is falling.

Gareth treads softly up behind me. 'You're not thinking of making love naked in this, are you, Sadie?' he whispers.

'Now that you suggest it . . .' I turn, grinning. 'Indoors,' I add, in case he should have misunderstood.

Gareth leads me upstairs to the bedroom. There's no longer a tatty mattress on the floor but a double bed, dressed in a duvet embroidered with gold stars, and a raspberry velvet throw, a bed fit for a princess and her prince. We make love. Twice. Then I lie with Gareth's body curled around mine, and his arms snug around my waist.

Now what? Can I really be happy, allowing Gareth to wander into and out of my life whenever he likes? Can I settle for what he appears to be offering me, the odd day or weekend of fun and passion, interspersed with weeks of separation during which he might, or might not, bother to get in touch? It's no good. I need long-term commitment. I don't do casual flings.

'I suppose this is just sex to you,' I begin.

'Is that what you believe?' Gareth frowns. 'It isn't just anything. It's everything to me. Sex, yes, but it's also friendship and love.' He pauses, running his fingertips across my cheek. 'I love you, Sadie.'

My eyes mist with tears. 'I love you too.'

'Will you marry me?'

My throat constricts. I shift my arm, and pinch an inch – more than an inch actually – of one of my rolls of belly fat.

'What are you doing?'

'Pinching myself.'

'"When two people are head over heels in love, marriage can strengthen the bond between them." You see, I haven't forgotten what Topsy said about marriage that day we first met. She made quite an impression on me.' Gareth smiles. 'It's taken me a while to realise it, but you're the woman I want to spend the rest of my life with.' He watches me, anxiety etched on his face. 'You've gone very quiet.'

'Yes,' I breathe, 'I'll marry you. Yes, yes, yes!' I yell out my decision to Gareth, the twins, Homer, Alvin and probably The Neighbour From Hell in his hospital bed, and it's all that Gareth can do to restrain me from ringing Helen and Annette. 'When?'

'As soon as possible,' he says. 'Getting married is like buying a house. Having made an offer and had it accepted, I want to make sure the deal goes through.'

Gareth's offer isn't the only one. When Helen and I put the development on the market, we are inundated with offers. We accept one, a little under the asking price to take account of the slightly less than perfect finish in the kitchen, but it falls through a month later, by which time all the others have mysteriously evaporated. We can't understand it.

Marcus re-advertises for us, and we try again. I flood the stair carpet with Vanish to remove the stain that one of Alvin's furballs has left. I send Homer back to live with Annette and Sean. Helen brings her coffee and bread machines, and switches them on to fill the house with welcoming aromas. I notice that she has surreptitiously lost the coffee grinder that I bought in the car-boot sale.

In spite of all our work, there are no offers this time. Marcus suggests that we add a wardrobe to the main bedroom, remove some of the tat – that was his exact description – from the back garden, and paint out some of the gerbera, which would be okay if he hadn't kept on about how fantastic it all was when he came to talk to us about marketing the property. Helen and I discuss the possible changes. Should we compromise our design for the sake of a quick sale? I say yes. Helen says no, absolutely not.

I can see her point. Helen is no longer a property developer. She no longer craves a second child either. When Michael moved back in with her, he agreed that she could have a baby. With Michael's opposition removed, Helen discovered that she didn't want one that much after all.

Helen is now an aspiring interior designer. She's starting a college course next September, so that she can acquire the skills to set up her own consultancy. She wants me and Gareth to employ her as our advisor when we set out on our new partnership – as developers, and husband and wife.

I still can't believe that I am about to marry Gareth. What if he has a last-minute change of heart? What if he doesn't turn up for the wedding? I'm not being unduly pessimistic. He's done it before.

Sunshine and April showers. A perfect day for a wedding. Dan collects the twins, and Helen arrives at nine in the morning, bringing a lacy blue garter and a bottle of champagne. She pours one glass for me to drink with my Shredded Wheat, and one for herself.

'I thought you were bringing Charlotte with you,' I say.

'She's spending some quality time with Michael. Now that she's not doing so many activities, and he's less driven, they're together much more. It makes me feel quite envious,' Helen witters on as she rifles through the pile of unopened post that's accumulated on the table during the past week, but I'm not really listening.

'What am I going to do if Gareth doesn't turn up?'

'He'll be there,' Helen promises. 'You'd better open some of this,' she adds, handing me an envelope that bears an Italian stamp and my mother's upright handwriting. 'Go on, open it. What does it say?'

'Hang on a mo,' I say, ripping it open to find a letter along with a cheque and a photo.

Congratulations on your news, although it came as quite a shock that you'd even consider getting married for a second time. A property developer, you say? (Maybe I did exag-

gerate a little.) *I'm so sorry that Roberto and I can't be at your wedding as we're moving into our new home, the most beautiful villa overlooking Lake Garda.*

I glance at the photo which tells a rather different story. My mother, dressed in a bikini top, sarong and strappy sandals, stands in front of a tumbledown shack with several scraggy hens at her feet. I read on.

You and Gareth and the twins must come and visit us as soon as you can – we're planning to convert the chicken shed into an annexe for guests. Con amore – that means 'with love' – Mum.

'That's nice of her,' Helen says, looking over my shoulder. 'You'll be able to have a family holiday at last.'

'Holiday? She's expecting Gareth to do her building work for nothing,' I argue, but then I start thinking how it would be a great adventure for Lorna and Sam, and how they don't get to see their grandmother very often, and how I could drop a few hints about the quality of Gareth's finishes . . .

'Don't worry about it now,' Helen interrupts. 'Go and shower and get dressed, or we'll be late.'

I'm in the shower when the phone rings. Helen starts hammering on the bathroom door.

'Let me in!'

'It's Gareth, isn't it?' I step out of the shower, and stand dripping on the mat.

'Open the door, Sadie!'

I slip the lock. The door flies open.

'We've done it,' Helen cries. 'We've sold the house!' She grabs a towel from the radiator and chucks it at me.

'That was Marcus. We've had an offer, full asking price, cash buyer, no chain. Do you remember the woman in the red top, the one that clashed so badly with the gerbera paint? Come on, Sadie, you must remember her.' Helen's voice softens. 'I suppose your mind is on the wedding, not how much profit we've made.'

'Profit?'

'Five thousand pounds!'

'How do you work that out?'

'The difference between the price we paid for it and the offer price, minus the cost of the first kitchen.' Helen gazes at me. 'It's a rough estimate.'

'You've forgotten the solicitor's and estate agent's fees, the money we owe Gareth, Jim and Michael, and the cost of materials for the new roof—'

'Underfloor heating for the bathroom, flocking machine hire,' Helen interrupts. 'It isn't going to be much to show for a year's hassle, is it?'

'It's going to be a massive loss.'

'Cheer up, Sadie. It doesn't matter, does it? Money isn't everything.'

'It is when you haven't got any.'

'Let's put it down to experience. We made mistakes, but you'll know what works and what doesn't next time.' Helen plies me with more champagne as I dress and put on my make-up. She wasn't happy when I told her that I wasn't going to spend hours in Kingston looking for a new outfit, that I already knew exactly what I was going to wear ...

Before we leave the house, Helen hands me an envelope.

'What's this?'

'A wedding present from me and Michael.'

'Money?' I gasp, opening the envelope.

'That's to pay for a survey on your next house.'

'It's too much.'

'Keep it! Michael's just invested in a new range of dog toys, on Annette's advice, and he can't get enough of them. Your sister might not be able to navigate from one end of the High Street to the other, but she's a remarkably astute businesswoman.' Helen grins. 'You and Gareth will be able to make an offer on the property next door, now that you've sold this one. There's a *For Sale* board up outside number thirteen. I guess The Neighbour From Hell isn't planning to move back. It's the perfect opportunity – the front garden's been turned into parking, but the rest of the house can't have been touched for years.'

'How can I think about that now?'

'You're right. We'd better go.' Helen looks me up and down, tweaks a curl, straightens my bow tie and hands me a bouquet of plastic roses. 'You look,' she searches for an apt description, 'amazing.'

I don't feel so good. When we arrive at the Register Office, I angle my hoop so I can slip out of the passenger seat of Helen's car. The champagne that I drank earlier seems to be fizzing back up my gullet. My hands are shaking. I step onto the pavement to cheers from the small crowd that has gathered.

Everyone is here. Almost everyone – Dan and Wendy, Sam and his new friend Matt, Lorna, Charlotte, Annette and Sean, Michael, Tom, Kath and Desmond, and Kate – but not Gareth, or Niall. I glance at my watch. There are five minutes to go before the ceremony. Where on earth are they?

Kath greets me first. She looks as nervous as I feel, remembering the last time that she dressed up for her son's wedding, I expect. She eyes me uncertainly, then smiles.

'I'd forgotten,' she says. 'Gareth told me that you were a magic operative, Sadie. What a talented daughter-in-law I shall have.' She takes a swig from the hip flask she is holding. 'Would you like some?'

'No, thanks.' I feel slightly sick.

Sam and Lorna run up and start chattering non-stop. Sam is wearing his Christmas disco gear – he was more than relieved when he discovered that he didn't have to wear what he thought was a tartan skirt, and pleased when I said that, as Lorna would have Charlotte to talk to, he could invite a friend. Matt might prefer playing football to Jackie Chan, but Sam has learned to compromise.

Lorna is wearing her dream dress, a purple satin bridesmaid's gown.

'Dad says we're going to stay with him while you and Gareth are on honeymoon,' she says.

We aren't going far. Two nights in a hotel on Brighton seafront, if Gareth turns up.

'I'm very grateful,' I say, turning to Dan and Wendy. Dan takes my hand and pecks me on the cheek.

'All the best, Sadie,' he says. 'I really mean that.'

'Love you, Sis,' says Annette, pushing in. Annette is heavily pregnant now, and she's put on a lot of weight, the consequence of an unfortunate craving for Marmite and Liquorice Allsorts on toast.

'Guess what, Mum?' Lorna says, clinging onto my hand for attention. 'Auntie Annette's taking eternity leave from school.'

'Don't you mean maternity leave?'

'No, eternity,' says Annette. 'I shan't be going back once I've had the baby. I want to spend all my time with him, or her.'

I smile wryly, recalling the sometimes mind-numbing tedium of looking after small babies. She'll soon change her mind.

Sean, in a suit instead of the Lycra shorts that I half-expected, comes forward to shake my hand, before retreating again to speak to Dan.

'I'm beginning to feel like the Queen,' I say, when Tom presents himself.

'I had to come when Dad told me that you and Gareth were getting married,' he says, smiling.

'Mum, how can you marry Gareth if he isn't here?' Sam cuts in.

'I can't, can I?' I am beginning to panic. 'Where is he?' All kinds of possibilities flash through my mind, the best of which is that his rugby friends have put him on the overnight train to Edinburgh. I jam a lid on my jealous thoughts, and concentrate on willing him to turn up. I am aware that Michael is talking to a woman at the door to the Register Office. He looks at his watch and walks towards me, frowning. At the same time Helen, who's just returned from parking the car, puts her arm around my shoulder.

Michael shakes his head. 'The Registrar says that if the marriage can't go ahead right now, then it won't happen today.'

'I'm so sorry, Sadie,' Helen says.

I don't know what she's talking about because I can see Gareth pounding along the pavement towards us with Niall puffing along behind him.

'Gareth!' I wave.

A flicker of surprise, then amusement crosses his face before he yells, 'Sadie! Wait for me!'

'He's here,' says Helen. 'Mikey, go and tell the Registrar. Bribe her if you have to. Quickly!'

'Are we going inside now, Mum?' says Lorna.

'Yes, Gareth's here.' I try to give Lorna a hug over my hoop, then I turn to Sam. 'When I start crying in there,' I say, nodding towards the entrance to the Register Office, 'it'll be because I'm happy, not sad. You understand?'

Sam nods.

'I love you, Sam.'

'I love the way you love me, Mum,' he says softly.

I bite my lip, determined not to break down into a blubbering heap just yet.

'Sam, hurry up or you'll miss the wedding,' Lorna calls from the door.

'Go and join the others,' I say. 'I'll wait here for Gareth.' I keep my eyes fixed on my tardy groom who slows to walk the last few strides up to me, allowing Niall to overtake. Niall gives me a sheepish smile and dodges into the Register Office behind Sam.

Gareth fixes my eyes with his. 'I'm not too late, am

I?' he says, offering me an arm, and a bristly cheek that carries a faint scent of railway station.

'I hope not. Michael's talking to the Registrar.'

'You're angry with me ... I don't blame you.'

'I'm not angry,' I say, looking him up and down. He's wearing a morning suit – no, part of a morning suit, and his left ankle is bound by a padlock and chain. His boots are splashed with mud. I reach up and fiddle with the daffodil that he's wearing in the top buttonhole of his wing-collar shirt, instead of a tie. 'I'm just relieved that you made it.'

Gareth's face suddenly breaks into a grin, and my heart turns over. 'I woke up with a hangover in Milton Keynes this morning, not a pleasant experience. Niall booked a taxi to New Malden, and we were halfway to Maldon in Essex before we knew it.'

'Serves you right for having such loutish friends,' I say, stroking the skin at the side of his neck, and feeling for the throb of his pulse.

Gareth's hands are around my back inside Topsy's hoop, his fingers massaging my buttocks as he pulls me against his body, crushing my breasts against his chest. His mouth is on mine. I close my eyes, clutch at Gareth's waistcoat, and lose myself in the most intoxicating kiss ...

'Hey, you two, you can do that later,' Helen calls out. 'We're all waiting for you.'

'I can hardly tear myself away,' Gareth murmurs, but he does. He dips a hand into his pocket, pulls out a handful of cherry blossom, and scatters it in front of us as we walk arm-in-arm into the Register Office.

'Come on, Sadie Keith. Let's get married.'

I can hardly believe it. My eyes are already burning with tears. There were times, terrible times, when I doubted that I would ever take full possession, but now the hottest, most desirable property in the world is mine. All mine.

Under the Bonnet

Cathy Woodman

'Funny, truthful and original . . . I loved this book'
Jill Mansell

With a struggling second-hand car dealership in South
London, Juliet and Andy Wyevale don't have it easy.
And it's not just the business that needs a jump-start –
their relationship could do with an overhaul too.
Andy's always too busy with work to help with the
kids, and what's more, he's losing his hair and gaining
a paunch. Although Juliet loves her husband dearly,
she knows the passion leaked out of their marriage a
while ago.

So when Andy hires Steve, a gorgeous young
mechanic with an appetite for fast motorbikes *and*
older women, the sparks begin to fly. Will Juliet risk it
all for a tumble on the tarmac? Or will she realise her
family needs her now more than ever?

0 7553 0956 1

headline

No Going Back

Lynda Page

Looking back over the past forty years, Judith Chambers realises she has led a sad and lonely life. Her parents never loved their only daughter, and by forcing Judith to stay at home they stopped her from making friends or finding happiness.

Then her father's death gives her the chance to spread her wings. At first, she struggles to survive in the outside world, and just as she is making headway, an unexpected visitor forces her to deal with difficulties she is ill equipped to cope with. But for Judith Chambers there's no going back.

Don't miss Lynda Page's other sagas, also available from Headline.

'A welcome read for fans of Cookson and Cox' *Daily Express*

'Full of lively characters' *Best*

'It's a story to grip you from the first page to the last' *Coventry Evening Telegraph*

'A terrific author' *Bookseller*

0 7553 0879 4

headline

Now you can buy any of these other bestselling Headline books from your bookshop or *direct from the publisher*.

FREE P&P AND UK DELIVERY
(Overseas and Ireland £3.50 per book)

Under the Bonnet	Cathy Woodman	£5.99
No Going Back	Lynda Page	£5.99
The Captain's Daughters	Benita Brown	£5.99
A Lucky Break	Lynda Page	£6.99
The Girl From Number 22	Joan Jonker	£6.99
Second Chance of Sunshine	Pamela Evans	£5.99
A Mother's Love	Lyn Andrews	£6.99
Always I'll Remember	Rita Bradshaw	£5.99
In Love and Friendship	Benita Brown	£6.99
Three Little Words	Joan Jonker	£6.99
Love and War	Dee Williams	£5.99
The Chandler's Daughter	Victor Pemberton	£6.99
Every Time You Say Goodbye	June Tate	£6.99

TO ORDER SIMPLY CALL THIS NUMBER

01235 400 414

or visit our website: www.madaboutbooks.com

Prices and availability subject to change without notice.